DIVISIBLE MAN™

THE ELEVENTH HOURGLASS

by

Howard Seaborne

ALSO BY HOWARD SEABORNE

DIVISIBLE MAN
A Novel – September 2017
DIVISIBLE MAN - THE SIXTH PAWN
A Novel – June 2018
DIVISIBLE MAN - THE SECOND GHOST
ANGEL FLIGHT
A Novel & Story – September 2018
DIVISIBLE MAN - THE SEVENTH STAR
A Novel – June 2019
DIVISIBLE MAN - TEN MAN CREW
A Novel – November 2019
DIVISIBLE MAN - THE THIRD LIE
A Novel – May 2020
DIVISIBLE MAN - THREE NINES FINE
A Novel – November 2020
DIVISIBLE MAN - EIGHT BALL
A Novel – September 2021
DIVISIBLE MAN - ENGINE OUT
AND OTHER SHORT FLIGHTS
A Story Collection – June 2022
DIVISIBLE MAN - NINE LIVES LOST
A Novel – June 2022
DIVISIBLE MAN - TEN KEYS WEST
A Novel – May 2023
DIVISIBLE MAN - THE ELEVENTH HOURGLASS
A Novel – October 2023

PRAISE FOR HOWARD SEABORNE

DIVISIBLE MAN - THE ELEVENTH HOURGLASS [DM11]
A *BookLife from Publishers Weekly* Editor's Pick - "A book of outstanding quality."

"A lean, fast-paced, and unpredictable story...An accomplished supernatural thriller from a series that keeps on delivering...Will Stewart is one of the most believable unbelievable characters currently running in fiction."
— *Kirkus Reviews*

"...thrilling...an effervescent pace...littered with slabs of wicket humor... relentless action...full of fun...truly compelling." — *The BookLife Prize from Publishers Weekly*

DIVISIBLE
MAN - TEN KEYS WEST [DM10]
"The best possible combination of the Odd Thomas novels of Dean Koontz and the Jack Reacher novels of Lee Child."
— *Kirkus Reviews*

"The soaring 10th entry in this thriller series is as exciting as the first...Seaborne keeps the chatter fun, the pacing fleet, and the tension urgent. His secret weapon is a tight focus on Will and Andy, a married couple whose love—and bantering dialogue—proves as buoyant as ever."
— *BookLife*

"The author effectively fleshes out even minor walk-on characters, and his portrayal of the loving relationship between his two heroes continues to be the most satisfying aspect of the series, the kind of three-dimensional adult relation-ship remarkably rare in thrillers like this one. The author's skill at pacing is razor-sharp—the book is a compulsive page-turner..."
— *Kirkus Reviews*

DIVISIBLE MAN - NINE LIVES LOST [DM9]
"Seaborne's latest series entry packs a good deal of mystery. Everything Will stumbles on, it seems, dredges up more questions...All this shady stuff in Montana and unrest in Wisconsin make for a tense narrative...Will's periodic

sarcasm is welcome, as it's good-natured and never overwhelming...A smart, diverting tale of an audacious aviator with an extraordinary ability."
— *Kirkus Reviews*

DIVISIBLE MAN - ENGINE OUT & OTHER SHORT FLIGHTS
"This engaging compendium will surely pique new readers' interest in earlier series installments. A captivating, altruistic hero and appealing cast propel this enjoyable collection..."
— *Kirkus Reviews*

DIVISIBLE MAN - EIGHT BALL [DM8]
"Any reader of this series knows that they're in good hands with Seaborne, who's a natural storyteller. His descriptions and dialogue are crisp, and his characters deftly sketched...The book keeps readers tied into its complex and exciting thriller plot with lucid and graceful exposition, laying out clues with cleverness and subtlety...and the protagonist is always a relatable character with plenty of humanity and humor...Another riveting, taut, and timely adventure with engaging characters and a great premise."
— *Kirkus Reviews*

DIVISIBLE MAN - THREE NINES FINE [DM7]
"Seaborne is never less than a spellbinding storyteller, keeping his complicated but clearly explicated plot moving smoothly from one nail-biting scenario to another...The author's grasp of global politics gives depth to the book's thriller elements...Even minor characters come across in three dimensions, and Will himself is an endearing narrator. He's lovestruck by his gorgeous, intelligent, and strong-willed wife; has his heart and social conscience in the right place; and is boyishly thrilled by the other thing. A solid series entry that is, as usual, exciting, intricately plotted, and thoroughly entertaining."
—*Kirkus Reviews*

DIVISIBLE MAN - THE THIRD LIE [DM6]
"Seaborne shows himself to be a reliably splendid storyteller in this latest outing. The plot is intricate and could have been confusing in lesser hands, but the author manages it well, keeping readers oriented amid unexpected developments...His crisp writing about complex scenes and concepts is another strong suit...The fantasy of self-powered flight remains absolutely compelling...Will is heroic and daring, as one would expect, but he's also funny, compassionate, and affectionate... A gripping, timely, and twisty thriller."
—*Kirkus Reviews*

DIVISIBLE MAN - TEN MAN CREW [DM5]

"Seaborne...continues his winning streak in this series, offering another page-turner. By having Will's knowledge of and control over his powers continue to expand while the questions over how he should best deploy his abilities grow, Seaborne keeps the concept fresh and readers guessing...The conspiracy is highly dramatic yet not implausible given today's political events, and the action sequences are excitingly cinematic...Another compelling and hugely fun adventure that delivers a thrill ride."
—*Kirkus Reviews*

DIVISIBLE MAN - THE SEVENTH STAR [DM4]

"Seaborne...proves he's a natural born storyteller, serving up an exciting, well-written thriller. He makes even minor moments in the story memorable with his sharp, evocative prose...Will's smart, humane and humorous narrative voice is appealing, as is his sincere appreciation for Andy—not just for her considerable beauty, but also for her dedication and intelligence. An intensely satisfying thriller—another winner from Seaborne."
—*Kirkus Reviews*

DIVISIBLE MAN - THE SECOND GHOST [DM3]

"Seaborne...delivers a solid, well-written tale that taps into the near-universal dream of personal flight. Will's narrative voice is engaging and crisp, clearly explaining technical matters while never losing sight of humane, emotional concerns. Another intelligent and exciting superpowered thriller."
—*Kirkus Reviews*

DIVISIBLE MAN - THE SIXTH PAWN [DM2]

A *Booklife from Publishers Weekly* Editor's Pick: **"A book of outstanding quality."**

"Seaborne...once again gives readers a crisply written thriller. Self-powered flight is a potent fantasy, and Seaborne explores its joys and difficulties engagingly. Will's narrative voice is amusing, intelligent and humane; he draws readers in with his wit, appreciation for his wife, and his flight-drunk joy...Even more entertaining than its predecessor—a great read."
—*Kirkus Reviews*

DIVISIBLE MAN [DM1]

"Seaborne's crisp prose, playful dialogue, and mastery of technical details of flight distinguish the story...this is a striking and original start to a series, buoyed by fresh and vivid depictions of extra-human powers and a clutch of memorably drawn characters..."
—*BookLife*

THE SERIES

While each DIVISIBLE MAN ^{TM} novel tells its own tale and can be read on its own, many elements carry forward. **The novels are best enjoyed in sequence.** The pivotal short story "Angel Flight" bridges the third and fourth novels and is included with the third novel, DIVISIBLE MAN - THE SECOND GHOST. "Angel Flight" is also published in the ENGINE OUT short story collection along with eleven other stories offering additional insights into the cadre of characters residing in Essex County.

Publisher's Note: DIVISIBLE MAN novels contain harsh language and are intended for mature readers. An edited PG-13 version is available for younger or more sensitive readers in the **Large Print Edition.**

SUPPORT YOUR LOCAL BOOKSELLER

The entire DIVISIBLE MAN ^{TM} series is available from major online retailers as well as the many local independent booksellers who offer online ordering for in-store pickup or home delivery.

Search: "DIVISIBLE MAN Howard Seaborne"

For advance notice of new releases and exclusive material available only to Email Members, join the DIVISIBLE MAN ^{TM} Email List at **HowardSeaborne.com**.

Sign up today and get a FREE DOWNLOAD.

ACKNOWLEDGMENTS

Thank you, Robin, Rich, Ariana, Stephen Parolini, David, Carol, April, Claire, Kristie, Rebecca, Steve, Rebecca and Daniel, Stacy, Sharon, Bill, Judethe, Nikki, Sue, Mark, Edith, Tom, Marjorie and Ken, Phil and Mary, Willy, Jimmy, Greg, Margaret and Paul, Julie, Mike, Mary, Donna, Chryste and Mary, Dorothy and Sam, Denise, Arnie, Vic, John, the never-forgotten Mark Patton, Dave, Jeff, George and Barb, Earl, Frederick and Dan, Helen and John, Martha, Stephen and Gordon, Stanley and Adena.

For all the parts and pieces.

Thank you
  .

Author's Note

Events and characters in this story refer to people we met in the short story "Engine Out" and the short story "When It Matters," both of which are published in the short story collection, *Engine Out & Other Short Flights*. It is not critical that you read both before embarking on this adventure, but it is entertaining.

*For the genius program director
who ran the old horror films
on Friday Night Shock Theater.*

PREFACE

THE OTHER THING

It's like this: I wake up nearly every morning in the bed I share with my wife. After devoting a religious moment to appreciating the stunning, loving woman beside me, I ease off the mattress and pick my way across the minefield of creaks and groans in the old farmhouse's wooden floor. I slip into the hall and head for the guest bathroom two doors down—the one with the quietest toilet flush. I take care of essential business, then pull up to the mirror. The face offers no surprises. I give it a moment, then picture a set of levers in my head—part of the throttle-prop-mixture quadrant on a twin-engine Piper Navajo. The levers I imagine are to the right of the standard controls, a fourth set not found on any airplane, topped with classic round balls. I see them fully retracted, pulled toward me, the pilot. My eyes are open—it makes no difference—I can see the levers either way. I close my hand over them. I push. They move smoothly and swiftly to the forward stops. Balls to the wall.

For a split second I wonder, as I did the day before, and the day before that, if this trick will work again. Then—

Fwooomp!

—I hear it. A deep and breathy sound—like the air being sucked out of a room. I've learned that the sound is audible only in my head.

A cool sensation flashes over my skin. The first dip in a farm pond after a hot, dusty day. The shift of an evening breeze after sunset.

I vanish.

Bleary eyes and tossed hair wink out of the mirror and the shower curtain behind me—the one with the frogs on it— fills in where my head had been. The instant I see those frogs, my feet leave the cold tile floor. My body remains solid, but gravity and I are no longer on speaking terms. A stiff breeze will send me on my way if I don't hang on to something.

The routine never varies. I've tested it nearly every morning since I piloted an air charter flight down the RNAV 31 Approach to Essex County Airport but never made the field. The airplane wound up in pieces and I wound up sitting on the pilot's seat in a marsh. I have no memory of the crash. The running theory is that I collided with something—something I recently found in a winter woods under a crush of broken trees. I believe that object—whatever it was—saved me and left me this way. I may never know how or why. The object is long gone. As time passes, the memory of its discovery plays like a dream.

Since the night of the crash, whenever I picture that set of levers in my mind and I push them fully forward, I vanish. Pull them back, and I reappear. It applies to things I wear, things I hold, and even other people in my grasp.

A gimmick? A party trick? A useful tool for espionage—assuming I knew anything about espionage? I don't know.

There's one aspect of this *thing* that I may never understand. On a fogbound Christmas Eve I held a dying child in my arms and made us both vanish. I found out later that the child stopped dying. That when this *thing* envelops a child stricken by cancer sometimes—often—it leaves the child whole and healthy.

Don't ask. I have no idea.

This *thing*—what I call *the other thing*—saved my life. It allows me to disappear. It defies gravity. It cures where there is no cure.

Those things don't scare me.

Far scarier things greet the dawn every day.

PART I

"**Y**ou need to get your ass over here like *right now*." Pidge delivered the command in a breathless whisper.

"Why?"

"Earl's holding a baby hostage and the cops are here. *I am not shitting you!*"

"What?"

Pidge ended the call.

I rolled the creeper out from under the Piper Navajo wing where I'd been wiping a film of dirt and oil off the bottom side of the flaps.

"Well, that's weird." With no one else in the hangar, I got no argument.

I tossed aside the oily wad of paper towels and levered myself up off the floor. I left the cleaning supplies because, dollars to donuts, this would add up to a waste of my time and I'd be back at this task soon.

The big hangar door hung open, perhaps a little optimistically. Despite the mid-May date on the calendar and a bright sunlit sky, the morning temperature had barely topped 40 degrees. The airport MOS predicted mid-sixties, but it would be afternoon before such glorious warmth crept in.

Still, the air was fresh, and the crystalline sky promised the best a Wisconsin spring had to offer. Lingering traces of what were once snow piles between the hangars melted into the grass. I liked the way the open door caught the sound of student pilot runups or morning charter flights departing. Ordinarily Pidge would have been piloting one of those charters, either in Earl's Piper Mojave or one of the Beechcraft Barons he operated, but she was in the home stretch of having one arm in a cast. The break she suffered during a misadventure in the Florida Keys did not set properly and had been re-broken and reset using an assortment of pins and screws. Being grounded accounted for her presence in the Essex County Air

Service office at 9:15 a.m. In lieu of flying, Pidge updated charter records, tutored students studying for written exams, and relieved Rosemary II of some of the scheduling, but mostly she drove everyone from the building or else insane. Thanks to an earthbound Pidge, not much has been seen of Earl Jackson, the operation's owner, and my former boss. Earl either locked himself in his office or found cause to spend long hours in the engine shop arguing with Doc, the chief mechanic. Rosemary II confided in me that despite the way Pidge and Earl mimic a crate of nitroglycerin on a roller coaster, Earl plans to offer her the chief pilot title before some regional airline lures her away. At twenty-four, she has all the ratings and twice the skill.

Earl's holding a baby hostage and the cops are here.

This I had to see.

EARL STOOD with his feet planted wider than his bowlegged usual. His stance suggested a linebacker ready for the snap of a football. His elbows rode high and away from his fireplug frame. In the scarred and gnarled claws he calls hands, sure as hell, he clutched an infant at arm's length. The bald-headed pair stared at each other.

"Hey, Will." Del Sims, the smallest cop on the Essex Police Department patrol roster, stirred coffee in a mug a few feet from Earl and his hostage. The scent of Rosemary II's mysteriously delicious blend warmed my senses.

"Del." I stopped inside the tinted glass doors to the Essex County Air Service office where, until just short of two years ago, I had been chief pilot. "What's up?"

"Not much. You?"

I shot a look down the hallway. Pidge's mop of short blonde hair poked out of the second office door. She fought to keep a full-blown laugh from slipping through the devilish grin on her face.

"Hey, Earl." I pointed at the bundle in a tiny blue onesie. "Who's your dance partner?"

Earl said nothing. Despite the permanent expression of rage on his aged yet ageless face, I got the distinct impression that the infant was winning the staring contest. I got an equally distinct impression that Del, in full uniform and armed per department policy, was more interested in his coffee than the child. A second glance at Pidge's grin confirmed I'd been had. Still, I wasn't sorry for getting suckered. I wouldn't have wanted to miss this scene.

I contemplated grabbing a photo.

I was about to question Del when the doors behind me swung open and Rosemary II struggled into the office with an armload of grocery bags. I grabbed the door for her. She shoved one of the bags into my hands.

"Uh!" She adjusted the load. "Thank you, Will. I—" She stopped. Her deep brown eyes darted from me to Earl to the baby to Del then back to me, returning laden with questions.

"Beats me." I shrugged before she could ask.

"Earl Jackson, what on earth are you doing?" Rosemary II lowered two loaded paper grocery bags to the floor and darted forward. Before Earl could answer, she swept the child out of his grip. "That's no way to hold a baby!"

I swear the child giggled. Earl remained rooted to the floor with his eyes locked on the kid. Rosemary II cuddled the infant against her chest. Like dawn, a bright smile spread and creased the smooth milk chocolate skin on her face. "And who are you, little one?"

Rosemary II is not much older than me, but she is everyone's mother at the airport. Radiant in that role, she instantly communicated to the infant that its fortunes had changed for the better. It grinned up at her adoring face.

"He's mine. I'm sorry." A meek voice came from the hallway leading to the restrooms. "I'm so sorry. I really, *really* had to go. It's been hours."

A wild shock of long red hair atop a girl with a slender physique emerged from the hallway. The hair framed a face pale enough to have been rendered in marble, with skin as smooth. Shy but piercing blue eyes warily regarded the fresh assembly of strangers.

I knew that face. So did Pidge.

"Kelly?" Pidge hurried up behind me. She looked astonished. "Jesus, Kelly, why did you come back here? Are you under arrest?"

Kelly Pratt darted a glance at her friend Pidge, then at me, then at the woman holding her child. Her expression betrayed the same undertow of ingrained fear I had seen the first time I met her and the last time I saw her, yet she seemed different.

Pidge ducked past me and took her friend in a hug, then sternly gripped her arms. As if Del wasn't standing three feet away, she whispered, "You can't be here. You can't be back here."

The Police stoically sipped his coffee. Something told me he had no idea who Kelly Pratt was or why her presence in Essex might have just blown up an elaborate and somewhat illegal plan executed for the young woman's own protection.

"I had to come." Kelly turned to face Earl's withering glare. "Mr. Jackson, I had to come. It's your wife. I think someone wants to hurt her."

2

—————

"Kelly Pratt." I repeated the name into the phone for Andy. I strolled down the hall, past Earl's closed office door.

"Back up the truck, Will. What do you mean a hostage situation?"

"Oh, yeah, that. Pidge walked in and saw Earl holding a baby and Del standing there in his gear and she swears she heard Earl tell Del not to get any closer, but in retrospect, I think Earl was talking to the baby."

"Why was Earl holding Kelly's baby?"

"Kelly had to go potty. Bad. She was on a bus all night. And then she hitchhiked from the stop on 34."

"She hitchhiked?"

"Or tried, until Del picked her up. What else are you going to do when you see a girl hitchhiking with a baby? Kelly begged Del to take her to the airport."

"I'm sorry, Will. I'm trying to get up to speed here. Why was she hitchhiking? More importantly, why did she come back to Essex? Did she come looking for Pidge?" Andy knew the story of Pidge's friendship with the girl, and of how Pidge had come to Kelly's rescue.

"Actually, she came for Earl." I explained Kelly's message about Earl's wife —his ex-wife—Candice.

Candice Hammond Stubowsky Day Jackson O'Connor Thorpe. I don't know why, but the laundry list of Earl's ex-wife's married names stuck in my head like lyrics looking for a song. Candice owned Renell Lodge in northern Minnesota, a rustic dream she inherited from one of the husbands—I forget which—where Kelly had been hiding since Pidge persuaded me and Earl to help the girl and child escape an abusive boyfriend. Andy knew the story of what happened at Halloween, a story I liked to entitle *Attack of the Killer Zombie.* Andy's title of

Criminal Child Abduction by Three Idiots carried less appeal but landed more on point. The abusive baby daddy could have proven a genuine problem if he had not sacrificed his custody standing by being sentenced to state prison, thanks to the stash of drugs found by the cops after he crashed his pickup truck.

After the Killer Zombie made him crash his truck.

"Hurt Candice how? Who?"

"Dee, I have no idea. The baby started fussing and Kelly went to feed it—"

"Him. If I remember correctly, the baby is a boy. Seth, I think."

"Right. Anyway, Kelly set up in the pilot's lounge to—you know—hook the kid up."

"Breastfeed, Will. It's called breastfeeding and you need to get a little more comfortable with the concept." A lot of new concepts introduced themselves since Andy let me know she was pregnant.

"I know what it's called. And I am perfectly comfortable with the concept. And totally respectful." It was half true. My mind wandered a bit when thinking about Andy in that way. "Anyway, Kelly's feeding the baby. Rosemary II is making Kelly something to eat. Earl locked himself in his office. Del is finishing his coffee. And I called you because—"

"You want to know if Kelly is in any legal jeopardy over the abduction."

"Bingo. I don't think Del knows who she is, but he will certainly remember what happened last Halloween. He was there. I was hoping to head off trouble."

"Off the top of my head, no, there shouldn't be any trouble. Technically Kelly committed an unlawful abduction of a child subject to shared custody, but the ex-boyfriend hadn't filed anything. Lucky for her, we got him on the drug charges before we knew she had fled the state. But if the boyfriend hadn't been in prison he could have filed for custody, and she'd be subject to an open fugitive warrant."

"Can you let Del know? Right now, he's hanging around to drink Rosemary II's coffee, but he says he wants to talk to the girl."

"I'll call him. Please call me when you find out what's going on. Please?"

"Will do. Love you."

"Will."

"What?"

"Don't get tangled up in something here. You have that thing coming up. On Thursday. With Lewko."

"Me? Never."

"I mean it. You know how important it is."

"Love you, too."

3

I joined Pidge behind the front counter. We watched Del answer Andy's phone call. He listened for a moment, then waved at us and pointed at the door. He tucked his phone between his ear and shoulder, freed up his hands to pour himself a to-go cup of Rosemary II's coffee, then slipped out the front door still chatting with Detective Andrea Stewart, my wife.

"Was that Andy?"

"Yeah." I sent Pidge a look that attempted to scold. "Hostage situation?"

"How was I supposed to know it was Kelly? I walked in and saw a cop and Earl holding a baby." She poked my arm. "Come on—you gotta admit. That was priceless. You had to see that." She wasn't wrong.

"Looked to me like Earl was the hostage."

"What did Andy say?"

I explained Andy's assessment of Kelly's standing with the law. Pidge blew out a sigh of relief and chased it with a few choice words for the still-incarcerated ex-boyfriend.

"How did Earl wind up with the baby?" I asked.

"I wasn't here for that part. Rosemary II ran over to the Piggly Wiggly. I was in the back. Earl must have been the only one in the office when she came in. When a girl's gotta go, she's gotta go. I guess she handed the kid off to the only warm body in sight." Pidge gestured at the closed pilot lounge door. "How long does it take to feed one of those?"

"Beats me. I suppose I better learn—" I caught myself before I let Andy's pregnancy slip. Andy and I had decided to hold back any announcement until her condition approached obvious.

"Better learn what?"

"Um…I suppose I better hang around and learn what's going on. Being a co-conspirator and all."

"Do you think?"

"HE'S SUCH A BEAUTIFUL CHILD." Rosemary II sat on the floor beside the cushy leather sofa with her legs curled under her body. She gently stroked the back of the blue onesie. The baby lay belly down on a faded yellow and blue blanket, sound asleep.

He seemed cute enough. He had no hair to speak of. His fair skin reflected that of his mother. For his sake, I hoped his genes favored her. His biological father was hawk-faced and mean looking.

I dropped into one of the fat recliners. Pidge sat on the sofa beside Kelly who threw her arm around her friend and issued a deep squeeze mindful of the cast on Pidge's left forearm.

"Kel, what the fuck? Why did you come back here? You could've gotten in a lot of trouble."

"I need to talk to Mr. Jackson." Kelly looked for Earl in the empty front office outside the pilot lounge door. Pidge glanced at Rosemary II. Kelly followed the glance. "Is he coming back?"

Rosemary II gave the sleeping infant one more gentle stroke, then leaned close to breathe in the scent of his bald scalp.

"Heavens, it's like a drug." She pushed herself upright. "Of course, dear, but best not to talk in here. It might get loud. Let's all step out and let this little one sleep. Will, push that coffee table up against the sofa in case he rolls, would you?"

"On it."

After moving the furniture, I joined Pidge and Kelly at the office front counter. Rosemary II went to fetch Earl. When she returned alone, she carefully pulled the door to the pilot's lounge closed.

"He's making some calls. How long does the child usually nap?" Rosemary II asked Kelly.

"He's a sleeper. He'll be down for at least two hours." Kelly suddenly lifted her arms and pressed her wrists against her shirt. "Oh, gosh. Sometimes they just don't want to shut off. I'll be right back!" She scooped up the baby bag that had not left her side and hurried toward the restroom.

Earl stomped down the hall and joined us. He cast a sharp eye around the office and the lobby.

"Where is it?"

"*He*, Earl, is sleeping." Rosemary II gestured at the pilot's lounge. "So, keep your voice down. Is someone going to explain to me what this is all about?"

Earl looked at Pidge, who looked at me.

"What?" I frowned. I waited. No one relented. "Fine."

I told Rosemary II the story of how Kelly was on the verge of letting herself be enslaved by an abuser, trapped by their shared child, and how Pidge brought the problem to me, and I engaged Earl in a conspiracy to separate Kelly from her dangerous ex-boyfriend on the opening night of the Essex Fall Festival—on Halloween night. I left out the part about how I made Kelly and the baby vanish inside a dark funhouse ride. And the part about how Pidge took off with Kelly and the baby, pursued by the enraged ex-boyfriend. And how I chased the boyfriend's pickup truck and made myself reappear on the truck's hood, scaring the bejesus out of the shithead because of the zombie makeup I wore for my role in the haunted funhouse. The ploy caused Kelly's pursuer to lose control and roll his truck. Pidge delivered Kelly to the airport and Earl flew her and her baby to Minnesota and into the care of Earl's ex-wife, Candice. The cops scooped up the ex-boyfriend along with possession with intent.

I was about to explain Andy's assessment that violating the law by abducting her own son was a near miss for Kelly—that she was safe—when Kelly returned from the restroom. Earl lifted an accusing finger in her direction.

"I warned you about getting your panties all wet for your ex and coming back here." I thought he might scare the girl into the kind of helpless catatonic state he had induced in her when they met last fall.

She surprised me and, I think, everyone.

"Don't you snap at me, Mr. Jackson. You're going to listen to what I have to say. Candice always told me not to let you scare me. So...just you *don't*. Scare me, I mean." She swallowed hard and stared at Earl who tucked away his finger. "I've had a lot of time to think about this, Mr. Jackson, and you're probably not going to want to hear it, but if I live a thousand lifetimes, I don't think I can ever thank you enough for what you did for me and Seth. You and Candice. You took me to her, and she didn't just take me in, she gave me life. Neither of you have ever asked anything in return, but if you did, I would give you anything, so just you don't...yell...at...me." The last few words escaped a quivering lower lip. Kelly rubbed tears from her eyes.

Rosemary II made a move toward hugging the girl, but I closed a grip on her arm. Kelly wasn't finished.

"Now you *listen to me*." She rubbed her face again. "Two nights ago Candice came into my room and told me to pack whatever I could carry and get the baby ready. She said there was no time to explain. I didn't know what to think, but I did as I was told. She said someone was coming for us. I don't know, but it was super scary. I put what I could in this bag. Mostly it's baby stuff. And then she rushed us out of the lodge and into her Jeep and she drove us into Big Fork and made me get out in front of the courthouse and she told me to stay there out of sight until the pharmacy across the street opened. She said that's where the bus stops. She gave me a bunch of money to buy a ticket and she told me not to come back and not to tell anyone where I was going. Just go somewhere safe, she said. You know how she is. She's always so strong and tough. I didn't know where to go, so I bought a ticket to Minneapolis and when I got there, I bought a ticket here to Essex because I had to see you, Mr. Jackson. Something is wrong. Something bad has happened. Candice needs help and you're the only person I could think of who can help her."

Earl curled his claws into fists and mounted them on his hips. He stared at Kelly for a long minute, then lowered his gaze to his shoes. The modulated low rumble of his voice had nothing to do with a sleeping baby in the next room.

"She tell you to come get me?"

"No, sir. The opposite. She said I shouldn't tell anyone. She said I should stay away."

"And you came straight here?"

"Yes, sir. The bus to Minneapolis yesterday morning—then we had to wait all day for a late bus last night to get here. We got out at the highway stop this morning and hitched here—at least until the policeman picked me up. I told him your name and got him to bring me to you."

Earl showed Kelly the leathery top of his bald skull while he locked his gaze on his steel-toed work boots.

"And she didn't say nothing about nothing?"

"No, sir. She wouldn't hardly talk to me." Kelly waited. None of the rest of us dared move. "I think she was scared, Mr. Jackson. I never seen Candice scared of anything, but I think she was scared and not just for herself. I think she was scared for me and Seth. Whatever it was that was coming, I think it was coming for her, but she was afraid it might come for me and the baby, too."

Earl's head bobbed once. He lifted his face at the girl. She flinched. Beneath Earl's crags and creases, I saw his judgment of Kelly shift. A curt nod paid her the compliment of both belief and gratitude.

Earl turned to me. "I tried calling. She ain't answering her cell and the line for the business says it's out of service."

"That makes no sense," Kelly said. "The summer season is starting in a couple weeks. She told me she was booked through October."

"Boss, you don't think this is blowback for that old Queen Air you and I pulled outta there. I mean—that outcome was pretty damned public. Anybody with an interest in the airplane and its cargo saw it spread all over cable news."

"What Queen Air?" Pidge asked.

"Tell you later." I watched Earl think about it for a moment. He didn't take long.

"Pidge, get 619 out and gas her up. Will?" He paused. "You in?"

Worst idea ever. In just two days I needed to be in Memphis, and the day after that in Evermore, North Carolina to connect with Spiro Lewko and engage in what might be the biggest test of *the other thing* yet. There was no way I could just charge off on a mission with no plan, no schedule, no idea of duration. Too much had gone into preparing for Evermore. The stage had been set recently in New York City where the world watched Lewko and a child vanish in front of dozens of phone cameras. In a single stroke, Lewko became the focus of a world-wide media frenzy that might otherwise have landed on me. More importantly, the scheme made it possible to organize the still mysterious curative aspect of *the other thing*. In a few days, in Evermore, it would be tested on two dozen eager, desperate children.

Andy would kill me.

"Lemme grab my overnight kit."

I started for the door when Kelly hooked a gentle grasp on my arm.

"I'm coming, too."

"The hell you are." Earl's growl left no room for negotiation.

Kelly's voice gained strength I didn't think she had. "I am, Mr. Jackson. I'm coming, too. You can't say no. You saved me. You and Cassidy and Will saved me, but Candice changed my life. What she's done for me made me know I am a person, *a real person*. What I was before would have run and hid. But a real person helps someone who needs help. I won't go back to being a non-person. *I won't.* I'm coming, too."

Earl stepped directly in front of Kelly. This time she did not flinch.

"I am not taking no baby. That's that."

"The baby can stay with me." Rosemary II put her arm around Kelly.

"He's been taking formula," Kelly said. "I started him…"

Earl looked into the eyes of one of the few forces of nature that he could not overcome. Rosemary II stared right back at him.

"You heard the young lady."

Earl turned and marched toward his office. "Wheels up in twenty, Will. Anybody else wants a ride, they best not dawdle."

4

I told Arun Dewar that I'd be gone for 24 hours, a bald lie passing for an optimistic estimate. He rose from his office chair in the Foundation hangar and chased me through the lounge. He reminded me of the flight to Memphis scheduled for two days hence and launched his standard information overload about the coming trip. I waved him off. As I hurried out through the main hangar Arun shouted after me.

"Today is Tuesday!"

"All day long."

"Memphis on Thursday!"

"I'm guessing it will be there all week, but sure, Thursday. Send the itinerary to my email."

"Which you never read!"

I paused at the hangar door. "Great system, eh?"

I RETURNED to the Essex County Air Service office with my flight bag. The white and blue Beechcraft Baron sat at the fuel pump. Pidge was nowhere in sight. One of the kids Earl hired to park airplanes and pump gas fueled the aircraft. I hurried through the front office to Rosemary II's coffee station and filled a thermos. I stole most of a fresh pot, for which I expected a sharp word or two from the front desk. Rosemary II ignored or didn't notice me. She and Kelly were huddled over a baby bag. Kelly busily explained various pockets and components. The look on Rosemary II's face mixed pride in the young mother's diligence with sadness for the obviously meager contents. I knew without guessing that Kelly would find the bag brimming with supplies upon her return.

I hurried past the ladies to Earl's office, but his desk chair and the cluttered space were both empty. I headed into the machine shop adjacent to the main hangar where I spotted Pidge. Sight of her stopped me in my tracks.

"Pidge! Jesus Christ, what are you doing?"

She looked up from the workbench. She had tightened the blue cast on her left arm in a vice and held a hammer in her right hand.

"What does it look like? I want this goddamned thing off."

I dropped my bags and hurried forward.

"Are you nuts? You need to have that taken off by a doctor."

"Really?" She drove the hammer down onto the cast. I winced. She didn't. "Oh, look. It's cracked. Gee, how did that happen?" She rapped the hammer on the cast again. And again. I jerked the weapon out of her hand.

"Are you crazy? You're going to break your arm and then you're stuck in this thing for another eight weeks." I tossed the hammer out of reach. Too late. She tightened the vice. The cast cracked. "Alright! Alright! Hold on a second. Jesus, you're going to crush your own arm."

She unwound the vice and wiggled her arm free.

"Come on. Help me get this piece of shit off." She clawed at the broken cast.

"Hang on." I found a pair of tinsnips.

"That's what I'm talking about. Cut this puppy off."

"Didn't you have an appointment next week? Why are you doing this now?"

She didn't answer. That's when I noticed her overnight bag by the door.

5

I flatly refused to allow the freshly cast-free Pidge to take either pilot seat. There was no combination of coercion, bribe or threat that would induce me to climb in the back seat of an airplane with her and Earl sharing the controls. The only possible outcome to such an arrangement would be fiery death, and that's before the airplane ever left the ground. I claimed the pilot in command seat and designated Earl copilot. I told Pidge if she didn't like it, I would pick her up and carry her back in the office and lock her in the supply closet. She muttered a few of her favorite words but agreed to ride in the rear with Kelly.

I completed the aircraft preflight and stowed the bags. Earl showed up less than a minute after I determined we were ready. During that minute, I launched a rapid text message to my wife sketching out my departure and promising an explanation soon. Earl and Kelly appeared on the ramp just as I hit Send.

Allowing for startup, taxi, runup and takeoff—we launched within a few seconds of Earl's declared twenty minutes to wheels up. I banked right after tucking in the wheels and activated the autopilot while I opened a conversation with air traffic control.

We climbed into a bright cloudless sky at 130 knots.

6

Renell Lodge has its own runway, a charitable term for a narrow east-west cut in the Minnesota north woods. During my last visit, Candice declared the usable runway to be three thousand feet long. Calling it twenty-five hundred would be generous, and the sixty-foot trees at both ends don't do pilots any favors. Navigating to the nearly hidden runway required us to first fly to Big Fork Municipal Airport, a one-runway airport just north of its namesake town. Over the departure end of runway 33, we turned on a course of 285 degrees and used time and speed to find the right spot. On the way, I noticed a cluster of buildings and homes—not much more than a wide spot in a narrow road—that represented a dot on the map called Beaudry, the nearest facsimile of civilization to Renell Lodge. I made a mental note of the town in case we needed help.

Renell Lake, better described as an oversized pond, provided a decent landmark. After we found the landing strip, I circled the lake to read the wind direction from ripples on the water. I also studied the log lodge overlooking the water and the cabins tucked in the surrounding woods. I saw no vehicles or people. Except for the landing strip a quarter of a mile north of the lodge, the landscape contained nothing but trees, lakes, and marshy meadows. Canada lay to the north, fifty or seventy miles away.

I slipped from the circuit around Renell Lake into a downwind leg for landing from east to west. Although I throttled back both engines, I did not lower the gear or flaps. I eased into a descent and flew two wide left turns until the Baron lined up above the trees on the right side of the runway. Earl said nothing about the still-retracted landing gear or my apparent intention to land in the trees.

Just above the treetops, I leveled off and nudged the throttles to avoid bleeding off airspeed. The Baron steadied at 120 knots. Trees flashed past beneath us. Off the left wingtip, the runway streamed by.

"It's paved." I had no idea. When Earl and I were here, we landed on packed snow. Earl didn't comment. "Looks clear. No standing water or debris."

Less than 150 feet below and to my left, the short, narrow asphalt strip looked less than inviting. I saw no other aircraft or equipment. I tipped a slight left bank and held my altitude and speed. After a few seconds, the lodge and cabins appeared ahead of the nose. I raced over the lodge roof, shedding altitude to make the low pass count. The Baron shot over the small lake where I added power to climb and return for landing.

Earl twisted in his seat as we buzzed the lodge. "If she's down there, she knows we're here."

7

"Thanks for not killing us." Pidge jabbed my shoulder with her elbow as she climbed past the front passenger seatback.

"That landing was so good, you should put it in your logbook, too." I followed her out the door and onto the wing.

Earl popped open the baggage door. He reached inside. "Leave the bags for now." He pulled something from his overnight kit and stuffed it in the pocket of his leather flight jacket. I caught a glimpse of flat gray steel—his Colt M1911A1 semiautomatic pistol.

"Don't close it." I hopped off the wing. He stepped aside. I reached into my own bag and dug down until I found a pair of small tubes resembling flashlights. The tubes had a single slide control positioned to be operated by a thumb while gripping the unit. The devices each contained a small electric motor and went by the brilliant name of BLASTER—*Basic Linear Aerial System for Transport, Electric Rechargeable*—at least in my head. Andy insists the name needs more time on the drawing board. I tucked both devices in my jacket breast pocket, then fetched two black six-inch carbon fiber model airplane propellers from the bag and stuffed them in the same pocket.

Turnaround at the end of the runway had been tight, but I thought it prudent to park the Baron facing back the way we came in case we needed an expeditious departure. I joined Earl where he stood at the wingtip. He scanned the woods all around the airstrip and between us and the lodge.

"Feel like we're being watched?" I asked.

He grunted. "Anybody who says they feel like they're being watched is full of shit."

"Right." I looked down at the bulge in his jacket. He followed my glance and tapped the leather.

"Bears. They come outta hibernation and they're groggy and hungry and lookin' to hump another bear. I don't want to be mistaken. Let's go." Earl marched toward the tree line. He didn't mention what we both noticed—Candice did not meet us at the airstrip.

We followed a two-wheel track through the woods. Dark green pines cast black shadows on the leaf bed. Deciduous trees had yet to bud and fill in the shadows. Sunlight took the opportunity to reach the forest floor where it enticed green sprouts to rise through layers of decaying leaves. The temperature read just below fifty when we landed. Despite the early afternoon sun, I did not think it would go higher. I expected to see more snow. Isolated patches of white peeked from under fallen logs or in ravines. Except for a choir of overly energetic spring birdsong, the forest lay quiet.

Earl took the lead, pounding his bowlegged way forward like a man on a mission. Pidge walked beside Kelly, who hooked her friend's arm and pulled it against her body. I brought up the rear thinking that if something threatened us, I would grab both Pidge and Kelly, vanish, and get off the ground before anyone got hurt. Earl could fend for himself.

The first structure we encountered was the smallest of Candice's cabins. The log-walled square looked sufficient for a single room with a fireplace. Except for the main lodge and the boathouse, I'd never seen the inside of any of the Renell structures.

"Kelly, you said the season was about to start. When do the paying guests arrive?" I asked.

"Memorial Day weekend. We've been working for the past few weeks to get ready. Lots of cleaning."

"Did Candice seem worried about the start of the season?"

"How do you mean?"

"Troubled. Maybe having problems with suppliers? Deliveries? She cooks for the guests, which means bringing in a ton of food. Was that all coming together as expected?"

Kelly looked uncertain. "I don't know. Candice always goes into town for groceries. I cleaned the cabins. Tidied up the grounds. I don't know about all that other stuff."

Earl diverted from the track. He jogged onto the small cabin's narrow porch. He cupped his hands around his face and pressed against a window. After a moment, he tried the door. Locked.

"I can get the keys," Kelly offered.

"Nah." Earl rejoined us.

The roof of the main lodge building peeked through the trees. Earl hurried forward. We skirted the cabins between us and the lodge without stopping. As we stepped into a broad open yard, I noticed the taillights of a Jeep Wrangler at the far end of the lodge. I was about to mention it when everyone stopped.

"What the fuck?" Pidge closed ranks beside Kelly who lifted both hands to her face. The hair on the back of my neck jumped to attention.

We stared at what had been a pair of double doors lending entry to the main lodge. Both doors hung in tatters. The wooden frame was shredded. Shattered glass littered the porch.

Claw marks tore into the wood all around the door frame and marred what was left of the doors. Wood panels and muntin bars were ripped apart. In some spots, the gouges looked as much as an inch deep. Both doors were in shambles. The left had been torn from its hinges. Pieces lay on the porch and in the yard between us and the building.

Earl slipped his hand in his pocket and kept it there. He climbed the steps to the lodge porch and carefully stepped over broken glass and through the opening.

I moved past Pidge and Kelly and eased up behind Earl.

"Her Jeep is here."

"I seen it."

I followed Earl into the lodge. He stopped.

"Mother of God." Earl's hoarse growl raised goose flesh on my arms.

A great room dominated the main lodge building and overlooked the small lake. The room offered scattered secondhand furniture, fostered a corner library, and served beverages at a small bar that doubled as a check-in desk.

None of it had gone untouched.

Long slashes scarred the wooden walls. Books had been torn from their shelves. Tossed hardcovers littered the floor, many of them shredded. Loose pages wiggled in a breeze seeping through shattered windows. Moldings around the window frames showed raw claw marks. None of the liquor shelves behind the bar survived intact. Bottles lay on the wooden floor halfway across the room, some broken. A glass display frame full of photographs hung askew. Photos of past guests—many of them black and white prints dating back decades—lay sliced and shredded. The lodge walls once held the usual collection of taxidermy. A few deer heads remained in place. The rest, torn and split open, lay on the carpet. The furniture had been ripped. Tufts of stuffing skittered around on the bare wood floor, pushed by a breeze that intruded through broken windows.

"Earl," I said quietly, "I don't see any blood. Do you?"

He shook his head.

"Is this fur? Animal fur?" Pidge pinched something from a split in the shattered door frame and held it up.

"Maybe from one of those animal heads." I pointed at a severed deer head that stared at me with black glass eyes.

Kelly's ivory skin turned a shade paler. Her blue eyes bulged, wide and unblinking. "Where's Candice? Do you think she's okay?"

Earl stepped to the girl and put a hand on her shoulder.

"If she's here, we'll find her. Where are those keys?"

Kelly lifted her eyes to a set of stairs that rose to a half landing, then to the second floor. The walls appeared unmarked. Whatever had done this had not climbed the stairs.

"Candice keeps them in her office. Upstairs."

"Show me."

"Boss, you think it's safe?" I gestured at the second floor landing.

"I think whoever or whatever did this is gone." Earl turned to Kelly and spoke so gently I thought a stranger had joined us. "Honey, you show me. Show me where she keeps the keys. I'll be right beside you."

They moved to the lodge stairs and climbed. Earl led the way and kept his right hand in his jacket pocket.

"Will, c'mere."

I picked my way back across the shattered front door glass to where Pidge had returned to the wooden porch. She studied the gravel and dirt yard where cars pulling up to the lodge might park.

"You see any tracks?"

"I see tire tracks. Candice's Jeep Wrangler is parked at the back. Those might be hers." I pointed. "Looks like some other tread patterns, too."

"Not that kind of tracks. Animal tracks."

"You mean like a bear?"

Pidge huffed. "Bear, my ass. No fucking bear did this, I don't care how horny or groggy or hungry they are."

"What then?"

She glared at me. "You gonna make me say it?"

"Out loud."

"Fine." She held up the fur she had pinched from the door. "Fucking werewolf."

8

E arl returned with Kelly and a fist full of keys. He singled one out, held it up, and showed me the black molded plastic end that said Jeep.

"Nobody upstairs." He pocketed the keys. "We're gonna look for Candice, but we gotta assume that something came here to do harm, so I want reinforcements." He pulled out his phone.

"Who're you calling?" I asked.

"County sheriff." He thumbed in three numbers, then listened for the connection. Earl did not survive decades near aircraft engines with his hearing intact. His phone speaker volume was loud enough for me to understand the 911 operator who asked him to describe his emergency.

While Earl delivered a terse version of events, I poked deeper into the lodge. A dining room capable of seating a couple dozen at one long table joined the great room. The destruction diminished in volume but not in violence. Chairs had been flung away from the table. Claw marks cut into the wooden table surface. Shattered dining room windows overlooked a narrow deck and the roof of a large boathouse and the lake beyond. Sashes and frames hung in splinters.

Double swinging doors separated the dining room from the lodge kitchen. I expected to find more destruction within. If this had been an animal—and I had strong doubts given the vicious vandalism—surely food would have been an attraction. Yet the doors showed no claw marks.

I was about to push through the doors when I heard a thump. I froze and looked at Pidge and Kelly who had followed me. I lifted my finger to my lips.

"Don't go in there!" Kelly whispered urgently.

I held up one hand and mouthed the words *Stay Here*. They paid no attention. Both Pidge and Kelly tiptoed around the big dining table and formed up behind me. I rolled my eyes at them, then pressed one side of the double kitchen doors slowly open, just far enough to see most of the left side of the room. I let the door ease shut again, repositioned, and did the same to the other door. Nothing looked out of place or waited in ambush in any part of the kitchen that I could see. Nor did I see any damage.

I pressed the door open and moved through.

The kitchen was tidy, untouched. Candice's cooking space contained modern fixtures fronted with abundant stainless steel. Pots and pans hung from hooks over a central island. The white tile floor looked new, utterly spotless. On the wall opposite the door to the dining room, a pair of upright freezers and a refrigerator dominated, also looking new. Beside them stood a solid steel door.

"What's that?" I pointed.

"That's the dry pantry," Kelly whispered.

I was about to tell them both to stay put when Earl pushed through the door behind us. Pidge spun around and threw her finger against her lips and shushed him. Earl dispensed a withering glare and slid past her.

I pointed at the dry pantry door.

Earl nodded. He pulled his hand from his pocket and swung his Colt down by his side with the muzzle aimed at the floor. He eased silently past me. When he reached the wall beside the door, he raised the pistol to a ready position held firmly in a two-handed grip. I set up on the opposite side of the door, facing the wall. He tipped his head once in my direction.

I closed the fingertips of my left hand on the doorknob and applied pressure. The knob turned. Not locked. Earl stepped back and tipped the weapon's muzzle slightly upward. If someone startled him, an accidental discharge would put a hole in the ceiling.

I twisted the knob and jerked the door wide open. It momentarily blocked my view of Earl who jumped into the door frame.

Someone shrieked.

"DON'T SHOOT!"

I leaned in to look past Earl who fixed his aim on something dark in one corner of the shelf-lined pantry.

"Don't shoot! Please don't shoot me!" A man's voice with a heavy eastern accent lifted out of the dark.

"Wait!" Kelly cried. She pressed past me. "Don't shoot him! That's Mister Minelli!"

I fumbled for a light switch and didn't find one. A string tickled the back of my hand. I tugged it. A bare bulb lit up.

In the back corner of the pantry behind a makeshift stack of boxes, rice bags and canned goods, a fleshy bespectacled face mounted wide, terrified eyes.

Earl lifted the gun skyward and removed his finger from the trigger guard. "Who?"

9

"I din't see nuthin'." Minelli used both hands to lift a coffee mug to his lips. The brew inside was straight Macallan 12—my father-in-law's favorite, although Louis Taylor qualifies his choice with something about *double cask*. Minelli found an intact bottle behind the bar. After pouring and taking a substantial gulp, he repeated the phrase. Minelli sounded like a low-level mob soldier under interrogation. I tried to place the accent. Not New York. Something else.

Out of shape and overweight, it wasn't easy to guess his age. He had thick black hair cut short on the sides and moplike on the top. His abundant beard stubble showed no hints of gray. A ruby tint to his nose suggested intimacy with the scotch in his coffee mug. If forced, I might have gone as young as twenty-five or as old as forty.

After affirming that he wouldn't be shot, Minelli pushed past all of us and made a beeline for the bar.

Earl hooked Kelly's arm and walked her out of the great room and back into the lodge dining room. Pidge and I followed. Low and out of earshot, he asked, "Who is this guy?"

"That's Mr. Minelli."

"Local guy? Some kinda caretaker?"

"No—uh, I mean—he helps sometimes with like heavy stuff. But he's a guest."

"I thought the season hasn't started."

Kelly shook her head. "It hasn't. He's been here for about a month. Candice made a special arrangement because he's writing a book about Minnesota minerals or something. He's really nice."

"And he was here the whole time? Even when Candice evacuated you?"

Kelly shrugged. "I guess."

Earl walked back into the great room. Pidge, Kelly and I did our duckling imitation and followed him.

"Who are you?" Earl didn't point the gun at the man, but he didn't put it away either.

"Ray Minelli. Who are you?"

"Candice is my ex-wife. Her car is here. Any idea where she is?"

"Which husband are you?"

"Jackson. Kelly here says you're a writer or something."

Minelli smiled. It lent a friendly twinkle to his eye. He tipped an appreciative nod in Kelly's direction. She smiled back at him.

"She's a sweetie, ain't she? I'm just a fucking cab driver from Philly. Or I was. 'Til I got shot by some scumbag trying to rob me for a lousy thirty bucks." Minelli leaned back and for a moment I thought he was going to lift his shirt to show off a scar. Instead, he pointed at a spot on his ribs. "Missed my heart by a red—" He cut himself off, glancing again at Kelly and then Pidge. "—by a hair. And that was it. No more cab driving for me. I got disability and I hit the road."

"And you came here."

"Yeah. A couple years ago. Then again last year. This year I asked Candice if I could come early and stay the whole season. And yeah, I'm workin' on a book. Don't let this Grays Ferry accent fool you. I can read. Big words and everything."

Earl pulled out a chair opposite Minelli and sat down. "The whole season? That ain't cheap."

Minelli tugged up one corner of a grin. "I got a settlement from the cab company."

"Why don't you start at the beginning?"

Minelli opened his mouth to reply, but a startled look washed over his face. "Holy God, Kelly! The baby! Is the baby okay?"

"He's fine, Mr. Minelli. Seth is just fine."

Minelli closed his eyes and threw his head back. "Thank the Holy Mother!" He threw an abbreviated sign of the cross over his forehead and shoulders. Earl waited, then repeated his question. Minelli settled in his chair. He downed another gulp of scotch, then poured more into his mug.

"Scared the ever-loving piss outta me. Jesus, Mary, and Joseph, I'm so glad you're okay, Kelly. Honest. I didn't see youse two yesterday and when all this started last night, I got scared for you and—where's Candice?"

"You tell us," Earl said.

Minelli shrugged extravagantly. "I came back from a hike in the woods last night and wasn't nobody around. Candice always said to go ahead and fix my own supper, so I did, and that's when it started." He jerked his thumb at the destruction. "Jesus Christ! Did you see all this?"

Earl didn't answer.

"I was in here eating some supper. You was gone, Kelly. And Candice. I figured youse went into Beaudry and I was kicking myself because my car is there and they called and said it was done and I could'a got a ride, but it's no big deal. I was in here eating and that's when something went past the window."

"Something?" Pidge asked. I glared at her, signaling her not to blurt out her pet theory. "What kind of something?"

"The hell do I know. It was dark and it was a big motherfucker and it moved fast. Pounding on the deck. Right out there." He pointed at the deck beyond the smashed windows. "I didn't even see it at first, it was like it was part of the dark, but then it moved all of a sudden like, and BAM!" He slammed a fist on the table. "It was gone. And I just about crapped my pants. I couldn't fuckin' move. I don't mind telling you, back in Philly when that ni—I mean—that guy shot me, I didn't even think about it. I was never scared. Not even when they told me it just missed my heart. But last night I thought I was gonna pee myself. I sat there and I wasn't even breathing. And then, BAM!" He slammed the table again. "All hell broke loose at the front door. I don't even remember getting outta my chair. Next thing I knew I was diving into that pantry. The door don't lock, but that's a solid goddamned door. And that's it."

"What?"

"That's it. That's where I stayed. I heard this place getting torn apart, and I prayed and stayed put. I sat there for hours after it was over. I guess I fell asleep, and then I heard an airplane fly over and here we are. I din't see nuthin'. The whole time. 'Til youse got here. Now you're telling me you can't find Candice?" A fresh tide of worry flooded his face. "Jesus, we gotta find her! Was that you in the airplane?"

Earl didn't answer, so I did. "Yeah. That was us. Are you saying you haven't seen Candice for two days?"

Minelli made a face like he was thinking about it and the effort hurt. "I guess. Sometimes it's like that. She comes and goes. Been nice having Kelly and the baby around. But yeah, sometimes I don't see Candice for a day or two. She's busy gettin' ready for summer. I guess it was day before yesterday—last I saw her." His failure to mention Candice abruptly hustling Kelly away in the middle of the night made me think of something. "You said your car is in Beaudry?"

"Getting fixed. I snagged the exhaust pipe on a stump last week. Everybody drives an SUV or pickup truck around here but not me. Crown Vic. A classic. I took it to a shop in Beaudry so some guy can weld a new bracket. 'Sposed to be done now."

"Why are you here?" Earl leaned forward to add weight to his question.

"Told you. I been coming here the last few years. It soothes me. And this year I decided to write a book."

"What kind of book?"

Minelli smiled. "Mineral substrate and the collision of the gneissic Minnesota River Valley subprovince and the Superior subprovince at the end of the Archean Eon." He grinned, like he had just told his favorite joke.

"You some kind of professor?"

"Nope. Told you. Cab driver. Six years."

"Mineral what the fuck?" Pidge asked.

"I was a geology major in college. You know who hires geology majors in Philly?" He gave it a beat. "Cab companies." He let the punchline settle. "Look, I'm happy to tell you my life story, but I'm worried about Candice. It ain't safe out there. We need to find her, and I don't wanna be outside after dark."

10

The Itasca County Sheriff's SUV that rolled into the yard had a jarring effect on me that had nothing to do with the crime scene.

"Shit." I slapped the breast pocket of my flight jacket. "I gotta call Andy."

Earl waved for me to follow him. "If she hasn't filed divorce papers by now, another fifteen minutes ain't gonna make a difference."

We stepped across shattered glass on the porch.

The deputy—his shirt tag said Reitman—looked too young for the uniform he wore or for the gun strapped to his hip. Not quite as short as Del Simms, he had close-cut dark hair over a face he might shave every third or fourth day. The wire rimmed shades tried to infuse authority but perched on a narrow nose and unblemished skin they only made him look younger. I suspected his quick arrival meant he drew the short straw and patrolled the farthest reaches of the county. That or he worked out of a substation in Big Fork or maybe even Beaudry, although what I'd seen of Beaudry suggested the tiny settlement would be lucky if it had a tavern to go with whatever service station harbored Minelli's Crown Victoria.

He lifted the dark glasses to stare.

"Holy cow." He ignored Earl and me. "Hooo-leee cow."

Deputy Reitman climbed the porch steps in a daze. At the door, he reached up and stroked his fingers over the claw marks dug into the wood. "What the hell...?" Earl and I said nothing. We waited for the deputy to shed his astonishment and notice us. When he did, he pulled a note pad from his pocket and consulted scribbles. "Did you call this in—uh—Mr. Jackson?"

"Uh-huh."

"Were you here when this happened?"

"Do you see any scratches on me?"

The kid looked, then got the inference. "I mean—any idea what did this?"

"I do." Pidge appeared in the door frame. I cringed. "Fucking werewolf."

Reitman caught himself reaching for his pen to make a note. He stopped and re-examined the claw marks. Pidge held out her hand.

"Tell me that's not wolf fur." She lifted fibers toward the deputy as if she thought he might sniff them. He tipped his head away and did not pluck the hairs from her fingers.

"I'm not much of an expert on animal fur. Where'd that come from?"

Pidge pointed at the door frame. The deputy looked at her, looked at the frame, then looked at Earl who said nothing.

"Don't fucking believe me?" Pidge moved to the other side of the broken frame. "Here. There's more." She pointed but did not touch. Another tuft of gray hairs lodged in the fractured wood. "You need to take a sample of that and get it analyzed. Bet you anything it comes back with both wolf and human DNA."

"Might have been a bear," Reitman replied politely ignoring the crazy. He studied a line of claw marks.

"A bear? Really?" Pidge charged forward and positioned her hand over the deep scratches. "Five fingers. That's human!"

"Bears have five fingers—five claws on each paw," I said. Pidge glared at me. "Sorry. They do."

"Son, we got a bigger problem than her imagination." Earl moved to the edge of the porch and squinted into the trees surrounding us, trees that were starting to make me feel claustrophobic. "The owner of this lodge is missing. And if all this was meant for her, she's in big trouble."

BETWEEN A COLD STARE from Earl and vigorous hand signals from me, Pidge took the hint and backed off her werewolf theory long enough for Earl and me to tag team an explanation of who we were and how we came to arrive at Renell Lodge looking for Candice Thorpe. Deputy Reitman took dutiful notes and asked questions. While he appeared more concerned with recording enough to write a novel, he could not stop shifting his gaze to the damaged building or throwing a curious glance at Pidge. At the end of the explanation, Earl and I walked him through the lodge and introduced him to Minelli, who filled in blanks about himself and his presence, and the events that drove him into the kitchen's dry pantry.

Three pages of notes later, Deputy Reitman folded over the cover of his notebook and returned it to his shirt pocket. For a moment he seemed at a loss.

"So?" Earl lifted his wristwatch. "Clock's ticking."

"You mean…?"

"Let's go. Let's get cracking." Earl pulled out the wad of keys he had obtained from Kelly. "We gotta check all the cabins."

"Is there any reason Mrs. Thorpe would be hiding in one of the cabins?"

"Other than a fucking werewolf on the loose?" Pidge asked.

"Her vehicle is parked in back," I said. "I think the Boss here is right. She could be hiding. She could be hurt. Or both. We made noise when we arrived. It says something that she didn't come out to greet us."

"Right."

"One more thing." Earl reached for his back pocket and produced his wallet. He slipped a card out from under his driver's license. "That's my concealed carry permit. Minnesota reciprocates with Wisconsin." He patted his jacket pocket. "I just don't want you surprised, son."

"Right." Reitman examined the card. "I appreciate the heads up. Keep it in your pocket. Let's have a look around then."

WE SEARCHED for the better part of the next hour, starting inside the lodge. Candice's office and four guest rooms occupied the second floor of the main lodge. Candice kept a small apartment behind the kitchen at the back of the lodge building. The outbuildings included a big boathouse at the water level, and 12 small- to medium-sized cabins. Unwilling to be left alone, Pidge, Minelli, and Kelly trooped behind me, Earl, and Deputy Reitman from building to building. The boathouse, which had housed a parked Beechcraft Queen Air twin-engine airplane for more than two decades, had been restored to its original intent. It sheltered a row of canoes numbered to match the cabins, racks of lifejackets and oars, and assorted gear. A snowcat vacationed under a tarp in a back corner having completed its winter duties. A chain ran from a steel loop in the boathouse wall down the shallow slope to the water where a raft floating on empty steel drums bumped against the shore. Nothing inside or outside the boathouse had been damaged. The small cabins were untouched. Minelli, after refusing to enter until someone turned on the lights, conducted a tour of the cabin he occupied. Complex topographical maps were pinned to the walls. A desk carried stacks of books and an unhealthy supply of assorted whisky representing the Scottish, and whiskey from Irish and American distilleries. A power cord ran from a laptop to the wall socket.

"There's no internet." Minelli tapped the laptop. "I'm off the grid. I use it strictly for writing."

I asked, "Mr. Minelli, did Candice give you any indication why the main phone line for the lodge comes up as 'out of service'?"

"It is? No idea. She's got a computer up in the lodge with some kinda internet connection for the phone, reservations, and such. She let me use it once or twice to look up a reference. But I had no clue the phone was out."

"The number is not in service." I tapped the phone in my pocket and again felt the jolt of a reminder to call Andy.

"Like I said. No idea."

"Memorial Day weekend is in a couple weeks. Just seems weird that she's on the verge of having this place packed for the summer and the phone isn't working."

"That ain't all." Minelli shuffled his feet. "I don't know if it's relevant or any of my business, but Candice had a cow last week on account'a some of the local kids she hires on for the summer ditched."

"Ditched?" Reitman reached for his notepad.

"Dropped out. Gave their notice. Whatever. She can't run this place with just her and little Kelly, there. She hires on local kids every summer."

"Did the kids give her a reason?" Reitman asked.

"Nope. Just left her high and dry."

Deputy Reitman made a note, then concluded there was nothing more to be found in Minelli's cabin. We moved on.

I LET the search party finish off the last three cabins on their own. Keeping them in sight, I hung back and dialed my wife.

"Hi, gorgeous."

"Uh-huh…" There was no mistaking her tone.

"Busted?"

"Like Capone. Will, I thought you were not going to get tangled up in this. You know you cannot miss Evermore on Friday. People are counting on you."

"Who ratted me out?"

"Arun sent me an email with your itinerary for Thursday. He asked me to print it out and make sure you see it. He practically begged me to get you back in time. Naturally, I had to ask what he meant. He told me that Pidge told him about going to Minnesota with her friend Kelly for a few days. So, then I called Rosemary II. Turns out she has a new baby."

"You should go over and test drive it—er—him."

"Don't change the subject. Where are you?"

I explained everything up to the minute, including Pidge's theory that one of the Universal Studios monsters from the days of Lon Chaney had trashed the lodge.

"I think that's highly unlikely, but please tell me you are seeing the bigger picture here."

"Of course," I assured her, "and that would be…what? You mean Lewko?"

"Yes, I mean Lewko. Will, this thing in Evermore on Friday—it's kinda *huge*. Everything that happened in New York set this up."

"For Lewko."

"For a lot of other people, too."

"I know. I know." Andy didn't need to remind me. The stage had been set for weeks. Friday and the weekend were to be the first mass application of *the other thing* to children who needed more than radiation therapy, more than chemo, more than known medicine had to offer. Despite the potential positives, the approaching arrangement planted a growing knot in my gut. I could hardly complain. It was largely my plan. Still, the date loomed on the calendar like an iceberg dead ahead.

"You're not trying to…you know…run away from this?"

"No. I'll work it out. I fly Arun to Memphis on Thursday. I'll hop over to Evermore from there. That gives me two days here to try and sort this."

"You mean Candice?"

"Yeah. Someone made a mess of this place." I described the destruction. "The question is, did she run from this? Or did this take her?"

"Is there anything I can do?"

"Good heavens, no, Dee. You've got enough going on."

"Just promise me you will be careful."

"Earl is armed to the teeth and I'm a card-carrying coward. First sign of trouble, I'm gone."

"Don't be glib. I know you. I just want you to be safe. Not just for me."

She let silence punctuate that new and dramatic aspect of our lives. After a moment the blue blood running through my wife's veins compelled her to ask if Candice left behind any signs or clues.

"Nothing. Her Jeep is here. It's parked behind the lodge. She delivered Kelly to the bus stop, then she probably came back. Thankfully, there's no body or blood, so that strongly suggests that whatever made a mess of the lodge didn't find her. We hope."

"Tell me you're not staying there tonight."

"I'm not staying here tonight."

"Are you just saying that?"

"Yes, because you asked me to. But I do agree in principle. Just need to work out the details. What do you hear about the trial?" Andy had a big court case grinding through final pre-trial motions. I leaped to the change in subject hoping it would lift me off the hook and keep her from stressing over the travel obligation looming ahead.

"Nothing. And don't change the subject."

I tried…

Silence fell between us. The alternative of dwelling on the destruction would only make her worry. After a moment, we sought neutral ground. We talked about her schedule for the rest of the day. I told her I would rather sleep in my own bed tonight. She lowered her voice and said something over the phone that I chalked up to intriguing new hormonal mood swings. Nevertheless, it caused me to sincerely wish I was back in Essex.

WE DID NOT FIND Candice Thorpe on the property, or at least on the three or four acres that contained the lodge structures. Renell Lodge encompassed several hundred acres of woodland with the lake at its center. The expansive wild terrain could easily swallow up search resources far beyond the six of us.

If Candice was out there, I doubted we would find her alive or in one piece. I mulled the idea of conducting an air search on my own. The notion ignited a stark memory, one that had not jarred me for a while. Pink and white jackets on a bed of leaves. Two tiny girls found dead in a woods. The stark flashback stopped me in my tracks on the trail between cabins. Pidge nearly walked into me, then asked why I looked like I'd seen a ghost. I brushed the question off but could not escape the growing fear that I might be called on to find Candice in much the same way I once found two murdered children.

11

Deputy Reitman told us to wait in the lodge while he called in a report. He assured us he would not leave, then retreated to his SUV. Earl tossed off a 'follow me' gesture. He passed through the dining room and into the kitchen.

Earl stopped at the dry pantry door. He pulled it open and jerked a string to turn on the light. Shelves of canned goods and cooking supplies lined the walls to our right and left. The back wall had been stacked with boxes of paper goods and more canned foods. Earl appraised the makeshift fort Minelli had constructed in the rear corner.

I gave him a minute before asking, "What are we looking at?"

Earl grunted. Then he sniffed the air.

"Guy said he hid in here last night when all hell broke loose while he was eating his dinner."

"Yeah?"

"Scared shitless. Makes himself that hidey hole. Then shivers in the dark while someone tears the lodge apart. Then he's too scared to leave. Eventually falls asleep. He's still in here when we fly over. What time was that?"

"Around 1:30."

Earl leaned over the remnants of Minelli's protective wall. He sniffed the air again. "Figure dinner around 8. Then we fly over at 1:30. That's seventeen and a half hours."

I knew the answer but asked anyway. "What are you saying?"

"Can you go for seventeen and a half hours without taking a piss? Can you just fall asleep for most of a day on a hard tile floor?"

"There's no dishes out here, either." Pidge startled me. Behind us, she cracked open a plastic bottle of peach iced tea she had conjured. "If he was eating dinner when the werewolf showed up, where are the busted dishes and leftover food? There's nothing out here."

Earl paid Pidge a glance that bordered on respect.

"What are you thinking, Boss?"

"I'm thinking I don't like that guy."

12

When I returned to the littered great room, I found Kelly crouched in the center of the floor. She carefully pulled snapshots from under shards of broken glass. I kneeled beside her to help.

"Candice said these were all guests. Mr. Minelli said some of them might be famous people." She paused and regarded the damaged frame dangling from the wall. At least a dozen of the snapshots remained attached to partially shredded cork board. Half of the frame remained as well. The glass and the other half of the frame littered the floor. She drew her riotous red locks away from her face with one hand and lifted the photos off the floor with the other. She delicately placed the photos in two stacks on the bar. Intact and torn. "Some of these are really old. I think we can fix the ones that are torn. Most of them."

She touched the damaged photos reverently.

I knew this girl only briefly and only as a victim. Slim to the point of skinny and not much taller than Pidge, she couldn't go much more than a hundred pounds soaking wet. When I met her, she had been afraid to speak, afraid to move, afraid to think for herself. Pidge never told me how long she'd been with the ex-boyfriend, but it was long enough to graduate from his immersion course on control, intimidation, and the consequences of a violent temper.

She was different now. She looked stronger, healthier. I felt the change more than saw it, although her speech to Earl back at Essex County Airport left no doubt. Even now, as she regarded the torn mementos with sadness, she did not look helpless.

I added a few more photos to her pile. She surprised me once again with my first name, and with a hand on my forearm.

"Will, can I ask you something?"

"Anything."

She looked directly up at me. No flinching. No hesitation. Her hand stayed on my forearm, but utterly devoid of need. My ego tried to chime in with a suggestion that she wanted more than my attention, but the idea didn't carry water. Her light grip was a connection, a sign of confidence.

"At the festival—in the haunted house—you told me to keep my eyes closed."

"Did you?"

"Uh-huh. The whole time."

I had a bad feeling about where this was going. Her escape had been planned around slipping her and her baby out the back of a funhouse ride while her boyfriend loaded up on beer. We hadn't expected him to attach himself to Kelly as if handcuffed. When they appeared together, I had to use *the other thing* to extract her. *No matter what, Kelly. Eyes closed.*

"I was so scared. I felt like some animal caught in headlights. Frozen. I felt—this is going to sound bonkers."

"That's okay."

She looked down at her hand on my arm and I thought she might pull it away, but it stayed. If anything, her grip tightened.

"I thought I was dying. I felt cold. Like my body was—letting go. Like my heart stopped and I didn't know it and that was the end and that's what it feels like just after it's—you know—over?"

That was the cool sensation you feel when the other thing *makes you vanish, kiddo.* I never imagined how she must have processed the sensations of disappearing, but bless her heart, she obeyed my command not to look.

"You know, Kelly, there are all kinds of expressions about how being brave isn't doing something dangerous without fear, but rather doing something dangerous despite fear."

"Duh. Total cliché, Will." She smiled hesitantly. I returned the smile and she relaxed. "I just wanted to tell you what it was like. I wanted to tell you ever since—you know—that day. And it's been so different here. I'm going to sound like one of those born-again people because I keep saying it, but Candice changed everything for me. She made me braver." She dropped her gaze for a moment. "But I feel like I'm letting her down because…because I'm really scared. I feel it again—around the edges. That fear."

I waved my free hand at the room. "You'd have to be an idiot not to be scared of this, right?"

"Certifiable." She laughed. A release, albeit brief. Kelly's hand squeezed my arm again. "I don't want to go back. To being that helpless."

I covered her hand with mine.

"You're here. That says all that needs to be said."

Deputy Reitman entered through the smashed doorway. Kelly pulled her hand out from under mine, but not before giving my arm a second squeeze. The deputy took stock of Pidge at the far end of the room and Kelly and me. "Folks, I gotta ask. What are your intentions? Because I'm not sure I can allow you to stay here."

"Why?" I asked.

"For starters, it's a crime scene. Property damage. Vandalism. Just being here disturbs the evidence."

Earl appeared in the doorway to the dining room. He huffed. "What? You sending out a goddamned forensic team? They gonna go over this place with swabs and microscopes and fingerprint powder to find out who broke some windows and trashed some furniture?"

"Well, no...but with the owner absent, I don't think any of you have permission to be here."

"Bull." Earl didn't need to get anywhere near the deputy to be in his face. Reitman, half a room away from the boss looked like he wanted to take a step back. Earl pointed at Kelly. "That girl there is a member of the staff and at this moment she's senior staff. And Mr. Minelli has paid up accommodations. We will, too." He fished a money clip out of his pocket, peeled off a bill and handed it to Kelly. "Rooms for three, please."

I looked around. *Where's Minelli?* I wondered if he was busy packing his bags to beat it after declaring he had no wish to stay here after dark.

"All the same, I can offer you a lift over to Big Fork. There's the Timberwolf Inn and the Antler Lodge, and we got a Country Inn and Suites down in Grand Rapids."

"We got our own lift over at the airstrip," Earl said.

"Speaking of which," Pidge said, "I was thinking it might be a good idea to take the Baron over to Big Fork for the night. Just to make sure nobody gets any ideas about scratching up any of that tender aluminum." She gestured at the gouges in the wood around the door. "You know—just to be safe. You two can stay here and me and Kelly could go. Deputy, do you know if either of those joints have a Jacuzzi?"

"Timberwolf has a great restaurant and bar."

Pidge looked at Earl. "I say we do it to keep the airplane safe."

I thought Earl would dismiss the flimsy ploy without appeal. Instead, he scratched the leathery backside of his scalp and studied the floor for a moment. "Might not be a bad idea."

Pidge perked up, surprised. She looked at Kelly whose worried expression signaled she did not share Pidge's enthusiasm for leaving.

"What if Candice comes back?" Kelly asked.

Pidge crossed the great room and threw an arm around Kelly's shoulder. "Those two big strong men will be here. You and me—we grab a shower, get some decent food, hang out in the bar. Sounds better than sweeping up broken glass."

"No. I want to help find her," Kelly protested.

"You should go," I said. "We won't be organizing a search tonight. There's nothing to be done here. Come back in the morning."

Minelli appeared in the open doorway. "Who should go?"

"The ladies are flying out to Big Fork." I instantly wished I hadn't put it that way. I expected Minelli to ask for a seat on the plane. Maybe because of his deception about the dry pantry, I didn't like the idea of him going with Pidge and Kelly.

Earl shared the same wavelength. "Mr. Minelli, I was thinking about your car. Deputy, what say you give this gent a ride over to where they're fixing his car?"

"Fixed. It's finished. Ready for pickup in Beaudry." Minelli turned to Reitman. "Farwell Brothers. They did some welding. You know them?"

"I do." Reitman didn't comment further, but I read disapproval in his short answer.

"They said they'd stay open until seven. It'd be great if I could hitch a ride."

"I don't have a problem with that. Then you won't be staying here tonight?"

"I dunno. I wasn't up for it before," Minelli waved at me and Earl, "but if these guys are sticking it out, I feel like I owe it to Candice to keep an eye on the place. In case she comes back. I wouldn't want her to find it like this and me gone, too."

"All right, sir," Reitman said. "You ride with me."

Everyone headed for the door. Earl, Pidge, Kelly, and I remained on the porch. Minelli waved at us and climbed in the deputy's SUV. We watched the deputy turn around and pull away.

Kelly spoke first.

"Mr. Jackson, I don't want to go, but if we are leaving, I'd feel better if you'd walk up to the airplane with us."

"First things first, young lady. That computer in Candice's office. Does she have passwords on it? Can you get into it?"

"Her bookkeeping software is password protected, but she let me use the computer any time I wanted. She let Mr. Minelli use it, too."

"What about reservations? How does she keep track of bookings?" Earl asked.

"Reservations are built into the website."

"It's not protected?"

Kelly shook her head. "It is but I can show you."

13

Framed photos of Candice with hunters, fishermen, and cabin guests covered most of the wooden walls of her office. In the photos, her lively blonde hair and her attractive features lied about her age. Even in photos I recognized as recent, the camera gave a pass to the tiny lines that bordered her sparkling eyes. In a few photos, an infectious smile stole the show. I caught Kelly staring at a picture of Candice as she leaned on a porch post, her head turned slightly, and her eyes narrowed to a squint, as if she heard an interesting bird call just before the shutter snapped.

"Hey," I said. "We'll find her."

Kelly broke her connection with the photo and smiled faintly.

Candice's small desk was ornate and constructed of wood dark enough to be nearly black. A modern mesh office chair snuggled up to the desk. A bank of muntin-barred windows filled the wall behind the chair. The windows over-looked the boathouse and lake. I noted a pink fringe on high cumulus clouds. Evening approached.

Kelly slipped around the desk and into Candice's chair. She set aside a clutter of papers and envelopes, most of which were imprinted with a cartoon sun logo. From under the clutter, she found and squared up a small silver laptop. She lifted the laptop lid and brought the screen to life. I dropped into a wingback leather chair, the single occasional chair facing the desk. Earl leaned on the door frame.

"What's she using for internet?" Pidge leaned over Kelly's shoulder. The question drew a blank. Pidge nudged Kelly. "Let me."

They swapped seats. Pidge pulled out her phone and laid it on the desk. She found a wireless mouse and woke it up, then worked through something on the screen. Seated where I was, I couldn't see. Pidge seemed confident.

"She was using a Wi-Fi hotspot on her phone. I can do the same. Gimme a sec."

"Don't we need Candice's phone?" Earl asked.

"It works with mine." Pidge laid her phone on the desk beside the laptop. She fiddled with settings on both the phone and the computer. "There. We have internet. What do you want to know?"

"Look at her reservation system."

Kelly pointed at the screen. Pidge clicked the mouse, then hesitated. "It's asking for admin access. Username and password. I thought you said it wasn't locked."

"It's not." Kelly pulled open the top left drawer. She reached for a curled Post-It note, but froze. "Oh, no." She lifted a phone in a garish pink protective case from the drawer. "This is her phone."

Earl put out his hand and took the phone from her. He pocketed the device, then pointed at the post-it note. "That what you're looking for?"

Kelly peeled the note off the drawer bottom. "Uh-huh. Username is Admin. Password is cthorpe83."

"That's the year she married Thorpe," Earl said.

Pidge typed. Her expression went from pleased to startled. "Whoa. She's got a shit ton of cancellations."

"How many?" I asked.

"Um...all of them." Pidge rotated the laptop. Earl and I leaned forward to look at a screen laid out like a calendar, but with rows of spaces marked with cabin numbers. In red at the head of each entry, the word "Cancelled" had been entered.

"Not everyone." I pointed at an entry at the top. "Scroll left. Back. Back. More. Stop. There. Two of them aren't cancelled. One for Minelli. One for someone named Yuan."

"That's Dr. Yuan. Oh, gosh." Kelly drew sharply erect. "I completely forgot."

Pidge rotated the screen back. She worked the mouse and tapped the keyboard.

Earl squinted at Kelly. "Spit it out, girl. Forgot what?"

"Last week, Candice told me that Dr. Yuan and his wife were booked for the week after Memorial Day, but he called and persuaded her to open a reservation early. She said he was a regular visitor—Candice said they're a super nice couple from St. Paul—and she let him talk her into it. Candice wanted me to clean and prepare Cabin 9 for them, but I never had time before all this happened. I never got to it."

"Well," Pidge said, "this makes it look like they're still coming."

"When?" I asked.

Kelly didn't need to look at the screen. "Yesterday. Last night."

14

Pidge rotated the Baron less than halfway down the runway, easily clearing the trees at the end. She banked sharply and flew a circle around the lodge property, finishing with a low pass over our heads. She rocked the wings and ascended into the twilight.

Earl and I shouldered our overnight bags and hiked back to the lodge. He didn't speak. The fresh mystery of the cancelled bookings hung in the air. Before closing the laptop, Pidge opened Candice's Outlook email program, which also lacked security protection. The program revealed an inbox filled with unread emails. Nearly all were angry or disappointed. A few were hostile. Each message responded to a form email sent by Candice in which she expressed profound disappointment at having to cancel the customer's reservation *due to unforeseen circumstances.* The email promised no charges were imposed on credit cards holding the reservations. The time stamp on Candice's message was near midnight yesterday. Earl pointed out that Candice sent her cancellation notice while Minelli cowered in the dry pantry.

Nothing explained the *unforeseen circumstances.*

Pidge returned to the reservation site and scrolled ahead on the calendar. The entire summer had been marked "Cancelled."

"MAKES NO GODDAMNED SENSE." Earl's utterance broke his silence as we reentered the yard in front of the lodge. "None of it makes any goddamned sense."

"What about Minelli? You think he's involved?"

"I sure as hell don't think it's Pidge's goddamned werewolf up in the office sending emails."

"Me neither. It wasn't a full moon last night." Earl tossed me a scowl. "Just saying."

"Gimme your bag." Earl held out his hand. I slipped the backpack off my shoulder and handed it to him. He studied the sky. "We got about an hour of light left. I think you oughta do your thing and have a look around. Make sure we don't have someone in the weeds."

"Why? You get the feeling we're being watched?"

Earl ignored my attempt at humor. He dropped down and picked up a splinter from the broken lodge door. He kneeled and used the sharp end to draw in the dirt.

"Here's the lake. Here's us. Do a semi-circle around until you hit the water, then go another fifty or a hundred yards and repeat, expanding outward." He drew concentric half circles radiating out from the lake.

"I can do that." I fished a power unit from the backpack and snapped a carbon fiber prop in place. Earl tossed his pointer away and put his hand on my hand, the one holding the power unit.

"Not here. Not out in the open. I get the feeling we're being watched."

The fissure in his lined face was probably recognizable as a grin only to those of us who know Earl.

"I'll do it inside, then. Go off the back deck."

Earl picked up the bags and headed inside. He spoke as he walked.

"Good. Best we both get inside. On account it's quiet out here...too quiet. And I got a bad feeling about this. And I'm getting too old for this shit. And I was born ready. And you're a loose cannon. And..."

He kept going. I never knew he had it in him, but he muttered every stupid movie line I've ever heard and some I hadn't on his way into the dining room. He was still reciting as he disappeared in the kitchen, leaving me smiling.

15

F *wooomp!*
    I vanished on the move. My last step tapped the wooden deck with enough force to launch me clear of the rail. The steep drop between the lodge and the boathouse immediately put me fifty feet in the air. I pulsed the power unit in my hand to change trajectory from a climb to level flight just above the treetops. The lake spread out ahead of me. The unseen spinning prop threw wind up my arm.

The boathouse passed under me. I adjusted my track to match the shoreline. There were two cabins on the water's edge on either side of the main lodge building. I cruised over the mossy roof of each, over the sooty crowns of their brick chimneys.

My first visit to Renell Lodge took place in the last days of winter a little over a year ago. The still frozen lake became a runway for the old Queen Air that Candice asked Earl and me to pull out of the boathouse. I remember thinking at the time that the lodge would be a nice getaway for Andy and me. Quiet days walking in the surrounding woods. Canoeing. Romantic evenings by firelight in the cabin. I liked what I'd seen of the cabins. The big beds and thick comforters covering them looked inviting.

Oh, and darling, they have werewolves. I smiled, thinking of how I'd pitch the idea to my wife now.

The breeze rippled my clothes and hair. Just past the second cabin I turned left and flew inland along an arc scribed outside the small cluster of cabins. Rising terrain forced me higher, but I kept my altitude to within fifty feet of the treetops.

Twilight remained bright in the sky, but the woods darkened quickly. I wished we'd started this sooner.

I used the roof of the main lodge as an anchor and flew the classic *Turns About A Point* maneuver we teach student pilots. I adjusted for a light wind from the west to keep the ground track perfectly round. Before too long, I reached the lake again on the opposite side of the lodge. I gave myself high marks for the maneuver because I arrived at the shore just beyond the second cabin on the other side of the lodge, an indication that I'd flown a near perfect half circle. Following Earl's suggestion, I extended fifty yards, then turned inland for a wider arc.

I reasoned that if someone were hiding in the woods and watching us, they wouldn't be very far out. Using this logic, I did six circuits, expanding fifty to a hundred yards with each until my search pattern radiated roughly five hundred yards from the lodge. When the pattern reached the airstrip, I changed the plan.

I followed the arc until it crossed the unpaved dirt road that constituted the public entry and exit to Renell Lodge. There, I turned and headed north above the road. Deputy Reitman had come and gone this way, so I didn't expect to find anyone or anything on the road or parked beside it. My expectations were met.

I flew nearly three miles to where the lodge driveway joined a narrow asphalt highway. To the east, somewhere down that highway lay the tiny burg of Beaudry. I didn't know what lay to the west.

If Candice met a dark fate on the highway, she probably would have been found by now. She also would have been in her Jeep, which remained parked at the lodge. If her fate was off-road, there would be little hope and not nearly enough battery power in my handheld unit to search the thousands of acres of woods sprawling in every direction.

Three miles of driveway to the lodge, however, offered a smaller search area. I went left a couple hundred yards, then began the return trip.

I climbed higher. Three hundred feet above the treetops rendered a decent view into the forest below. I was surprised to see several two-wheel tracks winding through the woods. Perhaps employed as hiking trails or snowmobile trails or paths for four-wheelers in the summer, these weedy routes did not look recently traveled. In some spots, standing water glistened.

Scattered open meadows broke the endless landscape of trees. Cattails marked wetlands. The land undulated, and modest ravines cut wandering paths through the woods, sometimes carrying fresh water in small streams that bubbled over polished rocks.

I found the crashed car in one of the ravines.

Reflection threw up a glint of light from glass and clearcoat paint. Nose down in the ravine, the sedan might have been hard to find on foot. From above, the metallic silver car stood out like a beacon.

The black and blue BMW logo on the trunk aimed up at me as I descended between tall trees. The front bumper rested under water, partially damming a small runoff stream. Tire tracks showed it had rolled down the side of the ravine. The sedan narrowly missed trees that could have stopped it.

Within fifty feet I spotted the claw marks.

My heart hammered.

Sliced through the metal above the driver's door, a spread of punctures tore teardrop holes in the steel roof. The windshield and side windows were smashed. Puncture and tear lines marred the doors. Both doors were open.

There was blood.

Handprints smeared the passenger door edges. Someone pulled their own wounded body out of the car. Or fought being pulled from the car.

I eased down. I pulsed the power unit to bring myself to a halt half a dozen feet from the open passenger door. The front bucket seats were bloodstained but empty. Travel bags had tumbled into the footwell, driven forward by the steep angle at which the car had come to rest.

Touch nothing. Andy's stern professional warning sounded in my head.

I searched up and down the stream that bubbled under and around the kidney-shaped grilles of the car. There were no signs of passage, at least none that I could see. Someone could have stumbled away on the stones in the water. Movement in the stream would leave nothing to catch my eye. Blood would have washed away.

Blood, however, revealed the escape route of the car's occupants. Dark stains painted the grass and leaves running up the ravine slope opposite that which the car descended. The driver and passenger got out of the car and scrambled up the side of the ravine.

I followed. I wished I hadn't.

At the top of the ravine where the land flattened into dense woods, I found them. At first, they were nothing more than a dark mass tangled among downed branches on a bed of leaves. The smell of blood met me the instant I realized what I was looking at.

Two bodies. Intermingled. Spread over an area larger than the car.

Torn apart.

I heard loud huffing. It jolted me, thinking that what had done this was nearby, crouched in ambush. Then I realized the sound came from my own desperate breathing, my fight to suppress nausea.

Little of their clothing escaped staining, explaining why I hadn't seen them from the air. There were no bright school jackets to catch my eye this time. There were no individual bodies, only large and small masses. A hand. A head. Dark hair. Long. A woman's.

Feet.

Deep gouges in the wood at the lodge implied the kind of damage that could be done by whoever or whatever wielded these claws. This scene left nothing to the imagination.

Torn apart.

I flexed every muscle I had, fighting to retain control. Fighting the urge to run. Fighting the urge to slide the power unit control to full power and shoot into the clean, clear, bloodless sky as fast as the batteries would take me.

Ten feet above the carnage, I focused on the work to be done.

I used low power to rise straight up until I cleared the treetops. I killed the power but continued coasting upward. My search path had been west of the lodge road. I estimated. 300 yards? 350?

I searched for and recorded bearings. The lodge road. The highway. The lake.

Higher and higher I ascended directly over the bloody scene. The dark mayhem quickly blended back into the forest like a secret to be kept, but the car remained a beacon.

When I saw the rooftop of the lodge in the distance and the lake beyond it, I drew a mental map. The lodge. The road. The highway. The wandering two-wheel track through the woods that the car had driven. Proportions. Three to two. The distance from the lodge to the crime scene was three. The distance from the lodge road to the crime scene was two. I mapped the ravine in my head. It angled toward the lodge from the northwest. The stream at the ravine bottom emptied into the lake just beyond the second shoreline cabin.

A search party starting from the lodge road could not help but stumble on the ravine. From there, finding the car would follow.

I aimed the power unit at the lodge roof and generated full speed. A cleansing wind peeled the smell of death off my skin and clothes.

16

"Mark this." I laid my phone on the lodge bar. Beside me, Earl leaned on his elbows. Two tumblers containing amber liquid joined us. His held iced tea. Mine held scotch. Between the tumblers, my iPad displayed the Fore-Flight map page with the screen set to Aerial Map. "Bearing three three zero from the lodge. Two and a half miles."

"Got it." Pidge spoke from my phone speaker. On her end she hovered over her iPad. She studied the same aerial view. "I see the ravine."

"There's a track—runs roughly east-west. See where the track meets the ravine?"

"Affirmative."

"Okay. Drop your pin there."

"Done."

Earl leaned toward the phone. "Keep it simple. You saw something shiny in the woods. You couldn't tell what it was. Don't get specific. You were moving too fast to make it out. You told us about it when I called after you landed. This call. Got it?"

"Got it."

I closed the iPad. "We'll call it in. Be ready to back us up. Remember. We called you to see if you landed. You told us what you saw. We went to investigate."

"Affirmative." The line fell briefly silent. "This is serious shit."

"Stick to the story. Get it straight with Kelly, too," Earl commanded. "Don't tell her what we found because you don't know. All you know is you saw something, and you told us about it when we called. Better if she doesn't have to lie to the cops."

"I got no problem lying to the cops."

"'Cause you've had a lot more practice," Earl said.

"Tell me you're not staying out there tonight."

"We won't be alone," I checked my watch. "In about an hour I think we'll have most of the Itasca County Sheriff's Department here with us along with staties, so don't worry about it. And Earl's got his .45."

"Got any silver bullets in that .45?"

Earl refused to answer.

"We're fine." I didn't think anything was fine. I thought that if I tried to sleep at all tonight, I might vanish first and tether myself to the roof. "Gotta go."

"Over and out."

I gulped a burning slug of scotch. Medicine.

Earl knew the moment I reappeared inside the great room that something terrible had happened. The first words I said to him were, "It wasn't Candice." I couldn't be certain, of course, but the circumstances strongly suggested that the victims were the unfortunate Dr. Yuan and his wife.

We waited twenty minutes, not saying much. Then Earl turned my phone to face him. He touched the keypad icon and tapped 911. It rang twice, then an operator recited her incantation for disaster.

"Nine one one. What is your emergency?"

17

A sheriff's department lieutenant sat us down at Candice's scarred dining room table. The evening breeze whispered through broken windows and enhanced a chill embedded in the back of my neck. The lieutenant, a burly man in his forties with two arcs of forehead invading a thinning hairline, cast a glance at the tumbler in my hand.

"How many of those have you had?"

"Not enough." I swirled a thin puddle of golden liquid at the bottom. My grip on the glass kept my hand from shaking.

Earl and I explained what had happened, starting with our manufactured call to Pidge and how her observation prompted me to hike out and discover the scene in the woods. How I raced back to the lodge to report it.

"What time was that?" Lieutenant Turinski—according to the tag on his ballistic vest—hovered his pen over a notepad identical to Deputy Reitman's.

I pulled out phone. "The call to Miss Page was at…7:12. I made it out to the car and back in about twenty minutes. Then Mr. Jackson called 911."

"Why didn't you call from the scene?"

"Have you been to the scene? For starters, I wasn't certain whatever did that was not still out there."

"But you found the wreck straight away? From here?"

I pushed the iPad toward him. "We use this for navigation. It has an aerial view. I worked from what our pilot saw." I recited the description we assigned Pidge. *Something down in the trees.* He asked for and I gave Pidge's real name and her mobile number. He wrote the information in his notebook.

A cluster of official vehicles parked in the lodge yard under flashing emergency lights. Red and blue danced off the lodge walls and the trees outside. In the dining room, the strobe effect played off some of the woodwork.

Turinski seemed in no hurry.

"Did you touch anything out there? Pick up anything? Maybe try to see if someone was still alive."

"No one was still alive. And no, I didn't touch anything. My wife is a detective with the Essex PD. I'm a slow learner but she's a patient teacher."

He smiled thinly. "Mr. Jackson, you said you were married to Mrs. Thorpe?"

"Number three."

"I know Candice. Lovely lady. She lets me and my boy come out here and fish. You haven't heard from her? Either of you?" We shook our heads. "But you came up here looking for her?"

Earl answered with a two-syllable grunt. I took up the slack.

"The girl who works here, Kelly Pratt, she's close with our pilot, Miss Page. It happened just like we told Deputy Reitman. Somebody or something spooked Candice into moving Kelly out of harm's way. Kelly came to us for help—to Mr. Jackson specifically. He's the one who introduced Kelly to Candice last fall."

"We're going to want to talk with Miss Pratt and Miss Page. I'll send a unit up to Big Fork. Mr. Jackson, are you still close with Candice?" I wondered about that myself. There had been a moment last year just before I flew the Queen Air off the iced-over pond when it looked like an old flame had been rekindled. Earl racing to her rescue again suggested the ember still glowed.

"Close how?" Earl wasn't biting.

"Close. Involved."

He huffed and gave his shoulders a shake. I think it was a chuckle. "We was married three weeks right after Vietnam. That should tell you it never got started, but that don't mean it ended, either. You said yourself, she's a lovely lady. That's all I got to say."

Turinski spent another twenty minutes gathering background. He used his phone to snap images of our driver's licenses. He asked for my wife's contact information at the City of Essex Police Department, and for the name of her supervisor. Eventually, he folded his notebook and secured his pen. "We'll do everything we can to find Mrs. Thorpe."

"And what about that horror out there?" I asked.

Turinski shook his head grimly. "The first two deputies up there lost their dinner. I hear it's bad. The county coroner is on his way. I called BCA. We can use the help. This sort of thing doesn't happen up here." He waved at the obvious destruction around us. "There is no dancing around it. What happened to the lodge was violent, but it might have been intended as a threat. What happened out there was a threat carried out."

"And you don't have any idea what did this?"

"I'm not going to speculate, Mr. Stewart—although I doubt it's what your young lady pilot told Deputy Reitman."

Earl stood up. "What about a search? For Candice?"

"We need to know more. And when we do, then we can talk about a search. There's a lot of empty woods up here. I'm not ready to call in people and dogs to search for Mrs. Thorpe in a million acres between here and Canada. I want to be sure she didn't take off for Minneapolis or the Caribbean."

"Her car's still here," Earl snapped.

"That needs to be reckoned with. She could have left her car to throw us off the trail." Turinski read the objections bubbling up from Earl and me. "Make no mistake, gentlemen, this is real, and it is serious, and we are grateful for your extra efforts. Just the same, I'm probably quoting your detective wife, Mr. Stewart, when I tell you both to sit on the sidelines and let us do our work."

"Hold up there, son." Earl put his hand up as flat as his bent digits allowed. "What's that supposed to mean—throw us off the trail?" Turinski looked uncomfortable. Earl put no effort into patience. "Spit it out."

"Well, there is one more thing. I'm stepping outta my lane here, so please keep what I'm about to say under wraps. Can you do that for me?"

"Yes, sir," I said quickly. Earl remained motionless.

"Did Mrs. Thorpe—Candice—did she say anything to you about financial trouble?" Turinski asked.

"I haven't talked to her since we were here a year ago. Boss?"

Earl's head moved back and forth minutely.

Turinski studied us both. If he saw reason to suspect a lie, he didn't let it stop him. "The Sheriff's Department is processing a foreclosure on the lodge. The bank's taking possession."

I didn't think anything else could jolt me. I should have known better.

Earl placed his hands on the table as if to hold it down. Or to launch himself. "That ain't right."

"I'm afraid it is. I shouldn't be telling you. My understanding is that Candice —Mrs. Thorpe—doesn't have any kin, but since you're got the closest thing to a family connection to Candice, I'll read you in. I got the paperwork from Charlie Pelton at the bank—and before you ask, I can tell you foreclosure is the last thing on earth Charlie would want—for anybody, let alone Candice."

"When?" Earl demanded.

"The department got the paperwork this morning." Turinski dropped his eyes. Earl did not. He stared bullets into the sheriff's lieutenant. "You know how these things work. It would have been a long time coming. Word is she's been missing mortgage payments for some time now. Can you shed any light on that, Mr. Jackson?"

Earl didn't move.

"I 'spose not if you haven't talked to her for over a year. But you need to consider all angles. If she's in that deep, it might speak to why she up and disappeared. And why she might not be out in the woods at all."

"Ain't so."

"It happens. People think they can stall it by avoiding being served the papers."

"Candice don't run from nothin'."

"Mr. Jackson, she clearly ran from something." Turinski gestured at the lodge great room. "Running won't make any difference to the bank, as you probably know. We'll just nail the papers to the door—or what's left of it—to make it official."

Earl didn't argue.

Turinski dropped a pair of business cards on the table. "If you hear from her, or think of anything, my number is on the card."

The lieutenant excused himself to join the deputies and investigators gathering in growing numbers outside the lodge. I wanted a refill for my tumbler but decided the scotch had done its job. To keep my hands busy, I fetched a bottle of peach iced tea from Candice's refrigerator. As I returned, I heard vehicles drive out of the yard and away from the lodge. I made a guess that they were headed to the BMW parked in a ravine, to where Dr. and Mrs. Yuan were spread all over the woods.

Two sheriff's vehicles stayed in the yard and remained lit up. The light show grew annoying. Earl and I retreated to the kitchen. I fetched some cold cuts and cubed pineapple from the refrigerator. We parked on a pair of stools and picked listlessly at the food. I stayed away from the meat.

Earl hardly spoke.

I fiddled with ForeFlight on the iPad, checking weather, pretending to plan for the trip Arun had scheduled for Thursday. The flight was a run to Memphis in the Education Foundation's Piper Navajo—she of the recently cleaned flaps. Memphis is a decent airline hub. My plan, yet unannounced, was to have Arun return on a direct flight to Milwaukee or Green Bay. From Memphis, I intended to fly to Evermore, North Carolina, to Spiro Lewko's almost imaginary company town. The billionaire was expecting me. I didn't much care what he expected, but others gathered there who needed me. People whose lives depended on me.

"She could'a asked me for money." Earl chimed in out of the blue to derail my train of thought. "I would'a handed it over in cash."

"I guess that explains the *unforeseen circumstances* in her email, and all the cancellations."

"Does it? Why cancel all that revenue? That don't explain nothin'."

Never argue with the Boss.

He picked at the pineapple and said nothing more.

18

We didn't know what to do with ourselves. We stalled in the kitchen for a while, then put away the food and returned to the great room. I suddenly felt compelled to pick up the pieces. Earl abruptly stomped out to the porch and called to the deputies in their units and told them to turn off the goddamned lights, they were giving him a headache. They didn't argue. With that success under his belt, he informed them that he was getting a broom to clean up unless they had objections. They voiced none. He invited them to get off their asses and help. They politely declined.

I took up where Kelly left off. She had recovered many of the fallen photos from Candice's memory display. Kelly's two stacks sat on the bar. I set about picking up the remainder. I thought they would be old prints, possibly brittle, maybe even faded Polaroids which, if damaged, would be irreplaceable. Instead, regardless of age or whether they were in black and white or color, the photos were uniformly printed on crisp new photo paper. The color prints had the dry semi-gloss patina of toner, suggesting they had been rendered by a laser printer.

Fewer of the photos suffered tears than I first feared. I added several damaged snapshots to Kelly's stack. Most had fallen intact when the frame and glass containing the display had been attacked. Photos that remained on the wall were fixed by thumbtacks on a dry cork board. With the windows gone, sooner or later the room would be exposed to dampness. I decided to save not just the ones on the floor, but all of them. I took down the survivors in the broken frame. In the end, I completed the two stacks Kelly started—the intact and the torn. Of the torn, I felt confident that Kelly and I had collected all the pieces.

Earl found a broom, dustpan, and garbage can. He scooped up piles of broken glass from the floor, the entrance, and the porch.

I lingered at the bar and sifted through the Renell Lodge photo DNA. The older images were the most interesting. Everything predating the Vietnam and Civil Rights era had been printed in black and white. Pre-World War II photos showed guests arriving in boxy cars sporting curved fenders from the Bonnie and Clyde era. Some of the cars were piled high with trunks and gear held aloft by ropes and leather straps. Men wore suits and hats; women wore skirts that tantalized with a glimpse of knee. Faces tried to be stoic for the camera, but a few broke the mold and projected broad smiles. And why not? Simply arriving at the lodge in those days must have been a triumph. I wondered what passed for roads in this part of the country before World War II. These vacationers may have traveled hundreds of miles on the kind of unpaved two-wheel tracks I'd seen in the woods. The journey itself probably comprised half the trip. Atop one of the pre-war cars, I spotted a potbellied stove. Camping at its finest.

Color joined the collage in the post-war era of cars with giant chrome grilles, fender skirts, and fins. One jolly group gathered at the back of a green Chevy station wagon parked outside of the cabin I recognized as Minelli's. Three boys and two girls—the image of walking mischief—grinned at the camera while seated in a row on the wagon's dropped tailgate. Behind them, the interior of the car was stuffed.

Cars weren't the only props. People posed on the Renell cabin porches holding rifles. They posed on the pier against the lake backdrop showing off fresh-caught fish. They balanced on the raft in dated swimwear. They rowed numbered canoes. Men, women, and children.

I wondered who the photographers had been. Someone started the tradition not long after the War to End All Wars, a full decade before the world had a second go at catastrophic annihilation. Several photos bore handwritten dates as captions, sometimes in white ink. The oldest images had been scanned from cracked and faded originals.

Earl finished sweeping and collecting broken glass. He fetched a mop and bucket. He cleaned spots where shattered liquor bottles spilled their contents on the wooden floor. Damp mopping awoke the scent of brandy and gin.

"You gonna stand around pickin' your nose all night?" He swept the mop past my feet.

"Matter of fact, no. I'm thinking of going up to one of those rooms upstairs, boarding up the door, and trying to get some sleep."

Earl ceased mopping. "If it'd make you feel better, I could look around and see if Candice has a gun you can slip under the pillow."

I cast a side glance at the deep slices in the woodwork.

"You really think a gun would stop whatever did this?"

"You mean *whoever* did this. And yes, I'm willing to give the sonofabitch a couple .45 slugs to think about." He shoved the mop into the pail and left it standing at attention. "On the other hand, if you don't mind missing some of your beauty sleep, I got a different idea."

"I'm not going out in the woods to look for Pidge's werewolf."

"Me neither. Let's see if that Jeep runs."

19

Candice's Jeep Wrangler kicked over on the first turn of the key. I half expected we'd find the engine wiring torn out or the fuel tank slashed open. After throwing our overnight bags in the back, Earl backed the dark green vehicle out of a sheltered parking spot at the end of the building. The deputies waved at us after our headlights swept over them.

"Looks like they're not holding us here as suspects." I waved back.

"Don't mean we're not." Earl had a point. I didn't think Andy would rule out a bunch of newcomers any too quickly.

He maneuvered us onto the unpaved road that wound past the cabins and into the woods. In short order we passed the west end of the landing strip. Not long after that, we crossed a junction formed by a rough track. Earl slowed down and looked to our left. Heavily trammeled grass and lines of tire tracks showed where the county sheriff and a variety of vehicles had turned off to reach the ravine where Dr. Yuan's BMW ended its run. Someone had dropped an orange cone to mark the turnoff.

Seeing the lane disappear in darkness made me wonder. "Why do you suppose they turned off here?"

Earl didn't answer. He looked at the dirt road ahead of us, and then at the overgrown path to our left. The route to the lodge was well-maintained. The turnoff was not. Diverting from the lodge road had not been a simple wrong turn.

Half a mile away, emergency lights flashed through silhouettes of trees, throbbing beats of red and blue.

Earl dropped the Jeep in gear and drove on.

We met two vehicles on the way to the highway. One was a large square utility vehicle with Sheriff's Department markings, the kind that carries tools, highway cones, and assorted equipment useful in the variety of emergencies encountered by law enforcement. The second was a white van with an outline of the state of Minnesota on the front side door. I assigned the van to the Minnesota Bureau of Criminal Apprehension but didn't have time to read the lettering on the decal. Both vehicles squeezed by us without stopping.

During my aerial search, I estimated the distance from the lodge to the county road at three miles. Bumping over the rough road through the woods made it feel a lot longer. I began to wonder if we missed a turn when more lights signaled through the trees. We cleared the woods and stopped at the narrow road where two more Sheriff's Department SUVs parked bumper to tailgate, lights flashing.

Earl huffed. "Great night to rob a bank in Itasca County." A pair of deputies chatted outside their vehicles. I waved. They didn't.

They held us up for ten minutes before radio exchanges with Lieutenant Turinski granted us leave. He wasn't happy that we'd stolen a vehicle that might contain evidence.

I looked over my shoulder when Earl pulled onto the highway. "Does it seem odd to you that they'd just let us wander off like this? Strangers from out of town?"

"Nope." He held up one hand. "You see any razor-sharp claws here?"

"That's a myth. Bears don't have razor-sharp claws. They're rather blunt."

The pavement felt refreshingly smooth after the ride through the woods. Earl accelerated away from the parked deputies.

"What're you, the goddamned nature channel? *Bears have five fingers. Bears have blunt claws.*"

"Some people watch the golf channel on a Sunday afternoon. Bears do have five fingers and the claws may be huge, but they're not razor-sharp like you hear all the time in grizzly attack stories. It's power that tears people up, not sharpness. You want sharp? Talk to a mongoose, but don't get too close."

Earl cracked something that resembled a smile.

"What do you make of this foreclosure business, Boss?"

The smile went away as fast as it had arrived. "It's a load of crap. Candice has money."

"I don't know. The hospitality business isn't easy. Maybe she got overextended."

"That woman can pinch a nickel until Jefferson cries for mercy. Not one of us husbands ever held the purse strings. I know for a fact that ever since she got title to the place, she's kept it in her name, no matter who came or went."

"Whatever is happening, it's been going on for a while. No matter what people think, banks don't want foreclosures. It's bad for business, bad for business relationships. And they don't want the property that comes with a foreclosure, or the headaches of disposing of it—especially something as niche as a hundred-year-old resort. I can't imagine that Charlie the Banker guy didn't do all he could to avoid the foreclosure option."

"You'd think."

The road stretched laser straight into the distance. Tall, dark trees lined each side. Our headlights, even on bright, didn't seem to reach very far. I kept an eye on the roadsides for deer, the kind that pause to wait before bolting just to make sure you hit them.

"So, where are we headed?"

Earl stared over his two-handed grip on the wheel. He had a look I'd seen when he calculated the hours left on an engine that had taken to consuming oil.

"I was thinking we'd see how Minelli got along picking up his car."

20

Farwell Brothers Auto Repair and Welding. The sign over the corrugated half-circle Quonset style shed displayed faded red lettering against a pocked and rusted white background. The aged state of the sign matched the building. The Century fence surrounding the property looked newer. I noticed a digital keypad beside a door to a shabby add-on office. Blue LED lettering spelled out the status of a modern security system.

The rest of the property looked like something out of Candice's photo collection. Old vehicles crammed the space on either side of the semicircular building as well as the back lot. Pickup trucks with snowplow blades. A dozen cars. Half a school bus. The shell of a truck cab. A powder blue Volkswagen Beetle, the old-school bug, not the rerelease. Countless roofs and hoods stretched into darkness suggesting a business focused less on repair and more on salvage. Illumination on the property came from a blazing pole lamp at the front of the building where a stark blue-white security light protected a cracked concrete pad hosting the only two vehicles that appeared mobile—a jacked up Ford F-250 with a tall bed cap and a crouching new Chevy Camaro in gloss black.

A sliding gate in the fence forbade us entry to the property. A sign hanging in a small window beside the larger shop door said, *Closed.*

"Don't see any Crown Vics. Do you?" I asked Earl.

"Nothing with Philadelphia plates." Earl can be funny if you listen carefully.

We sat in the idling Jeep across the road from the Farwell Brothers shop. The business marked the western boundary of the metropolis of Beaudry, population 237 as of 2020, so stated a sign just beyond the Farwell Brothers' fence. Looking at the town's meager cluster of buildings, I suspected that the census had been taken on a holiday when extended family was visiting.

"He must have picked up his car before closing time. If he headed back to the lodge, we would have seen him. So, unless he took off for the big city, I would look for him down there." I pointed at the other end of town, four buildings away. Neon red and blue advertised a brand of beer I wasn't familiar with. Roundhouse.

Earl eased off the clutch and put the Jeep in motion. He aimed for the extravagantly named Beaudry Public Brew House that marked the other end of civilization. The building dominated the street. Two stories tall, the tavern sat even higher on an exposed concrete basement that forced patrons to climb a set of steps to reach the front door. I looked for but did not see an ADA ramp and wondered if regulations didn't reach this far into the wilderness.

A rank of cars angle parked in front of the tavern. Earl slipped into an open slot. Two cars down, a drab Ford Crown Victoria nosed up to the building. Minelli's car looked like an unmarked police unit from the eighties or nineties.

We found Minelli at the squared-off end of the bar. He faced the door in what I think of as the "mobster seat," the chair with its back to the wall so that no one can sneak up from behind. As we pushed through the heavy front door into the beer-scented atmosphere, Minelli dipped his head toward a man sitting on the next stool. He spoke, but stopped abruptly when he caught sight of Earl and me. He added several more words before lifting his face to us and waving. The man beside him slipped off the stool and wandered in the direction of what I assumed was a pool room in the back half of the building. The clack of billiard balls informed my guess.

"Any news of Ms. Thorpe?" Minelli asked as we approached. He sat at the end of the bar with the newly empty stool to his left. The bar then took a 90-degree turn and ran the width of the building. Earl took the corner stool. I slid onto the next one in. The bartender, a man who easily tipped the scales at 300 pounds plus, ambled toward us from the other end of the bar.

"Nope." Earl propped his elbows on the polished wood. "Coke."

"Same." I followed Earl's lead. The bartender moved away to squirt fountain cola into glasses filled with ice and pure profit.

Minelli leaned closer and lowered his voice. A sound system pumped country music into the bar, but at a level akin to white noise. Despite the slim population of the town, the room was nicely filled for a Monday night. The rumble of conversation filled the bar. I had trouble hearing Minelli.

"I din't say nothing about nothing." He looked around. "People gossip. Story gets out about what happened out there and who knows what people will think. Like that little blonde cutie of yours, calling it a you-know-what. Crazy shit like that gets around faster than a November cold." Minelli nodded at us like he'd done us a favor.

Earl accepted the Coke he ordered and sipped. "Does this place serve food?"

"Hey, Leo!" Minelli signaled the barman. "Couple menus here."

Leo produced two laminated cards and slid them in front of Earl and me. My stomach rolled at the thought of burgers and chili dogs. I waged war in my head against fresh flashes of imagery representing the remains of Dr. and Mrs. Yuan. I pushed the menu aside.

Earl tossed his on mine and called out to Leo. "Club sandwich, please. Extra mayo."

Leo nodded. Folds of flesh under his chin bulged in and out. He looked at me for an order, but I waved him off.

"We're not taking someone's seat here, are we?" Earl tipped his head toward the pool room. "Saw you chatting with a pal when we came in."

"Billy Farwell. Trying to justify charging me two C notes for welding my exhaust pipe back on. He did a good job, but I resent covering the man's bar bill." Minelli chuckled. "Outsiders who talk funny get the upcharge."

"You coming back tonight?"

"To the cabin?" Minelli blew out a heavy sigh and ran fat fingers through the curled black hair on top of his head. "I dunno. One hand, I'm worried sick about Candice. Other hand, I'm not too much a man to admit that business last night scared the shit outta me. I know Candice keeps a double-barrel up in her office, but I ain't no hero. I got no experience with guns." Minelli cast an obvious glance at the pocket of Earl's flight jacket. "Although right now having one's not a bad idea."

Earl didn't acknowledge being tagged as armed. "Wouldn't blame you for staying away. We're grabbing a bite and heading back. Gotta ask you, though… you mentioned going on the internet on Candice's computer. I was hoping to get into her reservation system. See what's coming. You know anything about how I can do that?"

Minelli pursed his lips and did a slow head shake, No.

Earl sighed. "I'm worried about people showing up in the middle of all this. Season doesn't start for another week or so, but Candice might'a booked early arrivals."

"She never said nothin' to me. She just let me use her laptop to download a couple geology reports."

I asked, "Do you happen to know if she has a printer hooked up?"

Another headshake.

"Maybe Kelly knows," Earl said. "Somebody comes in early and stumbles into that mess, boy howdy. Bad for business."

We lapsed into the kind of silence that falls between strangers sharing a bar. I used the mirror behind rows of bottles to study the faces in the room. Mostly men. Nobody younger than me. Some looked tired. Too many looked over-weight, nursing beverages that shared the blame. There were smiles, though, and laughs. The place had low, warm lighting and a communal feel to the crowd.

Earl's sandwich came. It looked well made. Leo had kitchen help somewhere.

Minelli ordered another bourbon. I once again noted the ruby tint in his bulb nose, the web of red veins spreading into his cheeks.

Earl's suspicion of the man was palpable. In counterpoint, Minelli's concern for finding Candice felt sincere. I wasn't sure what to make of the man. Cab driver. Geologist. South Philly street smarts. Author. Alcoholic. He fit in with the faces in this room, but something about him echoed the incongruent Crown Vic sedan squeezed in a line of jacked pickup trucks and SUVs outside.

Leo drifted over and waited until Earl had a mouthful to ask how he liked the sandwich. I diverted the barkeeper from Earl's angry glare.

"Leo, the boss and I have business interests in the area. We're looking for a reliable bank. Candice—Mrs. Thorpe out at the Renell Lodge—mentioned a fellow named Charlie Pelton. She didn't say which bank. Do you know him?"

"I heard Candice is missing."

Earl grumbled something through his mouthful. I translated. "How'd you hear that?"

"Ernie Reitman's boy works as a deputy sheriff. That's Ernie down there in the Carhart jacket. Word gets around. You talk to Candice?"

"Not lately. And yes, we heard the same."

"Miss Candice is a great lady." Leo pulled a rag from an apron pocket and needlessly wiped down the bar. I wasn't sure the rag was the cleaner of the two.

"She is." I waited. Leo continued rubbing the varnished mahogany.

"Guy came in a couple years ago. Had one of those big plastic jugs, like you get cheese balls in?" I nodded to pretend I knew what he was talking about. "And he's got this sign on it. Raising money for his sister's kid. One of those special whatyacallit kids."

"Special needs?"

"Yeah, that's it. Raising money for extra care and what all. The kid needs one of them powered wheelchairs. Costs a friggin' fortune, those things, you know what I mean? The guy asks if he can leave the jug, maybe raise a few bucks to help the kid. I don't run no charity here, but if people wanna put a buck or two into it, I got no beef. If it's a good cause, you know what I mean?"

"Amen."

"So, I let him leave the jug and it was here most of the summer. And you could see a few bucks getting dropped in it regular like. Guy came in a few times to check, but he didn't collect because it looks better if there's something in the till, you know what I mean?"

I knew what he meant.

"But he's not raising a fortune, no way. Maybe a couple hundred by the end of the summer. And then Candice comes in one night and shoots some pool and has her supper and all. Nice lady. Everybody loves her. And the next day the guy comes in and guess what?"

"There's bunch of money in the jug."

"Nope. But two days later, Candice comes in again for lunch. Middle of the day. She's not a regular or anything. Mostly she stays out at the resort. But here she is twice in a couple days. It was noticeable, you know what I mean?"

I did.

"And guess what? The next week when that guy comes in, he finds a roll of hunnerds down at the bottom of the pile. Over five grand. More than enough to get the kid the chair." Leo leaned back and nodded his head once like he just stuck the landing.

"Candice."

"That's what I'm talking about, you know what I mean?"

Earl finished his sandwich. He had paid no direct attention to Leo during his story, but that didn't mean his ears weren't tuned to the bartender's frequency. He pushed the empty plate forward. Minelli nursed his latest bourbon. I noted that he had been listening, too, but he pretended he had not. He hung his attention on the television mounted above the mirror behind the bar. A soccer match played out, back and forth.

"She never took credit. She never said a word about it. Kept it secret." Leo began rubbing the bar again.

A secret except for the bartender who probably told this story to anyone who would listen, including two complete strangers.

"Charlie Pelton," Earl said to Leo. Leo looked surprised, perhaps because it wasn't the reaction he was looking for. Nor was the weathered map of what looked like malice on Earl's face. I tagged in.

"The banker Candice recommended." I glanced at Minelli, who remained fixated on the soccer match, then back at Leo. "She never mentioned the bank."

"Charlie's family owns Sun Lakes Bank over in Big Fork." Leo collected Earl's plate. "Good guy, you know what I mean?" Maybe it was our failure to express more awe over Candice's anonymous generosity, but Leo didn't seem happy at the change of subject. He walked Earl's plate to the swinging door at the other end of the bar and disappeared.

"I do know what you mean." I leaned closer to Earl and spoke so that only he could hear. "I think I'm going to disappear into the men's room. If he comes back, see if I can get a refill. Anything comes up, you got my number."

Earl grunted, holding his gaze in the direction Leo had gone.

I took one more look at Minelli, who remained enthralled by European football. And yet I had the feeling that if asked he could not tell me the score or even who was playing.

I headed for a dark hallway that led to the pool room. Halfway there, a carved wooden sign on a door said, *Dudes.* I looked at another door. *Dudettes.*

Cute.

21

*F*wooomp!

I watched myself vanish in the mirror above the men's room sink. A cool sensation joined the chill that had been lingering on the back of my neck since I found human remains in the Renell Lodge woods. My feet broke contact with the tile floor, but I used a grip on the porcelain sink to pull myself back to earth. I tapped the breast pocket of my flight jacket and felt the familiar bulge of two battery powered BLASTERs.

Fishing in the left jacket pocket, I pulled out a Bluetooth earpiece. I snuggled it into my right ear and fixed the mic stem against my cheek. If a call came to my phone, I could take it with a touch of the earpiece, solving the problem of taking a call on a phone screen I can't see.

I pushed away from the wash basin and rotated. With my left hand, I fixed a grip on the doorknob. In the vanished state, doors can be trouble. I can't just pull a door open by grabbing the knob. All that does is pull me into the door. I need leverage—in this case my right hand on the wall.

Another problem arises when a door is blind and public. I learned the hard way not to put myself in the path of a door that can swing open without warning. The outcome resembles a pinball taking a paddle hit.

Whoosh! The door flew open. I jerked my left hand clear. A man in a red flannel shirt and faded jeans stepped through, narrowly missing me.

Case in point.

The man moved to the nearest urinal. I grabbed the door's edge before it closed. The visitor stood with his back to me. With no interest in his business at hand, I let the door swing me into the hallway. Luckily, no one moved up or down the dark hallway, but this wasn't the place to stay for long.

I tapped the floor with my toes and rotated my body parallel to the ceiling. When acoustic tile bumped the back of my shoulders, I spread my arms and planted both hands on the facing walls.

A light tug propelled me forward.

The pool room had four tables, three of which were in play. Thankfully, the ceiling rose three feet higher than the hallway, abundant clearance above the shooters and spectators. The pressed tin ceiling and the room's dimensions suggested it may have been intended as a hall for wedding receptions or dances, but the placement of four pool tables in the center and random video poker games along one wall removed the question of public rental. High-top tables dotted the perimeter of the room. Leo operated a second bar in the back, as well as a connection to the kitchen. A young woman showcasing a crevasse of cleavage moved back and forth behind the mahogany, laughing with a row of young men lined up behind beer mugs in various stages of empty. The ranks leering at her looked ten years her junior. There were girls, too, though not many and nowhere near in proportion to the men. A group of four young women clustered around a table exchanging commentary with each other as if the young men watching them did not exist.

Billy Farwell sat at a table in the corner watching a pool match play out. My second look at him filled in blanks from the first impression. He wore a dark blue shirt with an embroidered name above the left breast pocket and nondescript gray pants with black grease stains on the thighs. The dirty hat on his head advertised CAT equipment. I guessed his age to be around mine. Four- or five-day-old beard stubble did little for blotchy pale facial skin. He had dark, narrow eyes set on either side of a nose sporting a sharp hump halfway down the cartilage. If he was an extra in a movie, it would not have been a gothic film about a werewolf. Perhaps a drive-in feature about biker gangs and beater cars in a desolate desert town. He held a brown bottle in one hand and tipped his chair against the corner intersection of two walls. From under the bill of his cap, he watched the pool match through hooded eyes.

The cluster of girls paid no attention to Farwell. They stole glances at the match. Not at the roll and strategy of the billiard balls on the felt, but at one of the players. Each time he positioned himself for a shot with his back to the ladies' table, their eyes settled on him. It was easy to see why.

I'd seen a man like this once before, not too long ago. Over six and a half feet tall, his muscles strained the fabric of a t-shirt. He wore jeans that had been stretched over bulging leg muscles. Cords flexed under his skin when he moved. The pool cue in his oversized hands looked like a child's toy. Long dark hair touched the muscles that bulbed above his wide shoulders. The romance-novel hair helped hide the size of his head, which was not much wider than his neck; upon too much scrutiny his head looked small in proportion to the bodybuilder's physique. His skin had healthy color, although a pale forehead betrayed a habit of wearing billed caps outdoors.

The ladies could not get enough of him. If he sensed their eyes on him, he didn't show it.

I hung at the hallway entrance, considering my options. Except for a sprinkler system pipe running down the center of the room, the ceiling offered nothing to grip. Lamps with fake Tiffany shades hung over the pool tables, creating obstructions. My intention had been to eavesdrop on Billy Farwell, given his acquaintance with Minelli and the conversation they abruptly terminated when Earl and I walked in. Since Billy appeared to be one of the advertised Farwell Brothers, I thought the other might be present. Maybe they would chat about Minelli.

But Billy Farwell sat alone. Farwell shared his high-top table with his beer bottle, from which he drew a slug every ten or fifteen seconds. I concluded that time spent hanging above his head would yield nothing of interest.

I was about to push back toward the *Dudes* room when a glass hit the floor and shattered.

"New girl!" The room erupted in cheers.

Looking both startled and sheepish, a tall girl with short black hair stood over the scene of the crime, a shattered beer mug that had tumbled from her overloaded tray. She cringed at the attention her accident generated. She cast a worried look at the woman tending bar, who pointed at a broom and dustpan leaning against the wall.

The girl hurried to deposit her tray at the bar, then fetched the cleanup equipment along with a metal wastebasket stored near the broom. Although blushing furiously, she ignored lingering chants of "New girl!" and maneuvered the broom under feet and chairs to collect the shards of glass in her dustpan. The debris renewed unwanted shouts when she dumped it in the metal wastebasket with a loud crash.

"Just take it out back," the bemused woman behind the bar said. She pointed at a door under a red Exit sign.

The teenaged server hurried to comply. She replaced the broom and dustpan, then grabbed the wastebasket and made for the exit.

I shoved hard against the side walls of the hall and coasted across the room. I reached the Exit sign above the door just as she pushed the latch bar and shoved her way through. Whether through frustration or miscalculation, she threw the door wide open. It banged against the back wall of the building. She hurried out the door and down a set of steps while the door rebounded. I grabbed the top of the jamb and swung my way through. My feet hit a concrete stoop. I grabbed a rail made of plumbing pipe.

The door clicked shut behind me. The girl hurried across a gravel driveway to a dumpster.

Fwooomp! I reappeared and settled on my feet, then quickly dropped to a seated position on the stoop.

"Excuse me."

She issued a frightened squeak and whirled toward the sound of my voice.

I threw up both hands. "Sorry! Sorry! Didn't mean to startle you. My name's Will. I'm a friend of Candice—Ms. Thorpe—out at Renell Lodge."

She hesitated, weighing the creepy aspect of the situation, precisely the reason I sat down. I hoped that planting my butt on the steps disarmed the moment. We were alone behind the tavern. A yard light hung on the back wall, but it served mainly to paint shadows that contributed to a slasher movie vibe.

She lifted a plastic lid and poured the wastebasket into the dumpster. Her bad luck continued. The dumpster was empty. The broken mug landed on bare steel and added a new chorus to her embarrassment.

She turned to face me. "I know Candice. Everybody knows Candice." Still hesitant. I didn't think she wanted to return to the bar the way she had departed, not with me blocking the steps. She glanced at the side of the building where the driveway offered passage to the front parking lot. Or a chance to run. Then she took a second look at me. "I heard she's missing."

"Yeah. That's why I came here with my boss. He used to be married to her. We're trying to find her. I'm sorry for following you out here, but it's only to ask you something. Do you know any of the kids who worked summers for Candice? Or were planning on working for her this summer?"

She chuckled. "Do I? Yeah. Me."

"You worked for her?"

"Last three summers. Best job ever. Way better than this." She waved the wastebasket at the tavern. "Is she okay? Have you heard anything?"

"No. Nothing specifically about Candice." I bit my tongue against mentioning the events at Renell Lodge. "Do you mind telling me why you decided to work here instead of the lodge this year?"

Her body language changed for the better. She relaxed and dropped the wastebasket to the ground. "This was the only thing I could get without driving all the way to Big Fork. Believe me, not working at the lodge wasn't my decision."

"What do you mean?"

"My dad. He knows people at the bank. He told me not to plan on working at the lodge this summer. That there was, I don't know, problems. We got in a big argument over it. I wanted to go out and apply with Candice anyway, but he wouldn't let me."

"Did he say why?"

She shook her head. "He just said he knew something he wasn't supposed to say. He's friends with people at the bank. He told me I better apply here and do it quick, because I wouldn't be the only one from the lodge out of luck and looking for work. He was right. My friends who worked there—they heard the same thing. Lizzy—my friend, Lizzy—she got an email from Candice saying her job wasn't available this year. She was kinda not nice about it." She clutched her hands together nervously. "I really like Ms. Candice. Are you sure she's missing? Are the police involved?"

"I don't know if she's missing or just doesn't want to be found. Honestly, I don't know enough to say anything with certainty. But you're right. She's a great woman. Like I said, my boss, the guy at the bar out in front who looks a little like a gargoyle, he was married to her."

She smiled. "Which one?"

"Jackson."

"Ah!" She counted on her fingers. "Number three."

"Yup. I give that woman a lot of credit. What did you do at the lodge?"

She smiled. "A little bit of everything, but mostly lifeguard when kids were swimming. You know—sign out the canoes for the corresponding cabins, hand out life jackets, camping, that sort of thing."

"Sounds nice."

"Beats cleaning up vomit here."

I stood and brushed off the back of my jeans. "Hey, I appreciate you talking to me. I'm gonna stroll around to the front so you can get back in there. Don't let them give you shit." I hopped down the steps to clear the way for her to return to the back barroom. "Thanks."

I set off purposefully to dispel any lingering creepiness. Halfway down the length of the building, she called after me.

"Will? Um...hold up a sec." She trotted out of the light to where I stood in shadow, a sign of budding trust. I clasped my hands and waited. "If you see Miz Candice, would you ask her to call me—I'm Val. I just—I want to know she's okay."

I bowed slightly. "Nice to meet you, Val. And yes, if I see her, I will tell her to let you know she's okay."

Val smiled again. It might have been the shadows on her face, but her expression adopted a sad hue. She looked like she wanted to say more. When she hesitated, I spoke instead.

"Val, go straight home tonight. Don't go out alone. Not until this gets sorted." I didn't wait for her to ask why.

22

I reentered the tavern through the front doors. My entrance ignited a flash of puzzlement on Minelli's fleshy face. Earl remained stationed at the bar behind a half-finished Coke. My drink had been refilled, but much of the ice had melted creating a two-tone effect in the glass.

"You get lost?" Minelli asked when I sat down.

"Yeah. Took a wrong turn."

Earl pointed at my watery Coke. "You gonna finish that?"

I noticed a couple of bills on the bar. Earl had settled the tab. I looked at my watch. Almost ten. I should have been more tired than I was. The notion of sleep held no appeal.

"Nah." I waved off the drink.

Earl leaned toward Minelli. "You going back?"

"One more for the road. Then, yeah."

Earl lowered his voice. "You might want to skip the one for the road. There's a couple sheriff's deputies at the entrance to the lodge and you ain't gonna want to glide in smelling like a distillery."

Minelli's eyes widened. "What's going on? Did they start a search?"

"Nope."

"Did they find her?"

"Nope. You know somebody named Yuan?"

Minelli held a blank expression.

Earl said nothing for a moment. He could not have timed it better. A commotion broke out at the other end of the bar.

A man in a Carhart jacket held up his phone and cried, "Holy shit! Holy shit! Somebody got killed out at the lodge."

People clustered around. An excited babble broke out. The man with the phone said something about hearing it from his kid. I heard Candice's name.

Minelli watched the breaking news, then looked back at Earl, who slid off his stool.

"Wasn't her." Earl pointed at Minelli's drink. "Like I said, the place is crawling with cops. Drive careful."

We turned and left.

23

"I don't like that guy." Earl didn't need to say it. His body language spoke volumes. Nevertheless, he nearly spit the words over the Jeep's steering wheel.

I didn't comment. I settled in the shotgun seat to watch the empty highway flow under our wheels like a gray conveyor belt. Tall, dark trees crowded us from either side of the road. Stars punctured the night sky, although the forecast called for overcast later. No moon. At least, not yet. When it did show up, I didn't think it would be full. And what would Pidge make of that?

Earl, unlike my wife, pegged the speedometer at precisely 55 miles per hour. The man is not a conversation connoisseur, but there are times when he expects a gap to be filled. After a moment he glanced at me.

"What?"

"Whad'ya find out back?"

I told him I had hoped to eavesdrop on the Farwell brothers but found only one and he wasn't chatty. I described the shattered beer mug incident and subsequent conversation with Val. I finished with the part that bothered me.

"This whole foreclosure—"

"Bullshit."

"—thing…I can't see any way that a bank would pull the trigger on something like that if they didn't have grounds. These guys are regulated up the wazoo. And if it's a local, family-owned bank, well they're usually the ones that bend over backward to help someone—especially someone like Candice. I mean, look at that story Leo told. Do you think there's anyone in this part of the county that hasn't heard that?"

"Sure sounded like her."

"You don't suppose somebody came looking for all that cocaine that was in the Queen Air, do you? Somebody who maybe thought it was her fault and she owed them?"

Earl scoffed at the idea. "Only ones looking for those drugs were those two clowns that showed up waving that hand cannon around. Last I heard they're both guests of the state of Minnesota. Nah. That's old news."

"So where did all of Candice's—?" I let the question trail hang unasked because at that instant, I remembered something.

Earl turned his head. His expression said he just landed the same fish.

"Her desk," I said.

"Yup."

Earl pushed the Jeep up to 60 miles per hour.

24

"Sorry, no one is allowed to enter." The deputy aimed the beam from his flashlight at Earl's face.

"You want to get the goddamned light out of my eyes, son. How'm I supposed to drive off after you ruined my vision?"

The light beam fell slightly.

"Like I said, no one is allowed to enter. This is a crime scene under the jurisdiction of the Itasca County Sheriff's Department and the Minnesota Bureau of—"

"Yeah, we know, we know. We're the ones called you fellas out here." Earl's thumb jerked in my direction. "He's the one found the bodies in the first place."

The Jeep idled in the middle of the road. The deputies had moved their Chevy Tahoes face to face across the entrance to Renell Lodge, blocking the dirt road. I hadn't noticed it before, but a carved wooden sign mounted on rough pine logs welcomed guests to the lodge. The sign was set back, clear of the highway right of way. Seeing it, I realized this was the first time I'd ever entered the grounds like any other guest.

"You?" The light swung up to my face, blinding me. I put a hand up to shield my eyes and give the guy a hint.

"Yeah, me. I found them."

The light fell again. The deputy, this one looking a few years senior to Reitman, came closer. He leaned on the driver-side sill and adopted a less authoritarian posture.

"We're hearing some crazy shit on the radio. What'd you see up there?"

"Nothing good."

"They're saying animal attack. Mountain lion, maybe."

"Only if the mountain lion is seven feet tall. The same thing tore up the lodge. Have you talked to Deputy Reitman?"

This deputy grinned. "Junior? No. I heard he filed a report earlier today, though. Vandalism at the lodge."

"Well, then somebody vandalized a couple people, too. Look, deputy, this man is Candice Thorpe's ex-husband. She's the owner of the lodge. We're as close as you're going to get to somebody in charge of the property—somebody that's not law enforcement, I mean. Lieutenant Turinski talked to us earlier and he was okay with us being on the grounds. Can you give him a call?"

"I can, but I won't. He's the one issued the orders—*after* you fellas left. Nobody in or out unless they're with the department, the staties, or the BCA. Sorry."

"You got a lot of people here tonight?"

"Half of northern Minnesota law is here—another reason we don't need visitors taking selfies and posting 'em on Instagram. I'd appreciate if you'd move along."

Earl closed a two-handed grip on the wheel and leaned back. The deputy pulled himself upright, away from the open window. He aimed his flashlight at the pavement. Conversation over.

"Deputy." I ducked down to see his face. "I saw what happened to the lodge and to those people. If I were you, I wouldn't park like that. I'd have those vehicles ready to beat it. If whatever did that comes around here again, your only hope is to be inside your unit and to outrun it."

The deputy glanced at his SUV, then back at the civilian whose advice carried zero weight. His expression made sure I knew it. "You have a good night, now."

Earl dropped the Jeep in gear, swung wide to the right, then performed a U-turn and motored back the way we had come. We drove without speaking, as if the sheriff's deputies were watching and listening. The highway ran straight as an arrow for miles. We traveled for several minutes before Earl slowed. He downshifted through the gears to avoid showing brake lights. We decelerated to a crawl. Still on the pavement, he turned off the vehicle lights.

My eyes acclimated to the starlit road quickly. The woods on either side of us stood black and forbidding. Earl eased off the pavement and rolled down one side of a small ditch and up the other. He goosed the accelerator to push the vehicle over some small shrubs. Twigs and branches scraped the Jeep's belly and snapped loudly beneath the tires.

Earl lurched the Jeep far enough into the trees to give us confidence that chrome or metal would not reflect passing headlights. He killed the engine.

"Think you can find your way from here?" Earl asked in the dark.

"What—through the woods?"

"No, dummy." He jerked his thumb skyward. "You know."

"Oh. Sure. You coming?"

Silence.

Earl has known about *the other thing* since I used it to leap out of an airplane he and Pidge were flying—and by leap I mean without a parachute. Since that incident, he has not asked for a close-up demonstration, let alone a ride. I found myself fighting a grin in the dark.

"Might be best if I stay here with the vehicle. Keep an eye on it."

"Bullshit. You need to come with me."

He muttered an objection to having his insides scrambled.

"It's not a Star Trek transporter. C'mon." I hopped out of the Jeep and stepped around the front to his side.

"What about my sidearm?" Earl climbed out and quietly closed the door. He patted his jacket pocket.

"It's fine. Just don't fire it. If you do, we're both royally screwed."

He pocketed the keys. I plucked a BLASTER from my flight jacket and snapped a prop in place.

"The hell is that?"

"Basic Linear Aerial System for Transport, Electric Rechargeable. It's how I get around." I held the unit up and made the prop spin.

"That little thing? You gotta be shittin' me."

I decided now wasn't the time to give a lecture on the characteristics of weight, mass, and inertia. I made a note to have Lane Franklin pigeonhole Earl for twenty minutes on the topic next time she stopped at the airport. Watching the girl lay some science on the old man would be fun.

I pulsed the BLASTER and made the prop whine. "Keep your fingers clear."

He didn't move. "Nah. You go on ahead. I'll hoof it through the woods."

"Earl, it's at least five miles. You'll break a leg in one of the ravines. C'mon. There's nothing to this. Andy's done it. Pidge has done it. Piece of cake." It was all I could do to keep a straight face. "Hell, I took Pidge out the window of a skyscraper in Chicago on her first ride. She loved it."

"Like hell she did." He took a hesitant step forward. "So, what do I gotta do for this? Rub my ruby slippers together?"

"Nope. Just stay in contact with me. If we get separated, you drop."

"I ain't holding your goddamned hand."

"I'm not asking you to go steady, Boss. Here." I stuck out my elbow. "Hook your arm through mine. Wait!" I popped open the Jeep and grabbed our overnight bags. "We're sleeping at the lodge tonight, right?" I handed him his bag. "Hold that against your chest."

He grunted at me but did the same as I did. I held out my elbow again. He hooked his arm through it then poked his hand in his pants pocket. I tightened the link between us and checked the space overhead. A few thin branches, but otherwise clear sailing to the stars.

"Now wha—?"

Fwooomp! I shoved the levers in my head to the wall. We vanished. A cool sensation flowed over my entire body. He jolted.

"Jesus H. Christ!"

"Relax." I pushed off the leafy woodland floor. We immediately rose through a gap in the trees.

"JESUS H. CHRIST!"

Earl's elbow lock on my arm turned to iron. We maintained a slow vertical glide up through branches on the verge of budding. The Jeep roof fell away beneath our feet. The woods, though quiet, was not silent. Something chirped. Something chittered. In the distance, a loon sang a lonely song.

The treetops slipped past us. The night sky opened above and around us. A solid carpet of forest stretched into endless distance. Above it all, from horizon to horizon, stars in their billions offered ancient light that grew brighter as our eyes adjusted.

I stretched out my right arm and held the BLASTER horizontally. Using the thumb slide control, I added power. The prop spun on the electric motor's whine. I aimed for where I knew we would soon see the lake, and then the lodge.

An owl called.

Another night creature repeated an agitated cry all the way to the lodge.

"JESUS H. CHRIST!"

25

We landed on the lodge deck overlooking the lake. I eased down and planted our feet firmly outside the dining room windows that had been smashed. Beyond the railing, the boathouse roof showed signs of dew. Beyond that, the lake shimmered with reflected starlight.

I searched the lodge interior for signs of law enforcement. The lights were on. Nobody home.

Fwooomp!

Earl thumped back into gravity's grip. He steadied himself, then tugged his arm out of mine.

"*That is the goddamnedest thing.*" Earl patted himself and checked his extremities. "*The goddamnedest.*"

"Christ, Boss, did you think I left some of your organs up in the air?"

I stepped through the vacant window frame. I was glad that Earl had swept up the shattered glass. Our footsteps remained silent. We slipped into the kitchen and deposited our bags.

During our descent, I looked for the deputies that had been holding down the fort. Both vehicles were gone. In the distance, lights near the fatal ravine scene created an otherworldly effect, like a UFO landing site in a Spielberg movie. I had feared Turinski would establish the lodge as a command post. I could not guess why he hadn't but was glad we didn't need to move through the building in the vanished state.

Lights throughout the building interior had been left on. Some in the great room and dining room. Some in the upstairs hallway. We tiptoed up the stairs to Candice's office. I flipped a switch at the door reasoning that one additional light would not be noticed. A floor lamp with a faded and brittle shade lit up in the corner of the room. Bugs that had wandered in the broken first-floor windows swooped in to orbit the light.

Earl paused. He fished the ring of keys from his pocket and placed them on a hook beside the door. I made a guess that was where Kelly had fetched them earlier. Earl moved around the desk. He ignored the laptop, still positioned on the blotter. He scooped up the papers we had shoved aside, squared them, and patted them flat. One by one, he paged through a mix of papers and the envelopes they had arrived in.

"These are past due notices. Missed mortgage payments. A couple months' worth. Maybe more." He laid half the wad of documents aside. "These here are bank statements." He held one of the documents up to see it better in the soft yellow light. He made a hybrid grunt and growl sound.

"What?" I tried to see what caught his eye.

"She's got a butt-load of cash withdrawals. Here. Fifteen hundred. Here. Thirty-three hundred. She was taking cash out regular-like. That's why she's short."

Earl dropped the hand clutching the bank statement to the desk. He stared into the distance. "It don't make sense."

"Why would she take cash knowing it shorts the mortgage payments?"

Earl poked his tongue into his cheek and squinted. He shook his head.

"Boss, she had to know it would put her in jeopardy. Plus, this Charlie the Banker guy would have reached out to her. How much cash are we talking about?"

Earl re-examined the statement. "This one's close to nineteen grand." He thumbed through the sheets. "This one's another twelve."

I gave up trying to read over Earl's shoulder. I slipped around the desk and dropped in the wingback chair. A novelty hourglass occupied a table beside the chair. A label on the top of the hourglass said *Activate at the eleventh hour*. A similar label at the bottom said, *When sand runs out, PANIC*.

Earl stared, not focusing, perhaps searching for explanations in his memories of Candice. I wondered if these actions fit the woman he knew. People change. A year had passed since he last saw her. Decades since they exchanged wedding vows that endured for three whole weeks.

"That woman can pinch a nickel until Jefferson cries for mercy. That's what you said. From the way you described Candice, she ran a tight ship. Yet she leaves sensitive bank statements scattered all over her desk. That sound right to you?"

Earl didn't answer. That was answer enough.

26

"The judge ruled against the last of the defense motions. That's it for the pretrial proceedings. Jury selection is scheduled for two weeks from now."

I drifted above the lake with Andy's smooth voice caressing my ear via the Bluetooth earpiece. Earl remained in the office. His compulsion for details drove him deep into the bank statements. I told him I wanted to cruise out over the crime scene to see how much of Minnesota law enforcement had joined the party. Lost in the paperwork, he didn't notice me leaving.

My watch read just past midnight when I sent Andy a text.

If you're still up, call. If not, ILY.

I launched off the same deck Earl and I had arrived on. Andy's call rang in my earpiece when I was less than a third of the distance to the ravine. I answered and simultaneously reversed and made a direct line to the lake where I brought myself to a stop thirty feet above the water. I pocketed the BLASTER and let myself float, silent and serene, grateful for the interruption. I was curious, but not anxious to return to the murder scene.

"Thank God," Andy added. "They've deposed me three times now. Trying to poke holes in my account and discredit my report."

"Always tell the truth. It's easier to keep your story straight." Andy's quote, not mine.

"Well, of course I'm telling the truth, Will." She missed the homage.

The case dogging my wife involved Clayton Johns, a former star running back in the National Football League who enjoyed sex with underaged and sometimes unwilling girls. Andy had been first on the scene when Johns was found naked and unconscious with a girl who later tested conclusively as having been raped by Johns. The laboratory proof deflated the defense claim that Johns had been drugged by a man named Derek Santi, a psychopath and serial killer. Santi had, in fact, drugged both the girl, and then Johns, but the laboratory evidence did not lie. Johns had his fun before passing out.

The pool player at the Beaudry Public Brew House reminded me of Santi—a head, albeit small, taller than anyone else in the room and a body buffed to comic book proportions. A candidate for the pro wrestling circuit. Like the pool player, Santi had been something of a human caricature—if he could be considered human at all.

Andy described moves made by the district attorney that deftly undercut defense motions designed to dispose of evidence, eliminate witnesses, and as a last resort, change the trial venue. As the defense tactics sequentially failed, Clayton Johns' legal team fell back on the last resort of the guilty. Delay. Delay. Delay.

"You still there?"

My mind had been wandering.

"Yeah. Still here. I'm out over the lake. I wish you could see this." I described the stars overhead, and their reflections in the water below me. It felt like floating in space.

"What's going on?" Andy was less than starstruck. I explained everything that had happened since we last spoke. "They brought in BCA? Right away?"

"Yeah. This is ugly, Dee. I don't want to describe it."

"I'm so sorry. Truly. I'm sorry you had to see that."

"Nobody should have to see that. So, uh, change of subject please. How are you feeling?"

"Strange. Normal. Mostly. Then weirded out. Then overwhelmed. I was at the office and—don't laugh, Will—I was suddenly flooded with emotion. Just this…I don't know…gratitude for life, and for you, and for us." A hitch caught her voice. "It's hard to describe. I had to go out in the sally port for a good cry. And don't you give me any static about hormones or emotions because I'm warning you, that pendulum can swing the other way."

"I tread on eggshells."

"I wish you were here."

"Me too. I'm sorry for getting caught up in this, but—"

"Stop. I get it. It's for Earl, and for Kelly, and for Candice. I hope I can meet her sometime."

"She's a legend around here. Which is why this doesn't make any sense." I told Andy about the foreclosure, the bank statements, and the cash withdrawals.

"It sounds like she has money trouble."

"Yeah, but enough to make her sacrifice the lodge for cash?"

We speculated back and forth for a few minutes, but nothing helpful bubbled to the surface. Andy introduced a new topic.

"Leslie texted."

Special Agent Leslie Carson-Pelham.

I think of Leslie as my pet FBI agent, a designation that would surely earn me a bullet if she ever heard me say it. She alone, in the vast intelligence and law enforcement apparatus of the federal government, knows that I can vanish. For that reason and, I suspect, possible benefits to her job, she likes to stay in touch.

"What does our favorite fed want?"

"She's meeting you in Evermore on Friday."

I wondered what Spiro Lewko would think when I showed up with the FBI at his built-from-scratch company town in North Carolina.

"Okay. Well, this puts a little more pressure on things."

"Sorry."

"It's fine. I got this. Did Leslie say why she's going to Evermore?"

"Leslie never says why she does what she does. But she has your best interest at heart. If she weren't a lesbian, I'd suspect her of being hot for you."

"Right. Which is why I suspect her of being hot for you, dear."

"Then maybe I should consider a change in orientation. I mean, look what happened thanks to messing around with you."

The conversation became playful, which made me forget where I was and what I was about to do. I painted a mind picture of Andy curled in a corner of our sofa under the fuzzy blanket she likes, the one I sometimes heat up in the drier for her, an act that sustains my Best Husband Ever rating. I imagined her rich waves of auburn hair, the light caramel color of her skin, and the way the slender flow of her neck always draws my eyes deeper.

Okay, this was not good.

"Sweetie, I'd love to keep this up, but we're both up past our bedtimes. You're sleeping for two now."

"Are you going to be able to sleep tonight? Is it safe?"

"Probably 'no' on both counts, but worst-case scenario, I'll do *the other thing* and tether myself to a treetop."

"Don't you dare. What if you reappear in your sleep and fall?"

I talked her away from that panicked thought by shifting the topic to a possible return schedule, which I had no business estimating. Eventually we traded declarations of love and wishes for good sleep and ended the call.

I remained suspended between a sky full of stars and the glittering reflection of those stars on the lake below me. The enchanting perspective perfectly accented the light ache induced by missing Andy.

27

To say the murder scene was lit up would be to say that New York City turns on a few lights after dark. Giant bars of searingly bright halogen lamps had been erected at the cardinal points of the compass around the ravine. A second ring of lights circled the terrible end of Dr. and Mrs. Yuan. On telescopic stands, the lights had been raised to roughly twenty feet in the air. In the damp night air, the hot bulbs launched wisps of vapor. At ground level, electric power generators muttered a single-note requiem for the dead. The lights both cast and burned away shadows. Every blade of grass and fallen leaf gained definition. Half a dozen people in luminous white hazmat suits moved within the circumference of illumination. They worked their way inward, toward the BMW and the central span of gore spread on the forest floor.

Uniformed deputies formed the next ring around the scene. They stood in clusters and lines watching the forensic investigators work. On the east side of the ravine, emergency vehicles crowded the trees. The boxy van I'd seen earlier dominated. It had been backed up to the ravine slope and the rear doors had been flung open to expose a cache of orange cones, toolboxes, ladders, ropes, and countless other emergency necessities. At least a dozen smaller vehicles, some of them marked, some not, parked beneath the trees. A few continued running their emergency lights, lending a disco ball touch to the nightmare.

Just above the treetops, I cruised a slow circle around the outermost ring of human presence. I wasn't worried about the whine of the BLASTER, which is sometimes mistaken for a small electric drone. Generators covered the noise.

Judging the deployed resources from above, no effort had been spared. I never would have guessed a northern Minnesota county had so many deputies on its roster. If the department maintained a reserve or auxiliary officer program, they had called them in. There had to be two dozen uniforms circling the site.

My Bluetooth earpiece announced an incoming call. Since I couldn't see my phone to read the caller ID, my generic pickup line served both Earl and Andy.

"I'm here."

"WHAT THE FUCK!"

Pidge.

"What are you doing up?" I veered left, away from the crime scene, back toward the lake. I'd seen enough and didn't want to risk someone hearing my voice in the night sky.

"Freaking the holy horsefuck out. It's goddamn breaking news. Animal attack. Two dead. Jesus, Will, you told me not to say anything to Kelly, and now she's bawling her eyes out." I heard something in the background that could have been a wounded animal or a broken dishwasher. Hard to say. "You gotta talk to her. Here."

Before I could object, a stream of sobs flowed into my ear. I heard my name mixed in, along with Candice's name.

"Kelly, listen to me. Listen. It's not Candice."

"*Wha—wha—who—whoizit?*"

"It looks like it was Dr. Yuan and his wife."

Fresh sobs erupted. "*Why?*"

"I don't know. Maybe they arrived at the wrong moment. I don't know. But it wasn't Candice."

"*Wuh—wuh—where is she?*"

"We don't know yet. Listen to me. Give the phone back to Pidge and go get a drink of water and get settled, because I need to ask you some questions, okay? Can you do that?"

Silence.

"Hello?" I suddenly realized I hadn't checked my phone charge, nor could I until I either returned to the lodge or landed and reappeared. "Hello?"

"I'm here." Pidge returned to the line.

"How did you find out?"

"They interrupted Late Night."

I hadn't seen any news crews at the scene. The nearest network affiliate might be—I had to think—International Falls? Minneapolis? "What are they saying? Do they have video?"

"No video. They're saying there are reports of an animal attack. Two fatalities. They're telling people to stay indoors. Like that would help."

"Did they mention Renell Lodge?"

"I don't think so. They said it was near the Big Fork Park and Pine-Something State Forest, and the Red Lake area—whatever that is. Kel totally freaked out. I might've missed a couple details. The talking heads think it might be a mountain lion. Idiots."

"This was no boating accident."

"What?"

"Sorry. A line from *Jaws.* It was no mountain lion."

"Duh. Fucking werewolf, Will. I'm serious. Where are you and Earl?"

"Earl is at the lodge. I'm fifteen feet above the treetops about a quarter mile from the crime scene, headed back to the lodge. I came up to check things out. They've got everybody but the National Guard out there. If this is all over the news, the place is going to be crawling with media in the morning."

"I'm flying in to get you the hell out of there."

"Put Kelly back on." I wasn't ready to argue with Pidge about a pickup.

"You're on speaker."

"Kelly, you there?"

"Uh-huh. Suh-sorry for the waterworks. I'm just really scared for Candice."

"That's what I want to ask you about. Did Candice mention any financial trouble? Did she seem worried about the lodge?"

"No. Not at all. We were super excited about the season opening. She talked about being booked up. She kept saying it was so nice to have me there to help. We talked a lot about summer coming—how it was going to be great."

"No money issues? You didn't see her cutting corners? Hoarding cash?"

"I didn't have anything to do with the money side of things, so no. Why are you asking these questions?"

I saw no premium in keeping it a secret. I explained what Turinski had said about the foreclosure.

"That's not possible," Kelly protested. She sounded like Earl. Not just wishful but endowing her conviction with certainty equaling a law of physics. "Candice loves the lodge. She loves her life there. She would never risk it over money."

"That's the picture Earl paints, too. And if she really did have money problems, Candice knows Earl is loaded. She could have gone to him at any time for anything. What about a man named Charlie Pelton? Did you ever meet him?"

"Mr. Pelton at the bank? Sun Lake Bank?"

My eyebrows went up. "Yeah. You met him?"

"Candice took me and Seth with her over to Big Fork a month or so ago. I needed a few things at the Walgreens. She said the bank called and needed her to come in."

"Do you know what for?"

"She has a safe deposit box there. She said she practically forgets it exists except for the twenty bucks they charge her every year."

"She needed to get in the box?"

"No. They needed her to come in. Mr. Pelton said they were doing something with the locks, and they needed her to stop by with her key. It only took a few minutes."

"So, just in and out? No long conversations? They didn't make you wait while they had a discussion?"

"Uh-uh. Just in and out."

"Did she seem upset? After talking to Pelton?"

"Uh-uh. He was super nice."

"But how did she seem?"

"Uh…like Candice. Fine. She joked with him about needing a locksmith to get into his own bank."

I was stumped.

"Will, what's going on?"

"I do not know, Kelly. I honestly do not know."

"I keep trying to tell you people, it's a fucking werewolf."

"Yeah, Pidge, I'm not ready to buy a ticket to the drive-in, but on that note, I'd just as soon you don't fly in here tomorrow. You'll only be met with a bunch of angry sheriff's deputies and then you two will probably spend a couple hours explaining yourselves. Worst case, they impound the airplane for God knows what reason. That reminds me. Did any deputies track you down?"

"For what? We didn't do anything! That guy in the bar downstairs was being an asshole." Pidge's leap to the defensive did not surprise me.

"I don't know who you beat up downstairs. The lieutenant we spoke to said he was going to send someone to interview you both—just to firm up our story of how the car was found. I think when this turned into a full fire drill, he either didn't have extra bodies or he forgot. Don't be shocked if cops show up and want to talk to you about how you found that car and told me and Earl all about it."

"Right. Okay. Forget what I said. I'm still flying in to get you in the morning."

"Don't. Seriously. It's not worth the paperwork. We've got Candice's Jeep. They're going to want us outta here, anyway. Earl and I will drive over to Big Fork."

"What about Candice?" Kelly asked. "Are they going to look for her?"

"One way or another," I replied.

I didn't think it would be the way Kelly hoped.

28

When I departed the lodge for my crime scene overflight, the lodge's interior lights had been on,. Earl had been nose-deep in bank statements.

When I returned, the building had gone dark. Surrounded by black trees, the lodge could be distinguished only by its geometric shape and proximity to the boathouse below it. Earl—or someone—had killed every light on the property.

I immediately eased back on the BLASTER power to reduce the noise it generates. I approached from over the empty yard where the sheriff's SUVs had been stationed earlier and were now conspicuously absent.

I cut the power and stopped the small prop. A glide carried me over the lodge roof. I slowly rotated my body and studied the shadows and varying shades of black below. Something else had changed. It wasn't only the incandescent light from the lodge that had gone dark. The starlit sky I had enjoyed above and below while I floated over the lake now offered no pinprick lights. Overcast clouds pulled a shade across the night sky, significantly reducing the ambient light.

Earl would not have gone dark without a reason.

I pulsed the power unit and returned to the deck at the back of the lodge. Not breathing, I looked and listened. Nothing moved. Nothing generated sound. The world lay silent and still. I bit down on an impulse to call out for Earl, easily imagining him scolding me for being an idiot and hollering his name while he was trying to avoid detection.

I rotated slowly to scan every shadow, every dark angle and nook. Without reflected starlight the lake became a black hole. Stone steps descending to the boathouse were faintly visible. Nothing moved on those steps or on either side of the boathouse. Beyond that, only black. The night sky in this part of the state lacked light pollution to reflect off the gathering clouds.

I held the BLASTER upright and gave it the least reverse power possible. The prop awoke and spun slowly. I descended. On my way down, I passed the windows to Candice's office. The glass surrendered faint and confusing reflections, but no visual access to the dark interior. The unit pushed me down until my feet silently touched the wooden deck outside the dining room.

Decision time. Appear or remain vanished?

I listened. Nothing.

Maneuvering through interior spaces in the vanished state is not easy. Control requires finesse with the BLASTER, or else pushing and pulling from one grip point to another—and with either comes the risk of colliding with something.

Fwooomp! I elected to reappear and let gravity press my feet to the floor. I secured the BLASTER and stepped through the empty window frame into the dining room.

I stopped and listened.

Nothing. No heavy breathing. No scratching of claws on the wooden floor. No animal sounds.

I became aware of the light rustle and creak of my leather flight jacket. The sound reassured me. If I could hear that, I would probably hear someone or something else moving in the dark.

Now what?

Find Earl.

I did not expect to locate him in Candice's office. Turning off all the lights in the building meant he had moved out of the office, down the stairs and into the first-floor great room and dining room. He could be anywhere.

I skirted the long dining room table. On my way to the great room, I collided with the chair Lieutenant Turinski occupied while interviewing us. Chair legs skidded loudly on the wooden floor.

Shit! I froze. I waited. I listened.

Nothing reacted to my stupid, loud error. I stepped sideways and eased past the chair.

I was about to turn into the great room when Earl growled at me from the darkness on the opposite side of the door.

"Pretty dang clumsy, buddy."

I froze. The steel barrel of a Colt .45 automatic emerged from the black, followed by Earl's hand, arm, and the faint outline of his bald head. He lifted a crooked digit to where his lips would be, then moved the same digit to point at his ear, then at the deck outside.

Heard something outside.

He pointed at himself, then at the broken windows.

Going outside.

He pointed at me and made a *poof!* gesture with his hand.

Do your thing.

I heard the mime commands expressed as Earl's voice inside my head.

I pointed at myself, then at a path through the great room, out the front door, and around the end of the building.

I'll circle around.

He nodded.

Earl crossed behind me and disappeared into black. I crossed the floor to the front door. A few feet from the still gaping opening—

Fwooomp!

—I vanished on the move. I tapped my toe on the last step to generate a slight upward vector. It was a bit much. I had to grab the top of the door jamb to redirect myself under it. Adding an extra push, I heaved myself across the porch and into the yard.

On the glide, I retrieved the BLASTER from my flight jacket pocket. I snapped a prop back on the electric motor shaft and tested the unit. All good.

I added power and angled my wrist to the left. Sensitive to the noise the unit made, I kept the power low, which limited my speed to a brisk walk. Seconds stretched. It took forever to circle around the end of the lodge. The land sloped away on a path that wound down to the pebble beach, the pier, and the boathouse. At the end of the lodge, the front porch became a second-story deck with a view of the water. Small tables and deck chairs were set up for guests. Coffee with sunrises. Cocktails with sunsets.

I cruised past the deck rail and emerged above the steep slope between the main lodge and the boathouse. Looking left, I spotted Earl's silhouette descending the stone steps to the boathouse. He held his gun at his side, the muzzle pointed at the ground. Whatever drew his attention had to do with the boathouse. I searched the building's roof and saw nothing.

Two paths joined the beach and boathouse to the main lodge—the steps Earl descended and the winding path down the slope. Anyone needing to ascend from the waterline would have to take one of those paths to stay stealthy. A direct route through the rough brush would generate noise.

Earl had the steps covered. I followed the walking path in case someone ascended from the beach to the lodge.

Tree boughs overarched my route. I dropped down until my toes scraped the chipped wood path. The switchback path went first west and then east. The total distance came to almost two hundred yards. I fought the temptation to add power for more speed. Noise from the prop and electric motor would not only alert an intruder, but it would also mask my ability to hear someone moving in the dark. I searched my left for a shortcut through the trees. Sparse pines with most of their branches near the top would have allowed it, but the shoreline had deciduous trees with low branches, most of them nearly invisible in the dark. A shortcut guaranteed noise. The path guaranteed clearance. I stayed on course.

By the time I reached the pebbled beach and a boardwalk that joined the pier and boathouse, Earl had rounded the end of the building. His bowlegged, bent figure and leathery bald head moved along the wooden wall several hundred feet away. Something drew him to the section of beach that sloped from the boathouse to the water where Candice's barrel raft floated at the end of a chain.

I cursed the clouds that had curtained a sky full of starlight. The raft floated as a shade of black on black, barely distinguishable.

Movement near the raft caught my eye. I heard splashing.

I aimed the BLASTER straight at the raft but kept the speed at a walk. I did not want to get downrange between him and a potential target.

Earl didn't wait.

He crouched and swung himself around the corner of the boathouse. I heard his voice. Whoever or whatever he saw reacted. I saw movement. I heard a thump. A splash.

Just as I goosed the power unit to accelerate to a closer look, the brush on the slope erupted. Crashing, snapping, and thumping announced movement of something huge. The intruder cut directly down the slope from the yard to the lake.

I slammed the BLASTER into reverse and stopped.

Pidge's werewolf broke out of the brush less than twenty feet from me.

Massive.

The bulk stole my breath. I made out a fur coat, a huge head, a long snout. It hunched over on huge, long arms that it leaned on as legs. Blade claws glinted at the end of curved fingers. The blades stabbed the earth.

Earl spun to face the threat.

The creature bolted toward him. Earl raised his weapon.

Straight at me.

"Earl don't shoot! I'm here!"

FWOOOMP!

I reappeared and dropped hard. My feet hit the loose pebbles and slipped. I fell on my ass. A jolt shot up my spine and reminded me of a once-broken pelvis. The BLASTER in my hand hit hard. I heard a snap and didn't have to look to know that I'd lost the prop.

The creature threw down one arm and dug its claws into beach pebbles, throwing a spray of them into the air. It halted. It turned its long snout over one shoulder and found me.

"Here!" I scrabbled backward. "Over here, asshole!"

Using the claw for leverage, the monster pulled itself around to face me. A massive arm slammed down onto the wooden boardwalk. Splinters flew.

I dropped the BLASTER and scooped up a handful of stones and hurled them. Tiny stones bounced off fur, ticked the wooden boardwalk, and pinged metal somewhere. I might as well have thrown feathers. The creature didn't flinch, but it did hesitate, and that's what I wanted.

Earl had the good sense to lower his weapon. The creature turned from me to

Earl and then back at me. Earl threw himself down the pebble beach and splashed into the water. A few feet in, he dove, disappearing in the dark near the raft. Movement shifted the darkness on the other side of the raft.

I scrambled backward on my butt.

"Hey!"

The monster gave me its full attention. It jerked the claw free of the board-walk and dropped down on all fours. The long forearms stabbed the stones. It took a step, then two, then hunched and threw itself forward with a horrible grace. In a second it would be on me.

I heaved myself into a kind of half sit up. My legs coiled. I drove my heels into the pebbles.

Bearing down on me, the monster threw a giant arm skyward to strike.

Fwooomp!

I vanished and fired my leg muscles like a cannon. The result hurled me backward across the beach.

The raised arm slammed down where I had been. Claws gouged. Stones flew.

The massive head shot from side to side, searching. I sailed backward. After a few seconds of fruitless search, the huge head rotated in Earl's direction.

Fwooomp!

I reappeared and dropped from a height of almost six feet, hard on my backside.

"Hey asshole! Here!" I scrambled to my feet and faced the monster, which drew itself erect long enough to let me know who was taller by a huge head. I waved my arms in the air. "Come and get me!"

It lunged. I turned and ran. I could hear the scratch of its pounding footfalls in the gravel. Without looking back, I gauged the shrinking distance between my back and those claws and—

Fwooomp!

—I kicked the ground and shot upward—directly into an overhanging tree branch.

The impact caught my head and shoulders. My legs sailed forward. My head flipped backward. I tumbled. Skinny leafless branches and twigs slapped my face and arms. I cleared the tree on a downward trajectory. I rotated at the last second to get my legs under me and then hit the ground running.

Fwooomp!

Gravity lent a hand and gave my feet solid purchase. I sprinted up the trail. A glance over my shoulder showed that I had opened distance on the beast, which strutted across where I had been a moment ago. It searched, then froze, then pivoted the long snout in my direction. I hit my stride in a pounding sprint up the hill.

I knew that if the beast followed, it would ignore the switchback trail and cut through the brush—so I did the same. My boots snapped small twigs. I slapped the brush aside. I darted past tree trunks praying not to hit a root the wrong way and break an ankle.

A few seconds later, behind me, sticks and branches crashed. The beast followed.

I didn't need much time or distance. Just enough to be sure that Earl found a safe place to hunker down. With that accomplished, I planned to vanish and head for a treetop.

I broke onto the trail and cut hard right. At a full run, I climbed the hill toward the lodge. A glance over my shoulder showed only darkness but the sound of the monster chasing me warned that the distance was closing. Halfway up the trail I heard it cease smashing through the brush and join the trail behind me.

This was going to be close.

Even at full speed on the open trail, I held no illusions of outrunning it. I'd seen it move, pounding those huge arms in a cadence with its legs. The image of a lowland gorilla at full gallop snapped through my mind. Fast. Too fast for a human on two feet. Candice would have had no chance.

The beat of its arms and legs drummed the earth behind me. I broke into the yard. I was just about to call it a day and vanish when a new shape materialized out of the darkness.

"GEDDOWN!"

Twin barrels of a shotgun swept up toward my face. I dove. I hit the ground just as two blasts and corresponding flashes strobed the night. I skidded and slid on the rough bark path and slammed into Minelli's legs.

I rolled sideways and frantically searched for the creature on the trail behind me.

Nothing.

A hand fell on my shoulder. I grabbed it and tugged myself to my feet.

Minelli snapped open the shotgun and tugged at hot spent shells in the breach to reload. He fumbled two fresh shells to the ground. I gasped for air and hunted for motion in the darkness.

Nothing.

To our right, where the cabins dotted the woods, pounding footfalls and crashing brush faded into the distance.

"Missed the sonofabitch." Minelli found the shells at his feet. He stuffed them into the barrel and snapped it closed. He hefted the weapon in hand. "Could'a used this bad boy in the cab. You okay?"

I doubled over and sucked air, nodding.

"What the hell wazzat?"

Still fighting for breath, I could not speak, but Pidge's voice didn't hesitate in my head.

Fucking werewolf.

29

"Stay here."

"By myself? What're you? Nuts?" Minelli waved the shotgun back and forth at the black woods. The creature crashing through the brush either stopped or had traveled out of earshot. "We need to get inside. Maybe one of the cabins. Do you know if Candice has any more of these bullets? 'Cuz I only found six."

"They're shells, not bullets." I turned and started toward the lodge. "Come with me or go lock yourself in your cabin. A door won't stop it, but the shotgun got its attention. I need to find Earl."

"You're gonna get your ass kicked if that thing comes back. Just sayin'."

I broke into a trot.

"Just don't shoot me in the dark."

I HURRIED through the dark lodge to the dining room, then through the windows onto the deck. My night vision had improved. Despite the absence of starlight or a moon of any quarter, I could make out the shape of the boathouse below and the black lake beyond. On the far side of the lake, the shoreline formed a darker than black horizon.

I took Earl's route down the wooden stairway from the deck. Stone steps ended at the boathouse door. To my right, bits of the grass and brush lay crushed by bootsteps. Earl's steps. He had moved along the back of the boathouse, then down the side of the building toward the water's edge. That's where I saw him when I emerged from the trail.

I did not follow his route. The door had three deadbolt locks above a knob with a lock, but none were engaged.

Inside, I found and flicked a light switch. Bare bulbs attached to the rafters lit up. Nothing had changed from my previous visit. Numbered canoes remained lined up waiting for guests who were not coming. The chain holding the raft against the shore snaked under the waterfront main door. I found the power switch and punched the green button. An electric motor fired up. Wheels and pulleys groaned. A door the full width of the building folded upward like a hangar door. Light spilled onto the shallow slope of pea gravel beach that separated the building from the water. I walked through a gap in the canoe ranks and stepped into the night air on the beach.

Earl heard something or someone down here.

I looked up and down the shoreline. This was the part where I was supposed to hunt like a frontier tracker until I found The Clue. A shoe print. A cigarette butt. A thread tangled on a bramble. A convenient shred of Earl's shirt caught on a twig.

Fat chance.

Water lapped the shoreline, pushed against the gravel by a light breeze. I saw nothing at the water's edge—no *eureka* clue to pick up and examine. No gotcha to send off to a forensic lab for analysis.

"Earl!"

I listened. No sound met my ear, not even the echo of my own voice.

Earl dove in the water when the creature took aim at him. Not a bad move. He had at least fifty-fifty odds that his pursuer could not or would not swim after him. But hiding in water only works for as long as you can hold your breath.

Unless.

The pier was too tall. Popping up under the planks could easily be seen from either side. The raft, on the other hand, floated on double rows of barrels. With a deck made of two by twelve planks, it also had a skirt of the same planks around all four sides. The skirt rode just inches above the water. A good place to hide and surprise someone.

Fwooomp! I vanished. My feet left the soft gravel.

I pulled my spare BLASTER from the flight jacket pocket and snapped my remaining prop in place. A short burst of power pulled me across a dozen feet of water to the raft. I stopped above the center.

Fwooomp! I reappeared and gravity regained its influence. My boots landed on the dry wooden surface. The raft bobbed under my weight.

I dropped to my knees and rapped on the wooden planks.

"Earl!"

Nothing.

"You under there?"

Nothing.

I stood up and studied the shoreline. Lights from the boathouse showed two sets of depressions in the gravel beach. Mine stopped well short of the water's edge. Earl's made a straight line from the corner of the boathouse to the water, exactly the path I'd seen him take. The angle wasn't direct to the raft, however. Earl moved to the left of the raft, the far side. If he intended to hide under the raft, why not take a direct path? Why take the long way around?

I turned and followed the line until it had me facing out toward the center of the lake, a tableau in shades of black.

Mud.

My gaze fell from the dark distance to near my feet. Along one side of the raft, a line of smeared mud ran parallel to the raft's edge. The mud remained glossy and wet.

Earl didn't climb onto the raft. So, why the mud?

I took a step closer.

Upside down to my eye, the message Earl left was instantly readable in the smear of mud he had scooped from the bottom and spread along the edge of the raft.

DO NOT FOLLOW

30

I called 911 and reported the attack. I gave my number and told the operator to have Lieutenant Turinski call me ASAP, which he did. When I told him whatever probably killed Dr. and Mrs. Yuan had just attacked us at the lodge, and that we had run it off, he barked orders for us to barricade ourselves in the dry pantry and wait for the cavalry. He told me to tell Earl to secure his handgun somewhere safe, like the kitchen freezer, so that a deputy didn't get the wrong idea. I told him Earl was missing and explained Minelli's use of Candice's shotgun. I got an earful about goddamned amateurs making matters worse. He snapped at me that if his deputies arrived at the lodge and saw someone with a shotgun they would shoot. His way of telling us to keep it out of sight.

We did none of what we were told. Minelli didn't lock himself in his cabin. He waited on the front porch for me to return from the boathouse, shouldering the shotgun and pacing like a frontier sheriff. He insisted he wasn't taking his hands off the weapon or hiding in the dry pantry again. I suggested that before the deputies arrived, securing the shotgun in the dry pantry might spare him another bullet.

Half a dozen SUVs rolled into the yard and discharged deputies with weapons drawn. I anticipated their arrival with every light in the building blazing. Minelli and I waited in the great room with our hands in plain sight. Minelli reluctantly followed my advice about the shotgun. He ditched it in Candice's office.

The deputies vetted us and then searched the grounds. The search included the waterfront I had just come from. I left the boathouse open and the lights on but said nothing about the smear of mud on the raft.

Earl's voice came through loud and clear in three finger-painted words.

DO NOT FOLLOW

I knew the man well enough to obey. I also went with my gut feeling that he wasn't interested in having the entire Itasca Sheriff's Department follow him either. Before departing the raft, I scooped water from the lake and washed the mud off the raft.

Fine, Boss. We're not following.

I wasn't sure where to follow.

After reporting the inconclusive search, a deputy handed me a radio through which Turinski ordered me and Minelli off the property. Minelli replied in terms befitting a Philadelphia cab driver. I said I'd leave in the morning. The deputies cleared out.

During the hours that remained dark, Minelli didn't sleep. He found a box of shotgun shells in Candice's office cupboard and perched himself on the second-floor landing. He stacked dining room chairs on the stairs and left every light in the lodge blazing.

I fought off a blast of deep fatigue that hit when the adrenaline wore off. I found another iced tea in the refrigerator and went back to Candice's office, only to discover that the desk had been cleared. The papers were gone. The laptop was gone. The bare wood held only her blotter. With no one else to appreciate my thoughts, I shared them with myself.

"This shit just gets weirder and weirder."

I waited out the dawn in Candice's office chair. If I dozed, sleep was brief and easily interrupted by jolting dream flashes of huge hairy arms swinging knife-like claws in my direction.

The small hours of the night offered no new revelations. When dawn broke, I called Pidge.

"EARL'S GONE." I planted my feet on the corner of Candice's desk and watched pink-gray light etch the treetops on the other side of the lake. Pidge's voice carried into my earpiece.

"What do you mean, *gone?*"

I recited the blow-by-blow description of events that followed our late-night phone exchange.

"I searched. I looked up and down the shoreline. Minelli and me and the cops searched the whole grounds. I tried his phone. No answer. He's nowhere."

"What the—?"

"I know. He dove in the water to get away from that thing. I thought he might hide under the raft. I even went out to look. He completely disappeared. The thing is…" I double-checked to ensure that Minelli was nowhere in sight, then explained what I had found on the raft.

"Are you sure that thing didn't get him?"

"Not if he left a message like that. And there's no dead body. That thing rips people apart. There's nothing subtle about it. It doesn't try to hide evidence. We didn't find blood or shredded clothing. Nothing."

"Did the old bastard drown?"

"Earl can swim, probably better than me."

"What the—?"

"This feels like Candice."

"What do you mean?"

"Earl disappearing. Like Candice. Her car being here makes a strong case that she isn't on the lam because of some stupid money problems. She's just gone. Like it's deliberate. And now Earl, too. And with that message...deliberate."

Pidge huffed loudly into her phone. "Now what?"

"I don't have a damned clue. We called the sheriff's department. They were pissed that we were here, pissed that we let the thing get away, pissed that they had to search, and double-pissed that we added another victim for them to worry about."

"What about Minelli?"

"Guy came through in the clutch, I gotta hand it to him. Although he might have been a little drunk at the time. I looked for blood and fur. His timing was great, but his aim sucked. There's no sign he hit the thing, which is hard to believe given the size of the target."

"Jesus, Will, what do we do?"

"I know what they want me to do. The sheriff's department and BCA both want me out of here. Minelli, too, but he told them to get lost because he's living here now. Says he's paid in full and he's not leaving. I can't believe he wants to stay here after last night. He was all set to bail when we saw him in the bar. He grew an alcoholic backbone and stiffened his resolve. But me? I'm being evicted."

"Can I finally come and pick you up? I mean—you heard the boss. Do Not Follow."

I squeezed my eyes shut and tried to think.

It wasn't like Earl couldn't take care of himself. Earl Jackson flew fighters in Vietnam, tore up brothels in Thailand, raised hell flying for diamond miners in South America, and mixed it up with drug traffickers in northwest Mexico. The man carried a loaded .45. Even with his eighties on the horizon, he wasn't a man I would mess with. Of the two of us last night, I considered him the more capable, discounting my ace in the hole with *the other thing.*

What would he want me to do now? We had come looking for Candice and now they were both missing. Earl was like the man who rescues the drowning swimmer, succumbing to the waves himself, leaving me high and dry.

"Hey." Pidge shook me out of my thoughts. "You still there?"

"I'm here. Just trying to figure out what to do next."

"I think it's pretty effing obvious. By the way, the TV is going apeshit. Ever hear of a wendigo?"

"A mythical creature of the First Nations people."

"Yeah, well wendigos are coming out of the woodwork because of the Indians up here."

"I thought a wendigo was lore from an eastern tribe. Iroquois or Algonquin. Up here isn't it mainly Chippewa and Sioux?"

"You got me. The rest of us are calling it a werewolf. Can't believe you fucking saw it up close and personal. Holy shit!"

"I'm not sure what I saw. It was dark. Listen, give me a couple hours. Don't do anything until I call you."

"Why? Why don't I just haul your ass outta there?"

I needed to think. The impulse to call Andy throbbed in my head, but the hour was early and these days, mornings were not her best time of day. Given the hour, Pidge almost didn't answer my call and she launched a barrage of choice words when she did.

I wasn't ready to give Pidge the answer she was looking for. I stalled.

"Hey, is Kelly there? I need to ask her something."

"I'm putting you on speaker." The phone audio changed. "Kel, c'mere. It's Will."

"Kelly, I know you weren't at the lodge for a full summer yet, but did you ever meet any of the other people Candice hired? Any of the kids who helped in the summer?"

"She talked about some of them. I think she wanted me to know who they were."

"Did she mention a girl named Val? I met her at the bar in Beaudry."

"Sure. I think. Val—you mean like a lifeguard?"

"Yeah."

"Sure. Candice said she, like, managed things by the lake. The canoes. The lifeguard thing. I think she handled campouts. Candice told me they do that sometimes. Mostly the kids. Overnights. That sort of thing. She said the grown-ups liked getting rid of the kids for a night."

"Did any of those summer employees come out to the lodge this spring? To check in? To fill out applications? Anything like that?"

"Uh-uh."

Pidge asked, "What are you thinking?"

"I don't know. Just…maybe if Candice talked to one of the kids…maybe she said something. Maybe they know something."

"I didn't see anyone," Kelly reported. "Sorry."

"Dude, lemme come and pick you up," Pidge persisted.

"Give me a little time. I don't disagree, but if you fly me out, where do we go? At least if I go get Candice's Jeep out of the woods, we have options."

"Options for what?"

"Good question. Talk to you in a couple hours."

I tapped the button to end the call before she dragged me into an argument.

31

M inelli snored in the chair at the top of the stairs with the shotgun resting
on his lap. Rather than untangle his barricade of chairs on the wooden
steps, I vanished and hopped over the railing. Just as I landed and reappeared on
the bare great room floor, a sparkling white late model Land Rover rolled up to
the lodge behind a sheriff's SUV. I knew without guessing that the sticker price
for this model topped six figures, so it wasn't driven by a county or state law
enforcement officer. The man who slid out from behind the wheel wore a suit and
tie and showed no sign of carrying a weapon. Thinning hair grown long on top
covered a bald spot. A full pot of flesh flowed over his belt. His face carried folds
and jowls at the chin line, and deep bags under the eyes. He lacked Minelli's
alcohol induced veins, but I swear I caught a distillery whiff when he clasped my
hand and shook it.

"Charlie Pelton." He pumped my hand and applied pressure while reading me
with eyes that didn't smile. "And you are?"

"Will Stewart. I came up here with Earl Jackson. He's—"

"One of Candice's ex-husbands, right?"

"Number three."

Pelton let go of my hand and looked at the damaged front door. "I heard it
was bad, but—my God."

The deputy who accompanied Pelton stepped out of his unit but did not
approach. From behind dark shades, he radiated a none-of-my-business vibe.

"Did you see it? Whatever did this?"

I had no interest in fanning the rumor flames. "That happened before we got
here."

"Huh." Pelton stared at the scars in the wood. "And where's Mr. Jackson?"

"I have no idea at the moment."

"Do you know if Mr. Jackson is laying any claim to the property or acting in any capacity on behalf of Ms. Thorpe? I only ask, well, because I'm here on official business. The deputies tell me that Ms. Thorpe hasn't been located yet. Terrible. Just terrible."

"I can't answer your question. What official business brings you out here, Mr. Pelton?"

"Sad business. Sad, sad business." He turned to the deputy and nodded. The deputy leaned into his vehicle. He extracted a folded paper and a silver staple gun. Under Pelton's watchful eye, he marched up the steps onto the porch and found a spot on the woodwork beside the front door. After unfolding the paper, the deputy positioned the Notice of Foreclosure and snapped two staples through it, one at the top and one at the bottom. He stepped back and took his phone from his pocket. After snapping a photo of his work, he returned to his unit. Without saying goodbye to Pelton, he drove away.

Pelton paid no attention to the departing vehicle.

"Can you reach Mr. Jackson by phone?" He scanned the grounds and the cabins.

I didn't answer—Andy's trick of letting others fill an awkward silence. Pelton didn't disappoint.

"He might be of help, you know. Mr. Jackson. For Candice."

"How is that?"

"Well, I can't divulge personal financial information, of course, but the situation is rather transparent. Candice and I are friends. She's told me about her, um, history. Of her husbands, Mr. Jackson is the only one living. And I understand he is a man of means. His arrival here is a bit late for the execution of this foreclosure, but surely, he would want to help Candice. Do you know anything about their divorce settlement?"

"Nope."

Pelton poked his hands in his trouser pockets.

"So, it's official. The foreclosure. What happens next?" I asked.

"Standard filing. Registration of foreclosure. Postings of notice for auction. Grace period. A sale of the property to satisfy the mortgage held by the bank. Just a darned shame. That's why I came out myself. I feel...I dunno...like something this hard ought not to be done anonymously. Not to a friend. Know what I mean?"

"Candice certainly doesn't deserve this."

"And there is no one in greater agreement with you than me, Mr. Stewart. Candice is a dear friend, an absolute angel. I have known her for, gosh, I don't even know how long. I helped write her husband's first mortgage on the resort."

Minelli walked out of the great room onto the porch.

"Good afternoon, sir." Pelton rushed forward with his hand out. "Charlie Pelton. And you are?"

Minelli blinked momentary confusion at Pelton, at the hand. "Uh…Minelli, Ray Minelli."

"Mr. Minelli, nice to meet you. Ms. Thorpe has mentioned you. You're a professor? An author?"

"Not a professor. Just a geologist scribbling things nobody will ever read."

Pelton backed up a step. "I understand you're a paid-up guest of the lodge, Mr. Minelli. I'm sorry to say—to both of you—that this property is now owned by the Sun Lakes Bank and as such, well, given what's been happening, the bank cannot afford to carry the potential liability of your presence here. I do apologize."

"Are you telling me I gotta get out?" Minelli asked.

"It's for the best. The bank will review your situation, although any question of a refund is between you and the former owner. Mr. Stewart, can I assume you were here on less official terms?"

"Just a guest of Mr. Jackson who was a guest of Candice."

"Then you understand our position."

"Your position being Get Out."

Pelton smiled an unfriendly smile. "I wouldn't put it so harshly. Take as much time as you need today. Nice to meet you, Mr. Minelli. Mr. Stewart. And please…when you see Mr. Jackson, have him call me at his earliest convenience. I'd very much like to ascertain his position."

Pelton fished business cards from his coat pocket and handed them out.

Minelli said, "Hold up."

Pelton paused beside his all-terrain luxury ride. Minelli dropped down the steps and approached. He waved a hand at the lodge.

"You got a property with a bunch of busted out windows and a ripped up front door. Last night I ran off whatever did all that. Who knows? Maybe it came back to do more damage. You're gonna have raccoons living in the pantry and birds dumping on the rugs. Why not let me stay on as caretaker? Go back to your bank and call up somebody to get a load of plywood and some nails out here. I'll hammer it over the busted windows and doors. Otherwise, it's all gonna turn to shit while you try to find a buyer."

Pelton glanced at the damage.

"I don't know, Mr. Maloney…"

"Minelli. C'mon, Pelton. Leave it like this and your value is going down the shitter."

Pelton hesitated. I wasn't sure if he sincerely debated the idea with himself or if he pretended to think about it for show. After a long moment and a little extravagantly, he smiled and said, "You may consider yourself retained. Perhaps in exchange for your lodging?" He pointed at the card in Minelli's hand. "Assess your needs and call me. I'll order whatever lumber you advise."

"Terrific. And screw you for foreclosing on that nice lady. No offense."

Pelton's face reddened. "I assure you. It's not my wish. Never in a million years would I wish this on Candice."

He mounted up, turned his Land Rover, and departed. I waited until the white paint and chrome ceased to glitter through the trees.

"You're really going to take up carpentry?"

"South Philly, baby. I know which end of a hammer to use on a kneecap. This mean you're leaving?"

"Looks that way. I don't have much choice. Might take one more look around."

"Want me to come with?"

I shrugged, trying hard to look like I didn't care. "Nah. I'm gonna try Earl's phone again, and then call for my ride." I pulled out my phone.

"Suit yourself." Minelli ducked back inside, then returned with the shotgun in hand. He winked at me. "Don't leave home without it."

He started in the direction of his cabin.

"Hey. I meant to ask. How did you get past those deputies last night?" I pointed at his Crown Vic, parked beside the small cabin.

Minelli winked at me. "Thought about what you said. I might'a had one too many, so I wasn't interested in touching my nose or reciting the alphabet backward for some cop. There's more'n one way in here. Course, that's how I busted my tailpipe in the first place." He pumped the shotgun in the air as a way of waving at me. "Don't leave without saying good-bye."

32

When sand runs out, Panic.

The sand had run out, but I couldn't figure out how to panic.

After Minelli wandered off, I raided the kitchen and dry pantry for something to feed a sudden onslaught of hunger. I found peanut butter, jelly and bread and wolfed down a couple sandwiches, chased with more of the peach iced tea Candice seemed to favor.

I took the last sandwich to the deck overlooking the lake and studied the shoreline. To my right, the lake merged with a wide marsh filled with cattails. Directly ahead, the opposite shore was lined with dense woods that rose to higher ground. The woods continued to the left, but the lake joined a stream that broke up the line of trees. In a summer of fun that was not destined to be, the stream might have offered nice canoeing for guests of Renell Lodge.

Finding nothing new in the view, I returned one more time to Candice's office and the most comfortable undamaged chair in the building. I raked through my options. Stay. Go. Trek back to the Jeep and set up camp in Big Fork. Fly another search pattern over the woods. Fly home. With each option, Andy's favorite question challenged me.

And then what?

Getting a room in Big Fork didn't constitute a plan. It only meant sitting in a room. Cruising around the woods looking for Candice (and now Earl) didn't make a lot of sense and it ran directly against Earl's mud-scribed command. Hiding out at the lodge to wait for a seven-foot-tall monster to show up again and tear me apart made the least sense of all, which made me wonder if Minelli might sober up from his alcohol-infused impulse to stay after dark.

Do Not Follow.

Follow where? Short of making Earl vanish and flying him away, I could not think of how he had done his disappearing act. Last I saw of him he dove, fully clothed, into the lake. I wasn't worried about him drowning. The man can swim. His move made sense at the time. The boathouse's main door was closed. He had no chance of outrunning the beast on the beach or up the slope and stone steps to the lodge. Slipping under the raft to hide in the space between the plank deck and the water might have been Earl's only option.

And then what?

That was the blank I could not fill in. Where did he go? What had he seen? Why didn't he return? What attracted him to the edge of the lake in the first place? If not for me drawing the beast away, he never would have escaped its claws. He had been caught in the open, looking at or for something I could not see.

I wondered if I might have been able to pursue the creature through the woods. Given how dark the night had gone, I had my doubts, although the thing was anything but stealthy. The fly in that ointment had been Minelli. I could not vanish right in front of him to race off after the creature—the werewolf, if I allowed myself down Pidge's rabbit hole.

Waiting around in Big Fork promised nothing—especially if Pidge's predictions of a media circus proved true. Staying at the lodge promised nothing. What did that leave?

I pulled out my phone and called Pidge. After giving in to her plan to pick me up, I left the office and went to the kitchen for my flight bag. It sat on the kitchen counter where Earl and I had dropped our bags last night.

Earl's bag was gone.

What the hell?

Lifting my bag off the counter instantly gave up the final surprise of a night that had gone deeply south before turning into day.

My flight bag clocks in at 27 pounds, a calculation I use for weight and balance purposes when flight planning. I know from years of experience what 27 pounds feels like.

This wasn't that.

I unzipped the main section. Nothing new. I unzipped the secondary section. The silver rim of Candice's laptop glinted up at me. Stuffed beside the laptop were the bank statements that had been on her desk. In a fat envelope between the statements and the laptop, I found the two stacks of photos Kelly and I had recovered from Candice's great room memory frame.

This could only have been Earl. He must have taken his bag and loaded the contents of Candice's desk into my bag when I made my recon flight over the ravine crime scene. He wanted me to take the laptop, the bank statements, and the photos.

And then what?

PART II

33

"You okay?"

I leaned on the wall outside the master bathroom. The farmhouse Andy and I rent employs a traditional layout of small functional bedrooms on the second floor. Prior to renting it, our landlord James Rankin, converted the smallest bedroom beside the largest bedroom into a master bath and walk-in closet. Of all the rooms in the house, it is the most modern.

Behind the door, Andy retched.

My stomach rolled. I fought an impulse to run.

"Want me to hold your hair?"

The toilet flushed. Second time in five minutes.

"Go away." She sounded out of breath. "You did this to me."

"I had help."

I heard water running. I checked my watch.

IT HAD BEEN late afternoon when Pidge greased the wheels of the Baron onto runway 24 at Essex County Airport. During the hour and a half that I waited at the lodge for my ride, I failed to come up with a plan for finding Earl or Candice. I failed to make sense of the gruesome murders of Dr. and Mrs. Yuan or the bank's foreclosure on Renell Lodge. Worst of all, I failed to conjure up an excuse to stay—one that didn't violate Earl's specific instructions.

Do Not Follow.

Pidge landed effortlessly on Candice's narrow strip and rolled to the end. She turned the Baron around without stopping the engines. I shoved my bag in the rear door, then hopped on the propwash-swept wing and boarded.

I took one last look at the forest and the lodge in the distance.

We flew home minus Earl, feeling defeated. Kelly sat in the back seat and said nothing the entire trip.

Fatigue gnawed at my bones when I climbed down off the wing in front of the Essex County Air Service office. Kelly's energy for hopping out of the back seat and hurrying across the ramp mystified me—until Rosemary II emerged from the office and met her halfway across the lawn with a bundle of baby in her arms. Kelly raced to a reunion with her child who would not remember the moment except as some visceral code for warmth and comfort embedded in his love for his mother.

I hung out just long enough to frustrate Rosemary II with my answers to her urgent questions about Earl. As a mission, our trip to Renell Lodge had been a colossal failure. It did not help that an explosion of lurid news about animal attacks preceded us, nor did Pidge's insistence to Rosemary II that we had encountered a genuine werewolf.

As quickly as I could, I parted from an increasingly worried Rosemary II and walked to the Christine and Paulette Paulesky Education Foundation hangar where the Foundation's Piper Navajo harassed me with its pent-up desire for flight. She was like a pet begging to be let out.

"Gimme a day." I patted her on the wingtip. "I need to sleep for the next 24 hours."

Arun hurried out of his office as soon as he heard me enter the lounge.

"Did you get my text?"

"Sure." I patted the phone in my pocket. He made a face.

"Perhaps I should rephrase. Did you *read* my text?"

"I'm supposed to read those things?" My incredulity was not well received. I groped for a change of subject. "Cassidy's back. Over at the office. She's booked out on a charter, though. Trying to clean up the mess she made of the schedule after being gone for a couple days. If you hurry, you can catch her."

Arun didn't bite. "I already texted her. And if you had read my text, you would know that Memphis is moved up. We leave at nine tomorrow morning."

"What? Why?"

Arun disappeared back into his office, then returned with a sheet of paper in hand. The hangar had once been home to a corporate jet and Arun Dewar sustained the image. I've never seen a neater, crisper young man. His Bollywood handsome features, constantly trimmed hair, flawlessly clean-shaved face, and warm skin tones paired perfectly with the ironed white shirts he wore. I rarely saw him without a tie. I have two. He seemed to have a trunk full of them.

The only thing more commendable than his decorum and his organizational skill in taking over the directorship of the Foundation from Sandy Stone was his patience with me.

He politely handed me the printed sheet of paper.

"Here's the new itinerary. Wait." He took the paper back. After carefully folding it, he stuffed it in my shirt pocket and smiled. "Be here at 9 a.m. tomorrow."

"On the dot."

ON MY WAY HOME, I stopped at the Essex County Air Service office. I left Candice's laptop, the bank statements, and the collection of photos in the care of Rosemary II. I asked her to give the works to her fourteen-year-old daughter Lane, and then have Lane call me after her homework was finished. Lane is a whiz with computers. I had questions I believed she could answer. I thought Rosemary II might protest her daughter's involvement, but her concern for Earl trumped her reservations. She took the package and said there would be no response until tomorrow; Lane had plans for late stargazing with the high school astronomy club. I headed home. Andy showed up hours later after an extra-long day. She collapsed with me on the sofa following a light dinner over which we beat and re-beat the dead horse that was any kind of theory about Earl and Candice. Andy threatened to find a second wind and start making phone calls to Minnesota law enforcement. I threatened to toss her phone in the garbage disposal and reminded her that her doctor already took a dim view of the stress induced by her job; she didn't need to add more. Earl was fine, I argued. Earl Jackson was more dangerous than whoever or whatever he might encounter. I shut down the discussion and pulled her into my arms for rejuvenating physical contact, which put us both to sleep. Sometime after dark we stumbled off to bed.

Andy occupied the bathroom when I woke up, saw the time, and dressed quickly. She did not open the door.

"Do you want me to stay? I can make some scrambled eggs."

The toilet seat snapped against the tank. I heard Andy retch again. A few minutes passed before she spoke.

"Go. Please."

I checked my watch again. 9:05.

34

"Any news?" Pidge caught up to me as I tightened down the oil cap on the Navajo's left engine. The airplane absorbed sunshine outside the Education Foundation hangar. On the far side of the Essex County Airport ramp a student pilot ran up the engine of a Cessna 152. Pidge raised her voice. "I mean other than the bizarre wendigo animal attack werewolf bullshit on the news."

"Werewolf was your theory, remember?"

"I didn't say it wasn't true. I'm just saying the TV news people have gone batshit whacko over it. Full-fledged panic."

When sand runs out...

I wondered if the forensic experts examining the bodies of Dr. Yuan and his wife found a more prosaic albeit gruesome cause of death than a Universal Studios monster. I wondered if Candice's rapid evacuation of Kelly and her baby had been prompted by said monster.

I wondered how on earth I could wing off to Evermore with Earl and Candice missing.

The answer to the last one was sharply obvious.

Pidge waved her hand in front of my face. "You there? Helloooh."

"Sorry. No. I got nothing. I called that sheriff's lieutenant, Turinski. Left a message for him to call. I imagine he's busy."

"This is some shit, Will. Fucking story made CNN. Itasca County is talking about closing schools. The Minnesota tourist industry is freaking out. The locals are putting officials in front of cameras to tell everyone that it's fine, blah, blah, blah, there's no shark in the water. Everybody grab your floaties and pile in. Meanwhile, mommies and daddies are cancelling their camping reservations in droves and gun nuts are loading up with silver bullets and driving north. It's some grade A crazy."

"I'm going back up there," I declared, surprising myself not by the decision but by saying so aloud. "As soon as I get back from this trip, I'm going back up there."

"You got a plan?"

"Hell no."

"Cool. Count me in."

Grade A crazy.

I gathered the empty bottle for the oil I had just added to the Navajo's left engine. On the other side of the glass wall that separated the hangar from the lounge, Arun hurried out of his office with his briefcase in hand and a laptop backpack over one shoulder. He glanced in my direction and spotted Pidge. He diverted toward the door that accessed the hangar.

"Head's up. Lover boy is on the loose."

"Shut up." Pidge's face morphed into a pleasant smile as Arun crossed through the hangar. Her crystal blue eyes sparkled.

"Good morning." Arun spiced the warm greeting with Arun's ever-present accent. Probably not their first Good Morning greeting of the day, though. Pidge didn't spend a lot of time at her own apartment lately.

Arun pushed his case and bag into the Navajo cabin, then strolled nonchalantly around the wing. Pidge beamed at him. She hooked his arm and lifted herself on her toes for a kiss. Not too long. Not too expressive. Tender and reassuring. I dubbed it properly British.

"Will tells me there is no news of Mr. Jackson."

"If it weren't so nice and quiet at the office, I might miss him." Pidge tried for humor and a dash of imp in her smile, but both failed.

"Don't be that way, love. You're worried about him. You know that."

Pidge didn't deny it.

I said, "I worry about whoever runs into him. I worry about Rosemary II ever giving up Kelly's baby—or Kelly, for that matter." Kelly had reluctantly agreed to join her infant son's lodging at the Franklin house. Rosemary II was delighted. "Is she settling in?

"She's trying," Pidge replied. "She can't stop worrying about Candice. She really loved living at the lodge. She wants to go back."

"Well, like I said, as soon as this trip is over, I'm going back." I looked at Arun. "You ready?"

Arun checked his watch. "Forty-six minutes ago. But then I always factor an allowance for your tardiness."

"Good to know."

Arun looked down at Pidge. "No offense to Will, but I wish you were flying me to Memphis."

"Me, too." I stopped. "Oh. Did I say that out loud?"

Pidge ignored me. She tightened her grip on Arun. "I love Memphis barbecue. Bring some home for me. Promise?"

"Can't," I interjected. "Carrying concealed barbecue across state lines is a felony." I walked past Arun, who had an *Is that true?* Expression on his face. I tapped his shoulder. "Let's go, buddy."

Pidge tightened her grip on Arun. "Let Will take the plane to North Carolina by himself. Come home tomorrow night. You can fly into Milwaukee. I'll pick you up."

"Let me think about it. I don't mind tagging along with Will. It's only another day."

This was my fault.

I had intended to send Arun home precisely the way Pidge pleaded. I made the mistake of telling Pidge the plan and mentioning the side trip to Evermore. Pidge told Arun, whose attraction to Pidge met its match in the magnetism of billionaire Spiro Lewko, a superstar in Arun's financial world. The moment I arrived at the hangar Arun politely inquired about tagging along while trying to conceal his excitement. Like the rest of the world, Arun knew about Lewko's Objects. He did not know my connection to them or *the other thing.* I doubt either would have been as compelling to Arun as the prospect of meeting Lewko.

I couldn't say no.

Pidge formed a pout with her lips, which compelled Arun to kiss them.

"I'd tell you to get a room, but we gotta go." I signaled for Arun to board. I smiled sweetly at Pidge. "Close up the hangar for me, will you, love?"

Pidge backed away from the plane. She watched Arun until he waved and climbed the airstair to board. When he disappeared in the cabin, she flipped me the finger. One for each hand.

35

It was a nice flight at 8,000 feet. By the time we reached Memphis, early afternoon convection launched marching battalions of puffy cumulus clouds. Blinding white tops gradually rose above our cruise altitude. The cotton balls were scattered and largely avoidable. The few we bore through caused the plane to lurch and streaked condensation on the windshield. I didn't mind. Approaching and colliding with a bulb of formed mist at 200 miles per hour remains thrilling.

Memphis Approach Control tried to persuade me to request a visual approach to Olive Branch, but I didn't bite. I suspected it was their attempt to vector me the long way around the Memphis Class B airspace. Instead, I asked for and received clearance for the RNAV 18 approach, which had the added benefit of making it easier to find the airport.

Three hours and seven minutes after takeoff, I eased the Navajo's wheels onto runway 18 at Olive Branch/Taylor Field. Seconds before touchdown, on short final over the airport fence, we crossed from Tennessee into Mississippi. I chose the small satellite field over Memphis International Airport because Arun's scheduled meetings were in Collierville, a suburb of Memphis less than fifteen minutes from the airport. It would have taken us that long to manage parking at the big airport. I also didn't mind avoiding the $100 ramp fees that pop up where the jets park.

Friendly tower controllers guided me to parking on a ramp populated with general aviation aircraft. A golf cart shot out to greet us. The ramp rat driver hopped out and gave us double orange wand guidance into a space close to the FBO office. When he approached my open side window to ask how he could be of service, I asked him to take Arun to the office straightaway. He said that our party had just arrived. Perfect timing. I threw Arun a wink.

Dumping the human cargo from a charter flight, or Arun from a Foundation flight, always brings a moment of relaxation to the cockpit. I double-checked that all the proper switches were in the Off position, the mags were off, and the battery was off. It can be annoying to return for departure to find an airplane with a dead battery. The gyros sang their descending one-note song as they wound down. A nice breeze, albeit warm for May, brought the scent of fresh-cut grass through my side window. I took an extra minute to check my phone for messages. Andy sent a *Sorry about this morning,* otherwise there were none.

Pointedly, nothing from Earl.

By the time I secured everything inside that I wanted secured, the ramp rat returned to see what else he could do for me. I asked for fuel, and he brought a truck around and topped off all four tanks under my casual supervision. With that accomplished, I entered the FBO and paid the bill and the tie-down fee. I asked the woman at the desk for a taxi service recommendation. She asked how long we planned to stay. I told her it would only be for the night, and that we'd be wheels up early tomorrow morning. She ducked into an office and produced a set of keys on a ring with a streamer that said, *Remove Before Flight.* Take the minivan parked in the second row, she instructed me. No charge. Just put some gas in it before you return.

I love small airports.

36

I napped briefly after hitting my room at the Courtyard by Marriott located on the Tennessee side of the state line. The nap did what it could to smooth out lingering fatigue and nagging disappointment over the unsuccessful trip to Renell Lodge. Just after 4 p.m. as a new hour of "Breaking News – Minnesota Murders" blazed across the TV in my room, Arun texted. The Collierville Schools delegation invited him to dinner. He asked, as he always does, if I cared to join. I sent back a kind thank you and declined. The hotel was within walking distance of a Red Robin. I needed exercise and the excuse to dine on the sort of red meat and greasy carbs that my wife suddenly found intolerable. I overate. I rationalized the excess would be worked off by the return walk to the hotel.

Back in the room, I sat at the small desk and worked up a flight plan to Hickory Regional Airport near Lewko's research village of Evermore, North Carolina. At 414 nautical miles, the flight promised an easy two-hour hop across the southern tip of the Appalachian Mountains. Nothing obnoxious popped up on the forecast weather. I texted Arun to suggest we meet at 9 a.m. for breakfast.

With a flight plan on file and a preliminary weather briefing downloaded, I closed the ForeFlight app on the iPad and set it aside. I dialed the Itasca County Sheriff's line and got a new recording advising me to call 911 if this was an emergency, then stating that the department "is not responding to questions about the current situation. Please file all media requests in writing. If you have business not related to the current situation, please listen to the following menu." I hung up. I reopened the iPad to Google and quickly found the phone number I was looking for. I dialed. It rang once.

"Leo!" The quick response and shouted name threw me.

"Is this Leo? At the Beaudry Public Brew House?"

"You ought'a know. You dialed."

"Sorry. Uh, this is Will Stewart. I was in two nights ago with an older guy. We're friends of Candice Thorpe. You told us a great story about her."

"Uh-huh."

"Leo, I know you pick up on what's going on in the county. My boss and I had to leave, but we're coming back up in a couple days. I was just wondering if there's been anything new."

"Heard your boss got disappeared. That's new."

"And you heard correctly. I didn't bring it up because the sheriff's department told us to keep it confidential."

"Turinski?"

"Yes. Lieutenant Turinski."

"Yeah, he's as cheap with information as he is at the bar. Running around like he's King Farouk. Doesn't tell anybody jack shit."

"So, nothing new."

"Plenty new. It's new that folks here are scared to go outta their homes. It's new that I'm closing up at sunset. It's new I'm losing my shirt on account of some goddamned native spirit animal gone all bloodthirsty. I got reporters and TV people jamming up my parking lot and harassing my customers and not spending squat at the bar. Plenty new."

"Right. Well, listen Leo, I'm coming back up in a couple days to look in a few places the cops haven't thought of. I know things they don't." A bald lie. "You're a man on top of things. I'd be grateful if you'd call me if you hear anything. I'll make it worth your time."

"This a good number for you?"

"It is."

"Good." He said nothing more. I thought he might, but then the line beeped three times to signal the call's end.

Just as I laid my phone on the desk, it rang. The screen announced Lane Franklin.

"Hey, Lane. Who're you gonna fly for?"

"The United States Air Force, God willing I can get an appointment to the academy."

"God and your local congressman. Fighters or heavies?"

"Transports. C-17 and see the world. Hi, Will!" Lane's bright voice fronted for an even brighter mind. I had no doubt she would knock it out of the park in academics and earn a military academy appointment if she wished. At fifteen going on thirty, Lane had experienced hard turns in life that might have dimmed a lesser soul's outlook. She had survived homelessness and a heinous abduction. She had seen a boy lay his first love at her feet and his fist kiss on her lips, only to be shot moments later in a terrible misunderstanding. Lane was the first to discover my use of *the other thing* when I broke her out of a burning building. In that instant, she and I established a bond that I still struggle to understand. In Andy, Lane found a big sister and a helping hand to womanhood. Lane also wants to fly, a point of pride for me and of minor conflict with her mother, despite Rosemary II's day job of managing an air charter service. Or maybe because of it.

"Pidge said you saw a werewolf. Is that true?"

"I'm not sure what I saw, but there is no denying it was big, it was powerful, it had claws that ripped the shi—the crap out of a building and came damn near to doing the same to me."

"And two people were killed by it? That's what they're saying on the news."

"Looks like."

"It's not a werewolf. There's no such thing. It's not possible." I found myself smiling at Lane's precise and practical take on the world. "I mean—the concept of a human transforming across species into a giant powerful beast like that—it's not possible."

"Hit me, kiddo. Why?"

She paused for a moment. My mind's eye saw the girl square up her shoulders, tuck her chin slightly and purse her lips as she took a breath and organized her thoughts. I see double when I see Lane. With each day, she grows more mature, more attractive. Flashing beneath that gathering poise, I still see the girl with too many knees and elbows, the bike-riding child I first met when Rosemary II took the job at the airport from the original Rosemary.

"Okay. Setting aside the biological challenges of a cross-species transformation, you have the law of conservation of matter. Pidge said you told her the werewolf was huge, seven feet tall at least. With long arms. Like a gorilla has long arms."

"That's about right."

"Estimated weight?"

"At least three hundred pounds."

"Then you would need to start with a human of the same weight and dimensions. The law of conservation of matter states that in nature, in a closed system, matter and energy can transform or change, but cannot be created or destroyed. If you run into a three-hundred pound seven-foot-tall werewolf, you have to start with a three-hundred-pound human. Simple physics."

So...maybe Leo the bartender? The notion expanded the smile on my lips.

"I did see someone that heavy. I will let the Itasca County Sheriff's department know we have a suspect. Can I give them your number?"

"No! God!" There she was. The teenager.

"I thought you were stargazing tonight."

"We are. We're meeting at the high school at 9. The weather is perfect. Venus and Jupiter are out. I'm totally excited. Miss Linden is bringing her personal telescope. It's way better than what the school has. But I wanted to call you first. I looked at the laptop you gave Mom."

"Were you able to get in?"

"Oh, sure. It's not password locked. If it had a password or passcode lock, I would have been out of luck. The lady who owns this laptop is not too concerned about security, but I suppose it's because she doesn't have much on the laptop. Just internet and bookkeeping."

"What about the reservation system? And email?"

"That's the internet part. Her whole reservation system is her website."

"Did you get into them?"

"Easy. I used the password you gave Mom. Did you know that all the reservations for the entire summer have been cancelled?"

"Yeah. We saw that."

"Did you know they were all cancelled at the same time? Like…all at once?"

"I didn't see that."

"Yeah. Totally. And did you see that email that she sent out?"

"Uh-huh."

"It's weird, right?"

"What's weird?"

"Well, the timing. She sent out the email *after* all the reservations were wiped. That's weird."

"Everything about this situation is weird. We have no idea why she trashed her whole season unless it was because of her money problems and the bank foreclosure."

"She doesn't have money problems."

I dropped my boots off the corner of the desk, laid my phone down and tapped Speaker. I leaned close. Lane had my attention.

"What do you mean, *She doesn't have money problems?*"

"Uh…well, I hope it's okay. I looked in her bookkeeping software. It's QuickBooks. That's one of the programs we learned in computer science."

"How did you get in? Tell me you didn't do that dumb movie schtick where you type a bunch of random stuff and then say, 'I'm in!' because you just broke an unbreakable code."

"No, God, no. That's totally stupid. No, I just tried the same username and password she uses for the reservation system. It worked. She really shouldn't do that. All the experts say you should use different passwords, but a lot of people just don't like to have to remember them all."

I almost slapped my forehead. We didn't think of testing the reservation site password on her bookkeeping program.

"Why did you say she doesn't have money problems?"

"I hope it's okay. I was kinda snooping."

"No, no, Lane! It's completely fine. That's why I gave it to you. I wanted you to snoop. Tell me what you found."

"Uh, well, this lady is loaded. She's got like forty thousand dollars in her bank account." I thought it was cute that Lane thought forty grand ranked as being loaded.

"That can't be right. Did you look at the bank statements?"

"Uh-huh. Mom's been teaching me how to balance her checkbook every month when she gets statements like that. It's a straightforward reconciliation, except she does it manually. But I don't understand."

"Understand what?"

"I don't understand why Ms. Thorpe would have a completely different set of books. Is this like some kind of fraud thing? Because her records in QuickBooks are completely different from the bank statements. And she has everything reconciled. In QuickBooks, it's super easy but it's a lot of trouble to go into that much detail for a false set of books."

"What about the mortgage payments? Did you see the past due notices?"

"Yeah. Hold on. I have the computer open on my desk." I heard Lane rustle papers near the phone. "I'm seeing the payment for April—in her QuickBooks company file—but I'm also seeing the past due notice from the bank for April. I don't really get it because she has the mortgage payment set up as an automatic withdrawal going *way* back, and it never shows up in the red."

I didn't speak.

"Will, is this some kind of racketeering thing? Like the way mobsters keep two sets of books?"

"Is there another set of books on the laptop?"

"No. I looked." I heard a mouse click. "I'm not seeing another company file. If she's totally scamming, it's not on this laptop. But I don't get it. Except for being audited by the IRS, who else but this lady is going to look at these records? I mean—is she like a crazy person? Just faking herself out?"

"Uh...I don't think she's crazy. But beyond that, you've got me. It sounds like you have it right. It sounds like she was keeping a completely different set of records. Weird."

"Oh!" Lane startled me. "That reminds me. Speaking of weird, I hope you don't mind, but you know all these photos? The ones in the envelope? There's some that are all torn up."

"Yeah. I know. I put them there. What about them?"

"These are all scanned and reprinted."

"I knew that, too. She printed them on photo paper. I think some of them were originally Polaroids, by the way they looked."

"What's a Polaroid?"

"It's a kind of photo from back in the day. The camera spit out the picture and you—I don't know—peeled it apart or something. And then after a minute or two the image would magically appear. It was a big thing. All the cool kids had one."

"That sounds awesome. So, yeah, these are reprinted. I found a folder with all the original scans. I hope it's okay—"

"Lane! It's totally okay. Seriously, why do you think I sent you the laptop? I really, *really* wanted you to poke around."

"Okay. Well, I found the folder and I got curious, like, mostly about the ones that were ruined. It was a good idea that she had them stored like that so they can be reprinted. Some of these pictures are like a hundred years old. I looked through all of them."

"The lodge has a lot of history."

"Yeah. Was there one that was totally mangled?"

"What do you mean?"

"Well, a bunch of them were ripped, but they're all accounted for. But there must have been one that was completely trashed, right?"

"Uh…I don't think so. I thought we picked up everything."

"Okay." She didn't elaborate. I waited. "Uh…it's just that, like, there's thirty-eight images in the folder but only thirty-seven photos printed."

"Maybe one of them was crap."

"No. I looked at it. The scanned original is as good as any of the other ones. I guess it's no big deal."

"Lane?"

"What?"

"Are you able to send me that image? The one that Candice didn't print?"

"Hang on." The line went silent. I heard her phone bump as she moved it. Then more silence. "There. You should have it."

A notification for incoming email popped up on my phone screen. I have no idea how she did that so fast.

"Got it."

"I have to go soon. I have to get ready for tonight. Is there anything else you want me to look at on this?"

"One more thing. Can you make sure everything is backed up?"

"Like in the cloud?"

"Yeah, whatever. Cloud. Flash drive. CD. Just so it's somewhere other than the laptop."

"Nobody does CDs anymore."

"I have been schooled. Just make sure it's safe, okay? And then give the whole works to your mom and have her lock it up at the office. Her office."

"Okay, Will. Love you! Bye!"

The phone triple beeped to announce the end of the connection.

Love you?

That was new. If not for causing a sudden knot in the center of my chest, I might have ignored it. Andy has long warned me that Lane fostered a crush on me, but I didn't think those were words she would utter as the product of a schoolgirl crush. I counter Andy's suggestion by claiming it's a dad thing for a girl with no father.

But to say it? The weight of her words surprised me.

I picked up the phone and tapped into the email she sent. The photo popped up on screen.

There's a photo of Lee Harvey Oswald holding the rifle he used to kill John Kennedy. In the backyard photo, he rests the rifle on his right hip, the same hip that mounts a handgun. He holds a packet of papers in his left hand. Flyers, perhaps. Or manifestos. He wears a black polo shirt and black trousers, or at least that's the rendering in the black and white photo. He also wears his pinched, superior expression on a clean-shaved face beneath his sixties-dad short haircut.

All three young men in the photo Lane sent me wore the same expression, the same dated clothing, the same look of supremacy and confidence. One of Candice's cabins formed a background—I thought it might be number 7, the one that Minelli occupied. A sixties vintage Cadillac with blinding chrome and sharp rear fender fins provided a prop against which three men posed for the camera. There were no rifles or handguns on hips. Two of the three dangled cigarettes from their lips. One wore plastic sunglasses. Of the three, something about the man in the center suggested dominance. Something about him gave the image an extra electric charge.

The photo had no date. Oswald's backyard photo was not in color—at least not the copies I've seen. This image had the oversaturated look of old Kodachrome. The snapshot didn't look terribly different from other guest pictures Candice had mounted from the same era. It may have been taken by the same camera that shot the image I found amusing of the five kids on the tailgate of the Chevy wagon.

The three men might have been college friends on a road trip if not for the hard-edged faces and aura of malice under their short-sleeved shirts. The photo revealed nothing to explain why it had not been included in Candice's display. It had no captions—no date imprinted on the photo border.

Lane is nothing if not thorough and observant. Maybe too observant. She's like a professional educator who cannot read a page of text without spotting the typos. Maybe this photo omission was a simple typo.

What concerned me more was the question of why Candice kept a set of fake business records. Whatever the reason, it couldn't be good.

37

Over the noise-cancelled rumble of the Navajo's twin piston engines, the Olive Branch ground controller issued my favorite clearance. "Cleared to Hickory Regional Airport via direct, maintain 4000, expect niner thousand 10 minutes after takeoff. Departure 125.8, squawk 0454."

I jotted the shorthand version on the clipboard resting on my thigh—

HKY D> 40 90^{10} 125.8 0454

—and read it back verbatim.

"Readback correct."

I let Ground Control know we were ready to roll. Six minutes later, under full power and accelerating, the Navajo broke its bond with Runway 18. We hit Blue Line on the airspeed indicator. The gear came up. I eased the aircraft's nose toward the bright morning air. The sky was ours.

"NAVAJO ONE TANGO WHISKEY, stand by to copy amended clearance."

We cruised high above a low layer of scattered cumulus that had been building over the hazy southern Appalachian Mountains. The air was smooth. The visibility, unlimited. To this point, the flight had been easy. ATC's abrupt call suggested that was about to change. It's not unusual to be rerouted. Any number of reasons can cause controllers to point a pilot in a new direction. I immediately added the option to cancel the instrument flight plan to my bag of tricks. If rerouting took us wandering, a simple solution was to decline further services from the air traffic control system and fly the balance of the flight under visual rules, assuming the weather permitted VFR operation, which in this case it did. Clear skies lay ahead.

"Navajo One Tango Whiskey, advise when ready to copy."

"One Tango Whiskey, ready to copy."

"One Tango Whisky is cleared to Charlotte Douglas International via direct Sierra Uniform Golf then the LINN THREE arrival, maintain niner thousand for now."

Huh?

Despite the glaring error, I copied the clearance to my knee board.

"Center, uh, this clearance assigns us the wrong destination. We are level niner thousand, direct Hickory Regional."

"Okay, uh…One Tango Whiskey, stand by."

That was a first. I'd never been assigned the wrong destination. Mistakes happen. I wondered if another aircraft with a call sign ending in One Tango Whiskey was flying in this sector. I felt confident the mix up would be revealed, and if not, I still had the option to cancel the flight plan and finish the trip on my own.

"One Tango Whiskey, no error. One Tango Whisky is cleared to Charlotte Douglas International via direct Sierra Uniform Golf then the LINN THREE arrival, maintain niner thousand. Advise if you copy."

"Confirming this is a clearance for Piper Navajo One Tango Whiskey?"

"Affirmative."

"Okay. I repeat, that is not our filed destination."

I slid erect in the seat and automatically scanned the aircraft instruments to ensure that I was still on course, that the engines were comfortable in their normal temperature and pressure ranges, and that the autopilot was still flying the airplane way better than I can. The rapid scan allowed me to set those items aside while I dealt with this hiccup from ATC.

"One Tango Whiskey, stand by to copy."

"Tango Whiskey, ready to copy."

There it was. They figured out their mistake.

I readied the ballpoint to take down the *amended* amended clearance.

"Tango Whiskey…Lima…Echo…Sierra…Lima…India…Echo."

What is that? A waypoint?

It had one too many letters for a GPS waypoint. I reached to punch the letters into the Garmin 750 navigation system when the obvious looked up at me from my own notepad.

LESLIE.

The controller, who by now sounded almost apologetic, asked, "Tango Whiskey, do you want me to repeat?"

"Negative." I looked at the previous line on my notepad.

CDI D> SUG LINN 3 90

I read the Charlotte clearance back to Center.

"One Tango Whiskey, readback correct. Expect lower in two zero miles."

Leslie.

I glanced back at Arun in the cabin, still nose deep in the paperwork from his meetings in Collierville, wondering if I should tell him that the FBI had redirected us to a landing in Charlotte. I decided it would require more explaining than I cared to burden myself with while setting up the arrival and approach.

He would find out soon enough.

38

Charlotte Douglas International Airport sports three parallel runways, all running north and south. The runways are spread far enough apart that one of the Essex County Air Service trainers could probably fly a pattern without conflicting with a similar trainer doing the same thing on the next runway over.

Approach control lined us up for a visual approach to Runway 18 Left, which was a relief to me because the general aviation fixed base operation on the field lay on the east side of the field. Reaching the ramp from 18L involved a simple left turn off the runway and then taxi direct.

Rows of NASCAR jets worth millions occupied most of the available parking. A single row near the FBO building seemed to be designated for us regular avgas burners. A lineman in an orange vest with orange wands guided us to parking where I killed the engines and completed my shutdown checklist.

Arun, bless his heart, is so used to arriving at unfamiliar airports that he never lifted his attention from the work spread on his cabin table to notice where we had landed.

I turned in my seat and landed a steady gaze on him as he stacked papers, folded his laptop, and packed his attaché case. It took him a moment to feel me staring at him.

"What?"

"Welcome to Charlotte."

"Right, well, good. A very nice flight, Wi—did you say Charlotte?"

"Yeah. Side trip." At that moment, a silver SUV rolled up in front of the Navajo. Civilian vehicles on the ramp inside the security fence at a Part 121 air carrier field are unheard of. This was not a civilian vehicle.

Special Agent Leslie Carson-Pelham stepped out from behind the wheel.

She stationed herself beside the open door of the vehicle with one elbow resting in the lowered driver-side window. Beneath her shock of short black hair, always swept up and to her left, she spread her slightly off-center smile and waved.

Arun stretched in his seat to look at the woman whose wave I returned.

"Side trip?"

"Yeah." I opened my seatbelt and stashed my iPad in the flight bag on the front passenger seat.

Arun settled back in his seat.

"Are we not seeing Mr. Lewko?"

"Pretty sure we are, but somebody went to a lot of trouble to see me first."

I slipped past Arun and opened the cabin door. Warm, humid air wrapped itself around me when I dropped down the airstair and stepped onto the ramp. I walked around the back of the left wing, around the tip, and met Leslie at the door to her ride. Arun poked himself out of the cabin and stood on the airstair watching us from a short distance.

"That was a neat trick. Hijacking us like that."

"Ooh. Not a word you want to throw around at airports, especially within earshot of the FBI. How are you, Will?"

We traded pleasantries, which I found a little strange for Leslie. She asked after Andy. I shared a few comments about the Clayton Johns case. I didn't bring up pregnancy or Minnesota or the connection I had to Breaking News.

"What's he doing here?" Leslie flicked her eyes in Arun's direction without turning her head. I noticed that she kept her voice low enough that it would not carry the thirty feet to where Arun watched us.

"You know Arun, right?"

"I know who he is. He doesn't know who I am."

"Really? He was at the house rebuilding party last winter."

"So was half the town. And he only had eyes for your little pilot friend. Why is he here?"

"We had a trip to Memphis."

"Right. I know. But what is he doing *here*? Does he know?"

Leslie left no ambiguity in her question. She did not approve.

"He's a financial geek. He begged me for a chance to meet Lewko." This did not please the FBI. Leslie's frown put me on the defensive. "I might ask the same. What are you doing here? And why the diversion?"

Leslie pulled a pair of dark glasses from her pocket and slipped them on. From behind them, she took a longer glance at Arun.

"Will, you're not thinking. He can't be here. You can't be here. And you certainly can't just traipse into Evermore."

"I *have* to be here. It doesn't work without me."

She huffed a bit of exasperation. "Well, of course I know that. But just the same, *you can't be here.* Are you following me? You can't be seen in Evermore. You didn't answer my question. Does he know?"

"No."

The look on Leslie's face told me I was digging a deeper hole.

"Did you tell him who I am?"

"Not yet."

The exasperation intensified. "My God, Will. Are you that much of a boy scout? Did you plan to just fly in to Hickory Regional and drive over to Evermore and pop in on Lewko? And then do your thing with a bunch of sick children?"

"Well, no—but kinda. I mean—not when you put it that way. I've been there before. I know how his system works, Leslie."

"Will, there are fourteen news networks and several hundred reporters camped outside Lewko's little fantasy town. Dozens of researchers and oncology specialists have arrived. The press is climbing into the shorts of everyone they can't readily identify. Photos. Identity. Specialties. The American Cancer Society has set up camp in an RV parked outside the city limits. Jesus, Will. Did you not think of any of this?"

I hadn't.

"And if you think there isn't a contingent from just about every intelligence service trying to gain access, and damn close to forcing it via subpoena, you're wildly out of touch. Every face, *every single face*, coming within fifty miles of Evermore is being documented. You'll be ID'd faster than you can say 'facial recognition.' The man who fell out of the sky and lived. Why do you think I diverted you? My own bureau has agents stationed at Hickory Regional."

"In my defense, I've got werewolves on the brain," I muttered.

"What?"

"Nothing."

"On top of that, you brought along someone who is not in the circle of trust. What were you planning on doing with him?"

I thought I knew, but the answer suddenly fell embarrassingly in line with her calling me a boy scout.

"Get rid of him. Send him over to the terminal and send him home. And then you and I need to lay out a plan to get you where you belong. This is not negotiable."

She avoided looking at Arun, who loitered on the steps to the aircraft cabin.

"What am I supposed to tell him?"

Leslie gave it a moment. She ran unpainted fingernails through her short black hair and gave up an audible sigh.

"Okay. Option A, I grab you and kiss you and we make him think I'm your salacious side piece. You swear him to secrecy and send him home."

"Yeah, that'll never work. Arun has met my wife."

"I'd take offense if I hadn't also met your wife. Plus, kissing you might make me gag."

"Thank you."

"Option B, I'm the FBI and I'm here to escort you into the research facility for an interview about what happened in Key West, and it's all classified, and he can't come along. Sorry."

"Do you think you can do that?"

"Do what?"

"Pose as the FBI?"

I let her make a face at me while I took an instant to think.

For some time, I've contemplated briefing Arun on *the other thing*. Until recently, I used Foundation trips as a means of visiting hospitals that specialized in children's cancer. On more than one occasion, the timing of my late-night escapades came close to getting caught. Arun is a brilliant young man, though perhaps too trusting. One of the reasons I favored the new plan of making Spiro Lewko custodian of the objects that, to the public eye, made children vanish as a cancer treatment, was the way it eliminated the haphazard approach I've used at night in random hospitals. An approach that Arun would eventually uncover.

Pidge knew. Earl knew. Would it be so bad if Arun finally knew?

Probably not. But the scope of what was happening in Evermore never occurred to me. This wasn't the time to bring Arun into the picture.

Shit.

I should have thought of all this sooner. I let the kid's starstruck view of Lewko sway me. I let my access to the billionaire feed my ego.

Leslie read the look on my face. "Let me handle it. I'll be the bad guy. I'll be the hard-assed FBI telling you what you can and can't do."

Ironically, offering to be the hard-ass revealed Leslie's tender side, which only made me feel worse.

"Nah. I'll give him the bad news."

39

Leslie drove from the airport to The All-American Pub, a bar with a slightly touristy feel that probably translated to a lively date night destination for Charlotte locals. She asked for seating outdoors where a patio featured blue metal furniture beside a quiet street. We took a table in the farthest corner. I had a moment to think that in her signature black blazer and slacks and my black t-shirt and jeans, we looked a little out of place, a little suspicious. The eager young man offering us a beverage didn't seem to notice. Leslie ordered iced tea. I asked for a Corona with lime. My empathetic abstinence on Andy's behalf extended only to the farmhouse lot line.

Leslie waited until the server darted off to fetch the drinks before pulling a tablet from her shoulder bag. She propped the device up so that the screen faced away from the restaurant interior. A few taps of the screen produced an aerial view of Evermore. The neat geometry of Lewko's by-design town showed off a mix of research and office buildings embedded in neighborhoods populated by Norman Rockwell homes.

"FBI surveillance satellite?"

"Google." Leslie pointed at a rectangle on the screen. "Lewko is housing the children in this converted office space."

"Office space? Seriously?" I pictured hospital beds in cubicles.

"Don't underestimate. In a matter of weeks, he gutted the building, built suites that rival a five-star hotel, and set up a first-rate oncology department equipped with just about every medical device money can buy. Because he has the money to buy them. He's got a full staff of doctors and nurses. Why are you not up to speed on all this?"

"He's texted me a couple times. I haven't really paid a lot of attention. And no, he hasn't divulged any technical details via text. I think a breach of security like that would give the man a heart attack."

"Did you make any arrangements with him?"

"You mean, beyond date and time? Not really."

"I assume the date is today. What time?"

"Six. Local."

"Where were you supposed to meet him?"

"Hang on." I pulled out my phone, opened it, and scrolled to the last text from Lewko. "He said come to his private residence. He's clearly assuming I will arrive via Divisible Man Airways."

Leslie did not smile at the joke. She'd heard it before.

"Once again, my point about bringing your young friend along."

"Touché." I felt bad about Arun. He took his dismissal with grace, but his disappointment was palpable when I told him to find his way to the airline terminal and fly home alone. I offered to reach out to Pidge so she could pick him up in Milwaukee. He waved me off, saying she had already offered.

"His private residence. I assume you know where that is?"

"I don't. Figured I'd ask for directions when I got there."

Leslie shook her head. "Honestly, it's like potty training a toddler."

"Hey."

"Fine." She raised her hands in surrender and apology. She then expanded the aerial view on her tablet so that the whole town plus the vast package processing center were visible. The rooftop of the package center nearly equaled the area of the small research town. Last I heard, Lewko had added twenty-six thousand jobs to the North Carolina economy. Leslie pointed out an undeveloped area north of the town. "This is his private residence. He has three hundred acres of woods here, with one of his homes at the center overlooking this small river valley. Just about no one has ever seen the place. There are no public photos of the interior. A few drone shots of the exterior have been published. The structure is a mashup of Frank Lloyd Wright and NORAD. Photos only show parts of a rooftop because it's built into the side of a hill. He made the builders and contractors all sign secrecy agreements."

"Sounds like him."

"So, he just expects you to show up here at six tonight?"

"I guess."

"And then what?"

"I assume we head to where the kids are. Do the thing with the pieces of debris, and then I'm outta there."

Leslie sat back thinking, staring at her small screen. She slowly closed the cover and laid it between us.

Our drinks came. The menus on the table remained untouched. We asked the server to come back in five minutes to take a lunch order.

"You're giving me a look that says it's not that simple."

"I don't trust him." Leslie made the declaration sound matter of fact. "I don't trust my own bureau. I don't trust some of the other alphabet agencies that have taken a serious interest in Lewko's Objects ever since they went viral at that gala in New York."

"How bad is it?"

"Bad." She sipped her iced tea. "There's been talk of declaring the objects a threat to national security. Talk of invoking the War Powers Act—although I'm not sure how that helps. I can't stress to you enough the kind of interest that those pieces of debris have generated. C'mon Will, you haven't been living under a rock. You must have picked up on some of the internet chatter at the very least."

"I don't surf. Factoids shooting back and forth between people in chat rooms hardly reflect reality. I go to bed at night and pray that conspiracy theories read like a joke book in the serious halls of power."

"They used to. Now they're recognized as the next trigger for violence or motive for extremism. People are making pipe bombs over shit they read on the internet. Doesn't matter how big the lie, how bizarre the theory, or how wildly unrealistic they are. Everyone's problem is now that there are genuinely stupid people out there believing these things. And since the vanishing act in New York went viral, the population is divided. Half sees a medical miracle. Half sees a hoax. And the fringe sees a threat that will take away their guns and their apple pie. And that's just the public side. On the serious side, the reality side, there are agencies looking at this as a potential new weapon."

"That's been the threat since day one. Why do you think I tried to say it was gone?"

"Yeah, well, it's too bad you're such a poor liar, Will."

I laughed. She chuckled. The mood lightened.

"So, tell me Leslie. Why are you here? Why are you my friend—assuming you are my friend?"

"I am." She lifted one corner of her crooked smile. "Lindsey. And Lee, of course. Lindsey mostly. He read me in. He saw the upside, and the downside. He understood how much damage someone like you could do, but he also met you."

"I got a good report?"

"No. He thought you were immature. But the funny part is that worked in your favor."

"I do think fart jokes are funny."

More smile, but it faded quickly. She sipped iced tea and let her gaze shift to the quiet street beside the outdoor dining spot.

"There is another option here."

I looked for a hint in her expression, but we both still wore our sunglasses. I had a feeling that I was about to hear the real reason I'd been diverted to Charlotte. I tried hard not to give the impression of bracing for it.

She removed her sunglasses and placed them on her closed tablet.

"And that is?"

"Don't go."

She let the weight of her words settle between us.

I played it out in my head and immediately saw her angle.

"Right. I don't show up. Nobody gets treated. The percentage that believes it's all a hoax wins. Right?"

"It might take some convincing, but yeah."

"What kind of convincing?"

She shrugged. "I don't know. Maybe a leaked report showing how the event at the Met was staged. A few well-placed experts who debunk the whole thing. Lewko made out to be just another crazy billionaire with too many toys in the attic. Fox News will run with that. They hate him."

Before she could elaborate, the server showed up with his pad in hand. I ordered a club sandwich. Leslie ordered a salad. We sent him packing with the menus.

"Where's this coming from, Leslie?"

"Upstairs." She threw up a stop sign hand. "No. Don't go there. I'm still the only person in the bureau who knows, Will. But they gamed this out both ways. Real or hoax. They gamed it out thoroughly. Real opens a nasty can of worms. Hoax puts it in a lock box along with the theory that Roosevelt knew about Pearl Harbor and Ted Cruz's father killed Kennedy. That's what I mean by upstairs. There would be a whole lot of relief if Lewko's Objects turn out to be a giant hoax. Of course, as soon as we confirm hoax, the conspiracy nutballs will instantly swing the other way and claim they are real and it's all a coverup, but you get the idea."

"Right. I don't show up. Lewko can't make kids vanish. Giant failure and embarrassment for him. Everybody on your team breathes a little easier."

"That's how the hoax scenario played out on the top floors of the FBI."

I tipped my chair back against a railing and folded my arms.

"That's why you diverted me. To wave me off."

"I'm not going to answer that."

The part of me that liked Leslie was being sorely tested.

"How good is your intel?"

"On what?"

"Lewko. How many kids did he bring in?"

Something flashed in Leslie's eyes. I wasn't sure I saw it or imagined it. If it was there at all, she tried hard to hide it. She fiddled with her sunglasses.

"Word is there are twenty-four. From local hospitals mostly. A few flown in on his plane. I'm not sure how they handled that. He had thousands of applicants on the site he set up. Thousands. Not just kids."

The numbers didn't surprise me.

"This war game—the one where I just walk away and it's all a hoax. Those kids just go home untreated, right?"

"Yes."

"What if I went in on my own? Without telling Lewko. What if I made it so he couldn't use the Lewko Objects, but I go in anyway? At night."

"Ignoring the probability that his little hospital is bristling with security cameras, those twenty-four kids are the most monitored cancer patients in the history of medicine. If you go in, and the survival rate shoots up to one hundred percent, don't you think someone's going to notice?"

She had a point. I said nothing.

"I suppose you could go in and just do a few random individuals…"

"Right. And who picks?"

She did not meet my eye or the anger rising there. She folded and unfolded the plastic sunglasses.

I fought the urge to get up and walk out. Or simply vanish and launch myself, which would have been incredibly stupid since I didn't have a BLASTER in my pocket. My flight bag and jacket were both in the car.

I dropped the chair back on all four legs and planted my arms on the table. I leaned toward Leslie, staring her in the face.

"Tell me one thing. Is this you asking?"

"Me?"

"Yeah. You asking me. You."

She shook her head. "No."

"Were you sent to ask?"

"No. I told you the truth. It's just a scenario that got played out in a conference room. A conference room full of very worried people. But nobody knows that I know you. Nobody asked me. I'm being straight with you. This could be an out. For them. For you. It's a choice you have. You need to know that."

"Okay. Noted. But I'm not bailing on those kids. Not if there's a chance for them. Sorry."

Leslie didn't move or speak. I was about to renew a vow that I would never play poker with this woman when one corner of her mouth curved upward. A fragment of smile flashed in her dark brown eyes.

OUR FOOD CAME. Thanks to my indulgence the night before, I wasn't terribly hungry. Flash memories of the horror at the ravine didn't help. The still missing Earl and Candice gnawed at me. In the past 40 hours I called the Itasca County Sheriff's Department twice and failed to connect with Lieutenant Turinski both times. Messages left did not generate return calls. I regretted leaving, but even at a distance and with the benefit of hindsight, I could not come up with a way staying in Minnesota would have helped. But I had another idea.

"Does the bureau have a presence in that double-homicide in Minnesota?"

"That wendigo thing? God, I hope not." Leslie froze a fork full of salad in mid-lift. "Why?"

I took a bite of sandwich. Leslie lowered the fork to her plate.

"No. Will, seriously, tell me you're not…"

It wasn't a bad sandwich. I took another bite.

"Oh, for heaven's sake."

I pulled out my phone and tapped until the photo Lane sent filled the screen. I held the phone up for Leslie to see.

"If I send you this photo, can you take a crack at identifying the people in it?"

Leslie examined the image warily. "That picture is from sixty years ago. What makes you think I can identify those guys?"

"Because they look like they belong on a post office wall. Three tough guys. A Coupe de Ville. It screams mob. Doesn't the bureau have a zillion mug shots stored up?"

"Two zillion. Fine. Send it to me. And I hate myself for asking this, but what have you gotten yourself into now?"

40

U.S. Highway 321 departs Charlotte on a route that arrives at Hickory Regional Airport in roughly 53 minutes. From there, another thirty minutes of driving delivers you efficiently to the outskirts of Evermore. Leslie's chosen route took two hours and twenty minutes by avoiding both 321 and efficiency.

Pulling out of The American Pub parking lot, she ordered me to vanish, insisting that I not be seen by a single traffic camera or random security camera. With gravity out of the picture, the seatbelt trapped me against the cloth of her rented Chevy's front seat. My legs occasionally drifted up to bump the bottom of the dash and if I forced myself to relax my arms wanted to float loosely extended. Oddly, trying to relax induced stress on my shoulder muscles which became painful after a while. I solved the problem by sliding my left arm under the seatbelt and gripping the panic handle above the window with my right hand.

I didn't mind taking the scenic route. We zigzagged through a mix of farm and forest. Occasional encounters with clusters of homes dropped our speed briefly, otherwise Leslie cruised a steady ten over the posted limit of either 45 or 55 miles per hour. Blue sky painted with high cirrus clouds escorted us all the way. The sun felt warm and made me sleepy after a meal. If not for a few flowering trees I would have identified the season as summer rather than spring.

We talked. I didn't set out to brief her on the events at Renell Lodge, but given the time together, venting my frustration became inevitable. She peppered me with questions about Candice that I could not answer, and I pressed her with questions about the law enforcement response in Minnesota that she could not answer. She apologized that her focus had been on the other national headlines I generated and said she had not paid much attention—for obvious reasons—to a reported werewolf running amuck in the north woods. She reiterated her promise to search the FBI archives for the identity of the men in the photo, but I didn't hold out much hope of that being relevant. Aside from suggesting that if it were her assignment she would look deeper into Dr. and Mrs. Yuan for possible involvement, she made no commitment. I took her lack of interest in my problem with Candice and Earl as a measure of her concern for the federal interest in Lewko's Objects and their potential for trouble.

When the conversation dwindled, I watched the scenery flow and wrestled my thoughts away from Earl and Candice and Lewko. We passed clusters of new development that sprouted on exhausted farms like mushrooms in a lawn after a rain. In the backyards of strikingly uniform saltbox mini-mansions, families built colorful play fortresses sporting swings and slides.

That's in your future.

Andy and I planned to know the gender of the baby. I had no ties to whatever people considered to be the "old school" reveal at birth. Andy, the practical partner in this endeavor, thought it only made sense to know, to be prepared, to shop accordingly.

A child. The depth of that concept mystified me, probably as it had billions of people before me. I had no clue what I was getting into. Ask me again in twenty years what it means to bring a child into the world, and I might have an answer that makes sense. Maybe this was a case of ignorance sustaining bliss.

Except for borrowing the daughters of Andy's sister Lydia for a few hours of "favorite uncle" playtime, I had no experience with children. Who does?

That's not so.

I had experience with children. Frail, sleeping, sick children. Sometimes alone. Often with a parent camped on a nearby sofa or spare bed in hospitals that are never dark, never silent, never peaceful. I had experience closing a grip on thin arms and legs in the night and pushing *the other thing* out over their fragile skin and bones, making them vanish, and then bringing them back again and praying that they returned without the disease that was killing them.

Until now, they were someone else's children.

I claim cowardice in the face of physical confrontation. I practice it where emotional confrontation looms. I don't want to know the names of the children. I don't want to know if what I do succeeds, because that would require knowing when it fails. I don't want to know what leukemia or lymphoma or neuroblastoma does to a child's body. One of the only times I tapped the great god Google out of curiosity, I inadvertently learned that more than 15,000 families each year are delivered the horrifying news that their child has cancer. My curiosity died on that laptop screen. Slipping in and out of hospitals at night, changing a life trajectory here and there, I had allowed myself a sense of accomplishment. After reading that statistic, I felt utter hopelessness.

A pair of shotgun barrels brushing death past Andy changed everything. Her obsessive pursuit of Gabby Calbert, one of the 15,000 children stricken, ended with an opportunity to hand the curative aspect of *the other thing* over to Spiro Lewko in full view of the public eye. My sometimes clumsy night forays could be transformed into an assembly line in Evermore. Twenty-four families waited there for the inaugural trial. Thousands waited in Lewko's hastily set up application process. I had no idea how this was going to work, but I was determined to make it work. Lewko had his motivation. I had mine.

Because in about eight months I would hold an infant in my arms and feel a connection beyond comprehension. That moment would finally teach me the full measure of devastation wrought by a cold diagnosis for thousands of families. And from that I might fully grasp what we were trying to launch in Evermore.

They should all have one, I thought, watching yet another yard fortress glide past.

41

———————

"This is as far as we go. Do you have your propeller thing?"

"BLASTER? In my jacket on the back seat."

Leslie rolled the SUV to a stop in the shade by the side of the road. North Carolina forest hugged the two-lane blacktop on either side. Trees arched their boughs over the road for as far as I could see ahead and behind us. Shafts of sunlight gave the empty back road a cathedral ambiance.

"I'm sorry. I side with your wife. That's a terrible name. Why not call it Rocket? Or Jet Pack? Or something like that?"

"Because it is neither a rocket nor a jet pack," I replied. "Although I think a jet pack would be terribly cool. Ever see Jet Man? The guy that—"

"Will."

"Right." I reached into the back seat and grabbed my leather flight jacket. Draped across my lap, the weight held me in the seat after I released the seatbelt.

Leslie reached into the footwell and pulled her tablet from between the seat and the center console. She flipped the cover and tapped the screen until she found what she wanted. Using two fingers to pinch the image, she adjusted the span of the aerial photo she had shown me over lunch.

"This is us," she pointed at the blue dot on a gray line of road, "and this is Evermore—about three miles that way." She pointed over her shoulder. I ignored her finger and used the tablet image to register Evermore three miles out on a course of 310 degrees. For bearing, I estimated our stretch of road aligning with 060 degrees. "This is the hospital. And this is the location of his residence. Somewhere up here. If you go to the town first, then follow Main Street, you get to where it goes left. There's a private road. Look for gate guards. That's the entrance. I assume he's expecting you."

"Ain't no party without me." I opened my door.

Leslie abruptly reached across me and grabbed the door. She jerked it shut.

"What?"

She pointed at the rearview mirror.

The white vehicle approaching from behind had the boxy look of an SUV. A Ford emblem rode the grille behind a heavy push bumper. A low-profile light bar, barely distinguishable from a luggage rack, topped the windshield. Less than a quarter mile back and closing quickly, I thought there was a good chance it would simply roll past us—until I saw blue and red flashes erupt.

"Cops or private security?"

"Private doesn't use the blue and red. County." Leslie pushed her tablet back down beside the seat.

"Open the sunroof."

She thought about it for the duration of a useless glance in my direction, then pressed the power switch that slid the overhead glass all the way back. Fully open, it remained a tight and awkward exit for me. I unsnapped my seatbelt.

"I'm outta here. I'll wear my earpiece. Call me if there's a reason. Where do you plan to be?"

Leslie watched the unit pull up behind us. I glimpsed a hatless deputy behind the wheel. "Not sure…"

"Let me know. You're my ride. You've got my bag in the back."

"Do you want it?"

"I can get by without it." I scrunched up my jacket and pulled it against my chest. Twin tubes of BLASTER with fresh batteries in the side pocket reassured me that I had transportation.

Fwooomp! The jacket vanished. The seatbelt tangled up beside me when it didn't retract. I pushed the belt aside and found the seat controls. I reclined the seatback to improve access to the open sunroof. Getting out of the vehicle remained clumsy and difficult. Leslie lowered her window and leaned on the sill like a girl at a drive-in, which helped. Even so, I still bumped her back with my knees.

I pulled my legs out by curling up in a cannonball posture. My feet snagged, then cleared the opening. Not quite ready to launch, and more than a little curious, I stretched out and fixed a grip on the edge of the sunroof glass.

The deputy took his sweet time, tipping his head down for long moments to enter and extract data from the computer mounted to his dashboard.

"What's he doing? Playing sudoku?" I asked the back of Leslie's head.

"Running the plates. Connecting with Avis. Running the name of the driver. Finding out that I'm—yup, here he comes."

A stout young man in a warm gray shirt and dark pants stepped out of his unit. He wore his ballistic vest under his uniform shirt, which magnified an already round torso. This guy would not beat the throw against a long lead-off for the department softball team. Above a square face and sharply geometric jaw, his head flashed pink in the afternoon sun, his hair having been cut boot camp short. His dark plastic sunglasses looked cheap.

"Afternoon, ma'am." He approached Leslie without a smile on his lips or in his tone. She ensured that both of her hands were visible,

"Good afternoon, Deputy…Masters." Leslie read the embroidered tag on his shirt. "How can I help you this fine day?"

He gave no sign of enjoying her convivial tone. "You can explain what you're doing here."

"Would bird watching suffice?"

I could not see Leslie's face, but her crooked smile was easy to discern in her voice.

"License and registration, please."

"How's this?" Leslie opened the palm of her right hand and revealed a flat leather wallet. She deftly did a one-handed flip to spread the wallet. She extended her hand to show the deputy her FBI identity card and the small gold badge with the eagle on top.

"Federal Bureau of Investigation. How do you do, Special Agent Carson?"

"Carson-Pelham. I do well, Deputy Masters. And you?"

"Fair to middlin'. Are you here with the advance team?"

Leslie snapped the wallet shut and palmed it again. She leaned into the casual pose on her open window. "That would be telling, Deputy. What brings you to this stretch of road. Are you part of…all of it?"

"I am. This road and most of the county roads around Lewkoville will be closed to the public for two hours before and after. That why you're up here? Scouting it out a'fore they arrive?"

"How much did they tell your department?"

"Just federal bigwigs coming in. They didn't say who, but we didn't hear nothin' from the Secret Service, so I'm gonna guess it ain't him. Or the veep. You being part of the federal family, do you know?"

"I only know what the bosses tell me, Deputy. Same as you."

"Amen that." His hand fell away from the holster. "At least I'm not down on that picket line. I don't know who's worse, the crazies with the signs or the media with the cameras."

"Makes one appreciate a nice quiet road like this. Well, I understand you checking me out. I would have done the same. I have a few more miles to scout before I report back. Anything else I can do for you?"

"No, ma'am."

"Good." Leslie leaned back, but then turned her head to Masters. "Oh, and Deputy, when you cross check my ID with your brass, keep my name off the open airwaves. Phone. Not radio. Got it?"

"Yes, ma'am."

Leslie settled in her seat and used the mirror to watch Deputy Masters hike back to his unit. She waited until he closed the door.

"Call me ma'am one more time and I'll yank that vest up around your ears, kid."

I pulled myself closer to the open sunroof.

"What's that about? Advance team? Bigwig? What's going on?"

"You forget. I'm with Fairytale Believers Incorporated. Beats the living shit outta me. You best be off, Peter. Go find Wendy and the Lost Boys. I'll call you if any of this starts to make sense."

"Later, gator."

42

I climbed trees as a kid. Trees. Barns. Silos. Anything to get off the ground until sufficient age and scraps of money earned working on a farm bought my first flying lessons. Trees imposed limits as the boughs and branches thinned near the top and would not support my weight. I never conquered a tree by poking my head above its crown.

From Leslie's rental I rose above the road until I encountered fully leafed-out branches. I mapped a path through them and pulled myself higher, hand over hand. Deputy Masters rolled his patrol unit beneath my unseen dangling feet. The throaty hum of his police interceptor V8 hinted at the vehicle's potency.

I worked my way up until an opening let me rise past the highest fluttering leaves in the crown. Treetops spread out all around me. The moment made me smile and briefly closed doors to chambers full of worry over Candice and Earl and the logistics of making children vanish. Alone and eight years old again, I conquered the top of a tree.

LEWKOVILLE. The deputy wasn't complimentary.

I skimmed over North Carolina forest that differed in shades of green from northern Minnesota forest. The fabricated town with its orderly streets sprawled where the trees and farm fields ended. An arterial road once traveled by Dr. Lillian Farris and me entered Evermore from the south. The scene on the highway was the inverse of Lewko's placid planned community. Evermore harbored tidy streets and gingerbread homes sprinkled around the manicured lawns of research buildings designed to look like quaint public libraries. The highway into town resembled a post-apocalyptic traffic jam. Vehicles clotted both sides of the two-lane blacktop, parked at angles, double-parked, and pulled off into fields. Tents and canopies had been thrown up at random among the glittering glass, chrome and clearcoat vehicle paint. Near the town border, twin rows of utility vans dominated both sides of the highway. The vans displayed bold graphics advertising television stations and networks. The media vans sprouted transmission antennas and nudged a police roadblock that established a border between Evermore and a clamoring hoard. Fanned out on both sides of the roadblock, a fluid crowd pressed a fence that looked temporary. Signs floated above their heads; many of the signs were professionally printed.

ACTS AGAINST GOD
YOU ARE DECEIVED
ABOMINATION
SATAN'S WORK
SAVE AMERICA

The signs bounced and bobbed for emphasis as their bearers wandered back and forth along the picket line. Because I'd seen something similar in front of my home, their presence induced a deeply unsettled feeling. These weren't individuals expressing a view. This was a mob, a frightened creature that had assimilated and subsumed the individuals, energizing fear over rational thought.

As I passed overhead, I realized that the police used the highway to separate two factions. Dueling crowds exchanged chants and counter chants. The larger faction waved professionally printed signs with block letters on fields of red and blue. The smaller faction waved handmade posters and hastily scrawled cardboard signs.

TRUST SCIENCE
LET THE CHILDREN LIVE
TAKE MY CHILD NEXT

I veered away from the front line and angled toward the center of town. Isolated in a different world, people on the streets and sidewalks moved on foot or bike or electric scooter, going about their quiet business in sunshine that encouraged shirtsleeves, shorts, and light summer dresses. In the center of town, small shops propped open their doors. Patrons populated sidewalk cafes and coffee shops, hunched over phones, tablets, and laptops. Sixty feet up, my brain hallucinated coffee aroma. I gave a moment's thought to dropping behind one of the buildings and reappearing long enough to grab a fresh brew. The moment didn't last. I reminded myself that there wasn't an angle or corner of Evermore without a camera watching.

The research building Leslie pointed out gave no indication of harboring the focus of the outside world's rabid attention. Like several other buildings in Evermore, Lewko's makeshift hospital was fronted by a quaint colonial exterior of red brick, white trim, and a pillared entrance. Peaked roofs formed a façade decorated with what I assumed were false gables. A full parking lot and a pair of private ambulances stationed near loading docks at the back of the structure hinted at the medical business within. I wondered if the interior had the same LCD paneled ceilings simulating the summer sky that I once saw in another Lewko building. Did the children in their new hospital beds sleep under stars?

I surveyed what looked like all glass front doors.

Gaining entrance wouldn't be hard. For visible visitors, access required high-tech badges resembling card-thin LCD screens on which AI hosts appeared. Watching people enter and exit the building, I calculated the height of the front doors and determined that slipping in over someone's head would work. Worst case, I would just walk in. Even when I cause a door to inexplicably open and close, few people question it, fewer investigate.

I didn't know what Lewko had in mind except to assume that whatever he had planned would be carefully orchestrated. And photographed. And recorded. And possibly scanned and tested.

The thought gave me pause.

What if I jumped the gun? What if I slipped into his five-star hospital and did my thing and then left? Skip the fanfare. Avoid the watchful eyes of his research team, and possibly examination by hidden scanners. I had not forgotten that Lewko purloined the tools and research of a team of college-aged tech nerds who first stumbled on remnants of the object that knocked me out of the sky. Lewko's own team would have advanced any research that had merit. How close were they to being able to see me when I am unseen? How close were they to being able to do what I do? Would my presence speed their path to discovery?

Maybe it would be best to deny Lewko's team a chance to observe the process in real time.

Get in. Get out. Gone.

That defeats the purpose. The thought came to me in Andy's voice.

A considerable effort had been put into creating the charade that the Lewko Objects caused a young girl to vanish in front of a thousand witnesses and cameras in New York. The charade protected me. More than that, transferring responsibility for the medical benefits of *the other thing* to the Lewko and his Objects eliminated the need to sneak in and out of hospitals in the night on random Foundation trips. Aside from being inefficient, sooner or later the meager tally of those I treated would fail to balance against the scores I had not.

I didn't trust Lewko entirely, but this plan was better than no plan.

I increased the BLASTER power, overflew the hospital, and accelerated toward the northern edge of the town. Main Street made a hard left turn that angled to the northwest in the direction of the huge Evermore package sorting and shipping facility—one of a dozen sprinkled across the country. The town's northern border had no police barricades or protesters, perhaps because the billionaire's private property abutted the city limits. A single narrow road entered his estate. As Leslie expected, a tasteful fence marked the entrance to the private lands. Gates and a guard shack provided security.

Beyond the gate, the road penetrated Lewko's private forest. I was instantly reminded of my search radius at Renell Lodge. Looking down through the trees, the electric shock that came with finding Dr. and Mrs. Yuan flooded back. I tightened my grip on the BLASTER and accelerated as if hurrying might outrun reminders of the gruesome discovery.

A river valley slid into view. More substantial than the aerial image suggested, a modest waterway snaked across the landscape in a basin between low hills. The road arrived at the southern crest of the hills and turned right. The pavement snuck under tall old growth trees before it emerged in an area that had been partially cleared. Structure blended into the hill overlooking the river. A wedge of flat roof joined the rising land. There were no lawns. Open meadows spawned fields of wildflowers. Gardens deliberately made to look anything but deliberate lined paths and surrounded the structural elements.

A wide swing over the waterway gave me a good view of three tiers of glass tucked in under wedges of roof. Stone patios extended from the glass, again in tiers. Stone steps descended between the levels. From each of the patios, paths radiated outward and wound through the gardens, eventually curving down the hillside until the paths reached the river. The entire layout blended seamlessly with the hill backing it. Portions hid beneath the canopies of old hardwood trees that were somehow undisturbed by the construction of this billionaire's lair.

I approached the largest of the stone patios, the one adjacent to the topmost tier. An array of modest outdoor furniture, metal chairs with bright striped cushions, offered seating and a beautiful vista beside a low stone wall.

Lewko's last text to me simply assigned our project a date and time and said *Come to my residence.* I had the date right. The angle of the descending afternoon sun said I had the time right, give or take a quarter hour.

No one occupied the patio on this level or either of the two levels farther down the hillside. I grew uncertain about the rendezvous until I spotted the items laid out neatly on the table closest to the wall.

An ice bucket contained half a dozen golden bottles of Corona. A dish with sliced limes nudged the bucket. I didn't know whether to feel complimented or creeped out.

I maneuvered to the table, grabbed the edge with one hand and secured the BLASTER with the other. Using the table as an anchor, I pulled one chair back. Sitting without help from gravity was pointless, but I suspected the beverage served as a signal—one I was happy to send. I maneuvered over the chair and pulled myself down using the chair arms. My butt contacted the cushion. I hooked both feet around the chair legs. My leg muscles did the job of keeping me seated, not that anyone could see.

I reached for the bucket and lifted an icy bottle of beer. Lewko thoughtfully supplied an opener, which I applied to the cap. The bottle remained visible in my hand. I jammed a wedge of lime in the bottle lips, twisted it, then tapped it down. The lime wedge torpedoed into the golden liquid and generated a small cloud of bubbles.

The first sip refreshed me. I set the bottle on the table but maintained a grip. The weight of the bottle helped to hold me down, which relieved my leg muscles.

A light breeze dusted the empty patio. Cameras I could not find watched the bottle rise, tip, drain, and then return to the tabletop. The first third of the beer was gone when one of the glass panels in the wall thirty feet from me motored open.

"I wasn't sure if you preferred Light or Extra." Spiro Lewko strolled out of the dark interior into dappled sunlight.

"You got the brand right. I'm surprised my data profile wasn't specific. What was it? Credit card history? Supermarket scanners?"

"I called your wife."

He came alone and empty-handed. Dressed in blue jeans and a white t-shirt over mildly beat up sneakers with no obvious brand name, he could have been the guy who sweeps the leaves off the patio stones. The arms he showed off and the drape of t-shirt over a flat abdomen attested to a personal trainer. His shoulder-length brown hair framed the wide dimensions of a face bearing a perpetual smirk. Andy told me that meme makers love to widen his mouth, sometimes grotesquely. I was glad my abstinence from social media spared me the image. Some things you can't unsee.

"Okay. Thanks. But the data thing is still creepy."

He took the chair opposite me and lifted one ankle to a knee. He shrugged. "The argument goes both ways. Convenient. Creepy. People protest yet they still give up their data willingly. I met a man once who worked in the automotive sector. This was back around '08 when GM filed and traditional brands were dropping like flies. Everyone thought it was the end of the automotive industry in America. I asked this man—he was in the software business, tangential to the retail side of it, vehicle window stickers, I think—I asked him what he thought of all the doom and gloom for automotive. He said, 'I don't know anybody buying a horse.' It's the same with the data people allow to be collected. There aren't many people loading shacks in the woods with canned goods, crushing their cell phones, and cutting their cable lines. People continue buying online, scanning grocery purchases, loading up credit cards. Do they really think no one looks at that?"

"They don't want to think so." I drained the first third of the bottle.

"What people *want* to think is a whole different discussion. Members of my family tree wanted to think they were being relocated to safe housing and at least busywork jobs while they rode the trains to the Nazi death camps." He paused.

"Sorry. Didn't mean to go that dark. How are you, Will? Are you alone? Are you also here, Andrea?"

"Just me."

"And your friend from the FBI?"

"She drove me, but no, she's not here. And what about us? Are we as alone as it appears?"

"I have a small personal staff inside, but that's all. Your presence is known only to me. I assume that's still the deal."

"It is."

Lewko reached across the table and took the partially filled Corona bottle from my hand. He moved it to his side of the table. "Hold that thought."

He looked back at the glass wall through which he had come. The same section he traversed motored open again and a woman in business attire stepped into the sunlight. Long black hair streaked with gray and tied in a ponytail draped one shoulder. She wore black-rimmed glasses on a pleasant, narrow face touched with minimal makeup. On her way to the table, I caught the tiniest tug of her eyebrows at the sight of her boss sipping a beer. She didn't comment. In one hand, she carried a slender electronic tablet which she handed to Lewko.

"They're coming." She spoke only to him and said nothing more as he examined the screen. His expression went from pleasant to something reflecting his one-word response.

"Shit." He handed the tablet back. "Please let everyone know I will head down to Gabby Calbert in ten minutes. I'll be right in."

The woman nodded and departed.

I followed Lewko's lead and waited until the glass motored shut again before asking, "Gabby's here?" I had last seen the girl who announced the vanishing act to the world when she disembarked Lonnie Penn's Gulfstream jet in Wichita. The idea of seeing her again, one month healthier, felt uplifting.

"What? No. We named the facility after Gabby. No, she's not here."

"Something doesn't sound good."

Lewko stood. "Finish your beer. We have to go. And no. It's not good. We'll talk on the way."

43

Lewko told me to meet him on the other side of the hill, where the driveway ended in a circle that I had seen on my way in. What I had not seen was a spur off the circle descending between two embankments. Below ground level, a rapid roll-up garage door covered access to underground parking.

After reluctantly leaving the chilled Corona behind, I conducted a short flight over the crest of the hill and took up a position above the driveway circle where it was just me and the birds for what seemed like ten minutes. At last, the garage door shot up and LED headlights appeared. A green metallic Jaguar SUV shot up the short hill and stopped on the circle. I was surprised to see Lewko himself in the pilot's seat. No driver. He leaned over and opened the front passenger door.

I maneuvered around to the side of the vehicle. Gliding in, I killed and pocketed the BLASTER, then reached in and caught the overhead passenger assist handle. After an awkward turnaround, I levered myself into the shotgun seat, fumbled with the seatbelt, and then closed the door while Lewko watched looking bemused.

"No. It's not as easy as you think." I snugged the belt to hold me against the plush leather seat.

Lewko stopped staring and dropped the Jaguar in gear. "That's what the astronauts say about their first couple days. Always kicking things. You don't know what to do with your feet."

I added chatting with astronauts to the list of billionaire perks. "What's the plan? And what just hit the fan?"

"The plan," he said, tapping the wheel twice for effect, "*was* simple. We'd spend the day tomorrow shuttling the kids into Imaging. Mom and dad wait outside—radiation, and all—while we bring in the Objects and you do what you do."

"They get to watch?"

"Yes. Along with a team of observers."

"Cameras?"

"Yes." I said nothing for a moment. He correctly read my hesitation. "There have to be cameras, Will. It's bad enough half the country thinks this is a David Copperfield trick."

"Cameras won't change that."

"True."

"What else are you recording? Imaging? What other readings are you taking?"

Lewko didn't look away from the windshield. There wasn't anyone to look at, but even so, he affected the posture of someone gauging the distance between truth and a lie. Or at least information that he wasn't anxious to share.

"Infrared. Low level radiation."

"Jesus."

"Not anything that can cause harm. Nowhere near the doses they're giving most of these kids."

"What about sound waves?"

He thought through his answer. "Yes. And yes, we piggybacked on that kid's research. The kid who found the objects."

"Did you pay him like I asked you to?"

The smirk spread into a smile. "Twenty million? Wasn't that what you asked me to pay him?"

"Sounds right."

"Yes. I paid him. And I hired him. The kid's got a head on his shoulders. And for the record he was lukewarm over the twenty mil, but over the moon for the job. He's on the team here."

Not bad, I thought. Lewko answered my next question before I asked.

"No. He doesn't know about you."

"Who does? On your team, I mean."

"Dr. Farris."

"Lillian? She works for you?" I laughed. "She kinda hates you."

"That she does. Which is why I persuaded her to sign on as a consultant. I don't want people around me who simply agree with me. I want people who think."

"Is she here?"

"She won't set foot in the place. Or the town. Or the state, I imagine. She works from New Mexico. And by the way, she thinks you're a terrible liar."

"That's well established. Who else knows?"

"Two of my top department heads and one member of my legal team, and before you criticize, that's half the number of people you've shared your secret with, Will. I think I have a better handle on the importance of keeping quiet than you do."

"Probably. But you're under a lot more scrutiny than me." I wasn't ready to feel sorry for the life of a billionaire, but there was no question that it wasn't a life I'd opt for. "I appreciate it, though. I do."

"Doesn't mean I wouldn't take you apart under a microscope if you'd let me."

"Good to know."

Lewko made a turn that aimed the Jaguar at the property gate half a mile away. He handled the vehicle nicely for someone I assumed had not driven since landing his first billion although I doubted that he would be seen on any city streets or country highways outside of his protected town. We descended a long slope through the trees. I had more questions.

"That's what the plan *was*. Now tell me what threw a wrench in that plan."

His expression turned icy. Andy told me that his younger-than-forty-something appearance and his long hair caused people to misjudge Spiro Lewko in boardrooms across the business spectrum, usually to their regret. The look he sent over the steering wheel was not one I'd like to receive across a desk or bargaining table.

"Timetable is moved up. We have incoming."

"Incoming what?"

He didn't answer.

"Look, man," I said, "my neck is on the line here—"

"Your neck? You're the guy who can just disappear. I'm the guy holding the bag."

"Don't put too much stock in the 'just disappear' angle. How safe do you think Andy would be if the wrong people—and I once counted you among them —got wind of me and decided to use her as leverage?" I felt anger rise, fueled by the squalling tiny inner voice that kept telling me I didn't want to be here in the first place. I didn't appreciate him withholding information. "Incoming what?"

He took and released a deep breath. "Texas."

"What? Texas Rangers? Dallas Cowboys? What?"

"The United States District Judge for the U.S. District Court for the Northern District of Texas. Amarillo. This afternoon a coalition of plaintiffs—a grab bag of front organizations—filed for an emergency injunction in the federal court in Amarillo."

"Wha...? Injunction for what?"

"To stop us. To stop us from giving treatment."

I didn't know what to say or ask. The words he spoke bordered on a foreign language.

He flexed his grip on the wheel. Blood evacuated his knuckles.

"I'll give you the nutshell version, Will—the one that will make you want to burn something. Groups with fancy names like *Defenders of Medical Integrity* and *Doctors for Transparency in Medicine*—that one I find terribly ironic—are arguing that we're introducing medical treatments that have not been tested or approved by the FDA. The FDA, they are arguing, is the only governing body that has the expertise and scientific authority to determine whether children should be subjected to this kind of experimentation or not."

"Hold on. Is this the same judge—?"

"Give the man a kewpie doll. Yes. Same guy that not long ago ruled that the FDA doesn't know it's ass from a Florida sink hole. He wasn't supposed to act on the motion until Monday morning. I guess he's a speed reader—since it's an 8,000-word complaint. He issued the injunction 46 minutes after it was filed."

"What does that mean?"

"It means he didn't read the damned thing. It means he knew what it said before he got it. It means the goddamned Texas Rangers and the U.S. Marshals are coming to shut us down. We don't have much time. We need to get you in position, and—oh, now what?" He swapped the gas pedal for the brake. I grabbed the overhead assist handle. The Jaguar shuddered to a halt.

Two vehicles sped towards us on the narrow road. Both vehicles—a white SUV with Evermore Security markings and a black Mercedes sedan—stopped in the road at angles that ensured we would not pass on pavement.

For a moment, I thought Lewko might dive for the shallow ditch and go around the roadblock. There was room. Brush might scratch the Jaguar's finish, but the off-road claims of the vehicle would be validated.

He sat static. A security officer in the SUV stayed behind the wheel. Two men jumped out of the Mercedes, both wearing dark suits. My first thought was FBI, but the suits and haircuts looked well beyond government pay grades. The men hurried toward Lewko's side of the Jaguar. The roadblock may have been a surprise, but the men were not. Lewko rolled down his window. I unsnapped the seatbelt and let it retract.

One of the two men leaned down and rested one arm on the door sill.

"What is it, Barney?" Barney didn't look like a Barney. He looked like a shark wearing a silk tie.

"Clarisse told you? The bastard ruled."

"Yeah. I know. We don't have a lot of time. We can—"

"You can't." Barney landed the command with confidence that told me he might be the one Lewko entrusted to know the truth about *the other thing*, about me.

"If we hurry."

"No. You can't go down there."

"What are you talking about?"

"They'll arrest you. On top of the injunction, the federal court sent a referral to the AG's office. Chris says his hands are tied."

"What referral?"

"State. They're issuing a warrant for the hospital. For you."

Lewko tightened his lips until they formed a thin line across his broad jaw.

Barney continued. "NC General Statutes 131E. Hospital Licensure Act. You're not certified. They're deeming us a critical access hospital, and we're not certified pursuant to 42 CFR Part 485—dammit, Lew, you get it. NC state patrol is on their way to shut it down. The marshals are bringing buses in for the kids and their parents. It's finished, Lew."

"Did you call the governor?"

"He's livid, but his hands are tied. The federal injunction kills us either way. The hospital licensure warrant is just twisting the knife. You know who you've pissed off. I came up here to stop you from going down there because the last thing any of us wants is to see Spiro Lewko getting hauled away in handcuffs on MSNBC."

Barney wore a hard look on his face that said he'd reach in for the vehicle keys if necessary. The fob lay in a cupholder in the center console and his gray eyes made note of it.

Lewko stared straight ahead. His grip on the wheel remained taut.

"There's more," Barney said. "Grumblings on The Hill."

"Heard it all before. They'll never call hearings."

"No. They won't. Because they don't want more spotlight on this than necessary, but the leadership is looking for ways to make you turn the stuff over to DOD or intelligence. Don't kid yourself, Lew. If they didn't think you'd raise a holy stink, they'd come in with writs and force you to hand everything over. This district court injunction has them turning cartwheels because it feeds the hoax angle. Bob thinks that's why they pressured the AG to add the hospital licensure. Makes this look like a con. You wind up on a perp walk for conning sick children and their families with a bogus hospital while they take everything out through the back door, leaving you with shit on your shoulders."

From a glance Lewko paid the second man, I took him to be Bob.

Barney reached in and closed his hand on Lewko's forearm. "Turn around, Lew. Drive back up to the house and break some dishes, and when you get your blood pressure back down, start making calls. People owe us. This bullshit of shopping for a judge in Amarillo won't stand at the next level. I'll go back and do what I can for the families. Open checkbook?"

"Yeah." Lewko turned to his attorney. "Buses? They're sending buses?"

44

"Anybody ever tell you not to drive angry?" I watched the speedometer digits flick higher and higher. Trees blurred past us. The Jaguar's 4-cylinder engine wound up like a blender.

Half a mile ahead, a hard right turn waited. Topping eighty miles per hour on his narrow driveway, Lewko wasn't going to make that turn. Not under control.

I unsnapped the seatbelt again. The car immediately and loudly chimed its discontent.

"Okay. Be an asshole. I'm outta here." I dropped the window. Just as I gripped the top of the frame, Lewko relented.

"Wait."

He let the speed wind down. Just short of the hard turn, he braked and brought the SUV to a stop. I pushed against the window frame to reposition myself on the seat. Lewko tipped his head down. His long hair fell around his face.

If I could have seen my watch, I would have pointedly looked at it.

"I'm going."

"No," he said without looking. "I need you to stay. We can still do what we need to do. It's all set up. Even if—"

"Even if what? Even if they take the kids? You want me to stay so you can do some imaging? Some testing?"

"It was part of the deal, Will."

"The kids were the deal. Period. And I'm going to make this perfectly clear right now. Don't play the threat card with me, Lewko. Don't. If you try to hold my wife or my friends over me all that will get you is a very short flight to a very high altitude. Do you understand me?"

He chuckled, which burned me. "Who's threatening whom?"

"I mean it. If there's so much as a hint of threat against Andy, I swear, I will forsake every moral signpost that woman has planted for me, and I will put an end to it."

His head shook. For a moment, I thought it was a spasm, but then he lifted his face and I saw the grin. It was a laugh, such as it was.

"God damn, you are a drama queen, Stewart. I wish I could see your face."

Fwooomp!

I dropped onto the seat and stared fire and brimstone at the man. He looked at me and chuckled again.

"Worth it. You gotta work on that."

I gave up and leaned back against the cushion. "Yeah, I know. Every time I try to do angry with Andy, she breaks out laughing. And I love her for it. Keep that in mind after I drop you from five hundred feet if you ever try to use her to get to me."

He waved a hand between us, still smiling. "Stop. Seriously. I get it. But I swear, next time I see her I'm telling her what you looked like just now."

Red flooded my cheeks just thinking about Andy hearing this from Lewko.

"I'm still going." I grabbed the top of the window again.

"Wait."

Here it comes. The pleading. The greater good speech. The reminder that there is an endless supply of children who can benefit. I swore to myself that if he used that last bit, I'd punch him.

"Why are you going out the window? You can open the door, you know." He pointed at the latch.

More heat in my face. I let go of the window frame and opened the vehicle door.

Lewko grabbed my arm. "Take me with you."

"Why?"

He released my arm. He dropped his eyes again and let the curtains of hair fall on either side of his face. A place to hide, I realized. I wondered if Andy might read the gesture as a sign of lying. Or would she brand it a sign of pure truth? I had no idea.

"Okay, fine. It's about testing you. It's about finding out how we can get those objects to do what you do. It's about finding out if we can control it. Replicate it. Build on it. It's all of those things. I told you the first time we met the properties of those objects open a path to the stars. So, yeah, it's all those things. But..." He paused. *Lies come easy. Truth is hard.* Andy's words. He struggled. "It's about those kids, too. I know the people behind this bogus injunction. I know the judge. I know their world view, and what they think of anyone who doesn't sign on to their values, their god, their purity. And I know what they will do to anyone who challenges those things. To hell with them."

He lifted his face from behind the curtains of hair and stared me in the eye. If it wasn't truth, it was the best imitation I'd ever seen.

"No."

He blinked. "What? Why not?"

"I'm not doing this with you hanging off my arm."

"Yes, you are. Because you can't get in without me."

45

F *WOOOMP!* I pushed hard. We vanished and immediately lost contact with the asphalt beside the parked Jaguar.

"Whoa!" Hooked on my left arm, Lewko tightened the squeeze using his pumped muscles. "What's with the thermal drop?" I tapped my toes to start a slow ascent. We had tree branches overhead. I selected an opening and pulsed the BLASTER in my right hand to establish a path.

"The cool thing? Beats me. Happens all the time, but you're right about it having some kind of thermal property. Summer or winter, my body feels the same thing, no matter how cold or hot it is. It's nice. What makes you think I couldn't get in without you?" I wanted to know in case I needed to dump him.

"The doors are acrylic with non-metallic mounts. You wouldn't be able to sever hinges or latches."

"How do you know about that?"

"Your wife. She told me how you got her and the Calberts out of that locked space on Remington's boat. Interaction with metals is something I'd like to study..." he quickly added "...if you're willing. Also, we installed air motion sensors. They're programmed to detect the movement of air caused by a body. Matched to motion sensors, the standard disruption of air caused by someone entering the building is accounted for. Try slipping in over someone's head, and we've got you. Oh, and there are filament sensors hanging from the ceilings. Smaller than spider webbing."

"Jesus." I steered us through the tree branches. We transitioned from a sea of leaves into an orange twilight sky.

Lewko gasped. "I know you think I only care about the scientific benefits but, *Will this is breathtaking.* Absolutely breathtaking. Humanity has dreamed this dream since—"

"Hang on." I aimed the BLASTER and slid the power control full forward. The electric motor and prop combination whined like a cheap drone. I rotated our bodies to minimize frontal area and reduce drag. We shot across the crowns of trees against a relative wind that grew to nearly sixty miles per hour, the fastest I've clocked myself.

Lewko did not utter a sound. I doubt it had anything to do with restraint.

46

The circus had come to town. Rows of law enforcement vehicles parked under their flashing emergency lights in front of Lewko's hospital. Two private buses lined the curb at the building entrance. Officers in gear meant for battle lined the sidewalk leading to the doors. A cluster of men and women gathered halfway between the building and the buses. Some wore suits. Some wore medical garb. All of them seemed to be gesturing and arguing.

"Looks like we're a little late," Lewko said. "Can you get us close? I want to hear what they're saying."

I considered describing the difficulties involved, but instead said, "I'll try."

I used a tight circle to bleed off the airspeed. Light pulses of reverse power further slowed us. I steered into the airspace above the argument.

"Closer."

"Shhhhh!"

I jabbed Lewko with my elbow rather than try to explain that the BLASTER attracts attention if used beyond a slow crawl. The men in battle gear wore bright yellow stencils that said U.S. MARSHAL across their shoulder blades. They were not amateurs, which accounted for their scrutiny of the sky as well as the perimeter.

We drifted into position.

"...absolutely insane. You have no right, no idea what you're doing..."

"...just children, my God, where is your humanity?"

"...want to exchange first rate medical facilities for a bus that doesn't even have a toilet? What is wrong with you?"

"Enough!" One of the suits put up a flat hand in front of the woman in scrubs protesting the loudest. He held up a folded paper. "Read it. Or don't. But this is happening. Now you can go back in there and get these people ready to move or I can send in these men with guns. Either way, I am here to *protect those innocent children!*" The man wielding the legal document shook it in his opponents' face.

The doctors and nurses attempted a final stare down over the paper held in the air at the circle's center. When that failed, a man in a doctor's coat snatched the document out of the holder's hand and stormed away. The others quickly followed.

"You're a disgrace!" The document deliverer shouted after the medical team. "You're a disgrace to your profession! Bringing children to this madman! Forcing them into a treatment that is illegal, immoral, AND AGAINST GOD!"

His face burned bright red under a glossy sheen of sweat. United States Marshals nearby found something else to look at or exchanged glances filled with doubt with their fellow officers.

Without asking, I tipped the BLASTER to a vertical line and sent power for slow revolutions to the prop. We rose toward a sky that had turned a stark orange and purple with the sunset.

"What?" Lewko whispered.

"How do we get in?" A marshal stood at each door. "Maybe we can reach the kids before they're packed up and pulled out."

I felt Lewko move, which I took as a head shake.

"There won't be time. We need the Objects."

"Really? Because I think the misdirection part of this is pretty much shot to hell."

"No. It isn't. Take me around to the back."

"Why?"

"To go in and get one of the Objects."

"And then what?"

I felt Lewko shrug. He really had not yet grasped the concept of communication without being seen.

"Then we hijack a bus," he added.

47

At the back of the building Lewko directed me to land on a loading dock. Twin overhead doors stood on either side of a man entrance. The door in the middle had a keypad. I maneuvered us to within reach. Above us cameras watched from either side.

"I presume you know the code," I said.

"Really? Hundreds of codes for hundreds of office and research spaces and just because I own the company you think I know them all?"

"Well then how—?"

"Relax. I know the master code." Even in the vanished state, I could see the smirk on his face. He tapped in a series of numbers, then paused, then a second series of numbers. The door latch buzzed then clicked. I put a flat hand on the wall for leverage.

"Pull it open."

We slipped inside.

We entered a receiving dock and storage space. Not large. Until becoming a hospital, the building served another purpose in Lewko's empire of enterprises. Stacks of cubicle dividers, desks and computer equipment filled roughly half of the space. Medical equipment, boxes of medical supplies, and stacks of paper goods and linens filled out the rest of the space. Single lights above two exit doors provided dim illumination. I looked for cameras and found two.

"Over there." Lewko tugged on my arm.

"Are you pointing?"

"Sorry. Over by those shelves. Beside the door."

I pulsed the BLASTER and we performed a short glide across the polished concrete floor. I grabbed the support for a set of steel shelves and used it to stop.

Lewko struggled to pull his arm out of mine.

"Hold up! You'll reappear if we break contact."

"That's the idea. You stay here. I'm going to get the Objects."

Before I could argue, he jerked his arm from inside mine.

Fwooomp! He flashed into view and nearly fell over backward when his feet found the floor. I grabbed the front of his shirt with one hand and held on to the shelf support with the other.

"So…what? I just stay here?"

"You got it." He pulled my hand from his shirt and straightened the fabric. Popping a flat grin on his face, he grabbed the nearby doorknob, pulled the door open and walked out.

I floated in the space by the door, wondering if the cameras had spotted him or if he knew their blind spots. After a few minutes that pretended to be hours, I studied the two cameras I could see, thinking the latter, and contemplating reappearing for a look at my watch. The problem was that the cameras were black orbs fastened to the ceiling. I could not be sure which way they were pointed.

But Lewko knew. He had to. He could no more afford to have himself seen appearing out of thin air than me.

I decided it was safe.

I pressed my boots against the floor and held the shelf support. I reached for the levers in my head and closed a grip to pull them back when—

A door on the other side of the room swung open. Two U.S. Marshals entered, a man and a woman. These two were not fitted out for a battlefield. Instead of body armor and web belts, they wore windbreakers with the agency lettering on the back. They did not enter with guns drawn. One held a cell phone. The other held a flashlight.

Without speaking they searched the room. They looked behind stacks of equipment, in dark corners, and directly at me in my slot beside the second door. They did their jobs well. Anyone visible attempting to hide would have failed.

Satisfied, they departed without speaking.

I realized that, for the most part, I'd been holding my breath, or at least had been afraid to breathe heavily. I blew out the air in my lungs and drew in fresh air. The near miss should not have affected me, but the nerves and tendons in my arms felt as if they were transmitting a low-voltage current. My chest tightened. I felt a tug at my center where I normally feel the strange axis around which I can rotate when I have vanished.

Something was not right.

Panic attack?

A shuddering need gripped me. My body—my whole being—wanted to do something. But what?

Unbidden, the image of the levers in my head leaped to mind and *I saw them moving.* They swept slowly toward me, away from the stops.

I threw an imagined hand over the imagined levers and pushed back. There was resistance. Impossible.

That's when I realized what was happening. I was being pulled out of *the other thing* just as I had once nearly been pulled into it. When Lillian Farris and I visited Lewko's storage facility to examine the object debris he had in his possession, that debris existed in the vanished state. As we approached, it tried to pull me into the same state. At that time, in the company of Lewko and his team, I could not afford to suddenly vanish. I fought back, and in the fighting, caused the vanished object to appear. Gravity pulled it to the floor of its storage cylinder, breaking it into pieces.

This was the same situation in reverse.

Lewko.

He had to have made it to wherever he stored the pieces and was now returning. I and the pieces existed in opposite states. Me vanished. The pieces not.

I shoved the levers to the stops again. Balls to the wall, as always, but this time I held pressure on them, pressure that was required because the levers fought back. The axis down my center vibrated, singing like a plucked bass string.

I swung around and grabbed the knob of the door beside me. I braced one knee against the wall and jerked the door wide open. Without looking, I pulled myself through, expecting to encounter a U.S. Marshal.

I entered an institutionally clean and thankfully empty white hallway. Glossy floor tiles stopped just short of being mirrored. Pleasant, recessed lighting lined the tops of both walls. A series of doors with placarded numbers ran the length of the hall, which ended in 90-degree turns at both ends, roughly thirty feet away in each direction.

The sensation within me grew more intense. I struggled to hold the levers and maintain my vanished state. Black bulb cameras marked the junctions at each end of the hall.

Jesus, Lewko, do you have enough cameras?

Footsteps approached. It had to be the marshals, either completing their search or retracing their steps.

The door behind me closed. I spun around to retreat and found it locked, secured by keypad access.

Shit!

The vibration down my center intensified. I felt myself losing the battle to remain unseen. I turned to face whoever was coming.

The footsteps drew nearer.

Lewko stepped around the corner and stopped suddenly. He held a small attaché case in one hand. He groped his chest. He studied his hand. He took a step. Then another.

The levers in my head slid halfway back and continued moving.

I threw everything I had into them.

FWOOOMP!

Instant relief. The pressure evaporated. The cords in my arms and legs that had been almost electric suddenly felt cool, steady. The core muscle down my center relaxed.

"What the—!"

Lewko vanished. Long hair. T-shirt. Jeans. Attaché case.

Gone.

48

"Lewko!"

"Will? What the hell?"

"Stay there."

"What just happened?"

I jabbed one hand in my jacket pocket and pulled out a BLASTER. Another jab brought out a prop.

"I'm stuck. I can't touch the floor."

"Just don't move. I'll come for you."

I snapped the prop on the shaft of the BLASTER's electric motor. Just as I lifted the device to propel myself forward, I realized I was already moving. I felt the tug at my core. I *thought* myself in Lewko's direction. Half a dozen times in the past, *the other thing* shot me off on a vector commanded by my subconscious. Try as I had, I could never replicate the effect—until I spent time in a New York hotel room with a case identical to the one Lewko now carried, possibly the same one. A case that held The Objects.

I felt a shred of control. Movement commanded by subconscious thought. The wires running down the back of my head vibrated in tune with the core muscle at my center. The sensations were alien, ticklish.

I pocketed the BLASTER and put my hands out. Better not to run into Lewko with a spinning six-inch carbon fiber scimitar in my hand. I imagined Lewko wiggling and flailing. My luck, he'd poke my eye out.

I opened my mouth to tell him to hold himself perfectly still. The words never formed.

Two federal marshals, the same two who had searched the facility, rounded the corner at the same end of the hall as the vanished billionaire.

They walked right into Lewko.

The woman threw up her arms and staggered to her right and bumped the wall with her arms flying. She looked like someone swarmed by bees. The man hit some part of the billionaire with his face and sprawled backward. Both scrambled away from whatever assaulted them. Both swore and groped the air.

"What the f—?"

"Who's there?!"

The woman threw open her windbreaker and jerked her weapon from its holster.

The man on the floor struggled to his feet while holding his left arm outstretched, swinging it back and forth. Blood ran from one side of his nose.

The woman tucked her weapon against her thigh, finger extended outside the trigger guard.

"What the hell?" She waved her free arm.

"Lenore, there's no one there." The man probed the air where he had just collided with Lewko.

I didn't think their gropes would find Lewko. They ran into him. Which meant he was on his way to me.

I had no choice. I needed to find him, yet the last thing either of needed was for the marshals to do the same. I didn't think using either of our names was wise.

"Marco!" I whispered.

"Polo!" Lewko answered, closer than I expected.

"WHO IS THAT?" the woman shouted. The gun came up.

I floated forward, arms extended. The hallway was at least eight feet wide, which meant we might float right past each other. I waved back and forth to cover as much airspace as possible.

"Marco!"

"Polo!" Closer now. To my left.

Something scraped the wall to my left. I veered and immediately caught my pinkie finger on cloth. His shirtsleeve. I closed a grip on the solid muscle of his bicep.

"WHO'S THERE?" Lenore the U.S. Marshal advanced, swinging her free arm back and forth like someone groping in the dark.

"Door," I whispered.

I rotated. The powerful vibration running down my center tugged us back the way I had come. I towed Lewko closer to the middle of the hallway to avoid bumping and scraping the wall. Behind us, the marshals advanced step by step, arms swinging. Lenore shouted at us. Her partner seemed content to cautiously pace forward in wide-eyed silence. He dripped blood on the glossy floor.

I stopped at the door. The keypad beeped. The lock buzzed. The latch clicked. Before I could set up for it, Lewko grabbed the knob, turned it, pushed—and thrust us back toward the center of the hall.

My rational brain worked on the geometry, but my subconscious dropped us to the floor where my boots connected and gained purchase. Lewko, still holding the knob, pushed the door open. We followed the door's arc into the receiving dock. Once inside, the door slammed shut behind us. Seconds later, running footsteps approached outside. Someone tried the knob.

"They've been in here once. They know the code. Let's go."

Lewko was one step ahead of me. I felt him move. A green button on a wall switch snapped inward. The big overhead dock door rattled to life and rose.

Behind us, the keypad beeped. The lock buzzed. The latch released.

"Hold on!" I jerked the BLASTER back out of my pocket and aimed it at the growing gap between the bottom of the door and the floor. I shoved the slide control full forward and rotated us both to a prone position.

The hallway door shot open. The marshals stepped through.

We swept down into the gap beneath the rising dock door. I cringed against the possibility of smacking the bottom edge or scraping the concrete floor, but my aim was true. We sailed through the opening and into the orange glow of twilight.

I aimed the screaming BLASTER straight up. We performed a tidy half loop and shot over the roof of the hospital building. The marshals followed the sound and hurried out onto the loading dock. I lost sight of them. We darted over the front entrance.

Too late.

The buses were gone.

49

"Do you see them? Which way did they go?" I rotated us in a slow, ascending circle.

I doubted the federally operated buses would run the gauntlet of protesters and the media at the south end of town. Something told me that people enforcing an injunction against treatment of sick children would not want media coverage.

"Doesn't matter."

"It does matter. We have to go after them."

"Will, I have The Objects. All of the pieces. That's what matters."

"Maybe to you, but I have a feeling that parents planning funerals for their kid six months from now would beg to differ. What route out of town attracts the least attention?"

"Take us back to my place and we'll sort this out."

"Like hell!" Anger blossomed. I wondered if Lewko understood what would happen if I let go of him. "Those kids came here full of hope."

"And I told you already. Hope kills. Now, take me back and we can regroup. The Luddites who did this won't get to play this card a second time. No appeals court will let this stand. We'll bring in another group. I'll buy a hospital if I have to."

"But *these* kids trusted you. And they don't get a second chance. I'm not letting them get away. If you're not with me, I can easily drop you—" I paused "—off."

"Exactly how do you plan to stop two buses escorted by U.S. Marshals?"

"I don't know. I'll cross that bridge when I get to it."

He said nothing. My anger intensified. "Which way, dammit?"

Silence. I threw my arm up and applied reverse thrust. We descended. As much as I wanted to, I wasn't going to drop him from three hundred feet. I might dump him from ten feet up. Maybe give him a pair of broken ankles to think about.

"Bridge."

"What?"

"You just said we'll cross that bridge when we get to it."

"So?"

"I know how we can stop the buses and get on board."

50

I recognized the stretch of road where Leslie had dropped me off. Not far from where Deputy Masters stopped to query us, I spotted the painted white roof of a bus. Fifty yards ahead of the bus, an SUV led the procession with emergency lights flashing. Now I understood why the road was closed. This was the planned exit route.

"There's one. Where's the other one?" Lewko called out over the wind and BLASTER noise.

I transmitted a shrug through our hooked arms. My thumb tried to squeeze more power out of the slide control on the BLASTER, but we were at the maximum. I felt the batteries wane. I had a choice: Lose time by changing units. Or keep going.

I kept going, aiming higher as the land rose to meet the same hills on which Lewko had built his lair.

The bus obeyed the posted limit of 45 miles per hour. We had a ten to twelve mile per hour advantage and pulled ahead. I searched through the overarching tree limbs for the other bus but saw only empty road. My eyes watered. I had not come prepared with a set of ski goggles.

The land crested. The river valley spilled to the left and right ahead of us. The road descended through the trees then turned parallel to the river. After a short distance, the road crossed the river via a steel truss bridge.

"There!" He moved, pointlessly pointing again.

Yeah, I see it. Painted black against the bleached gray of the road, the boxy steel bridge spanned roughly 200 feet of brown river water. The two lanes on the bridge originally handled carriages or horse-drawn wagons. A pair of modern sedans might squeeze past each other. Meeting an approaching bus would call for one party to stop and wait. That helped.

More importantly, I spotted the element Lewko deemed critical. Where the far end of the span regained footing on land, a set of railroad tracks ran tightly along the river. Post-mounted flashing light signals as well as the glint of clean steel rails told me the tracks remained in service. Drop gates protected both narrow lanes.

I dove for the river. We only had ten- or fifteen-seconds' lead. The other bus was still nowhere in sight. I feared it had already passed.

Another bridge to cross when we reached it.

I cut the power. Wind resistance slowed us. We descended over the last of the trees and passed over the slow-moving brown water. The river basin had a musty fish and mud smell mixed with the sweet scent of blossoms from plants and shrubs rioting along the shore. Remnants of twilight reflected in the surface of the water. The black steel trusses looming against a faded purple sky created an artistic portrait, something found in a gallery.

I reversed the BLASTER to slow us. Over my left shoulder, peripheral vision let me know that the two-vehicle caravan had crested the hill and joined the downslope to the river. Headlights winked on and off among trees on the silhouetted hillside. The lights turned right parallel to the waterway, then made a hard left turn to cross the bridge.

We eased to a stop where the bridge ended, just shy of the railroad tracks. The scent of creosote and heavy grease joined the night air.

I pocketed the BLASTER and grabbed the railroad signal post.

"How do you want to do it?" I asked.

"We don't want to be spotted until I climb aboard. Can you drop me close when they open the doors?"

"We aim to please. Listen, there's a problem when I'm near that thing. It wants to be in the same state as me and vice versa. It's a struggle when they're in opposite states. I don't know how long I can stay gone while they're not, so you have to move fast."

"How long do I leave them under?"

"No idea. I don't know if time matters. Let's give them at least twenty seconds."

"Got it."

I watched the headlights enter the truss bridge. "You know... just when I decide *not* to throw you under a bus, a bus shows up."

"Thanks," he said flatly.

THE SUV, unmarked except for a light bar across the windshield's brow, passed first. It rattled over the railroad tracks and turned right followed by a tight left that sent it up the hill again. Thick brush and fully leafed trees swallowed their taillights. Good. It meant they were comfortable with losing sight of the bus.

"Ready?" I wiggled my arm.

"Ready."

The big bus, a full-size cross-country type that seats its passengers well above the roofline of every other vehicle on the road, roared across the truss bridge, clearing the overhead steel cross members and anti-sway beams by just a few feet. In low gear, it sounded excessively loud given the way its speed diminished. I wondered if the marshals had forgotten about the railroad protocol.

The brakes squealed and then hissed when the bus stopped short of the tracks. I shoved off the post, betting on timing. We sailed fifteen feet toward the wall of aluminum and glass.

Come on come on come on.

The door swung open. I reached forward and grabbed the edge, then heaved Lewko through the opening. I heard something bang and felt an impact transmitted through his body. Possibly the attaché case. Lewko remained upright. I let him go.

Fwooomp!

Spiro Lewko landed on the second step into the bus. He gripped the shiny aluminum post and steadied himself. I reached for and grabbed the back of his jeans and pulled myself in before the driver heaved the door shut.

The driver acted by rote. Stop. Open door. Close door. Go. She pulled the door shut and released the brake even as she spotted Lewko. She shrieked. Her foot stomped the brake. The bus shuddered to an immediate halt.

"Evening," Lewko said politely. The woman stared up at him from a tight bucket seat that barely contained a body bulging against the blue and gray uniform she wore. Her eyes were headlights on bright. Lewko smiled. "Do you know who I am?"

Her jaw went slack. From the first seat, a child's voice rang out.

"That's Mr. Lewko! Look, Dad, that's Mr. Lewko!"

Lewko turned and nodded. The small boy wore a bathrobe over pajamas full of superheroes in dynamic poses.

They didn't even let them get dressed.

A deep thrumming grew down my center, the vibration generated by the conflict between The Objects, now visible, and me, vanished. I feared this. I worried that it might overwhelm me.

I tightened my grip on the imaginary balls at the top of the imaginary levers.

"What's your name?" Lewko asked the boy. At the same time, he lowered the attaché case to the floor and rolled the combination into the locks. He popped the case open.

"Luke! My name is Luke just like your name only without the Oh." The boy grinned at the billionaire. His skin stretched tightly across the bones in his face. His illness was obvious, but it did not diminish his smile.

The riders on the bus craned their necks to see what was happening. Under an outbreak of murmured excitement, adults leaned into the aisle. Farther back, people stood. A woman sitting across from the boy and his father shifted a bundle of child in her arms and reached for and touched Lewko's arm.

"Are we doing it? Are you here to do it?"

Lewko pulled a white-gray shard of what looked like broken Styrofoam packing, the kind that protects a new laptop, from the case. Two more rested in dark gray padding. He closed the lid.

"Yes."

The woman's composure broke. Eyes that were already red and damp spilled blobs of tear down her cheeks. She made a sound that merged laughter and crying. She squeezed the bundle in her arms. Chatter spread throughout the bus.

Lewko turned to the driver. "Are you going to be a problem?"

She shook her head vigorously. "No, sir. I just drive the bus. You do what you have to do for these poor babies. You have at it and Amen!"

"Can I have some light?"

She reached for and flicked on the bus's interior lights.

Lewko, despite his reputation as a recluse, slipped easily into commanding public speaking. He held The Object up for everyone to see, which automatically garnered attention.

"We don't have much time. I can't give you the detailed explanation you would have received at the clinic. I can't answer your questions, so don't ask. You know the gist of it. You saw what happened in New York. You know that the Amphitriton claims of a cure were false, but that results actually came from this. We don't know why or how it works. I make no promises. If you want out, wave me off. I'm coming down the aisle and you'll each get a turn. That good enough?"

Unanimous agreement erupted. On each side of the aisle, parents shifted in their seats, woke their children, lifted them onto their laps or changed them to the aisle seat. Bald heads peeked over the seatbacks. Mothers standing held toddlers on the aisle seat cushions. The disease killing them was starkly evident. For a horrifying instant, I thought of Lewko's ancestors arriving at the camps, stepping off trains and confronting the emaciated, the sick.

Yet, I could not believe what I saw in the faces. Despite disease, these faces glowed like spotlights. Eyes lit up like fireworks. Not just the kids. The parents. At night, when I did this trick in darkened hospitals, parents were often in the room, sleeping restlessly, revealing wear and worry. Those parents never knew. This was overwhelmingly different.

"Can you lock that door from the inside?" Lewko asked.

"I sure can," the driver replied like a soldier ready for battle.

I released my grip on Lewko's pants and pulled myself higher on the post at the front. If everyone stayed in their seats, I could easily follow Lewko by pressing myself against the high center ceiling of the bus, using the luggage racks on either side as grips to move.

Or not. I hesitated. Given the powerful vibration generated by The Object and the distance Lewko had been from me when he disappeared in the hallway, I wondered if staying close was necessary. Better to stay near the door if possible. I glanced through the front windshield. The escort SUV's lights climbed the hill. They had not yet discovered that the bus had stopped.

I nudged Lewko. He leaned toward the boy in the front seat and held out The Object.

"Grab this, will you Luke?" Lewko held the ends. The boy closed both hands around the top and bottom. I didn't wait.

Fwooomp! Relief from the vibrating tension shot up through my core. Luke and Lewko vanished. A loud gasp filled the space in the bus. Beside the boy, his father's eyes bulged. The man stared at empty space in the seat beside him. He raised a hand, wanting to touch, but froze, perhaps fearful of disrupting the process.

I forgot to start any kind of count in my head, so I guesstimated when twenty seconds had passed, then gave it a few more.

Fwooomp! Lewko and the boy reappeared. The vibration in my core returned.

Lewko broke loose an involuntary laugh. How could he not? Startled excitement lit up the boy's face.

"WOW!" the child cried.

Lewko didn't wait. He turned to the woman across the aisle. She pulled back wrapped blankets to reveal a small bald head. "Put him on the seat, please."

"Her. This is Lisa." She slid the bundle onto the seat beside her. I thought the sleeping child would wake, but she simply nestled against the back of the seat. The woman extracted a tiny arm. "Here. You can take her hand."

Lewko slipped the Object under the girl's limp palm and pressed his own hand over hers.

Fwooomp!

51

The marshals rolled up as Lewko reached the halfway point in the bus aisle. Despite igniting the emergency lights, they showed no urgency. They stopped on the other side of the railroad tracks. The driver stayed behind the wheel. The driver's partner stepped out of the passenger side. He adjusted the nylon windbreaker on his shoulders and strolled toward us.

The bus driver pulled back a sliding window on her side of the bus. A neat trick. It drew the marshal to her, not the door.

A hush enveloped the bus the instant the federal vehicle pulled up. Until that moment, as Lewko performed his miracle at each seat, the excitement on the bus approached grade school field trip levels. Now everyone in the front half of the bus hunkered down. Parents tightened holds on their children as if the marshals had come to separate them. Those in the back half, still waiting, craned their necks. New worry etched lines in their faces.

Lewko ignored the new development and continued his work. I divided my attention between Lewko and the driver, who leaned toward the marshal outside her window.

"What's going on?" the man asked. He was young and physically fit. I immediately estimated my chances in conflict with him at zero, except for possibly making him disappear long enough to heave him into the river.

"She's just a little hot on account of those hills. I thought I'd let her cool off a bit before we go up this side, that's all."

The marshal lifted himself on his toes and leaned closer for a better look. "Everything okay inside?"

"Right as rain. This'll just be a few minutes. Grab yourself a sit or a stroll."

The young man adhered to his training as a skeptic. He leaned back to look through the heavily tinted side windows. I knew he could see inside with the interior lights on. Spotting someone as recognizable as one of the richest men in the world—the subject of the very injunction his agency had been sent to support —was all but guaranteed.

And then what?

Would he draw his weapon and demand that the driver open up? Would he force the door? I weighed my options for stopping him long enough to give Lewko a chance to reach the last child at the back of the bus.

From the rear of the bus, Lewko turned in my direction with an impatient expression on his face. He used a loud voice. "I think we just need to give it a second and try again." He held the Object in his hands and flared his eyes.

Shit.

I had been distracted and failed to throw the switch.

Fwooomp! He vanished, along with a small girl standing on a seat cushion.

The marshal wandered back along the side of the bus, looking through the side windows at the passengers. He strolled to the midpoint of the vehicle. A woman in the seat ahead of where Lewko worked stood up and reached for her bag in the overhead compartment. She muttered something out of the side of her mouth and the man in the next seat stood up to do the same. Both fumbled with their luggage.

They're blocking his view.

Fwooomp! I brought Lewko back. He moved on.

Fwooomp!

"LET'S GET THIS MOVING, OKAY?" The marshal walked back to the driver's side window and rapped on the side of the bus.

"Yes, sir. I think she's about cooled down and ready. You go ahead and load up. I'll be right behind you." She waited until the young marshal remounted his shotgun seat. The SUV driver fired up the engine and pulled a tight U-turn. The bus driver checked the mirror. "How're we doin' back there?"

Fwooomp! Lewko reappeared near the last few seats.

"Almost there."

"He's almost there."

"Just about done." The passengers relayed the message up the aisle.

Fwooomp! I hit it again. Counted to thirty. *Fwooomp!*

"One more."

"Just one more."

"Last one."

Fwooomp! The vibration had grown weaker with the distance. I worried that my control weakened as well, but the last child vanished as I threw the levers forward. I counted off the seconds. I heard laughter from the child, a girl with a red bandana hiding her bald head. She reminded me of Gabby Calbert with her pirate bandana.

The marshals hit their car horn impatiently. The bus driver tapped hers in reply. She flicked her lights at the rear of the SUV. The marshals pulled slowly away.

"Are we there yet?" The driver searched her mirror.

Fwooomp! Lewko's long hair and white t-shirt popped into view at the back of the bus. He turned to start up the aisle but was stopped almost immediately by hands reaching for him. Grasping his arms. Shaking his hands. Hands that patted him on the back. For the first time since meeting the man, I saw utter bewilderment on his face. He struggled through the loving touches, responding with awkward nods and gestures, trying not to cringe.

The bus moved. I wanted to tell the driver no, then realized her play. She pulled slowly ahead to just short of the railroad tracks and stopped again. She put on her emergency flashers and slowly opened the door. Rules are rules.

Applause broke out. Then cheers. Lewko fought his way forward.

I swung back down into the exit well, ready to shove off through the open door.

Lewko reached the front. He started down the steps when one last hand shot out and locked on his arm, stopping him. The driver leaned over from her seat and with her other hand pulled Lewko down. She kissed him on the cheek.

"Bless you! *Bless you bless you bless you!*"

I pushed myself backward through the open door.

With The Object still in hand, Lewko jumped out after me. In mid leap, shielded by the open door—

Fwooomp!

—I made him disappear.

The bus driver closed her door and released the brakes, combining a loud air brake hiss with a joyful horn honk. The bus pulled forward carrying away muted cheers.

52

I waited until both vehicles joined the upslope and the taillights were obscured by tree branches and leaves. Not sure where Lewko had floated to, I didn't want to simply reappear. He could have been over the river by now.

"Marco."

Nothing. Trying to be funny?

"You there?"

I don't know if he was being dramatic or toying with me, but he made no sound for a full minute before saying, "Yeah. I'm here." His voice sounded choked.

"You need some time?"

He didn't answer, which was an answer. I waited. When something like a minute passed, I said, "I'm bringing us back to visible. You okay to land?"

"Yeah."

Fwooomp!

I dropped onto gravel at the side of the road. Lewko appeared to my left, near the steel truss bridge. He landed neatly on the pavement with the attaché case in one hand and The Object in the other. He didn't even stagger. I took a step toward him, but he held up a stop sign hand.

"Gimme a sec."

He turned his back to me and walked onto the bridge. Ten paces in he stopped and faced the river with his head bowed. His long hair curtained his face. The last hints of twilight hung in the western sky. To the east, stars switched on for the night. Against the geometric complexity of the steel bridge, Lewko stood in silhouette.

I felt a smug satisfaction. The billionaire's involvement with *the other thing* originated with potentials for advancements in stealth technology. Once he gained possession of the pieces that had embedded themselves in the wreckage of the Piper Navajo I crashed, his obsession shifted to possibilities for things as far-ranging and foreign to me as interstellar travel. I grasped the basics—that without having to overcome mass and inertia, ultimate speeds could be reached. Lewko even hinted to me once that he had his eye on breaking Einstein's immutable speed limit, that of light.

My distrust of the man grew proportional to his obsessive pursuit. My first encounter with him at Evermore showed me a laboratory out of a science fiction novel and a man ready to rationalize. Darkly.

Had that changed? When he agreed to become the healing center for *the other thing* a part of me attributed his motives to greed. Amphitriton, the pharmaceutical company that tried to claim a cure for cancer that was the inadvertent result of my random nighttime forays, fell into Lewko's possession for pennies. With the new technology in hand, Wall Street's first blush put the value in the billions at a single stroke.

Yes, there were forces aligned against him. They played their best hand by shopping for an amenable federal judge in Amarillo. I didn't see that ploy succeeding. Not after tonight.

Had something else changed tonight?

On that bus, Lewko touched real people, and they touched him back. Did the hands reaching into the aisle as he passed deliver more than gratitude?

I wasn't sure he had it in him. But one thing I was sure of was that no one could look into the eyes and faces of the children on that bus and walk away unmoved.

I gave him his moment on the bridge.

But not for long. We didn't have much time. We had a bus to catch.

"You good?"

He didn't answer.

"Lewko. The other bus. We gotta go." I walked onto the span, into a forest of heavy century-old steel trusses with their fist-sized rivets and meaty steam-age strength.

"We're not going after the other bus."

"Yes, we are. I'm sure we can find it. I'll call Leslie." I patted my phone and felt a sudden urge to pull it out of my pocket for a quick check. It had been quiet all afternoon. "She can find out where they took them. It's late. They'll want to find a place to keep them overnight. A hotel or maybe a local hospital. It might be harder to get into. We got lucky with that bus. The railroad stop was a stroke of genius."

"We're not going after the other bus, Will." He lifted his head and stroked his hair behind his ears.

"What are you talking about?"

"Control group."

I stopped. The words raced through my mind, producing the worst possible suggestion, one that I refused to believe.

"What do you mean, *control group?*"

"You know what I mean."

"Spell it out."

He huffed an exasperated breath that told me in no uncertain terms how hard it was dealing with people of lesser intellect. "Do I really have to?"

I said nothing.

"Fine. I don't like it any more than you, but we're not going after the second bus because they're the proof. They're the control group that proves the positive result."

"No."

"Yes."

"You're talking about a dozen lives! Children!"

"*Two dozen*, Will. The people claiming to be on a crusade to *save the children* were willing to sacrifice the lives of *two dozen* children with that injunction. Do you understand that? They're willing to call it a hoax, to fight us, to put me in jail. And you know perfectly well what follows. They're coming after *this*." He held up the case. "First, they get their hands on this and lock it away. Then they flood the media with how the kids we brought to Evermore received no benefit from the bogus cure. That was their plan."

"Bullshit."

"Not bullshit, Will. Don't tell me you haven't considered this. Because you fear their success. You fear them coming for you. Why else have you tried so hard to stay out of the public eye?"

He wasn't wrong. I wasn't about to admit it.

"I'll go back and cop to what I've done here. They'll arrest me. I'll be out of jail by morning and an army of lawyers will be all over them. I'll be on every news outlet telling them what happened here. And the world will medically monitor *all twenty-four kids*—both buses—and guess what?" He spread his hands triumphantly. I didn't have to guess. He didn't need to explain.

"No."

"Yes, Will. By making the move they did, they cut their own throats. *When these twelve kids live, we have them! We own them!*"

I gaped at him.

"You mean when the other twelve kids die."

"Or stay in conventional treatment until we can prove our point. Six, eight weeks, tops. Very few of those kids have such a short-term diagnosis."

"*Very few?* Which few? Which ones get to die?"

He averted his eyes. He looked out over the river. "We'll get an emergency hearing at the appellate court. I'll buy a hospital and get out from under this licensing bullshit. The control group test plays out and we hammer the result in the media. You stay protected."

"Don't you dare make this about me." I took a step toward him in the dark. "What's to stop me from just taking those pieces from you right now?" I could. I saw it in my mind's eye.

"Nothing," he said serenely. "Nothing at all. And then I'm out of the picture. Is that what you want? Me gone? Or would you rather use my money, my lawyers, my doctors, my hospital? *My ass to cover your ass, Will.*"

I didn't answer.

"Right." The smirk bloomed on his face. "We do this my way. Or not at all."

I said nothing. He waited me out.

"It didn't affect you at all, did it."

"What?"

"Looking them in the eye. Seeing them up close. Hurting. Dying, yet still so full of life. It didn't touch you at all."

He didn't speak.

I pulled the BLASTER from my pocket.

"Get your own goddamned ride home."

Fwooomp!

53

The problem with making a dramatic exit is what follows. I vanished close enough to a steel bridge support to reach out and grab it. A quick tug pulled me over the waist-high rail and into the air above the river. I shoved the power slide control with my thumb and aimed high, shooting almost straight up into the night sky. Lewko merged with the black-on-black shadows and structure of the bridge below me. He did not call out.

I climbed until the lights of Evermore appeared in the distance. Haze and humidity gave the lights a fuzzy quality. I reversed the power to stop the climb.

Now what?

You don't just brand twelve children a *control group* and then walk away to see who dies first or fastest. It was insane. Six to eight weeks? Six to eight weeks of deterioration, pain, nauseating treatments, hope and failure. Six weeks of parents *knowing* that the other twelve kids, the other bus, received a life-saving treatment while doctors and scientists and media pundits watch your child die. For what? To prove what we already knew?

The thrill of victory. The agony of defeat.

I was told once that was a narrative line to the opening of a sports program. Tonight, I felt both. Never, in all the stealthy visits I made to hospital rooms, had I seen the result so appreciated. By the time that bus reached its destination it would be carrying a load of suddenly hungry children, kids who may not have been able to hold down solid foods this morning. I knew that those parents, better than any doctor or scientist, would see immediate changes. I'd seen those changes. In Gabby Calbert. In another girl who all but attacked a vending machine in a hospital cafeteria. In a girl sprouting a fresh head of hair at a funeral in Brainerd, Minnesota. It can happen fast. I wanted to feel exhilarated for what we had done, yet I felt helpless and ashamed. Of Lewko and his cold calculations. Of the media and their relentless search for scandal to feed ratings. Of the federal judge who thought he knew better than doctors or science what a human body needs to survive. Of the mountains of dark money that moved to block us, invoking the Word of God and substituting *thoughts and prayers* for genuine healing.

Bastards.

I hung in the night air alone, churning these thoughts. Feeling failure. For the kids on the other bus. For Candice. For Earl.

I had no idea where to go or what to do.

PART III

54

My stupid phone battery died sometime in the afternoon, probably around the time I sipped Corona on Lewko's stone patio. I learned this after making a landing where the road crested the hill above the steel truss bridge. I would have landed on the bridge again, but Lewko's ride had not yet arrived, and I wasn't about to return and ruin my dramatic exit.

I should have checked the phone earlier. I keep an emergency backup battery in my flight bag. Plugging it in would have brought my phone back to life instantly—if I had my flight bag, which was in the back seat of Leslie's rental. If I hadn't been such a drama queen and bolted from Lewko's company—if I had taken him back to his hillside home, plugging in would have been quick, easy, and private—with a cold beer to cool my anger.

I assessed my options. Returning to Lewko was a non-starter. I wasn't about to endorse his plan to let half of the kids he had gathered slowly die to prove a point. Landing in Evermore meant cameras and facial recognition. I had no choice but to head for territory outside the eyes of the Lewko Empire. Without my iPad or phone as a map, I wasn't sure where to find the nearest cluster of civilization. Nor could I connect with Leslie.

I decided to start at the circus on the main road into Evermore. The highway south would eventually lead to something, a gas station, a motel, a convenience store.

Fwooomp!

I vanished, but before ascending through the tree branches again, I used the BLASTER to glide a short distance into the woods and deal with another need that had been pressing since consuming Lewko's beer.

Launching a stream of pee out of thin air usually cracked me up—at least the twelve-year-old in me. This time I didn't even crack a smile.

THE ANSWER to my phone problem revealed itself.

At the Evermore border, the highway remained clogged with vehicles, roadside tents, police, and protesters. The anti-treatment side of the fence had thinned substantially. A federal judge blessing their protest with an injunction must have been deemed enough of an accomplishment that the main body of protesters left. A few true believers still marched up and down the fence, holding the line against Satan, if their preprinted signs were to be believed.

The media vans remained present and active. Bars of lights illuminated on-air reporters standing in front of cameras with microphones in hand, delivering live and up-to-the-minute reports. I wondered what they had to say. More of the same, probably. Or perhaps reporting that the intensity of the protests had decreased. Or that federal buses are now reported to have moved the children to an undisclosed location. Or that—breaking news—nothing is happening.

A group of people lined up at a food truck featuring Mexican cuisine. My empty stomach chimed in with a list of demands. Someone down there probably had a battery phone charger I could borrow, at least long enough to check in with Leslie and arrange a rendezvous. Just about everyone had their phones out.

I descended toward the back of the food truck, toward the shadow the boxy rolling restaurant cast on the shoulder of the highway behind the truck. I maneuvered into darkness beneath an exhaust fan that nearly killed me with empanada aroma.

Fwooomp!

My boots touched the gravel with enough forward motion to make it look like I walked out of thin air. One of my better landings. I wished someone had seen it just as much as I hoped no one had.

I rounded the front of the truck and joined the line to order. Cameras all over Evermore were the reason I avoided the cafés in Lewko's town. Here, given the makeshift nature of the vehicle-clogged highway, the itch that comes with being watched faded. Still, I wished for one of the Essex County Air Service ball caps I keep in my flight bag.

Everyone in the food line stared at their phones. A few people shared phones and chatted back and forth about the images onscreen. Like sports fans, several cried out in favor of their team, or whatever image they watched.

"Yes!"

"Amazing!"

"Look at this! He fucking did it!" This last came from a young man in line who waved down two complete strangers to share his joy.

Everyone watched.

I leaned toward the man in front of me. He wore a windbreaker with a CBS television station affiliate logo, Action News 11.

"Excuse me for asking. What's the big attraction?"

He turned and tossed me a grin. "Lewko. He just gave that asshole federal judge the finger. Check it out." He held up an oversized phone.

There he was. Lewko, standing in the bus aisle. Leaning toward a small boy. Holding out The Object. Behind him, faces watched over seatbacks. Farther still, an empty space beside the passenger grip pole at the front of the bus marked where I had floated, switching *the other thing* on and off.

Phones. Cameras. Social media. Of course, it had all been recorded and now it was being posted. The billionaire Spiro Lewko at it again. Vanishing into thin air. Taking child after child with him and back again. Not some special effect, either. Captured by half a dozen different phones from different angles. Video of Lewko dispensing treatment against a federal order spread to Tik Tok and Twitter and Facebook. Miracles caught on camera, going viral.

"You can hate him but you gotta love him. Everyone's going live." The news crewman pointed at ranks of reporters lit up by their truck lights. "The feds are probably on their way to arrest the sonofabitch. That's a perp walk that will be all over the morning shows. Unbelievable. He just blew the lead story completely outta the water."

He swiped his iPhone. A new video played as if it had been shot in Cinemascope, except in a vertical format. Lewko flashed into sight, extracted himself from the grateful hug of an adolescent boy, then moved on to the next child, a toddler with a bright red ribbon tied around her hairless head.

Son of a bitch. I should have seen it coming. He did. He knew he was being caught on camera. He knew they would post it. One step ahead as usual.

"What other story?"

"Huh?"

"You said he just blew that other story completely outta the water. What other story?"

"That werewolf thing. It hit again. Couple hours ago."

55

The news crew guy had several cheap battery rescue backups in his backpack. They bore the Action News 11 logo and the tagline "News That Matters" along with the CBS eye logo. He insisted I take one with his compliments. They get a ton of them at the station, he said. I pocketed the small cylinder, thanked him, and offered to buy him a taco dinner. He gave a *pro forma* argument but accepted my offer when we reached the front of the line. I pressed him for details about the werewolf, but all he knew was that it had taken another life in Minnesota. He thanked me and carried his dinner off to his truck. I wolfed down a pair of tacos standing in the middle of the highway beside several dozen other people. The buzz around me continued. Everyone had a phone in hand. Everyone talked about Lewko sticking it to a federal judge who most people seemed to consider either a moron or outrageously biased.

After finishing off the tacos and depositing the wrappers in a litter-loaded barrel beside the food truck, I connected my dead phone to the rescue battery. The bite-from-the-Apple logo awoke onscreen, giving me a feeling of reassurance that I wasn't sure I liked.

The screen worked its way through a scroll bar. I walked away from the front-line action. I didn't get far. The march of notifications filling my screen stopped me in my tracks.

Missed call—Andy.

Missed call—Leslie.

Missed call—Leslie. (There were four more.)

Missed call—Pidge.

Then there were text messages.

Where are you? (Leslie.)

Call me. (Andy.)

WTF?! (Pidge.)

I walked off the road, slipped between a pair of parked law enforcement vehicles, and jogged down one side of a small ditch and up the other. The ditch prevented vehicles from straying off this part of the highway. On the other side of a one-wire fence, a field of ready-for-cutting clover stretched away into darkness. New dew on the cloverleaves glittered in the spilled light from the TV trucks. The dew soaked my jeans. I walked until my shadow lost definition, nearly halfway across the field. I turned around so that my phone screen wouldn't be a beacon in the darkness. This part was tricky.

Fwooomp! I vanished. The cool sensation washed over me. The phone in my hand disappeared with me. I lifted the phone and cupped my other hand under it, then dropped the phone. It flashed back into sight. I caught it and held it steady. It remained visible and responded to my touch. The screen woke up. I tapped in my access code.

First things first. Andy answered after three rings.

"Hi gorgeous."

"You wouldn't say that if this were a video call. I'm a wreck. Where are you? I'm getting news feeds about Lewko. I heard there was an injunction. I thought everything was supposed to happen tomorrow."

I explained, expecting her to join my outrage at Lewko's calloused handling of the situation. Andy was briefly silent, then conciliatory.

"Will, it's all going to work out. He won't let those kids be harmed. I really believe that. You've got to give this a chance."

I made a mental note to drag Andy along the next time I had to induce *the other thing* on a busload of afflicted children. She might not be so forgiving of the billionaire's strategic thinking after seeing their faces—their parent's faces. I wondered what the parents on the other bus were thinking as Lewko's viral videos hit their phones.

My wife changed the subject. "Did you see what happened in Minnesota?"

"I've been in radio silence for the last few hours. But I hear there's another werewolf killing."

"It's on the news. I tried calling Lieutenant Turinski, but he's insulating himself with voicemail."

"Was it at the lodge? That guy Minelli?"

"They're not saying a name on the news, but it sounds like it was on a highway. Someplace between a town called Bonnie and Big Fork?"

"Beaudry?"

"That's it. Beaudry and Big Fork."

It's expanding its territory. The instant the thought crossed my mind, I almost laughed, thinking about the criticisms I'd received for quoting nature programs on television. Here I was thinking about an inventive murderer like he was some kind of exotic species. Richard Attenborough narrating the hunting and mating habits of the North American Werewolf. Jesus.

Do Not Follow. Strangely, Earl's scrawled message gave me a gut feeling that he wasn't the new victim. I felt no less agitated by his disappearance, but a part of me argued that his disappearance protected him now as it had on the shore of Renell Lake.

"I need to talk to Leslie."

"She called. She's been trying to reach you."

"My phone was dead, but I picked up a charging battery."

"When are you coming home?"

"I wish I knew. How are you feeling?"

"Next time we decide to get pregnant, just take me down to Great America and put me on their roller coaster for a couple hours."

"Next time?"

"You know what I mean. I've never had so many ups and downs."

We talked. Or rather she talked, and I listened. Her job was to perform a biological miracle. My job was to shut up and listen, take the blame, take the hits, and offer apologies for anything and everything. I took some pride in recognizing that and patted myself on the back for doing it well.

I listened, commiserated, apologized.

The whole time, I imagined a gruesome scene several hundred miles northwest of her.

56

"You've been busy." Leslie less than surprised by my call. "Does this mean you and your federal pals are going to arrest Lewko?"

"I'd have to get in line. The state's making a move on him for running an illegal hospital. I like his countermoves, though."

Yeah, well you weren't there. I bit back the retort and instead gave Leslie the inside play by play. "Any chance you know where the other bus went?"

"I can ask. You did that right under the noses of the marshals?"

"Pretty much."

"I know those guys. I am *never* going to let them hear the end of it." Leslie laughed. "It sounds like your operation is shut down. At least for now. Are you staying?"

"I don't know where. I'm not going to Lewko's Batcave. I don't want to show up on a camera in Lewko's little village. It's getting late." For once, despite having vanished, I could see the time on the screen of my phone. I held it facing away from the road. "I might as well head back down to Charlotte. Can you come and pick me up?"

"What am I? Your taxi service? And yes, I'll come and pick you up."

"First, scare up a list of the kids on the second bus and tell me where they're taking them."

"Why? You think you can track them down and get to all of them? You do know that at least one of those kids is from Texas. She was named in the filing for the injunction. That's how they shopped the jurisdiction and found the right judge."

"So, I'll go to Texas if I have to."

"Why don't you cool off a little and see what shakes out in the next few days. I understand your concerns, but a few days will not hurt."

"Yeah. That's the thing. *Those kids are hurting every day*." I realized I said it sharply. She waited, saying nothing. Silence prompted me for the apology she deserved. "Sorry."

"Like I said. Give yourself a chance to cool down. The good news is that this development has the alphabet agencies regrouping. They know they can't confiscate the tech now and pretend it never existed. Doesn't mean they're out of it. It just means they need to reevaluate. And their focus is on Lewko and his mobilizing army of lawyers."

I wanted to agree with her but the idea of federal agencies wringing their hands over Lewko didn't diminish the letdown of allowing the second bus to get away.

I said nothing. She waited, then filled the silence.

"I'll drive you back to Charlotte. We can talk about your mystery photo on the way."

57

Another hour passed before I strapped into the front seat of Leslie's SUV. We met at a quiet intersection several miles south of the circus. Leslie picked a spot where a narrow country road crossed the larger highway into Evermore. Finding it at night on unlit country roads proved nearly impossible. I had to make several hops, landing each time to make my phone reappear and tell me where I was. Despite the navigational issues, I reached the rendezvous ahead of Leslie. She arrived from the south and made a left onto the smaller road, then performed a U-turn and rolled up to the stop sign where I'd anchored myself. I pushed off and floated to her car door, opened it, and pulled myself in. The usual fumbling with the safety belt followed. Settled in, I pulled the door shut. She waited for a break in traffic, then took off back the way she had come.

"Do you want to talk about it?"

"What?"

"Lewko."

"First tell me where the second bus went."

She shook her head. "That's a closely guarded secret after what Lewko did. The Texas people are livid. The North Carolina AG says he's issuing an arrest warrant for Lewko for the hospital thing. Texas wants to issue one for the parents of the girl from Austin. They want to charge them with child abuse for bringing her here and subjecting her to untested medical treatment."

Jesus Christ, I thought.

"Was she on the bus? The one we did?"

Leslie smiled. "Yes."

Well, at least there was that. I said nothing for a few miles. Leslie broke the silence.

"His name is Anthony Caniglierie. Ring a bell?"

"Who?"

"The guy in your photo."

"Oh. No. Should it?"

Leslie shrugged. "You tell me. I thought maybe you heard the name up at that lodge. By the way—did you see the news?"

"I did."

"You going to tell me about it?"

"I planned on asking you the same thing—but hold that thought. The guy in the photo—Anthony whatzisname—who is he? Or was he? The photo looks kinda old."

"The photo was taken in 1963, the summer before Kennedy was shot."

"That's specific. Did you get that off the car?"

"No. There's a record of Caniglierie and the two other men in the photo, Rudolph Morris and Gianni Martini, entering the country through Canada in the summer of '63."

"Johnny Martini? Seriously? These guys sound like the mob."

"Bingo. Caniglierie has been a loyal mob soldier and captain for over sixty years. He started out under the Bruno Crime Family, then survived the changeover to Philip 'The Chicken Man' Testa, then made the transition to the Scarfo Crime Family. Scarfo went to prison and Geno Morretti took over. This was around the millennium. Morretti got a ten-year prison sentence in 2011, but continued to run the organization from his cell, largely with the help of...drum roll, please... Caniglierie."

"Jeez. I'm going to have to rewatch *The Godfather*."

"Morretti just got out a year or so ago, and guess who was there to greet him?"

"Our guy. He must be in his eighties by now. Kudos for surviving all those bosses. I presume these guys clean house when there's a change in management."

"Sometimes. Caniglierie had an advantage, which relates to that photo and that specific timeline." Leslie paused. I suspected it was for dramatic effect.

"Okay? By the way, how long do I have to stay out of sight here?"

"Until I drop you off. I can't have some traffic cam catch me with you in an FBI rented vehicle. Too many possible connections to explain. Get comfy."

I grabbed the overhead assist grip with my right hand and tucked my left arm under the lap belt. It was as comfy as I was going to get.

Leslie seemed anxious to tell me her findings.

"Fine. So, why was Caniglierie's photo taken at Renell Lodge in 1963?" *And why was it the only photo not up on Candice's board?*

"That photo might verify something that has been long suspected, but never proven."

"You're dangling teasers Leslie."

She grinned. "I know. It's delicious."

"Get on with it."

She laughed. "In the summer of 1963 a Lufthansa flight leaving Brussels was stopped on the taxiway by a truck painted in Lufthansa markings. The truck was not authorized to be there, but remember, this is long before airports had the kind of security they have today. Some confusion followed. Just enough confusion for three men to board the plane with guns and get the crew to open the cargo door. One of the three then held the passengers and crew at gunpoint while the other two searched the cargo hold. Cargo bay? What do you call it?"

"The place under the floor where the luggage is stowed."

"Fine. The two men found four unmarked lock boxes, which they off-loaded into the truck. They closed the cargo door, signaled the third man to jump off, and then drove away, leaving the rest of the plane and passengers untouched. This is all before terrorists figured out the benefits of hijacking airliners. Nothing political about it. This was a straight up daylight robbery. The truck drove out the airport gate and was found burned four days later in the French countryside."

"What was in the truck?"

"When it was found? Nothing."

"What was in the airplane that ended up on the truck?"

"One hundred and twelve million in diamonds, gems, gold, and other assorted compact valuables. I think there were a couple stamps worth a ton of money. It was the largest robbery haul in history up to that time. And that one hundred and twelve million is the 1963 value. Today that would be, I don't know, a shitload of money. Plus, there's the appreciation of the assorted valuables. We might be talking half a billion in today's dollars."

I whistled my own appreciation.

Leslie continued. "Not one dime's worth of the take was ever found. Nor were the three men who did the robbery."

"The three guys in the photo?"

"Carniglierie and his pals were on a list of possible suspects compiled by the French and Belgian police. They were in Europe at the time. They had underworld connections to other known players. The Belgian police said that in addition to the three actors taking the plane, they estimated at least another two to three actors were required for logistics. Getting the truck. Painting the truck. Gate access. That photo of Caniglierie, Morris, and Martini corroborates evidence that the three men traveled from Europe to Montreal, and then entered the United States by crossing the Canadian border up around International Falls."

"With the loot?"

Leslie shrugged. "Like I said. The loot was never found. But here's the thing. Caniglierie's survival across multiple mob bosses is no accident. He has long been considered even more Teflon than Gotti. He never made a move for the top spot. He's been loyal to each succeeding boss. And he had something just about every one of the bosses found useful. They sometimes called him The Banker."

"Money."

Leslie tapped her nose. "Did you ever read Vincent Teresa's book? It's called *My Life in the Mafia.*"

"Never heard of it."

"It's practically required reading at The Academy."

"Who's Vincent Teresa?" The crooked smile on Leslie's face told me I just asked a pilot to describe a favorite airplane. She wiggled a little, settling in her seat.

"Vincent Charles Teresa may have been the single most important government witness against the mob in U.S. history. He wasn't just some soldier like Valachi. He ran at the top. He was brutal. An enforcer. A planner. He was loyal, too. Teresa got caught and went to prison and he kept his mouth shut and he probably would have served his time in silence except his associates made a mistake. They threatened him and then his wife. And that was that. Teresa accepted a protection deal he had previously and quite adamantly turned down."

"He ratted out the guys that did the robbery?"

"What? No. No, Teresa had nothing to do with Caniglierie. I don't think their paths ever crossed."

"Then what does Vincent Teresa have to do with—?"

"I'm getting there. Stop interrupting. In Teresa's book he talks about his days of doing bank and armored car jobs. And how the planning and prep for these jobs always took money. Money for cars. Money for guns. Money for staking out armored car routes or banks or whatever they were hitting. Most of the time, Teresa himself was broke. The man was an incorrigible gambler who generally lost everything he made. The robberies and bank jobs needed a money man. Back in the day, Caniglierie was a money man. People with a plan went to Caniglierie. He gave a thumbs up or thumbs down. Thumbs up, and the job got financed. And then a big piece of the take went back to Caniglierie and his bosses."

"And you're saying Caniglierie's seed money came from the Lufthansa job?"

Leslie aimed a pointed finger at the sunroof. "Ah! That was one rumor. There were others. Oil leases he stole off some family in Oklahoma. An armored car robbery. A job in Montreal. Nobody ever knew for sure. Some said he liked to cultivate the Lufthansa story because it remains one of the greatest unsolved cases in history. Caniglierie wasn't like Teresa. He never threw money around. He never went in for the flashy cars and flashy women. He wasn't a gambler. He collected what he loaned out, plus his piece of the action whether they scored or not. Woe betide anyone who didn't pay."

"*Woe betide?*"

"We have him on the books for a score of murders. In the late nineties we got him indicted. The case went to trial, but a jury acquitted him. Everybody knew it was jury tampering, but the prosecutors decided not to try him again. So, yeah, he has a reputation. Stone cold killer. Part of the legend he established early on because of what everybody thinks he did after the Lufthansa job."

"Which was?"

"After they crossed the border, Caniglierie's pals dropped out of sight."

"Probably living out their days on a beach drinking umbrella drinks and cashing in diamonds."

"That's one story. But none of the jewels ever turned up. A job like that, something's always getting fenced. That's how we catch the baddies. Not this time. The rumor, which Caniglierie also liked to cultivate, was that he killed both partners and took their shares. Nobody knows."

"He's still around?"

"Oh, yeah."

"Retired?"

Leslie laughed. "These guys don't retire. Well, maybe some of the top guys get to. Some of the soldiers wind up in nursing homes in Florida. The ones that can't quit wind up taking the big dirt nap. It's a rough business and there's no 401(k). No, Tony Caniglierie still has a hand in the game. He likes to tell the Bureau he's more concerned with his golf score than making a score, but he's too highly placed. And he has another huge problem."

I didn't bite. After a moment Leslie continued.

"The closest he came to a falling out with the mob was because of his son, Vincent. His only kid. Born around '67 or '68. Caniglierie groomed him for the business. The kid was a rising star—until we took him down for a double murder. And by we, I mean the FBI—although it ended up as a state prosecution. It was a slam dunk. He killed two kids, teenagers, in cold blood during a truck hijacking. Just some kids out necking in the wrong place at the wrong time. Caught on camera and everything. Vincent was on his way to a double-life sentence when he flipped. Total snitch. He got the full witness protection program treatment. That put a black mark on the old man, the kind that usually doesn't come off, but it happened around the end of the Scarfo run."

"Leslie, I gotta tell you, I am gawking at you right now. Seriously. You're a freaking wise guy encyclopedia."

"I did a stint with an organized crime task force a few years back. Too many years back, to be honest. That's where I met Director Lindsay. So, yeah, wise guys are kinda my hobby."

"Impressive. Go on."

"Some of what the kid—Vinnie—gave the feds helped bring down Scarfo. It's widely assumed that Caniglierie got his son to flip on Scarfo as part of a deal to help Geno Morretti who was on his way in. But even though Vincent refused to give up anything on his father, Caniglierie completely disowned his son. They say he even put out a contract on his own kid. Which is even more bizarre because his kid had a kid—a grandchild to Caniglierie—that Caniglierie took in and raised as a son."

"Another chip off the old block?"

Leslie shrugged. "I don't think so. We don't have much on the grandson. He didn't go into the business. He disappointed the old man. Caniglierie is quoted as saying the kid had rocks in his head. So, fast-forward to when Geno Morretti was doing his stretch—"

"His 'stretch'?" I laughed. "With Bugsy and 'da guys?"

"Shut up. When Morretti was incarcerated, it was Caniglierie who saw that his interests were protected, who paid out what needed paying out, who collected what was due, and who hurt whoever needed hurting."

"Still? The guy must be in his eighties."

"He is. And yes, still. He might have slacked off a little, now that Morretti is out of jail. But he's not out of it. Not by a long shot."

"Huh." I wondered, was the photo just a bit of Renell Lodge history? Infamous guests who once passed through? Leslie read my mind.

"That picture. It got your attention because your lodge lady didn't put it up on her guest board. Am I right?"

"Kinda."

"Maybe the lodge didn't want that kind of endorsement from that kind of people. Nobody says it to his face, but nobody disputes that Caniglierie is a murderer."

I let a mile or so pass in silence. Leslie seemed to enjoy sharing the history, but the story had played out and I was no closer to understanding the significance of Candice's decision not to include the photo. It probably didn't matter.

"You said you heard the news?" I asked.

"In Minnesota? Yeah, I saw it. Will, I don't think whatever is going on up there has anything to do with you or your friends. I think someone is doing some very bad shit and it's not much more than that. Really bad shit happens every day. There isn't always rhyme or reason."

"Do you have any details? I mean about this latest attack?"

She shook her head. "If you really want me to, I can ask. But frankly, I think you have more than enough to be concerned with."

"Under other circumstances, I might agree, but I have two friends missing, there are two people dead, and now a third person has been killed. I don't have a clue what to do about it."

"You're not supposed to do anything about it. That's the job of law enforcement. Ask your wife."

"No need to play the Andy card. I get it. But I feel a need to head back up there. It's what Earl would do."

"Earl?"

"One of the two missing. Ex-husband of the missing woman."

"Okay, that sounds like a suspect to me."

"No." I shook my head, then realized she wouldn't see it. "No, Earl Jackson charged in to rescue Candice—the ex-wife. When you factor in the foreclosure and other shenanigans happening *before* we learned Candice had troubles, there's no way Earl is involved."

"Don't be so sure. It's always the husband. Or the ex-husband. Just sayin'."

"All the same, I think in the morning I'll head home. And if Andy doesn't kill me for it, I'll head back up to Minnesota in the afternoon."

"Good luck with that. How's our girl doing?"

Raging pregnant.

"She's fine." To cover the lie, I spelled out some of the hassles connected to the Clayton Johns case. Leslie sympathized. We chatted about trial issues, defense lawyers, and the snail's pace of criminal justice in general. Leslie knew about the Johns case and asked questions. I answered what I could. The conversation made me wonder about Caniglierie's murder trial resulting in Acquittal By Jury Tampering. How does that even work? I thought about the photo of three young men leaning on a Cadillac. Full of menace. Were they flush with riches? And were the bones of two of them buried under layers of rotting leaves in the forest at Renell Lodge? It would be flat out crazy if while investigating the dismemberment of Dr. and Mrs. Yuan, the Itasca County deputies found 60-year-old bones tied to an unsolved Heist of the Century. Or rotting canvas bags filled with jewels.

"I don't get how someone can be untouchable like that," I mused. "I've heard about these guys being Teflon, but to be untouched for an entire career? Scores of murders, you said. How is that possible? Was he associated with Gotti?"

"Gotti was New York."

"Sorry. I assumed Caniglierie was too."

"Nope. Philly."

58

"No." Leslie hurried to keep up with me. She delivered the word with the weight and authority of the bureau that paid her salary. "You don't go anywhere near Tony Caniglierie. Period. Not even if you're inv—"

"Leslie, I'm not talking about interrogating him to build a case for prosecution. I just want to ask him about Renell Lodge. And if he knows a guy named Ray Minelli."

"I said No." We walked to where the Navajo posed on the ramp at Charlotte International. As always, the big twin looked like she would rather be cruising at two hundred miles per hour above the clouds. "Will, you don't have any idea what you'd be stepping into. Caniglierie is probably under investigation. Possibly under active surveillance. You could accidentally set off alarms that crash months, maybe years, of investigative work. Absolutely not."

"Then come with me."

Her hands flew up to erase that suggestion from the board. "Worst idea ever. There is no way I waltz into the Philadelphia field office uninvited. Or barge in on an organized crime task force and disrupt the prime subject of an investigation."

"Prime subject? Sounds like he's been a prime subject for sixty years. I bet they're getting close to an arrest."

She ignored my sarcasm. I opened the cabin and heaved my bag aboard. A departing 737 interrupted the conversation by thundering into the night sky. Leslie resumed her argument by shouting at me before the jet roar faded away.

"You wouldn't even get close to him. He doesn't know you from Adam. You have no business with him or his interests."

"Getting close isn't a problem."

She threw Andy's question at me. "And then what? How do you explain suddenly appearing in his office? Or his favorite restaurant?"

"Which is…?"

"How would I know? Look, Will, these guys are more secretive than the Royal Family. Even his top associates don't get an audience without a reason." She put a hand on my arm. "This isn't screwing with some fat billionaire, Will. I mean it. This is serious. And for what? A wild goose chase over a sixty-year-old photo that probably has nothing to do with some psycho running around in the woods?" Her grip on my arm tightened. "Promise me. I mean it. Promise me you will steer clear of him and his kind."

I don't like making promises I can't keep and I'm bad at lying, but I consider myself a master at the art of avoidance. I sat down on the airstair step, planted my elbows on my knees, and buried my fingers in my hair.

"Hell's bells. This day has been an abject failure. Lewko. Those kids. I screwed the pooch on everything." I stared at my boots on the ramp.

"Leave Caniglierie alone, Will."

I shrugged. "If it sets your mind at ease, I don't pass the checklist to fly tonight."

"The what?"

"The self-evaluation checklist. I'm safe."

"That's good."

"No, it's an acronym. I-M-S-A-F-E. It's a personal checklist pilots use to self-evaluate before flying." I ticked the check points off on my fingers. "Illness. Meds. Stress. Alcohol. Fatigue. Emotion. I'm stressed over Earl. I had a beer less than 8 hours ago, which breaches the minimum defined by the regs. It's late and I'm tired. And I'm pissed. Any single check mark should ground a flight. I'm hitting four of six. That's a championship in the NBA finals." I looked up at her. "You can relax. It's not safe for me to take off. I'm going to flop in the cabin and catch up on texts, sleep, and phone sex with my wife. Don't tell her I said that because she would never…"

"There are such things as hotels."

"Hotels have cameras and leave a paper trail. We've employed stealth this far. Why blow it now? It won't be the first time I sacked out in the back seats."

I stood and put one foot on the step, hoping Leslie would take the hint.

Her phone buzzed. She pulled it from her blazer pocket.

"Hang on." She tapped an access code into the screen, swiped and tapped, then touched and spread two fingers. I waited while she read a message. "It's from my office. I asked for the victim's ID. The one you asked about. In Minnesota. Do you know someone named Pelton?"

59

A *nother reason to track down that photo.*

Leslie's admonitions aside, I had absolute confidence in my ability to get up close and personal with a mob captain like Caniglierie. But I had no idea where to find the man. His home? A golf club? A high-rise apartment? An office building?

I had another problem.

After I watched Leslie retreat across the ramp, I closed myself in the unlit Navajo cabin and opened my flight bag. I pulled out my iPad and took the seat Sandy Stone favors, facing aft, directly behind the copilot's seat. A few screens in, I confirmed what my gut told me about flying from Hickory Regional to Philadelphia.

The route took me straight through the Washington, D.C. airspace.

"Well, that's not going to happen."

As if to pile onto my pessimism, my phone vibrated a reminder of the missed calls, voice messages, and texts waiting for my attention. The phone and the companion battery backup remained in my flight jacket pocket. Despite the nagging, I decided to let it recharge and then dive into the list of people who wanted my attention.

I lifted my feet to the seat in front of me and opened my iPad. The ForeFlight screen glowed overly bright in the dark cabin. The map page showed me the direct line between Philadelphia International and Hickory Regional Airport—a line that plowed right through the most secure airspace in the United States. I switched the destination to New Castle Airport in Wilmington, Delaware, which looked close to the South Philly neighborhoods where I hoped to find Anthony

Caniglierie. New Castle avoided the complications attendant to landing at a major airport in Class B airspace.

To skirt D.C. I built a route to the south of the capital. I tapped waypoints I hoped ATC would find amenable.

"I can't wait to read back this clearance," I muttered to myself, looking at the line etched across several states, the dot-to-dot connection of a dozen waypoints across several airways. "If they'll even give it to me."

My phone vibrated another reminder.

In a minute.

Weather. I switched over to the Imagery page and reviewed the Prog Charts. A stationary front ran from the Ohio Valley all the way to the east coast. The chart painted a line of alternating blue triangles and red half-circles just north of Philadelphia. Low ceilings and reduced visibilities dominated the map from New Jersey to Illinois. According to the forecasts the damned thing lived up to its name. Stationary.

"Crap." I articulated the technical term for airports with less than a mile of visibility and cloud ceilings that obscured the local radio towers.

This development placed new emphasis on the Stress, Fatigue, Alcohol and Emotion check boxes. None of those are good on their own but mixing them with solid instrument flying shakes up a potentially fatal cocktail.

I flopped back in the seat.

My phone nagged me again.

One of the many things I love about my wife is that she is not needy. When I am away, she rarely pressures me to call, to report in, to be there. But things had changed. Pregnancy called for vigilance on my part. If the missed calls belonged to Andy looking for reassurance or at the very least *connection*, I needed to respond.

I pulled out my phone with the battery backup still attached. A touch of the screen revealed a power level at 86 percent. Nice. A taco dinner worth the price.

Screen notifications revealed the caller who was so desperate to hear my voice.

Pidge.

Pidge.

Pidge.

Andy wasn't on the list. I tapped the screen. Pidge picked up the call quickly.

"Where the fuck have you been? I've been trying to get you for the last two hours."

"Hello to you, too."

"We got trouble."

"I saw. Pelton."

"Fuck that. We got real trouble. Kelly's gone."

60

Andy didn't pick up. I felt worse with each ring. There had to be a reason she didn't answer. I was sure she was sleeping. She finally let go after a long day and allowed exhaustion to swallow her. Desperate for rest, her head found a pillow and here I was calling her after eleven at ni—

"Will? Everything okay?"

"I'm so sorry. Were you sleeping?"

"No. I was in the kitchen making an omelet and my phone was in my bag. What's going on?"

"An omelet? At this hour?"

"With jalapenos and peppers. You created a monster. What's going on? Where are you?"

"I'm in the airplane, on the ground in Charlotte. Pidge called me. Did she talk to you?"

"Yes. Hold on. I need two hands for this." The line bumped when Andy put down the phone. I heard a dish on the kitchen counter and the snap of the stove burner being turned off. I heard a pan land in the sink. Utensils clicked against the plate. Andy came back on the line, speaking through a mouthful. "Ow! Hot!"

The phone audio bumped again. I heard a cabinet door, then water running. More clicks and clatters before she came back on the line.

"Sorry."

"You know about Kelly, then."

"Uh-huh. Pidge wanted me to call the department and put out an all-points bulletin, statewide."

"Did you?"

"Don't be ridiculous. The girl took one of your crew cars from the airport that Rosemary II let her use. That's not exactly grand theft auto."

"That's not the issue. Kelly is freaked out about Candice. She's on her way back to Renell Lodge and that's a terrible idea. There's been another killing."

"I know." She said it through another mouthful.

"You seem pretty chill about it."

"Gimme a minute to finish this omelet and then I'll light my hair on fire and call Homeland Security. Darling, what would you like me to do?"

She had a point. "I don't know. Light your hair on fire and call Homeland Security. No. Wait. Not the hair."

"The poor girl is worried. Especially after this latest killing. Taking the car and going back up there—okay, maybe not great judgment. But not a crime."

"Uh-huh. And by the way, it was the banker. The one that foreclosed on the lodge."

Andy thought about that for a moment. I waited.

"You know the rule about coincidence."

"There are none."

"Exactly."

"Pidge wants to fly back to Minnesota to intercept Kelly before she gets to the lodge."

Andy sighed. "Do the math, Will. It's...what? An eight-hour drive from here? Pidge estimates that Kelly left after everyone went to bed, so say around ten. That puts her at the lodge around 8 a.m. You're not going to make it."

"No, but late is better than Kelly doing whatever she thinks she's going to do alone."

"It's also not necessary. I already called Lieutenant Turinski and asked him to watch for Kelly. He said they have the lodge property sealed. There's nothing Kelly can do. She can't get in."

"You got through to the guy?"

"Of course." Andy doesn't brag, but when she does, I admire her finesse.

"What does he say about the latest killing?"

"I didn't ask because I knew he wouldn't answer."

"I told Pidge not to fly up."

"Good."

"Not until I get there. Then I'm going with her."

61

Despite fresh urgency generated by my conversation with Andy, I needed sleep before flying. I texted Pidge to tell her to wait to fly to Minnesota with me in the morning. I texted my plans to Arun. I didn't recall anything on the Foundation travel calendar, but I thought it wise to ensure that he wouldn't add something.

With nothing more to be done about Kelly, I unrolled the sleeping bag as a pad on the cabin floor. I squeezed into the narrow aisle for such sleep as I could steal. I optimistically set my phone alarm for 2 a.m. but after dozing fitfully, gave up at 1:21 a.m. Cool night air and a cup of coffee from the FBO revved my engine. I filed a flight plan and launched for the long trip home.

Four hours later, the Navajo rendered an I-told-you-so landing, rough and devoid of finesse, that expressed the airplane's low opinion of my decision to make a deeply fatiguing night flight from Charlotte to Essex County. With half of the flight in solid instrument conditions and half of that in constant chop, the trip wore me out. I spent the final hour watching the fuel gauges bounce toward empty. No matter how certain I am that the fuel on board meets and exceeds the distance to travel, I still grow tense when the gauges read low.

Runway 31 at Essex County disappeared behind me as I bled off speed and rolled to the end. Easing onto the taxiway, I got my first good look at the pink dawn that chased me across Lake Michigan. The last hundred miles had been in clear air. The eastern sky put on a show.

Ugly landing or not, I was glad to be back on the ground.

"And what the hell is all this?" I demanded of the only soul on board as I taxied across the ramp.

The Foundation hangar door hung open. The lights were on. Temptation to cut the engines and roll into the big empty hangar flashed through my tired brain. I killed the thought quickly. Too many things go wrong around dumbass decisions like that.

I rolled to a stop after swinging the Navajo perpendicular to the open hangar door. A quick run through the shutdown list rendered both engines silent.

I gathered my flight bag and headset and cracked the cabin door. The air felt 20 degrees cooler than the night air in Charlotte. I stepped down the airstair into the appraising gazes of Arun Dewar and Sandy Stone who stood side by side in the center of the empty hangar. Arun dressed for business as always. Sandy wore the uniform of a kindergarten teacher, tan slacks and a pink sweater with an embroidered kitten prancing on the front. She tied her blonde hair in a casual but practical ponytail. Her attire and appearance dampened my fear that I had completely forgotten about a scheduled trip.

I dragged my bag out of the cabin and hiked across the concrete on stiff legs.

"Did I miss a meeting memo?"

I expected Sandy to take the lead. She holds the official title of Director of the Education Foundation despite handing the duties over to Arun. Excluding some emergency, I could not conceive of a reason for her to be at the hangar. In a couple hours she would take command of her current crop of munchkins at James Madison Elementary School. Sandy normally greets me with a quick, easy smile. The smile was conspicuously absent.

Arun spoke first.

"Will, I—we—felt it was important to be here—uh, as it were—for your arrival. To speak with you about something."

Hard worry shot into my veins. "Is Andy okay?"

"Yes! Yes, of course. No, this has nothing to do with—well, I mean it isn't about—well, come. Let's talk inside." A sheen of sweat glittered on Arun's mocha brow.

"Okay, but I need to grab a shower and change and then Pidge and I are heading out. Did she tell you?"

Arun had already turned and started toward the lounge on the other side of the glass wall at the back of the hangar. He spoke without looking back at me. "Yes, I am aware. This will not take terribly long."

I studied Sandy hoping to glean a hint, but she simply nodded toward the lounge, suggesting I lead the way.

This could not be good.

THEY SEATED me in one of the fat leather chairs that surround a low coffee table in the hangar lounge. I plopped back and savored the plush embrace thinking it would be easy to fall asleep, and that I could not let that impulse gain traction.

"Is there coffee?" I checked my watch, feeling pressure to get moving. If

Pidge had the Baron preflighted, fueled and ready, we might arrive at the lodge around the same time as Kelly.

Arun waved a nervous apology in the air. "I'm so sorry. We just—I should have—"

"Sit, Arun." Sandy touched the young man's arm and gestured at the chair opposite me. "I'll put on a pot. Why don't you get started?"

I think Arun expected more support. Sandy's deft extraction of the rug beneath Arun's feet impressed me.

"What's up, buddy?" I forced myself to ignore the clock ticking loudly in my head. I settled in the chair.

"This is not an easy conversation to initiate, Will. It's rather personal. We are concerned." He paused. I folded my arms and ticked off a mental short list of my most recent offenses while trying to figure out which one warranted such extravagant attention.

Sandy worked at the coffee station with her back turned. I wondered how far her "we" extended.

"Concerned about...?"

Arun cleared his throat and fidgeted on his chair. I braced myself.

Arun Dewar is one of the sharpest individuals I know. It was only a matter of time before he tipped to *the other thing*. That Pidge had not let it slip with him already was astonishing.

Sandy's presence complicated the option of simply confessing and bringing Arun into the circle of trust. My worry over sharing the secret with Sandy took root in her vulnerability. Part of me would never stop seeing the wounded, desperate young bride that Andy and I retrieved from Montana and near death.

Arun, on the other hand...

More than once, I thought about having this conversation with Arun. Letting him in on the secret had an upside. Arun would make a good ally. The young man is a wiz at running the Foundation. He could manipulate logistics to make things much easier for me.

Thanks to Sandy's presence, I prepared to handle the situation by lying. Not the best option, given my ineptitude at the art of deception and my fatigue in the moment.

"Will, I—well—you are a bit of a father figure in my life." Arun locked his fingers together as if in prayer.

"You mean brother. A big brother. Jesus, Arun, I'm not that much older than you."

"Very well. A big brother. The point I'm trying to make is that I—we—Miss Stone and I care very much about you and about Andrea. Your wife is a lovely woman and I—we—hold her in the very highest regard."

"She's my best friend, Will. You know that." Sandy injected a stinging touch of accusation into her tone. She returned with coffee mugs in one hand and a fresh pot in the other. She poured a round. I scooped up the glorious nectar and sent an aromatic shot up my nose while I waited for the liquid to cool. I reminded myself to hit the head before launching on a new flight with Pidge. Hope of grabbing a shower faded.

Sandy shot Arun a glance full of *It's your play, Shakespeare.* Arun cleared his throat.

"We care for you both. Deeply."

"You said that already. Spit it out, buddy. What's this about?"

"Right." Arun drew a bracing breath. "It's a delicate matter, Will. And we choose to broach this matter out of concern for your happiness—for that of both you and your wife. I think you know what I'm getting at."

"I have no clue."

Arun huffed frustration. "I think you do. It's rather obvious. You haven't been very discrete."

Sandy leaned in. "Will, I never asked for the whole story, but the Foundation exists because of you. I know that to be true. And while the work we're doing with Litton's money is fantastic, my position has always been clear. Take the money. Take the airplane. Do whatever you want. I told you that from the start. I never wanted it. Bringing Arun aboard has been a blessing, but if we shut it down today—I'm sorry, Arun, dear—frankly, you can have it. It's not worth what this may be costing. I love Andrea too much. And I know she loves you with her whole heart."

"What is it you think is going on here?"

Arun threw one last pleading glance at Sandy. She issued reluctant approval. I felt the door to all exit options closing.

Arun cleared his throat.

"Please don't pretend, Will. It's not fair to us as your friends. And none of this is fair to Andrea."

"What does she have to do with it?"

"Don't be crass, Will. Are you going to make me spell it out?" Anger shaded frustration. I felt anger of my own stirring.

"Well, pal, either that or I'm going to finish this coffee and gather up Pi—Cassidy—and get moving. The clock is ticking." *When sand runs out, Panic.* "And on that subject—I gotta ask—is she in on this, too?"

Arun shook his head vigorously. "Of course not. I would never share something like this without speaking to you first. I only spoke to Miss Stone because it involves the integrity of the Foundation."

He lost me.

Sandy sipped her coffee and looked over the rim of the mug at Arun, who stared down at the mug in his hands. The young man squared himself up to me.

"Your affair with that woman in Charlotte has to stop."

62

I never understood the concept of deafening silence until I had an engine quit in flight. When an engine quits, a pilot experiences a split second of denial. In precisely the same way, I spent an instant in an alternate reality where the words that came out of Arun's mouth were not the actual words he spoke.

Deafening silence followed Arun's words.

Your affair with that woman in Charlotte has to stop.

I blinked at Arun.

I looked at Sandy.

I could not speak.

Arun, empowered, marched on. "I've been aware of the liaison since I saw her leaving your hotel room in St. Louis. And there have been many nights on the road when you left the hotel and didn't return until just before dawn. I kept a diary."

Of course, you did. I wrestled with laughter gathering in my chest like a summer storm. The laugh struggled against my diaphragm. I bit one lip and fought to hold a straight face.

Arun, keeper of the Infidelity Diary, made his case. "Then, of course, the fiasco of this most recent trip. I was disappointed not to be meeting Spiro Lewko. I don't believe you set out to deceive me, but obviously that woman made herself available for a rendezvous, and you diverted to Charlotte to pursue her. I must ask, Will, is she married as well?"

Ensnared in the perfect diction of Arun's prosecution, my mind jumped to the witness stand.

Defendant will answer the question!

Was she? I scrambled to recall whether Leslie ever mentioned a spouse or a partner. If she had, I failed to pay attention. Was Carson-Pelham a hyphenated married name?

Sandy spoke softly, but sternly. "Will, my priority is protecting Andy. I like you but I can't condone your actions or forgive you for doing anything to hurt my friend." With that embroidered kitty facing me, I felt like one of Sandy's kindergarteners being told that hitting is never the proper response to any situation no matter how much the little shit deserved it.

"Uh…" The utterance escaped my mouth without permission or attachment. I had no idea what to say.

"I would never presume to judge," Arun said, gaining momentum, "but good heavens, Will. Andrea is beautiful and charming and frankly, except for a man's rather disgusting instincts, I cannot imagine why you would risk your marriage. Furthermore—and this is not in the least about me, but it must be said—I do not appreciate being deceived with that flimsy story about that woman being a federal agent. I am uncomfortable acting as an accessory to your…affair. I do not wish to keep secrets. Not from someone as lovely and devoted as your wife. I won't. Not any longer."

Sandy issued a sad sigh.

They stared at me. Point made. Mission accomplished.

Arun stood. "This job means the world to me, but I'm not sure I can carry on if it means upholding a deception."

Having painted himself into the dramatic exit corner, he turned to go.

"Wait."

Deafening silence again.

I had to admire Arun. I'd never seen anyone with such a vault of integrity and the backbone to put it on the line. If Andy, the object of his honorable defense, were present she would hug him.

Andy.

"Hold on," I said. "Sit."

Arun sat.

I pulled out my phone and tapped the screen to life. My watch read just before 6 a.m. so I bet on my wife being awake. I touched the Speaker button.

"Will," Sandy, spotting the image on my phone screen, launched a protest, "I don't think—"

Andy picked up. "Hi. Where are you?" Standard greeting lately.

"I'm at the hangar. Got home twenty minutes ago. Surprise."

"Oh…that's…wonderful."

"You okay? You sound a little—did I wake you?"

"Uh…I'm fine. Morning…you know how it's been—"

"Hold that thought, love. I have you on speaker. I'm here with Arun and Sandy."

Both looked at me in horror.

"Oh. Hi, guys," Andy said. I noticed a hollow tonality to the call. There's only one room in our house that creates that effect.

Sandy and Arun returned awkward greetings. Both stared bullets at me.

"What's going on? Everything okay?"

I held up a hand to say *I got this*.

"Dee, Arun and Sandy think it's time to end the extramarital affair with Leslie. I thought I'd check in with you and see if you're in agreement."

Andy gave it a beat. I pictured her dealing with momentary bewilderment, but my wife is nothing if not quick.

"Do they mean me?"

I shrugged. "I would think so. Of the two of us, it would have to be you, what with Leslie being a proud lesbian."

I divided a steady stare between Arun and Sandy who both sat paralyzed.

"I'm flattered, but I really haven't had time for that sort of thing lately."

"And I appreciate that." I watched the melting, morphing expressions on my friend's faces. "But would it be okay if I keep working with Special Agent Leslie Carson-Pelham of the Federal Bureau of Investigation on matters related to the domestic terrorist assholes who shot the living shit out of our house?"

Arun's jaw fell a millimeter.

"You mean clandestine meetings? Strange rendezvous? Unexplained disappearances?"

"Yes, love. Weird shit going on at all hours of the night because those are the hours they keep at the FBI. The sort of thing that suggests an illicit affair."

"I don't see a problem with that. If you must, dear."

I love my wife for so many things but seamlessly picking up on the humor here ranked in the top ten. I wished she could see the faces staring at me. "Please say hello to Leslie for me. We should get together sometime. I've been so—oh dear—"

I waited a few seconds. The line went silent.

"You still there?"

"I just—oh—oh, no."

The phone clattered. Dropped. I heard the unmistakable sound of a toilet seat thrown up against the tank. Knowing what was coming next, my stomach performed a Dutch roll.

Andy retched.

Sandy and Arun ascended to new heights of looking horrified.

Andy coughed. The toilet flushed.

We waited.

Andy repeated the performance. A nausea coda. Another flush.

The dawn that chased me down runway 31 that morning was nothing compared to the dawn on Sandy Stone's face. I broke into a grin. Sandy threw her hands to her cheeks.

Arun, poor guy, sat without a clue, still sweating lightly.

"You okay there, Dee?"

We heard water run. The click of a towel ring on the wall.

"OH—MY—GOD!" Sandy leaped to her feet. I held the phone out for her. "Honey, are you pregnant?"

From Andy, a hesitant, "Well…?"

Sandy screamed. In the bathroom in our farmhouse home, Andy joined with a sound that might have been laughter. Or crying. Or both.

Arun, utterly bewildered, looked at me, then at the glass door to the hangar behind me. I turned around to see Pidge halfway through the door with her flight bag slung over one shoulder.

Pidge beamed at me from behind a fiery grin.

"You motherfucker!"

PART IV

63

Turbulence slammed me against the seatbelt. Despite sky blue cracks in the towering wall of clouds, the cockpit grew darker. An ugly blue-green tint shaded the cloud barrier ahead.

"NEXRAD paints a cell 40 miles ahead and 20 degrees off the right side of the nose." I didn't bother holding up the iPad for her to see. Pidge had turned off the autopilot to prevent it from fighting the rough air. She held a sharp-eyed squint on the instrument panel and a loose grip on the control yoke.

"That crap's ten minutes old." She proclaimed exactly what I was thinking.

"Right. Ask for a forty-five-degree deviation to the left. We'll hold that for about thirty miles, then we should be able to get in behind it. Big Fork is in a nice hole, but the lodge is on the fringe and it's not going to stay that way. This one is an outlier. There's a line forming behind it, but its slow-moving."

Pidge made the call. ATC approved the move.

Nothing about the forecast for northern Minnesota endorsed making the trip. The bad outlook prompted Pidge to come looking for me because the window for flight was shrinking. A pattern of thunderstorms formed north of the Canadian border and was projected to flow down through Minnesota and into Wisconsin during the day. The bad news was that it wasn't pushed by a rapid air mass. Held up by the stationary front I tangled with during the night, the mechanism generating storms over Canada did not advance. Like some malicious god, it sat on the other side of the border, created monsters, and gave them marching orders. Lightning, high winds, hail and general mayhem were predicted across three northern states.

Pidge's appearance and urgency ended my hopes of getting a shower and a decent breakfast. On the plus side, her demand to depart excused me from explaining to my wife why I just outed her pregnancy. I had a feeling I would hear more about that. On the minus side, Pidge had us airborne in Earl's E-55 Baron before I had a chance to review the weather briefing that she had downloaded. Looking at it, I'm not sure I would have launched.

A little under two hours later, we bored through gaps in the garish colors on the iPad's radar imagery. The Baron didn't carry onboard radar. We relied on the NEXRAD images transmitted through the ADS-B system, an amazing cockpit resource that comes with a catch. The images can be anything from three to fifteen minutes old, depending on a variety of factors.

"Jesus Christ!" My head brushed the ceiling. The seatbelt bruised my hips. The old broken pelvis injury spoke up in protest. "You want to stop hitting every speed bump in the road?"

"Workin' on it."

Despite the rocking and thumping, Pidge sustained a light touch on the controls. Her eyes danced from instrument to instrument, then back at the darkening sky over the nose. We both glanced at the afterimage of a lightning flash ahead and to our right.

"I don't get it," Pidge said.

"What?"

"Kelly taking off like this. Why didn't she say something?"

"Really? She hardly said a word on the way home. She's worried sick about Candice...and now Earl."

"Yeah, but she was over the moon to be back with the baby. Why take off like this? What does she think she can do that isn't already being done?"

I wondered that myself. In our company, the girl had been quiet. If she had ideas about Candice, she had not shared them. Kelly being Kelly, I understood her ingrained reluctance to make waves.

Pidge continued. "The whole time we were in Big Fork, she was itchy to get back to the lodge. I thought it was just, you know, about Candice. About being at ground zero. Do you think there was more to it?"

Spits of rain peppered the windshield. The shower stopped as quickly as it started.

"Beats me."

We rode through another veil of rain. Pidge deviated from scanning the instrument panel long enough to throw me a grin.

"So, when were you going to tell me you knocked up Andy?"

"I wasn't. Andy wanted to wait."

"Boy or girl?"

"We don't know yet. Listen, please let Arun know we're good. He meant well. I think he was mortified."

"Oh, he was." She laughed. "Me, too. You as a dad. That is batshit crazy."

I kept my whole-hearted agreement to myself.

ATC interrupted to ask if we were ready to resume our course. Pushing it a little. We'd barely gone fifteen miles. Pidge replied in the negative. To our right, the sky looked badly bruised. Lightning flashed frequently. I watched the radar imagery. Big Fork remained in a huge hole surrounded by painted cells, but storms were bearing down on the lodge. A channel into Big Fork from the south offered us entry.

If it stayed open.

"Your boyfriend thought I was fooling around with that woman from the FBI." I explained about the impromptu intervention by Sandy and Arun. Pidge laughed.

"The lez? My god, he can be totally oblivious."

"You knew she was gay?"

I got a *How dumb do you think I am?* look. The airplane jolted. I grabbed the top of the instrument panel. ATC asked again if we were ready to turn. This time they said they had traffic ahead and it was either turn or take a lower altitude.

"Take the lower," I told Pidge. She made the request and throttled back for descent even before the controller finished clearing us out of eight thousand for four thousand.

The ride was no better down low, but I began to see Minnesota woodlands through shredded clouds below us.

Then, in a flash, it was over. The plane burst into a bright sunlit sky dotted with innocent-looking balls of piled cotton beneath a blue dome. Cumulus towered all around us. It was like entering a mountain valley. The turbulence ceased. Drops of water raced up and to the sides of the windshield. Contact with the ground below remained patchy, but I didn't care. Enough space existed below the clouds to allow us to find the landing strip at Renell Lodge once we flew the instrument approach into Big Fork.

Pidge made the turn that ATC had been pressing us to make.

WE FLEW the approach into Big Fork in mostly clear air. Over the airport, we cancelled our IFR clearance with ATC and made the familiar turn to 285 degrees. Pidge didn't slow to 120 knots, and I didn't bother starting a stopwatch. She had marked the lodge runway as a waypoint on the navigation system, making the narrow strip easy to find.

On arrival Pidge circled the lodge property, untouched by the invading storms less than sixty miles away. I tried to find the BMW crash site and murder scene, but failed, which told me that the investigators and officers finished their gruesome work and were gone. It made me wonder—in what condition did they leave the forest site? The bodies had soaked into or mingled with the leafy floor. I shuddered to think they left any part of the victims. Even worse was the idea of scraping up every twig and leaf stained by blood, every clump of soil clotted with viscera.

From the right side of the plane, I could not see the lodge or Minelli's cabin or if his car was present. Pidge checked her side and said no. She lined up on a downwind leg for landing, ran through the pre-landing checklist, and dropped the gear and approach flaps. Her pattern was crisp, and her airspeed control was perfect. We turned final with the postage stamp-sized runway dead ahead. She reduced our speed to 80 knots.

"Fuck!" Pidge startled me. She pushed the throttles forward just as she had begun to flare out. I saw the problem the instant she cried out.

At intervals along the runway, cut tree limbs had been dragged across the asphalt. Not terribly large, but they wouldn't have to be to cause serious damage to a landing aircraft.

Pidge firewalled the throttles and slapped the flap and gear levers up. The Baron wallowed for an instant before surging confidently forward. My own hand impulsively reached for the throttles and closed a grip on hers.

"Seventy-five...eighty...ninety...blue line." I read off the speeds. By the time the airspeed needle reached the blue line on the glass—ninty-nine knots—the gear and flaps had retracted, and the plane leaped out of the trench cut into the trees for the runway. I let go of the controls. Pidge didn't comment on my override. She knew better. Her focus had been on not hitting the limbs strewn over the pavement or the trees on either side of us. My eyes had been glued to the airspeed indicator. If either engine had hiccupped below 81 knots—the single-engine minimum controllable airspeed—I would have pulled both throttles to prevent a catastrophic loss of control.

"Who does that shit? I almost didn't see them!" She pulled into a sharp left bank and looked back over her shoulder.

"I don't think it was the sheriff's department."

"What? Why?"

"Creating a hazard like that? If they wanted to close the runway, they would have made it highly visible. Orange cones. Or painting an X on each end. Those limbs looked fresh cut and dragged into place. Somebody doesn't want us landing there."

"Did you see The Blue Whale?" Pidge referred to the powder blue Toyota Sienna minivan that comprised one half of the Essex County Air Service courtesy car fleet. The 2004 model had close to a quarter million miles on it and wouldn't have been my first choice for an 8-hour drive to Minnesota, but Kelly had no choice.

"No. Take us around again."

She rolled abruptly to the right, changing our path so that I had a view of the lodge grounds off the end of the right wing. No sign of the van. The only vehicle in sight was Minelli's Crown Victoria, still parked in the shade beside his Cabin

Number Seven. I wondered about Candice's Jeep, sitting in the woods to the east, impossible to see from above.

"Now what?" Pidge asked.

I pointed at the darkening sky to the north and west. The predicted line of storms marched toward us. We'd been lucky to find the resort runway in the bubble of calm, sunny air, but that bubble was deflating.

"We can't stay here. Best we head back to Big Fork and see if we can get someone to let us put this in the barn before that line arrives."

64

Pidge greased the landing on runway 33 at Big Fork. She rolled out to the end and stopped, careful to call out and identify the flap handle before retracting them. More than one pilot has mistakenly lifted the gear by mistake. She reversed course and used the runway to taxi back to the only available turnoff. A short run took us to a ramp with half a dozen tie-downs painted on the asphalt. The airport had three private hangars, a small shack, no FBO and no fuel service.

Near the mowed edge of the airport perimeter a small herd of deer nervously watched us roll onto the ramp.

"Now what?" Pidge braked to a stop.

I wished for a better answer but had none. "We tie it down, I guess."

Her face reflected my thoughts. Tying the airplane to the ramp is a prudent safeguard against high winds, but it does nothing to protect the thin aluminum and Plexiglas from hail damage.

"Or you can drop me off. I go look for Kelly, and you bug out."

"Fuck that." Pidge goosed the throttles and rolled into a parking spot where she shut down the twin's engines.

I cracked the door for fresh air but stayed seated. I pulled out my phone.

"What are you doing?" Pidge stowed her headset and watched me dial.

"Calling Earl's phone. I've been trying it since that night." I held the phone to my ear for a moment, then gave up. "Direct to voice mail. There's also a missed call."

"From Earl?"

"No. Hang on."

I dialed the missed number. It rang for a moment, then went to a voice message: "Beaudry Public Brew House. This is Leo. Talk to me." Beep.

I hung up. "That was the owner of the bar in Beaudry. We should stop there on the way."

"Well, then let's get going."

WE WERE HALFWAY through tying down the aircraft when I spotted the car approaching. I finished knotting the rope in the eyelet under the left wing and then stood at the wingtip watching. A black Mercedes-Benz, one of the older sedans with round headlights and the land, sea, air star logo upright on the front of the hood, rolled up behind the Baron. The man who climbed out from behind the wheel wore an Australian bush hat with a chin cord tangled in a bushy gray beard. His abundant belly stretched the buttons of a flannel shirt. A down vest enhanced his bulk. He grinned through the beard.

"Morning!"

I met him near the tail. Pidge finished tying down the right wing.

"A nice one, what's left of it." I glanced at my watch, which read just short of eleven, and then at the sky growing darker to the west and northwest.

"That's a beautiful airplane," the bearded man said. "You folks staying long?"

"Uncertain. Long enough to get caught out in that, though."

He gave the dark sky due consideration, then poked a thick hand in my direction. "I'm Mike."

"Will." We shook on it. "That's Pidge."

Pidge waved from where she had climbed back on the wing to offload our flight bags.

"Pidge?" Mike asked.

"Flies like a bird and talks dirty."

"Fuck, yeah. Nice to meetcha, Mike."

Mike's grin broadened. "I got no quarrel with a woman who speaks her mind. Nice to meet you, Pidge. You folks comfortable leaving this beautiful bird out in the rain, 'cause the radar is showing some nasty weather coming."

"Not in the least. Got any suggestions?"

"Well, it happens I own that hangar over there, and if I call my son and get him to come and drag one of his useless old tractors out of the way, we might be able to squeeze you in amongst the rest of his junk."

"That would certainly ease my mind, Mike. Much appreciated."

Mike pulled out an old flip phone and lifted a finger in the air. "Gimme a sec."

65

By the time Mike's son Larry arrived and the two of them debated the Tetris game of fitting the Baron in a hangar filled with junk, I felt certain we had lost our race with Kelly. I found myself hoping the old van had given out and stalled Kelly somewhere, but Earl and Doc took good care of the vehicle. Doc said the Blue Whale would log half a million miles easily.

Kelly would reach the lodge ahead of us.

Larry, a rotund chip off his father's block, fired up a 1940's era Farmall Model M tractor and pulled it forward just far enough to stretch a chain from the rear hitch to the front of a newer tractor, a red and white International Harvester Model 806 with a cab. The 806 temporarily laced both battery and starter. Mike took the wheel of the second tractor and followed Larry out once the chain went taut. The cab of the newer model cleared the hangar door by mere inches. The operation took on a fresh new set of worries when it became clear our hosts did not have a tow bar that fit the Beechcraft nosewheel. Earl keeps a small towbar in the back of the baggage compartment, but it's not made to fit a tractor hitch. This forced some creative wrapping of the chain around both the tow bar and the hitch. The effort got the airplane moving forward but would not work in reverse. At least, not well. Earl's E-55 Baron can be pushed by one strong person on a perfectly smooth ramp. It helps to have two. With four, we managed to get the bird in the barn just as the sun slipped behind towering cumulus to the west. I smelled the coming rain in the air and felt a static charge on my skin.

Mike carefully lowered the split hangar door. None of us were sure it would clear the Baron's nose until it did.

"That oughta do her," he announced.

We traded phone numbers and I said I'd call when we were headed back this way. Pidge, who had been absorbed in her phone, shook her head at me.

"Mike, is there another option besides the local Uber guy? We're not having any luck connecting with him."

Mike laughed. "Donnie Stomgong? He drives school bus during the day. He'd be hauling the morning kindergarten right about now."

"Is there a taxi service? Or maybe a rental car office in town?"

"Here." He dug in his hip pocket and pulled out a key on a black fob. He tossed the key. I snatched it out of the air. The fob had the Mercedes-Benz logo. "Take Thunderbolt."

I followed his gesture to the old black Mercedes. "Mike, I—are you sure?"

"Sure I'm sure. What's the worst that can happen? You run off with her and I get to keep a quarter-million-dollar airplane?" He laughed. "Go on. Larry'll gimme a ride home. I don't suppose you two would care to join us for lunch?"

"I wish. We have pressing business up at the Renell Lodge."

Mention of the lodge darkened his otherwise jovial face. "You know about what's been going on up in these parts, do you?"

"Yeah. We do. Did you know Charlie Pelton?"

Mike nodded solemnly. "We was in the Lion's Club together. I knew his dad before him. I know his wife, and Larry went to school with his oldest. Terrible shame. Terrible to go that way."

Pidge scooped up her bag and mine and trotted to the parked Mercedes. She opened the rear door and tossed the bags in, anxious to leave. I waited a moment, feeling the man's sense of loss and trying to balance respect against an urge to see how fast that old car would go.

"Mike, I'm sorry for your loss and I don't want to be indelicate, but we have a friend who's been missing for a—"

"Candice Thorpe? She your friend?"

"A very dear friend."

"Christ almighty, I pray she didn't meet up with the animal that did Charlie. They say he was spread out all over the highway. Just awful."

"It is." I gave it a respectful beat, then said, "I really need to be going. Thank you both, again. Much appreciated." I made it halfway to the car before something struck me. I turned around. "You said highway?"

"The way I heard it. It was up by Little Dodge Lake on the county highway. They found his car by the road and him—well—all over the road."

"Not in his car? Do you know if he was pulled from his car? Or if the car was damaged?"

Mike tucked his moustache into the hair under his lower lip the way men with beards do, and men with no teeth do even better. "I can't say I know. It didn't sound like it. That's a pretty empty stretch of road."

"So…why would he park his car and be caught out in the road?"

Mike and Larry exchanged glances. Neither offered an answer.

66

I pushed the old Mercedes up past eighty. The highway between Big Fork and Beaudry ran straight through long stretches of thick woods. Spotting a parked patrol car seemed like it would be easy, but not guaranteed. I kept an eye out but did not let up. The rock-solid car rolled like a leather-appointed drawing room on wheels, sequestering Pidge and me against road and wind noise.

Beaudry Public Brew House snuck up on us. The trees parted and revealed the smalltown bar. I braked heartily and rolled into a slot in front of the building. The parking lot wasn't full, but nearly so. At least four utility vans carrying television station markings took up space on the gravel. Despite his grumbling, Leo did a good business off the werewolf scare.

"Why are we stopping here?" Pidge looked up at the bar through the Mercedes windshield.

"That missed call? From the owner, Leo?"

"Oh. Yeah."

"This should only take a few minutes."

"Make it quick. And see if you can get a couple sandwiches to go."

"One or the other, Pidge." I closed the driver-side door before she could choose.

LEO HUSTLED beer behind the bar. Most of the lunch crowd chose to eat at the bar, so I had to go to the end where chrome rails preserved an opening for the servers. I didn't need to wave or signal for his attention. Between passing out plates laden with burgers and fries, he caught sight of me entering. He rang up an order and made change, filled a mug with beer and slid it in front of a patron,

228

then swung down to my end of the bar to pick up a check with a twenty tucked under it. For a man of his bulk and weight, he moved with remarkable grace. I found myself thinking about Lane's physics of werewolf transformation. The creature that tore after me had a certain grace, too.

Leo swept past me and tipped his head for me to follow him. He exited the end of the bar and led me toward the back room, past the Dudes and Dudettes doors. He produced a key from a chain on his belt and opened a side door in the hallway just short of the pool room. We stepped into his office, a broom closet with a desk. I was thankful that he squeezed behind the desk or else we would have been chin to chin.

"You heard about Charlie?"

"Yes."

Leo dropped into a chair two sizes too small. "If that goddamned werewolf wasn't making my nut for the month, I'd be inclined to take a sudden vacation. It ain't safe around here no more. 'Course, it's not like I could leave. Christ, I'm shorthanded as it is, and then this happens."

"What happened?"

"The reason I called you." Leo looked up at me. I pulled out my wallet. "I don't want your money. You seem like a right kinda guy, so let's get that on the table right away. I ain't asking you for money."

"Okay."

"I knew Charlie. And Candice. Them were good folks, both of 'em. I don't know anything about that couple that got sliced up, but Charlie and Candice were as fine as the day is long."

"Why did you call me, Leo?" I fixed a firm stare on the man.

"On account'a being shorthanded. I told you. I got TV people up the ass out there and that little girl what Candice took under her wing shows up this morning and poaches my wait staff. I'm running my ass off out there."

I blinked. "What little girl?"

"That redhead. The one what's been living up at the lodge. I think she's got a kid. I seen Candice with her a couple times. Karen. Or some such."

"Kelly?"

He pointed a fat finger at me.

"Kelly came in here this morning?"

"That ain't the half of it. She came in here looking for one of my girls. Next thing I know, they're both gone. Didn't say a word to me about nuthin'. Just took off on me. Today of all days."

If you're so busy, why are you sitting on your ass here talking to me?

"This is why you called me? With this information?"

"You told me to let you know. And look, I meant what I said. Don't go reachin' for cash because that's not what I want. I want her back."

"Who?"

"Val. That gal from the lodge came in here, had words with Val, and—*poof!*—off they went. You're going up there. I want you to bring her back. Hell, I'll pay *you* for your time. I mean it. I need help, but it ain't just that. I want Val to be away from that place. I'd go after her myself, but this circus would implode. You bring her back here for me and I'll pay you for your time." Leo pulled a checkbook in a weathered leather wallet from the top drawer of his desk. He grabbed a pen, but I waved it off.

"Keep your money, Leo. I'm going up there because I'm worried about Kelly. Now I'm worried about Val, too. I'll see that they're safe."

"I can't imagine what good goddamned twist got into their panties to make them go up there at a time like this with that freak on the loose. Not after Candice and that couple. Not after Charlie."

"Is that it? Is that all you have for me?"

He looked up at me with worry glazing his eyes. "Pray Jesus that's all."

I nodded. He nodded.

I moved so that I could open the door at my back. With one hand on the knob, I hesitated.

"Leo, one more thing. That night me and my pal Earl were in here, there was another guy we sat with. His name's Minelli. You know who I mean?"

"City guy from out east? Tossing 'em back at the end of the bar? Yeah, I know who you mean. I hear he's the one was caretaking the lodge for Charlie and the bank. Guy's gotta be nuts to be staying out there by himself. Nuts or stupid."

"The night we came in, he was talking to—"

"Billy Farwell. Yeah. He did business with Billy and his brother, Dickie. A couple years now."

"You mean work on his car?"

"I dunno about the car. I just know they liked to huddle and talk business. Billy and his brother."

"Brother? I only saw Billy. Was his brother here?"

Leo looked at me like I'd just told him the sky was purple. In fact, when Pidge and I drove up, the western sky was purple, but Leo probably hadn't been outside since opening the bar.

"You're shittin' me, right?" Incredulity dripped from Leo.

"I don't think so…"

Leo chuckled. "I don't know how you missed Dickie. That sonofabitch is built like Arnold Schwarzenegger's brick shithouse. He was playing pool in the back."

67

"We gotta make a stop." I dropped into the driver's seat but did not start the Mercedes. I stared straight ahead, thinking, hearing Lane's calm dissertation on the transformation of matter in my head. It took me a moment to realize that Pidge was talking to me. "What?"

"I said—what stop? Where? Because in case you didn't notice, the whole sky is about to open up and we need to get out there and find Kelly before all hell breaks loose." She pointed out my window.

Purple. Gray. Black in some spots. Mean spirits lined up across the horizon. The wall of Mother Nature's fury bore down on us from the west. Flashes of lightning ignited deep in the clouds. The air outside the Mercedes had gone still in the way that the world holds its breath before a storm.

"Yeah. A stop. Down at the other end of town." I reminded her about Minelli and his car and the Farwell brothers. I said nothing about my conversation with Lane. Pidge was already too deep into her werewolf theory. The last thing I wanted to do was lend it a hint of scientific foundation, however absurd.

"There's time. I just want a quick look around. I want to see if they're there." I inserted and turned the key. The car started instantly.

WE PARKED in front of the Farwell Brothers Quonset-style building beside the black Camaro I'd seen during my reconnaissance with Earl. The jacked up Super Duty Ford pickup was gone. Pidge hopped out of the car and followed me to the single entrance door. I tried the knob. Locked.

Pidge cupped her face against the dusty glass window beside the door while I looked at the security keypad. The LED message I'd seen from a distance the night Earl and I parked across the street blinked a steady message.

ENTER CODE

"Doesn't look like anyone is here." Pidge abandoned peeping through the window and balled a fist. She hammered the metal door.

We waited. No one answered.

"You gonna…you know?" Pidge made a motion with her head, indicating the lock on the door.

"No."

I turned around and looked up and down the street. To my right, the long drive through empty woodland toward Renell Lodge. To my left, the few homes lining Beaudry's one and only street. Directly across the street, a house watched us with windows that may or may not have eyes. I did not underestimate the attraction two strangers in a foreign car might generate for a citizen of Beaudry.

"Do you want to bag this and come back after we catch up to Kelly?" Pidge asked.

The urge to hit the road tugged at me. Still, we were here, and Leo's announcement that I had been in the same room as Billy Farwell's bulked up brother tugged harder. I needed to know more.

"Come here." I stepped to the driver's door, opened it, and leaned in. I pulled the hood release. "Pop the hood for me, okay?"

Pidge screwed up a question on her face but didn't ask it. She went to the front grill and groped through the car's grill vanes for a latch release.

I ducked into the back seat and grabbed a BLASTER from my flight bag. By the time I walked to the front to join her, Pidge found the release and lifted the black hood, which angled up and stayed open.

I put Pidge on my left, between me and the balance of Beaudry. The open hood blocked the house across the street.

"Stay here. Pretend you're overhauling the engine or something." I reached into my pocket and pulled out my Bluetooth earpiece, which I snuggled into my ear.

"What are you—?"

Fwooomp! I vanished. The cool sensation wrapped itself around me.

"Oh," she said flatly, "that. Never mind. Don't take all fucking day."

"Just want to get a look around. Call me if anybody pulls up."

"I'm not staying out here in the rain." She made the declaration to empty air. I had already kicked off the ground and shot up past the Farwell Brothers sign on the front of the building.

I extended my arm and aimed the BLASTER at the back of the property. My trajectory flattened. I skimmed the curved, corrugated metal rooftop thinking it would be damned loud inside the building if the skies dropped a load of hail. The thought drew my attention to the approaching weather. It was not moving as fast as I feared, but it looked every bit as violent as I expected. Boiling cumulus raced toward the upper atmosphere, blindingly white at the top, dark and forbidding at the bottom.

I pushed the power control for speed.

The roof ended and revealed a two- or three-acre lot filled with rusting vehicle rooftops. Several small outbuildings fringed the lot. Channels between vehicle hulks created a maze that joined the outbuildings to the main building. The paths were man-wide and clotted with bits of junk. Boxes. Barrels. Rusting metal machinery. A wheelbarrow with no wheels. The white hulk of a washing machine from another era. A heavy scent hung in the yard. The ground looked like asphalt, but it was not. The earth had been saturated with spilled oil and grease. If anyone ever tried to clear and recover this property, it would require hazardous soil removal. Not that anyone would ever see the value. Not in Beaudry.

Despite the machine curiosities crammed into the space below me, I did not see anything out of the ordinary. Nothing fed the hungry itch in the back of my mind.

The first small outbuilding on my right had a single wooden door. The door hung open. I dropped down to search the darkness inside. Dim tool handles lurked in the black. Belts and chains hung from a rafter. Except for scythe blades hanging on a wall, nothing threatened.

A smaller building beside the first had no door. Rusting lawn tractors were crammed wheel to wheel inside.

I followed a channel between parked vehicles that looked like they had not arrived under their own power—at least two had no engines. The channel led me to the rear extremities of the lot where a pole barn dominated. A chain and lock secured the single roller door.

I dropped in front of the lock and grabbed the chain. Before making a move, I took a long slow look around and almost immediately found what I expected to find.

Cameras.

The Farwell brothers matched their modern security system with equally modern cameras mounted on poles at the corners of the lot, and on the back of their main building. Reappearing, even for an instant, was out of the question.

I turned my attention back to the chain and padlock that secured a handle on the big door. Easy enough. I tightened my grip on the chain and pushed the levers in my head. *The other thing* spread out from my hand. Links in the chain vanished until I eased off the pressure. The part that vanished stopped in mid-link, leaving the steel chain looking frayed and fuzzy. Exactly the effect I was looking for. I tugged. The chain resisted, then parted with a soft snap. I opened my hand and chain links fell to the ground, severed.

I pulled the remaining chain through the door handle and quietly lowered it and the padlock to the ground. The cameras would see what came next. It could not be helped.

I closed a grip on the end of the door and used my hand hold to force my feet against the ground. This gave me leverage. I pushed. The door screamed on rusted wheels riding a track at the top of the door. Six inches. Ten. A foot. I stopped and slipped through the open space into semi-darkness. Old Fiberglas roof panels attempted to provide light and would have if the sun had been available. The growing darkness outside diminished the available light inside.

Fwooomp! I dropped onto the packed dirt.

I took a moment to let my eyes adjust. In the interim, I tested my other senses. Nervous breezes outside caused the metal sides of the pole barn to tick and creak. Oil- and grease-saturated soil scent thickened the air. Burned metal joined the aromas. Welding. Recent welding.

Minelli's auto repair involved welding. Unless they approached from the rear, there was no way of getting a vehicle from the street into this shed. Not through the yard between the shed and the main building. Whatever bread and butter work the brothers did, they did in the big Quonset building. Work performed in this pole barn had a different purpose.

Silver tanks and hoses rose out of the darkness. Benches and shelves joined. Racks of tools. Grinders and other power tools mounted on heavy benches sat attached to big, slumbering electric motors. I've been around power tools. The engine shop at Essex County Air Service has many if not all of the machinery collected by the Farwell brothers.

The brothers had something I doubted anyone else anywhere had.

It stared at me.

A dragon.

At first—before my vision adjusted—I thought it might be some kind of loader or excavator. I expected closer inspection to reveal tracks, a cab, an engine.

No. That's a dragon.

It had a gator-like head. A neck. Vanes. Horns came to deadly looking points. A pair of webbed wings rose beside the hulking body. High behind the monster a spade tipped a long, horn-spiked tail.

The beast crouched motionless in the center of the dirt floor. I stepped closer, expecting to find a body covered in leathery scales. Instead, I found steel. Chunks of cut up barrels. Angle iron bones. Hinged joints. Rows of spikes made from the teeth of a farm combine. All of it sealed and joined by welding beads. As a sculpture composed of discarded metal, it looked brilliantly rendered. One of the Farwell brothers was an artist with steel. The dragon had a viciousness to it. Claws made from farm hay cutters gripped the dirt underfoot. Muscles formed from hammered steel bulged.

I marveled at the work. The beast's shoulders were even with the top of my head. The spaded tail almost touched the roof, causing me to wonder how they thought they'd get this thing out of the shop, which caused me to wonder if the tail or any other parts articulated.

I was nearly so caught up in staring at the thing that I almost missed its companions. On either side of the main attraction, a metal menagerie kept it company. A bison hulked in the dim light. A bear stood on its hind legs. A cat with saber teeth crouched. There were other pieces. Torsos. Unfinished limbs. Some of the work looked old and less sophisticated than the main attraction, the dragon. In a far corner, a steel barrel provided a simple round torso to something that might have been a cow or a horse. Simple. Almost crude. Something a critic might credit to an artist's "formative years."

I edged around the dragon, careful to avoid sharp corners and dangerous steel edges. At the back of the shop, in one corner, a tall shape crouched under a canvas tarp. I could smell the cloth, thick with oil and mildew, as I approached. And something else. Something like leather that wasn't leather.

In for a penny...

The broken chain in front would tell the brothers that someone had been in their shop. There was no longer any point in trying to hide the fact that they had entertained a visitor.

Planting my feet in front of the eight-foot-tall sculpture, I yanked on the tarp. Instead of giving way in a sweeping cinematic reveal, it snagged. I tried flapping it, but it refused to release.

More than a little disgusted by the filthy tarp, I crouched and lifted its hem over my head, trying hard to avoid contact with my hair.

Fur. That was the other smell. And I instantly knew what Pidge would say. And she would be right.

I ducked under the edge of the tarp, then stood and backed away, lifting and spreading the canvas.

The werewolf posed on the attack, arms lifted, claws out. The face was made of steel angles matching the snout I'd seen as it bore down on me on Candice's beach. Glistening black eyes stared straight ahead. Rows of razor-sharp metal teeth lined up under snarling, bared steel lips. The body burst with muscles and wore fur that appeared to be pieces of pelts stitched together.

Pidge's werewolf crouched on long feet made of spring steel. Potent arms ended in Freddy Krueger finger blades capable of tearing open the lodge and rendering the damage we had seen inside. Or producing the sliced and scattered bodies of Dr. Yuan and his wife. This was the monster that chased me up the path from the beach.

Except for one major problem.

This was a sculpture.

I lifted the pelts and saw welded seams. I recognized steel auto body panels, cut and bent to create a muscular body, but nevertheless originating either in

Detroit or Ohio or Japan. I pushed and pulled the arms, which remained rigid. Peeking under the metal skin, I saw framework. No pulleys. No sockets. No means of motion. I estimated the weight at several hundred pounds. This beast wasn't moving from the spot it occupied in the Farwell Brothers' shed, not without a front-end loader. I wondered if it ever had seen daylight—or if this was some kind of private obsession.

Random ideas blossomed and withered. Steam powered. Electric. Mounted on a vehicle of some sort. Animated by magic.

Nothing that raced through my head explained how this sculpture, a doppelgänger of the beast on the beach, had come to life and moved at a speed no man could match.

I fished my phone from my pocket and backed away, cringing at the tarp stroking the top of my head. I shot several photos, then quickly ducked out from under the filthy cloth. I brushed off real and imagined dirt and shook my head to clean my hair.

I shot more photos. The dragon. The bear. The bison. If someone was watching, or someone watched the security camera footage after the fact, they would easily see the photo flashes coming from inside the cracked-open shed door. I didn't care.

Time to go.

At the door, I turned and took one more look at the tarp in the corner. It was the only covered sculpture. I didn't think it likely that the brothers invited visitors into their shop, but if they did, a steel sculpture of whatever killed three people in Itasca County wasn't something they seemed inclined to show off.

The rigid shape in the corner was clearly stationery, yet as I stared at it, my imagination gave the tarp motion. The scrape of breeze-blown brush on the side of the building became hungry, raspy breath. Drool fell from glistening teeth in the open mouth. The blade claws made a scraping steel sound as they extended. It crouched to lunge.

"Jesus." I used the sound of my own voice to burst the moment of imagination. The tarp hung limp in the darkness.

Fwooomp!

I slipped back out the door, floated to the other end, and levered myself against the ground to slide it shut again. There was nothing to be done for the broken chain, but at least the door would not call out to the Farwell Brothers that someone had visited their steel zoo.

68

Pidge flicked through the photos in my phone.

"What the fuck!"

Random fat drops of rain tapped the windshield. It didn't even warrant launching the wipers. I checked my watch. Past noon.

"There's your werewolf. And dragon. And a bunch of other animals."

"Is that supposed to make me feel better? How do they get it moving? Was it —I dunno—hydraulic?"

"Are you hearing yourself? You think several hundred pounds of cobbled together washing machine parts that are made to look scary are somehow being operated like some Disney dinosaur? Do you have any idea how utterly impossible that would be?"

She shrugged. "You see robots on YouTube all the time."

"Pidge. Seriously. Take the absolute best robotic technology available and you still never come close to the kind of power and movement I saw. No way."

"Okay. Then we're back to one of those guys is a fucking werewolf."

If that's true, I know which one. I kept that thought to myself and shook my head.

"Nope."

"Then explain it to me."

"I can't. But it's not a werewolf."

"Yeah, it is. And one of those guys is it. And he made that sculpture thing to cover his own ass. Somehow."

"How?"

"I don't fucking know how!" She sat sharply up in her seat and looked at the side of the highway. "Did you see that?" She pointed. I glanced back over my shoulder.

"See what?" I let off the gas and braked.

I slowed to a crawl, veered right onto the shoulder, then pulled a tight U-turn. Pidge leaned forward, searching, probably for a werewolf that wasn't there. I drove slowly back the way we had come. We were alone on a long stretch of highway. The entrance to Renell Lodge lay just a few miles ahead.

"Stop!" She rolled down her window and pointed. "Wheel tracks."

A pair of indentations disappeared into the woods.

"Minelli said there was more than one way into the lodge property. I think that might be the way. Good eye, Pidge." I turned the wheel sharply.

"You're gonna drive this land yacht into the woods? I don't think that's a great idea."

"You're probably right. But I don't want to leave it by the side of the road. Let's at least get it out of sight."

"From who? I'd be pleased as punch if some county Mountie came along right about now. This shit is starting to scare me. And don't tell me we're walking through the woods, either, because if we don't get hit by lightning, we're at least going to get soaked. Why not just drive up to the main entrance?"

"Andy says the property is sealed off by the sheriff's department. Let's see how far we can get without damaging old Thunderbolt, here." I turned the wheel and eased down one side of a ditch and up the other. We followed the Mercedes hood ornament. Trees passed us on the left and right. I kept the wheels aligned with indentations that marked a previously driven path. A remarkably smooth surface passed under our wheels.

A short distance into the woods, the path made a sharp right turn in the direction of the lodge. I felt encouraged. The way stayed clear. We rolled forward.

I expected to encounter a stump or a ravine or a bubbling runoff creek at any time that would end our journey. Instead, the narrow path wound its way steadily forward. At one point, the ground simply vanished at a ravine. I thought we were finished until I eased forward and saw the trail descend a manageable slope. At the bottom of the slope, a runoff creek flowed toward the lake. The trail executed a hard right turn and continued parallel to the stream.

We followed the stream for what seemed like a quarter mile before finding a crossing. Stones formed sunken pavement. Clear water flowed over the stones, but there was no question that a vehicle could pass through the stream. Someone else had. Recently.

"See that?" I pointed at the entry point. "Tracks."

Dual wheel tire marks, the kind with heavy-duty treads, marked the muddy entrance and exit to the stone ford.

"Somebody's used this since winter," I added.

"Somebody used this in the last half hour. Probably whoever made Candice think she had to run for her life and is about to slice us up like two kids in the second reel."

"Aren't you just a ball of optimism."

I let off the brake and navigated the Mercedes down into the stream, then up the other side. No problem.

A shallow slope rose back to the forest level I considered normal. If my bearings were correct, the airstrip would be off to our right soon. Possibly not visible, but out there and a sign that we were getting close to the lodge.

We crested the slope and nearly ran into the back end of a truck.

"I know that truck. Belongs to our sculptors. Come on." I turned off the engine and climbed out. Pidge hurried to follow.

"Dude!" she hissed at me. "Never get out of the fucking car! Don't you watch slasher movies, for God's sake?"

The black truck, a heavy-duty Ford with dual wheels and an oversized cap on the truck bed, blocked the path ahead. Trees, both standing and fallen, eliminated any hope of circumnavigating the truck. I leaned past the rear quarter panel and studied the cab via the big mirror on the side. It appeared empty. I pointed at the tire tread.

"Matches what we saw back at the stream."

"Duh."

She had a point. Obviously, this was the vehicle that preceded us through the woods. I had to wonder, though, if this trail was the one Minelli mentioned when he evaded the police on his drunken return to the lodge. If so, he did a fine job of driving under the influence. We made the trip in the afternoon, albeit a dark afternoon. He did so in the middle of the night.

Minelli knew the way. Well.

I don't like that guy. Earl's judgment can snap like the lightning that flickered around us, but it is rarely wrong.

I checked the cab. Empty.

"Nobody home. Let's look in the back." I rejoined Pidge. She released the latch and dropped the tailgate, then lifted the cap window which had been painted black on the inside. Not tinted. Painted. Somebody didn't want anyone looking inside.

At first glance, it was hard to see a reason for secrecy. The truck bed was cluttered with canvas like the tarp covering the werewolf sculpture. Bungee cords lay on the tarp and on the steel truck bed. A toolbox sat off to one side. A black plastic case lay partially hidden by the tarps. I threw back the covering and pulled the case onto the tailgate.

"Look at this." Pidge pinched something from the truck bed. She held it up in the light from the Mercedes. "Werewolf fur. Same shit we found at the lodge."

I wiggled the plastic case into position and popped the latches. The lid came open easily. I flipped it over.

The case was empty, lined with spongy black foam. But even empty, it told a story.

"Gun case?" Pidge asked.

"Nope."

I recognized the triangle-shaped indentation in the packing foam. I'd seen the object this case protected. I'd seen it in action.

"That's a night vision rig."

69

"Where are you going?" Pidge asked sharply.

I didn't answer. I hurried back to the Mercedes and leaned in. I killed the lights, then stood still, listening. Pidge followed my lead, but with a stark question embossed on her blonde-framed face.

This time she whispered. "Will, what the f—?"

"Shhhhhh!" I carefully closed the car door so that the interior light would die. I then opened the back door and quickly dug through my bag, extracting two BLASTER units with propellers. I hurried back to Pidge and pulled out my phone.

"Keep an eye out. Watch for movement."

"Jesus Christ, you're freaking me out! Movement of what?"

"Your werewolf. He drove here in that truck."

I tapped the screen on my phone.

"Oh, fuck, are you kidding?" She whirled around and searched the woods around us. "Jesus, Will, you know this is the scene in the movie where the idiots about to die have no bars on their phone."

I touched the Speaker function. A voice joined us. "911, what is your emergency?"

"I need you to connect me with Lieutenant Turinski of the Itasca County Sheriff's Department. This is an emergency."

"What is your location? Are you imminent danger?"

"Stop asking questions. Connect me with Lieutenant Turinski. I have vital information about the two recent attacks."

"Please hold."

Pidge divided her bug-eyed stare between me and the woods around us. She hopped back and forth to check both sides of the truck blocking our view.

"Christ, Will, I told you. Never get out of the fucking car."

"The car won't help us. I've seen what it does to a car. Stay quiet."

I touched the phone volume control to reduce it slightly. We waited. The darkness pressed in on us. Fat raindrops fell around us, sounding like fallen bugs against the leafy forest floor. Or like someone approaching. The hair on my arms stood up. Lightning flashed above the trees.

A voice, still too loud, spoke from my phone. I hit the volume button again.

"Crime-Stopper Tip Line, how can I help you?" I couldn't speak. "Hello? Is someone there? We're here to help. Do you have information about a recent crime?"

I mustered patience. "Can you connect me with Lieutenant Turinski? He's in charge of the investigation into the animal attacks."

"If you can just give me the information, I will be sure that he gets it."

"Tell him to get his ass out to Renell Lodge. The werewolf is there. Right now."

"Sir, there's no need for language. Can you start with your name? Full name, last name first, please include middle initial."

I poked the call end button hard enough to fear I'd break either the screen or my finger. "Shit!"

The outburst did nothing to soften the terrified look on Pidge's face.

"Okay. Okay. Hang on." I steadied myself and dialed a new number.

It rang. And rang.

Come on, it's the middle of the after—

"You know, you could have given me a heads-up, sweetheart." Andy sounded calm, even sweet. It jarred me. I jittered between the panic welling up between me and Pidge and her casual response to the business at the hangar with Sandy and Arun.

"Sweetheart. Listen. Monkeybutt."

Andy said nothing, an indication that she heard and understood our code word for *shut up and take what I'm about to say as life and death serious.*

"What is it?"

"I need you to call Turinski in Itasca County. Got a pen?" I assumed she was at her office, but there was always a chance she was driving.

"Go."

"Tell him the werewolf is one of the Farwell Brothers from Beaudry. B-E-A-U-D-R-Y. It's a costume. Tell him it's at Renell Lodge right now. Tell him to get himself and his deputies and the whole United States cavalry out to the lodge immediately. Got that?"

She didn't answer for a second. Writing. Good girl. "Got it. Will, is this real?"

"As a heart attack. I gotta go. Pidge is with me. We're in the shit and we gotta get off the ground. That thing is around here somewhere."

"Go." Beep. Beep. Beep. The call ended.

"If anybody can get through to Turinski, she will." I shoved the phone in my pocket and traded it out for the Bluetooth earpiece in case she called back. With the earpiece inserted, I pulled out a BLASTER and fixed a prop on the power shaft. "C'mere."

Pidge didn't need to be asked twice. She grabbed my left arm and squeezed herself against me.

Fwooomp!

70

We broke through the treetops beneath gray scalloped clouds. Ghostly vanguard sheets of mist raced beneath the iron sky. Lightning stabbed the landscape with thunder blasting almost instantly, certifying the proximity of the strikes. The huge relief I felt in getting off the ground and away from the truck dissipated. This did not feel safe. Already, the treetops waved and swirled as microbursts of wind tore across the landscape and buffeted us. A few miles away, the clouds touched the ground. Walls of rain fell.

I couldn't be certain we weren't vulnerable to a lightning strike. I had no idea how a thunderstorm felt about me in the vanished state. Did I have a static charge? Positive? Negative? Was I a damned lightning rod? Would a strike blast me out of *the other thing* the same way a gunshot had?

I did not want to find out. Returning to Beaudry was not an option. We had abandoned the Mercedes for a reason, a reason carved in gashed steel in the roof and doors of Dr. Yuan's BMW. I'd seen what the creature did. Driving back the way we had come would be neither fast nor stealthy nor survivable. In the woods, it could cover ground faster than old Thunderbolt.

And we had to consider Kelly and Val. Without saying so aloud, Pidge and I both knew that those girls were well ahead of us, probably at the lodge, possibly being stalked. Or worse.

The lodge. Our only answer.

I wasn't wrong about the airstrip. I saw the cut in the trees about half a mile ahead. It gave me a bearing on the lodge. I rotated Pidge and me to a horizontal position and pushed the BLASTER power as far forward as the slide control would go. Prop blast rushed up my arm and into my face. I squinted against it and the drops of rain that stung my skin. On the forest floor, white marbles bounced off the ground. Those random drops of rain had turned solid. This was going to hurt.

We accelerated. Pidge pulled herself against my body. She covered her head with one arm and pressed her face to my chest. I tightened my arm around her and did what I could to protect her. Hail bit into my head, my arms.

I shut my eyes and lowered my head. Thankfully, the hail was random. Spitting, not pouring. These were bits of ice that had been thrown ahead of the storm, launched out of the clouds fifty to sixty thousand feet overhead, left to fall outside of the roaring updrafts inside the storm.

Keeping my head down, I was able to gauge my height above the trees. I caught glimpses of the airstrip and had an instant to be thankful for the tree limbs dragged across the pavement. Without them, we would have landed, and the Baron would have been parked in the open, fully exposed to ice rocks falling from the sky. God bless Mike, Larry, and that hangar.

I veered left. The lodge roof came into view. The cabin roofs. A dash of powder blue peeked through from under the carport roof where we found Candice's Jeep. The Blue Whale. Kelly and Val were here. Beyond the lodge, the surface of the lake sparkled with hail splashes.

The lake. The thought hit me like a flat-handed slap to the forehead. Of course. That's why Kelly stopped for Val. Val the lifeguard. Val the keeper of the canoes. Val the campout leader.

I made a hard cut to the left. We shot over the lodge roof and over the boathouse roof. I performed a tight turn over the lake and bore in across the raft, which tugged on its chain near the end of the pier. Wind broke white spray from the tips of choppy waves. Without that chain, the raft would be somewhere in the middle of the lake.

I swept in low over the beach and ducked under the raised boathouse door.

They left the big door open—they were in a hurry.

I reversed the BLASTER and stopped us. Hail tapped the roof.

Fwooomp! I dropped my feet to the dirt floor.

Pidge became weight against the grip of my left arm. I lowered her to the ground. She shook herself free and looked around.

"Holy shit! Good thing we didn't park the Baron here." She watched hail the size of a healthy strawberry splash into the water. "Are you seeing this?"

I wasn't. I stared at what should have been obvious to me the night I searched for Earl. This was the reason he'd been drawn to the water. It was right here in front of me.

"Will, we need to go find Kelly and that girl. Come on!" Pidge started for the door that led to the steps up to the lodge.

"They're not here."

"What?"

I pointed. "Look at this." An open space disrupted the neat row of canoes.

"They're numbered. One for each cabin. Everybody gets a canoe. Twelve cabins."

Pidge returned and stood beside me. She examined the row of canoes. "Okay. So where are number seven and eight?"

"That's why Kelly picked up Val. Val was the lifeguard. She ran the water-front operation."

"What? You're saying she and Val went boating? In this shit? They picked a rotten time for that."

"No. I'm saying that Kelly needed Val to take her to where Candice is hiding with Earl. Out there. Across the lake or downriver or wherever they go camping. Candice took the number seven canoe. It was missing the night I came through here looking for Earl. There was a gap in the line. I just didn't see it."

"You sure?"

"About Candice? Pretty sure. It explains why her Jeep was still here after she took Kelly into Big Fork."

"No, I mean about Earl."

"Earl was headed for the water when that thing came after us. It had gone dark. Overcast. And with no light pollution up here, dark is dark. That thing came out of the brush and went after Earl. He was busy looking at something in the water. I think that something was Candice in the number seven canoe. I think she came here looking for us because we flew over. I think she's been hiding out wherever Val takes people camping. One of those islands where the river joins the lake. Huckleberry Finn shit. That's why Earl left that note. *Do Not Follow.* Sonofabitch."

"And you think Kelly and Val took off to find them?"

I pointed at the gap, which was twice as wide. "Yeah. Now there's two missing. Kelly and Val took the number eight canoe. Jesus, I hope they're not out on the water now." I stepped to the door and squinted, but it was impossible to see across the lake. Hail splashes created a mist. Wind drove diving shreds of cloud across the sky just above the trees.

I looked around at the boathouse. "Pidge, this is lousy cover. We can't stay here. Even if we close the door, it's not going to stop that thing. I think we need to get up to the main lodge. Stay close. Hold onto me." I put out my hand. "We do this my way. Don't let go."

She folded her small hand into mine. I've seen Pidge tough, confident, dominant, and powerful. She projected none of those things at this moment. Nor did I feel any of them myself. I felt a knot of fear in my chest.

"What about Minelli?" she asked. "Where does he fit in all this?"

"I have a thought, and if I'm right it puts him smack in the middle of it. If I'm wrong, then he's probably as dead as Pelton and the Yuans. I want a look at his cabin."

"I'm not poking around this place. Not with that thing running around."

"Fine. Let's get up to the lodge. We can wait for Turinski there."

"If he comes."

"If he doesn't, Andy will send the Minnesota National Guard. Somebody's coming. She'll see to it."

"Alright. Let's do this."

THE HAIL SLACKED OFF. My guess that it had been tossed out ahead of the main body of the storm seemed validated. Rain continued to fall in big drops, but they were few and unsteady, as unsteady as the wind, which had gone from gathering force to hesitant and nervous. The treetops spun but did not lean. Gusts raced back and forth as if not knowing which way to go.

I didn't venture to the boathouse door, fearing what I could not see to the left and right.

Fwooomp! We vanished where we stood. I rotated us, then reached out and gave the BLASTER a hard shot of power. It pulled us rapidly out the door, quickly past any threat that may have been lurking on either side. We raced over the water lapping the shore, over the raft bobbing in choppy waves. I made a sharp climbing turn and aimed for the broken windows of the dining room. Minelli either hadn't gotten around to nailing plywood over the damage, or he never intended to.

I pulled up sharply over the deck and lowered us in front of the window.

"We stay hidden," I whispered to Pidge. She tugged my arm in the affirmative. "If Minelli is innocent of all this, he's hiding here in the lodge behind a pile of chairs with a shotgun on his lap. I want to get you settled upstairs, then I'm having a look at his cabin."

"Fuck that. The girl who goes off by herself always gets killed. I'm staying with you, dummy. Never fucking split up. Jesus."

"Okay. Let's go have a look."

Instead of entering the lodge, I kicked us off the deck and started a slow acceleration, this time not going to full power. The situation called for stealth.

We climbed above the lodge roof buffeted by the uncertain gusts. I leveled off and we cruised toward the cabins. Even from a distance, I could see the change to the building where Minelli's Crown Vic remained parked under a tree.

The front door was gone. The windows were gone. Pieces of both lay strewn across the yard along with furniture, books, papers, and boards. The scene resembled the aftermath video in small towns where tornadoes have had their way, except this looked as if the tornado tore the insides out of the building and left the structure standing.

I waited for Pidge's trademarked comment, but she remained silent.

We cruised a straight line to the cabin porch where, days ago, Earl checked the door and then the windows. Equipment cluttered the porch. Crow bars. An axe. A metal detector, the kind found in the hands of treasure hunters wandering up and down public beaches. That would have seemed out of place if not for the conversation I had with Leslie.

If the equipment didn't confirm my suspicions, the cabin interior did. The floor was gone. Nothing but framework over dirt, some of it dug up.

"Will, look. No claw marks."

"They didn't find it."

"Find what?" Pidge asked. "What is all this?"

"A shit ton of money in diamonds, gems, and gold. Stolen from a Lufthansa flight in 1963."

Pidge made no sound. A first. I let her think about it while I looked around.

Minelli's car sat outside. The Farwell Brothers truck sat in the woods. If they found what they were looking for, both would be long gone.

So, where were they?

71

P idge broke her silence. "And you said my werewolf shit was crazy."

I backed us off the number seven cabin porch and rotated. "We'll set up in the lodge and wait for the cavalry." Buffeted by bursts of gusty wind, we recrossed the yard to the lodge entrance. "Stay quiet."

I used power to hold a flight line straight through the lodge front doors—still not sealed with plywood, nor looking like they ever would be. There was no sign of supplies delivered to the lodge.

The instant we floated through the open doors, I looked up at the stairs to see if Minelli had rebuilt his chair fortress. The chairs remained strewn on the stairs, but a clear path indicated that he had come and gone at will.

I pulsed the power to divert us to the second-floor railing where we could see down the upstairs hallway. Best I could tell, the doors to each room were open. No lights. I considered the possibility of Minelli hiding there and decided not to venture into a closed space with a single exit.

We dropped down and explored the dining room, peeked into the kitchen, and cleared the deck outside the back windows. Back in the great room, Pidge tugged on my arm.

"Let me down. I need a drink." She wiggled.

I lowered us to the floor.

Fwooomp! She landed lightly on her feet and marched to the small bar. I took up sentry duty facing the yard.

"You gonna tell me about buried treasure?" Pidge pulled a bottle off the shelf and looked for a glass. Finding none, she twisted off the cap and took a shot from the bottle. Vodka. She made a face, huffed a harsh breath, then chased it with a second.

I pointed at the torn frame. "Remember all those photos?"

"The ones all over the floor? The ones Kelly was so upset about?"

I nodded. "Guests. Going way back, almost to the founding. Candice must have found a stash of photos and scanned them to preserve the originals. What was in that frame was reprinted from scans we found on her laptop, or I should say, Lane found."

"Yeah? So?" Another slug of vodka went down.

"Take it easy on that. Cops will be here soon. Anyway, the photos were torn up by your werewolf. Now...why would a werewolf destroy a bunch of photos?"

"Werewolves. They got no couth."

"Granted. But I think it was done to hide the removal of one particular photo. Kelly said she saw Minelli looking at them and he made a comment about some of them being famous. Turns out, that's true. And it's the one photo that we didn't find on the floor or anywhere else. And we know that because the original was still in the scanned photo folder on Candice's laptop, which Earl stuffed in my flight bag before he took off."

Pidge sent me a look that suggested her patience was getting drunk and wearing thin. "How does that translate to buried treasure?"

"Ah. A quick story." I told her what I had learned from Leslie about Tony Caniglierie.

"A hundred mil? So, today that would be...Jesus."

"Yup."

Lightning strobed through every window in the place. The thunderclap was instantaneous. We both jumped.

"Nice special effects," she said. "That would've been cheesy in a movie. So, you're saying these three guys come here, divide up the loot, then the one guy kills the other two and goes to Philly where he becomes a famous mobster? Then why is somebody looking for the loot here?"

"Not sure. Maybe they divided the loot, then had a falling out. Maybe the other two tried to double-cross the leader and he killed them but couldn't find their shares. Who knows? The other two disappeared. Could be buried out here in the woods. Whatever happened, I think Minelli, or whoever he is, believes it's still here. And what better way to clear the deck and have all the time in the world to search than to get rid of Candice and have the place put in foreclosure? Maybe he plans to buy it at auction."

"Foreclosure is the bank's decision. How would they know the bank was going to...oh."

"Yeah. The banker. Pelton. Who just happens to be the next victim of your werewolf. Pelton, who drives out on an empty road and gets out of his car, and the werewolf just stumbles across him. Right? Are you seeing the flaw in that?"

"He was meeting someone. His double-crossing partners."

I touched my nose. She took a hit from the vodka bottle.

"Jesus, Mary, and Joseph, what the fuck?"

"Candice's bank financials were in a shambles. Money gone. Mortgage payments missed. Yet her copy of the books don't show any of that. Seems kinda strange. Why would she have fake books? Or more likely, how could she wind up in that kind of trouble and not know it? Lane looked at her accounting file and said she was loaded. The bank statements say otherwise."

"She screwed up."

"I don't think so. I think Candice's books were correct and Pelton cooked the bank's books, made her money disappear, and then uncredited mortgage payments or whatever. How hard would that be? It's all computerized. A few strokes in the bank's computer records? Make a few withdrawals she didn't know about? I think his piece of this was to force the property into foreclosure so they —whoever they are—could grab it up and then spend the rest of their leisurely lives looking for lost loot."

"Jesus, Will, that's some nice alliteration."

Pidge was getting drunk. I needed to put a stop to it.

Lightning flashed, but this time it had a blue and red tint and no accompanying thunder. I searched the trees and saw headlights approaching under emergency lights.

"Ditch the bottle, Pidge." She capped and returned the bottle to the shelf, then leaned on the bar looking both innocent and guilty.

The Itasca Sheriff's Department SUV pulled up to the lodge and killed its engine, headlights, wiper blades and emergency lights. Lieutenant Turinski stepped out of the vehicle, ducked his head against the rain and hail, and climbed the porch steps. He stopped in the doorway looking in my direction, and not at all happy.

"Your wife called. She's a persuasive woman."

"Are you the cavalry?" I looked past the man. Lightning flashed again, but this time it belonged to the storm. "Where's the rest of you?"

"I don't like being told to—what did she suggest?—get my rear in gear, so to speak. You told her to tell me there's a werewolf out here?" He remained in the doorway and poked his head into the lodge. "Looks pretty much the same as it did last time I was here." He looked at Pidge, then at the bar. The frown on his already sour face intensified.

"The werewolf is Dickie Farwell. He, his brother Billy, and possibly that Minelli guy who was here, are all involved."

"Dickie?"

"Will." Pidge spoke up behind me.

"The plan was to get rid of Candice Thorpe and—"

"Will!" Pidge pointed past Turinski. He glared at her. She cringed. "FUCK!"

The beast came out of the trees behind Turinski, out of the woods made dark by the black storm clouds. It streaked across the yard at an astonishing pace, bounding forward on long hairy feet as if they were springs. For a harsh instant I thought the sculpture I'd seen had come to life. Huge. Coated in fur. A long snout. But the snout had a tech look to it. Night vision gear. The fur had a slap-dash look. It flapped in places. The arms were long and thick and tipped with wicked blades.

Turinski whirled and dropped his hand to his sidearm. He struggled with a flap or release, then tugged his weapon free and staggered backward. Too late. He threw up an arm.

The beast leaped and sailed onto the porch, swiping one huge arm as he flew. The blades caught Turinski's arm and cut through it. Pieces fell. The blow drove the blades into Turinski's neck and shoulder. He screamed.

Momentum carried Turinski and the beast into the great room. The beast skidded to a halt and shook Turinski off its claws. The man sank to the floor choking and spitting blood. Blood sprayed from the opened arteries in his neck. He slapped his remaining hand over the wound but had no time to either hope or suffer. The next blow brought the beast's other clawed arm down on his head, splitting it open. His body flopped to the floor in a flood of blood.

"RUN!" I whirled toward Pidge.

Gone. The back of her blonde head bobbed out the window behind the bar. She slipped on the deck, then disappeared. The beast stared in her direction. I staggered backward toward the windows at the deck overlooking the lake. "Hey asshole! Over here!"

In that instant I saw how it was done. Curved spring steel formed a long shoe sole that ran out in front of his foot creating a wide, stable foot. The design enhanced his speed like similar designs I've seen for amputees who like to run. The effect held him eight or ten inches off the floor, adding to his already substantial height. Steel plates covered in fur enhanced his bulk. His arms were weapons. Long, thick, with glints of steel plate under fur. Heavy blades substituted for fingers. A wolf's head covered his own head, but triangular gear formed the snout. Night vision. Or infrared. Or whatever such military gear offered. His prey had nowhere to hide—except perhaps under water.

The huge head and body turned toward me.

"Fuck you, dipshit." The voice from within was absurdly high pitched. Coming from the formidable and terrifying beast, I nearly laughed.

He leaped.

FWOOOMP! I jammed the levers to the stops and vanished in a burst that surprised me. I kicked the floor and shot up into the rafters as Farwell swept under me, swinging his arms. He staggered all the way across the great room and through the windows, onto the morning coffee deck. Tables and chairs tumbled out of his way. He skidded on the wet wooden deck, driving his blades into the wood for stability. Despite the costume and the steel and the springs under his feet, the man commanded a masterful grace. Even up close, it was hard to shed the impression of a living, lunging monster despite the exposed mechanism beneath.

He stopped and swung around, temporarily confused by my disappearance.

I threw my hands up to prevent my head from hitting the wooden ceiling. This seemed like a safe place to be. I made no effort to descend. I would have stayed if not for what he did next.

He searched the room for me, then suddenly shot a glance sideways. After only a second's pause, he spun and brought both arms down on the railing. Bending his knees, he flexed and flew over the second-story railing. He dropped to the ground below.

I might have been astonished by the move if not for the horrifying realization of what caused it.

Pidge!

I shoved hard against the ceiling and dropped to the floor. As I hit the wood, I bent my knees for a rapid launch out the same windows. The move failed. I collided with the top of the window frame. The impact stopped me cold. I pushed myself down and launched again.

The second leap shot me over the same railing as Farwell, but on an upward angle. With the BLASTER still in hand, I fired up full power. The prop screamed. I shot forward, pelted by rain and hail.

Beneath me, on the slope to the lake, branches crashed. I knew where he was going and why. I looked down at the stairs that descended from the lodge to the boathouse. Pidge's short blonde hair bounced and flew as she took the steps two and three at a time. She hit the bottom landing at the door to the boathouse and threw a glance over her shoulder.

Black bulk pounded down the hill after her. She screamed.

She jerked the boathouse door open and launched herself through. The beast slammed into the boathouse wall.

"GET IN THE WATER, PIDGE! GET IN THE WATER!"

I dove after them. In seconds Pidge cleared the other side of the boathouse, but instead of plunging into the shallow lake directly from the beach, she pounded across the boardwalk onto the pier and raced toward the end.

The beast dug its claws into the log wall of the boathouse and pulled itself around the end of the building. It sprang after her on seven- and eight-foot strides, closing the distance rapidly. Pidge reached the end of the pier and leaped without hesitation. The beast pounded across the wooden planks, drew up, and skidded to a stop. She landed on the raft floating just off the end of the pier. Without looking back, she dropped and slid across the raft surface and into the water on the other side. She sank out of sight.

The beast paused, backed up, then bounded through the air. He landed deftly, almost lightly, on the center of the raft. Without hesitation, he stepped to the edge and swung one arm in an arc that splashed down where Pidge submerged. He retracted the arm and slashed the water with the blades on his other arm.

I dove, thinking I might hit him in the back, maybe throw him off balance. Distract him.

It was a stupid idea. Vanished, I had no inertia to bring to the fight. If I reappeared and hit him, I might score a momentary distraction, but he was fast. I'd wind up flat on my back on the raft with steel claws in my chest. Even hitting him sight unseen, he stood a good chance of drawing blood, or eviscerating me just by swinging at whatever annoyed him in the air.

I searched for Pidge.

Stay under! For God's sake, stay under!

Farwell traded swings. Right. Left. Right. He slammed his claws into the water. Judging the length of his arms, they sank deep.

I lined up on the near side of the raft and—

Fwooomp!

—reappeared. Gravity grabbed me and I dropped into the frigid early-May water. Darkness swallowed me. I sank to the muddy bottom. There, I curled myself, and then kicked forward beneath the raft.

The BLASTER slipped my grip, but it didn't matter. I groped over my head for the raft. My hand struck a steel barrel. I pulled myself up under the wooden deck.

The beast above me paid no attention. He strutted on the edge where Pidge had submerged, tipping the raft under his weight. His arms smashed down through the surface, over and over. Unless she had gone deep, I feared one of these lunges would get lucky.

I looked for Pidge under the raft, with no luck. I grabbed a deep breath and dove under the barrel. Rising on the other side, the chain holding the raft slammed into my face and jerked my head back. I grabbed the chain. I counted that as a win. The chain was precisely what I'd been looking for.

I gripped the chain tightly.

I focused on the levers in my head. This had to happen fast and all at once.

Balls to the wall.

FWOOOMP! I vanished. I could not see it, but I could feel *the other thing* spread down the chain. I didn't wait. I jerked as hard as I could. The chain separated. At the same instant, my weight in the water vanished with me. I became empty space, water displaced. I might as well have been a balloon inflated under one edge of the raft. The balloon shot upward. I gripped the edge of the raft. The raft heaved upward. The deck tipped.

The abrupt motion threw the beast off balance. Already slanted under his weight, the raft angled even farther. Stuttering steps transmitted through the deck. He pinwheeled his arms for balance but lost control. He plunged off the edge and hit the lake with a huge splash. The raft slapped down level again. I swung myself onto the deck.

Fwooomp!

My body fell flat, face-down, onto the hard wood.

I raised my head. I pushed myself to my feet.

A torrent of flailing and splashing burst out of the choppy windblown surface. The claws broke the surface and pounded down, attempting to swim. The strokes had no effect. The steel arms drove him under. He either didn't think to peel them off or he couldn't. For a split second his face broke the surface. The night vision unit was gone. His wolf head hung saturated to one side. He gasped for air and hammered the water with his arms, desperate to float.

"GET IT OFF! GE—!" He sank.

He burst out a second time, springing off the floor of the lake. He cried out. Water choked off his words. He sank.

He broke the surface three more times, each weaker and weaker until the last attempt came from the claws alone, smacking together as if praying to hook the sky and pull him free.

Lightning flashed over the bubbles of his last breath. Thunder announced his end. Rain and hail turned the surface of the water into sparkling carbonation.

The steel body suit Farwell had crafted into a living nightmare held him under.

"Hey!" Pidge cried out. She threw one arm onto the side of the raft, spitting and gasping. "Get me outta here. It's fucking freezing!"

72

The second BLASTER power unit remained in my pocket, but in the melee, the prop went missing. Pidge and I had to swim back to shore, a task made harder because the wind hurried the freed raft in the opposite direction. Exhausted, we dragged ourselves up the pebble beach into the boat house. She wasn't wrong about the water temperature. Damn near freezing and not helped by the cold air swirling around us or the icy rain falling.

We trudged up the steps to the lodge where we climbed through the window to the dining room. I had no desire to take a second look at Turinski's body, sliced and spread on the great room floor. Without a word, we pushed into the kitchen. Pidge went to the big gas stove and lit all the burners. We dripped on the floor. I peeled off my lightweight nylon flight jacket, wrung it out over the sink, and draped it over a counter, hoping the soaking didn't ruin it. At least it wasn't my leather jacket.

"Pidge, take your jacket off. You'll warm up faster."

Shivering, drawing great gulps of air, she did as I suggested. She held it out for me. I twisted water out of it over the sink, then spread it on the counter beside mine. She leaned over the stove, rubbing her hands, shaking water out of her hair.

"Told you it was a fucking werewolf."

"You did."

She pulled her phone out of the back pocket of her jeans and laid it on the counter. I found a roll of paper towels and yanked off a dozen sheets and handed them to her. She wadded them up and dried her phone, then began drying herself. I did the same after pulling out my own phone. I wasn't sure about using it. Sticking it in a box of rice for a few days came to mind. Minelli had hidden behind bags of rice in the dry pantry, but I had no intention of hanging out here for a few days.

I was still thinking about the rice in the dry pantry when the pantry door swung open. Both barrels of a shotgun poked through ahead of Minelli's pudgy face.

"You kids okay?"

I silently cursed myself for being too far from Pidge to grab her hand and vanish. The black open barrels of the gun didn't swing in our direction, but I found it hard not to stare at them. Minelli put on a friendly face.

"I thought I better hide in here. Helluva commotion. That thing made a pass here a little while ago, before you got here, so I beat feet." He edged into the kitchen, still holding the shotgun at the ready. His finger lingered inside the trigger guard. "I thought it was gone, but then I saw what it did to Turinski." He winced. "Jesus Christ, what a fucking mess."

Pidge eased away from the hot stove. She edged toward me. Neither of us spoke. Minelli took another step into the kitchen.

"It's probably gone now, though. I think maybe we should go outside." The friendly veneer on his face wavered. He gave the shotgun a little nudge toward the doors.

"Let's wait." I gestured at my phone. "Turinski's whole department is about two minutes away."

Minelli squinted and shook his head. "Don't ever play poker, Will. Come on. Let's go outside. I'm going to keep this shotgun pointed at you because I don't know for sure you're not both working with that critter, okay? Just to be on the safe side. Also, don't get within reach of me or this thing will go off. Let's keep it about six feet, okay? Just to be on the safe side."

Pidge put out her hand. I took it and we walked through the kitchen doors into the dining room.

"Keep going." Minelli followed us.

Vanishing had the downside possibility that Minelli, startled, would fire. At this range the blast would tear into one or both of us. On top of that, the dining room ceiling offered nothing to grip and wasn't high enough to get safely clear.

"Did you find it?" I asked.

He said nothing. I pressed.

"What does a hundred million come to in today's dollars? What was gold per ounce back in 1963?"

"Keep going. I want to get outside, away from that mess in the big room."

Outside. Where a shotgun blast doesn't leave holes in the walls. Where blood spatter is washed away by rain. I saw limits to how far we could go before doing something.

We crossed the dining hall and stepped into the great room. The straight line to the door was blocked by Turinski's body. I led Pidge around the pool of blood and gore, past the bar. Pidge, walking beside me, turned her head in my direction to avoid looking at Turinski's remains. She sucked in a great gulp of air. Her hand closed a vice grip on mine.

The storm rose to a furious pitch. Trees surrounding the lodge heaved and spun in the wind. Broken branches sailed through the air and rapped the sheet metal on Turinski's SUV. Hail pattered the roof and bounced through the open windows. Lightning flashed, a strobe effect that froze water and hail in midair for a split second. Thunder shook the bones of the building.

"Out there?" I shouted at Minelli. I pointed at the doorway.

"Yes! We'll get in the cop car. Use the radio." I didn't think Minelli should play poker either, but if his charade bought time, fine with me.

I calculated our chances. Better to vanish after we cleared the doorway, while Minelli's angles were limited. The wind, rain and confusion would add to our chances.

In the past, in moments of extreme stress, vanishing joined with uncontrolled, automatic movement. Until I had one of Lewko's objects in my hand, I was unable to generate a similar movement. It had been purely fight or flight. I prayed for that now. The instant we stepped through the door, I intended to slam the levers in my head into full vanishing mode. If nothing else, I thought I could shove Pidge to the side, forcing her away from Minelli's reflexive shotgun blast. What I didn't like was the possibility that if a blast caught and killed me, it left her visible.

As all this ran though my head, a voice cried out in the swirling storm.

"DICKIE! DICKIE"

Pidge looked up at me. I looked out the door.

A figure darted across the yard.

"DICKIE! Where the fuck are you?!"

The figure stopped and backtracked. He didn't seem concerned about the wind or rain or hail or lightning. For a moment he stood in one spot and shouted in all four directions.

"Keep going." Minelli did not like that we had stopped.

Pidge and I shuffled toward the door. Minelli followed.

Footsteps pounded the porch boards.

A soaked Billy Farwell filled the doorway.

"Ray, I can't find Dickie!"

"Jesus, Billy."

"Seriously! I don't think he found those girls, either." Farwell shot a glance at me and Pidge. "What are they doing here?"

Minelli frowned as if someone just gave away the punchline of his favorite joke. All pretense evaporated.

"Dickie's dead," I said flatly.

Billy Farwell gaped at me. He wiped his dripping face on his soaked sleeve. "What?"

"He's dead," I repeated. It gave me a reason to stop moving. "He's in the lake. He sank. All that weight."

Minelli glanced at me. "Seriously?"

Billy Farwell took a step. "Ray, what the—?"

Minelli fired both barrels. The blasts tore apart Farwell's torso and dropped him in a heap. My ears rang as if someone slapped two flat hands on the side of my head. Pidge crushed my hand in her electrified grip. Stunned, I failed to do the one thing I should have done in that instant. Instead of vanishing, Pidge and I froze. Minelli didn't. He smoothly snapped open the double-barrel shotgun, tugged out the spent shells, and shoved two new shells into the breach. He snapped the barrel shut again before I could think straight.

Minelli calmly turned the gun on us.

"Well, that changes things. Is he really in the lake?"

I nodded.

"Huh." Minelli gave it a couple second's thought. "Okay. I guess that's it for you two, then." He heaved the shotgun to his shoulder and took aim at Pidge and me.

BANG! BANG! BAM-BAM-BAM-BAM!

I threw my arms around Pidge and twisted her away from Minelli. I cringed and squeezed my eyes shut, bracing for explosive pain that never came. The count was wrong. Too many shots. Clenching every muscle against phantom shotgun blasts, I forced my eyes open, amazed to remain standing, amazed to feel no pain, amazed that my life was not bleeding away.

In the smashed windows joining the breakfast deck, lightning flashed. Thunder joined the battle. A silhouette with a glistening bald head stood with his bowlegs apart and his Colt .45 smoking.

Earl Jackson's growl joined the storm.

"I don't like that guy."

73

The ladies made Earl and me strip down to our shorts inside the dry pantry while they did the same in the kitchen, the only warm room in the house. Candice didn't miss a mothering beat after she followed Earl through the broken windows. She produced warm, dry blankets and ordered everyone out of their wet clothes. A rap on the pantry door gave Earl and me the all-clear signal. We turned burrito in the blankets we were given and joined Pidge, Kelly, and Val at the kitchen counter where they too snuggled inside colorful quilts. Each wore caps of wet hair plastered against their skulls. All three looked pale, although with Kelly it was hard to tell.

Candice hurried around in a floral bathrobe, scooping wet clothing off the floor and shoving the heap into an industrial strength dryer at the far end of the kitchen. She darted through the kitchen doors and disappeared into the dining room for a few minutes, then returned with an armful of liquor bottles. Pidge lifted the vodka bottle from her grasp and opened it before the rest of the beverage service landed on the counter. Candice produced tumblers from a cabinet, then set about pulling food from the refrigerator. She spread dishes and jars across the counter.

"It's nice to see you again, Will. I never got a chance to thank you after the last time you were here. I have questions about that, you know." Candice tipped me a stern but friendly glance. "I'd like my late husband's uniform back, please."

"I had it cleaned. It's well taken care of."

"What new fuckery is this?" Pidge looked at me.

"Story for another day."

Candice handed Earl a bottle of peach iced tea, generating a look that might have been gratitude—or disgust—it was hard to tell. I poured a couple fingers of scotch and dumped a generous gulp down my throat where the warmth went to work from the inside.

"I have questions, too. Like…where the hell have you two been?"

Candice, Val, and Kelly all spoke at once. Earl grunted, signaling for order. He gestured at Candice. "Let the lady speak."

"WE HAVE a shelter on the third island downriver. Renell Lake is really just a wide spot in the river. Over on the other side there's a string of islands. In summer, Val takes campers across for overnights and cookouts." Candice turned and wrapped an arm around Kelly. "Child, I told you to go away and stay away, but God love you, here you are. Thank you for coming back and bringing friends."

Kelly let a tear run down her cheek in response. She hugged Candice.

"Why the island?" I asked. "Why didn't you take off that night?"

"The night I dropped Kelly off? That was the first time I saw it. It came for me—for us all. Before that, I suspected someone was coming to kill me, but I had no idea who or how or when and you just don't want to cry wolf."

Pidge giggled. Val covered her mouth and laughed.

"What?" Candice looked at them.

"Wolf," Val said. "You said you didn't want to—never mind."

Candice gently slapped the girl's arm, then continued. "After I saw it—and I put some of the pieces together—I realized the most important thing was to get this girl and her baby away. That's all that mattered to me."

"What pieces?" Pidge asked.

"I had an inkling a few days before. At the bank. It never sat right with me that Charlie Pelton wanted to fiddle with my deposit box. Oh, there's nothing in there of any value. I should have cancelled the darn thing long ago. But it just didn't sit right. I've known Charlie for a long, long time and he's always been a good…" Candice trailed off, reading my expression. "What?"

"Charlie's dead," I said.

"What? How?"

"Werewolf," Pidge said indelicately. I glared at her. "What? That's how it happened." Pidge glared back. I picked up the thread.

"Candice, I think Charlie Pelton was part of all this. At least, until his partners decided not to share. They probably didn't want the loose end. I'm so sorry."

Val said sadly, "My dad knew Mr. Pelton. He always liked him."

Candice gave Val an appreciative nod. She processed a moment of sadness for an old friend, and for the betrayal, then continued. "I suppose it makes sense. Like I said, it didn't sit right with me. So, last week, when I knew Charlie was out of the office, I went back to the bank and asked for access to the box. And everything was still there, useless old papers and things. And one more thing." She tugged an envelope from her robe pocket. Earl had already seen it. She handed it to me.

The envelope and paper inside were damp but not soaked. I carefully pulled out the document. Legalese comprised most of the document. Candice's signature at the bottom was certified by a notary stamp. Charlie Pelton, Notary Public.

"What is this?"

Earl chimed in. "Her signature that she dismissed the option to take out mortgage insurance."

My dumb expression asked the next question, which Candice answered.

"It's a paper that says that when I took out the mortgage on this place, I turned down mortgage insurance. You know. The thing that pays off the mortgage if anything happens to me. The paper says I turned it down—what sixteen or seventeen years ago? It's dated. Or, I should say, backdated."

"So?" Pidge asked.

"I never signed any such paper. I took the mortgage insurance. I know I did. I wasn't going to leave somebody with a debt if I passed. The paper is a fake. The payment history would prove it, unless that's been altered, too. I can only assume Charlie put it there. I didn't want to believe it, but I didn't fall off the turnip truck yesterday. Charlie asked to use my key for some kind of maintenance—"

"I told them about that," Kelly said. Candice gave her a fresh squeeze.

"Well, must be what happened. Charlie used my key to put that paper inside."

"Or he made a copy. The bank doesn't have a copy of your key," Earl said. "That's why they gotta drill your box if you lose your key."

"I don't really know—but with that paper in the box if something happened to me, the mortgage goes unpaid which puts the property in foreclosure. I won't say I'm a suspicious woman, but I got to thinking that somebody was on the verge of doing me harm, and that got me thinking about little Kelly here, and Seth. Then right after that, I was poking around in the upstairs guest room one night, lost in my thoughts, when I saw something from the window that scared the living daylights out of me."

"The werewolf," Pidge insisted.

"If that's what it was. I couldn't make it out. There's a pretty good view of the road out to the airstrip from up there. What I saw was big and fast and it was coming, but I guess it lost its footing or something because as quick as it was coming at me, it stopped and limped off into the woods."

"Dickie Farwell." Candice looked at me. I reiterated. "It was Dickie Farwell. Him and his brother cooked up the beast idea. They got a shed full of steel animal sculptures, and I guess one thing led to another. Kinda clever, if you can get past the part about using it to kill people. That first night he must've had a wardrobe malfunction. He was probably on his way here to do the deed when you saw him. Something must've gone wrong and made him break it off. That would be my guess."

Candice stared at Kelly. "You and the baby were asleep. It would have been all of us. All three of us."

Kelly nodded.

"They wouldn't have wanted Kelly around," Earl said. "In case you put her in your will or something."

"Lord, I guess so. I was—I was just petrified at the thought of you two here. You say it was Dickie Farwell?"

"And his brother Billy," I said. "You didn't see him when you came in through the window, but Billy's out there on the porch in the rain."

Candice looked at Earl who looked down at his hands. "He's right. I saw Minelli shoot him. Wasn't going to mention it."

"Well," Candice said, "I don't wish to speak ill of the dead, but those Farwell brothers have been long-term turds. Why on earth would they join in something like this?"

"They had incentive. Money. A lot of it. We'll get to that," I said. "Go on."

"That's it. That was the night I chased Kelly away."

"It was pretty sharp of you to realize the connection," I said. "Between the document, the bank's position, and the threat."

"I don't know about that. I wasn't too bright coming back here. I should have called for help, but what do you say? I wasn't even sure I'd seen what I saw. But after dropping off Kelly, I came back here. There's a second entrance that goes east from here. I used it to come back—in case that thing was still out by the main road. I wanted to reach some folks to tell them not to come. That's when I found all my reservations were cancelled. Somebody sent out an email to every one of my customers telling them we were closing for the season."

"Minelli," Earl muttered. Candice sent him a querying expression. "You gave him access to your laptop."

"Plus, you had all the bank statements, right?" Pidge asked. "They were all over your desk."

"The what?"

Earl issued a growl. "I don't think so. Bastards put 'em there after she was gone. When they came in and wrecked the place." To Candice's blank look, he added, "Bunch'a phony bank statements. That Pelton sonofabitch cooked up a history of false transactions to make it look like you were in deep shit. Probably took your money, too. It's gonna take some untangling. I'll help you with that."

A warm look shot between Earl and Candice. Pidge poked me with her elbow and grinned.

"Well, that night it came back. Got its wardrobe malfunction fixed or what-ever, and it came back. I spotted it coming again and didn't think twice. I wanted to warn Mr. Minelli but—well, that thing was out there. And here I worried about him the whole time. Asshole." Candice helped herself to a sip of the gin that she had poured. "I couldn't get to my car, so I snuck down to the boathouse and took a canoe. It was dark. Black as ink. I figured all I had to do was get out on the water and it couldn't reach me, and then in the morning I'd get help. Didn't quite work out that way. Once I got to the island, I was too scared to leave. I decided to wait. Then you all arrived. I saw the plane and I knew it was you, Earl. So, I came back that night. That's when I saw it chasing across the beach. And it almost got you."

Earl nodded but said nothing.

"You saw Candice," I said. "That's why you were angling toward the water."

"Yup."

Candice said, "He saw me and got in the water and then the two of us went back over to the island to figure things out."

"Figure things out," Pidge muttered, grinning. "Is that what the kids are calling it these days?"

Earl grunted. Candice frowned, but there was a spark of mischief in it. "When we got to the island, Earl told me about Dr. Yuan and his lovely wife. Oh, that was terrible. Just terrible. If I could have reached them in time—I wanted to charge right back here, but he said no. I wanted to call the sheriff, but—" Candice looked pointedly at Earl "—you said you thought Lieutenant Turinski was in on it."

"I said I didn't trust him."

"That's not what you said."

Earl bit his lower lip and threw his hands in the air.

"Anyway, we decided to let the investigation take hold. I guess they didn't get very far. And you were wrong about Gene Turinski, Earl."

Earl said nothing. We joined him in silence, all of us thinking about Turinski lying in the great room near Ray Minelli. When Candice produced her stack of blankets, Earl asked for the oldest one. He covered the lieutenant but left Minelli on his back staring at the ceiling. I stepped out of the room while Earl stood over Minelli. I wasn't sure he didn't spit on him.

"Did the Yuans have anything to do with the lodge, Candice?" I asked. "I mean—you weren't thinking of selling to them or anything like that, were you?"

Candice shook her head. "Why would that matter?"

"For starters, it would change the whole scheme of bumping you off to put the property in foreclosure. It would mean that even if they managed to force the foreclosure, there was another interested buyer who might interfere. Did the Yuans ever express an interest in buying the place?"

"No. No, not at all. They just wanted to come up early. It was—" Candice choked on the words that followed, words delivered in a tight whisper "—their tenth anniversary."

"Fuckers killed them just for driving in at the wrong moment," Pidge offered soberly.

"Yeah," I agreed softly. "They probably ran into Dickie. That would explain why they turned off the main road. Running scared. Right into that ravine."

"Bastards," Earl grumbled.

I checked my watch. The rest of the sheriff's department would arrive soon, along with, I assumed, Minnesota BCA officers. The call I placed on the radio in Turinski's SUV went straight to a dispatcher and not to some volunteer on a tip line. The report of an officer down didn't need to be vetted and filtered.

Candice sighed. "This was all because of me."

A round of rebukes pelted the woman. She reached out to grasp our hands. She held them tightly for a long minute. When she released us, she dabbed her eyes.

Sirens sounded, distant and hesitant under the wind and thunder.

Candice looked at the faces around the table until she landed on me.

"I don't understand Mr. Minelli. You say it's about money? Stolen money? I just don't understand."

"I do."

EPILOGUE

1

I waited. It wasn't hard. This wasn't my first rodeo.

I waited for the small hours.

The old man probably had the usual retinue of household servants—a cook, cleaning staff—but I saw only one. A guy celebrities and politicians call the "body man." If the old man's associates came and went on business, they were not present at this late hour. The weather sucked, so I doubted there had been any golfing on the course that joined the estate. The storm system that dumped rain and hail on Renell Lodge took several days to pound its way across the Great Lakes before swinging northeast. The violent storms petered out. Eventually the low pressure system that caused all the trouble in the first place spread out as a vast damp atmospheric event most people think of as muck. Low ceilings. Rain showers. Cool temperatures that mess up barbecues, graduation parties, and golfing. It wouldn't have mattered. I arrived after dark.

The old man's gated and guarded mansion joined a golf course with its own clubhouse, the den of an exclusive country club. I used their parking lot for the crew car I borrowed. Denied eighteen holes of sunny exercise, club members flocked to the clubhouse bar. I left them to their drinking, and the drunk driving that followed. My target was the eyesore on the far side of the course, just off the ninth hole. I don't know the architectural style, but the building fit my recent encounter with a werewolf. The vine-draped rock pile should have had roiling black thunderheads, flashes of lightning, and swirling winds as a backdrop.

Upon arrival, I scouted the old man's bedroom. It wasn't hard to find. A huge bank of windows overlooked the golf course. And why not? Murder, money, and power rewarded him with a wake-up view he craved. His Wikipedia page identified him a lifelong golfer, not the most common hobby for men in his profession, but not unusual. I had no idea if, in his eighties, he still played, though I assumed more than ever.

Finding him was not terribly hard. Google has changed the world, something my detective wife appreciates. Despite efforts to keep his personal data private, snippets of the old man's life appeared online. Newspaper stories. Golf club blogs. Social commentary. People treated him like a celebrity businessman, like a rich former actor or sports star. I wondered if they knew the truth or simply chose to look the other way. There are those who inexplicably admire men in his line of work.

I floated outside the bedroom after his body man turned the lights on and the bed down. Electric motors majestically closed twenty-foot-tall curtains, shielding the old man from outside eyes so that he could sleep in privacy on his oversized bed and his silk sheets. Just before the curtains cut off my view, the old man entered the bedroom. Alone. He reminded me of Bargo Litton, the poisonous billionaire I met once in a similar house near a similar golf course. These guys all read the same instruction manual.

After the curtains closed, I ascended to the roof and tucked myself behind a chimney, blocked from view by peaked gables. I chose that spot so I could reappear and surf my phone. I double-checked my research. There weren't many photos of the old man, but what I'd seen walking into the bedroom matched those available. In the few seconds I saw him, he walked erect. He looked fit. He radiated a menace cultivated over a long and dangerous career—the menace captured in an old photo of him leaning against a shiny Cadillac beside Cabin Number Seven at Renell Lodge.

After reconfirming his identity, I surfed the news outlets. Few continued the story of the werewolf now that the werewolf had been dragged from a not terribly deep Renell Lake, the drowned victim of his own steel accessories. A fake. A phony. For a day or two, the story had been splashy, but a dead man in a steel suit deflated the legend. Dickie Farwell, in the end, was no Lon Chaney.

A story with longer legs featured Spiro Lewko. The reclusive billionaire who wildly claimed to have a cure for children's cancer, and who had engineered amazing deep fake images of himself making kids vanish, had been arrested by federal authorities for violating a federal court order. State authorities in North Carolina discussed (but seemed reluctant to bring) charges against the man for running a phony hospital. The governor denied any special treatment for the state's largest investor. Lewko was never the darling of the conservative media. Now he was their punching bag. Pundits railed against his behavior. They showered him with snide commentary. They compared him to charlatan revival tent healers, witch doctors, and legendary con men. Anti-vax groups added Lewko to their hate lists and vowed to boycott Evermore products. Religious extremists denounced him as a tool of Satan.

Lewko, of course, said nothing. He returned to his reclusive state on his reclusive estate.

His one comment, as far as I could tell, arrived as a text message on my phone (which spent three days in a bag of rice; I cheered loudly when it came back to life). The message simply read:

Corona?

I admit, it made me smile. I wrote back.

With lime, please.

Under the noise surrounding Lewko and the accusations of medical malfeasance, if not malpractice, something slipped nearly unnoticed into tail end paragraphs of stories posted by the calmer media outlets. Children from the first bus were doing well. Anecdotes from family sources described unexpected energy and new nourishment patterns. Medical professionals withheld comment but vowed to continue monitoring.

That also made me smile.

I stopped fiddling with my phone when the battery dropped down to 7 percent. I tucked it away, vanished, and spent the remaining time floating outside the old man's bedroom window. Lights in the house winked out, except the ones on timers or the ones designed for security. The estate had a fence. Don't they all? The fence had a gatehouse, and the gatehouse had a guard. I checked on him once—mostly to give myself something to do. The uniformed private security officer sat in a comfortable-looking chair with a tablet on his lap and his hand in his pants. I didn't look closely at the flesh writhing on the tablet. Cameras and sophisticated night vision surveillance covering all angles ensured the guard his privacy. I left him to his business, but before using a quiet shot of BLASTER to depart, I checked the clock in his little hut. 1:29 a.m.

I waited for what felt like another hour, then I lowered myself to the deck outside the old man's wall of windows. One of the windows had a doorknob. The knob was locked, but with such potent security, and because no one in their right mind would ever threaten or harm this old man, there was no deadbolt. The locked knob proved to be no barrier.

I pushed *the other thing* into the latch, waited a few seconds, then gave the knob a tug. The bolt severed. The door moved. I crouched and cupped my hand, then opened the door. The severed bolt dropped. I grabbed it, patting myself on the back for the save.

I turned and tossed the severed bolt onto the grass below the marble deck.

The curtains met just inside the door. I slipped through and floated into the old man's bedroom. The curtains were surprisingly sheer, meant only for blocking unwanted eyes, not for room darkening. Thanks to light from security lamps around the property and light pollution from the city, I easily made out the furnishings and décor. The old man didn't have extravagant tastes. There were no priceless works of art on the walls, no grandiose self-portraits. I had no idea what the style of furniture was called, but it reminded me of pictures I'd seen of the royal yacht once used by Queen Elizabeth. Simple, yet elegant.

He slept under a black sleep mask. Made sense. Don't darken the room in case you need to rise in the night or deal with an intruder. Darken your eyes for the sleep you need.

Did he dream of the crimes that put him in this mansion? Of the men he was reputed to have killed—slowly and viciously? I wondered if those dying by his hand screamed or cried or called for their mommies like young soldiers are said to do in their last moments. Did tortured cries echo under that sleep mask? Or did he keep a little orange prescription bottle full of pills handy to silence the haunting voices?

It didn't matter. The answers to those questions, if there were answers, would not change my plans.

I had not done this in a while, but the steps were simple and familiar.

Fwooomp!

I reappeared just inside the curtains. My feet settled onto plush carpeting. Nice. Quiet. I tucked away the BLASTER that delivered me to the mansion from a parking lot at the golf clubhouse. I pulled a wad of cloth from my flight jacket pocket. The balaclava slid over my head. I adjusted it.

From a holster borrowed from my wife, I extracted the Berretta M.92a semi-automatic pistol she owns. Another pocket produced the legal, licensed suppressor she also owns. She once described the complex paperwork attached to owning the device. I wondered why she bothered but appreciated having it just the same. Like the last time I held this weapon, the magazine slotted in the grip contained home defense rounds, frangible bullets designed to shatter on impact so that when you're blasting away at some intruder, the shots you fire don't go through your drywall and into a neighbor's house or into the bedroom of a sleeping child. I screwed the suppressor snugly onto the barrel tip of the weapon. Comfortable with my grip on the gun—of the weapons she owns, this was my favorite to fire—I thumbed off the safety. If this went badly, I was ready without regret.

I walked to the side of the bed and ran into a glitch. The damned bed was huge. The old man slept dead center. I sighed. If this was the worst hiccup tonight, I'd be happy.

Looking more awkward than it was, I kneeled on the mattress and walked on my knees to within reach. Tremors in the mattress woke him. He reached for the sleep mask. I touched the suppressor to his forehead.

"I want you to think very carefully before making any sudden movements."

He froze. I held him that way for a long minute. Not speaking. Not moving. I pressed the round suppressor tip against his flesh.

Andy once grew furious with me for doing something like this. For that reason, I did not tell her where I was going when I left the house this morning.

Late in the day I texted that I had a last-minute, late-night flight, but that I hoped to be home in time for breakfast. Love you.

I did not lie. It was a last-minute flight. It would be a late-night flight. And I would be home for breakfast. I cannot lie to my wife.

I waited for the old man to fill the silence. He did not disappoint.

"Who the fuck are you?" He asked the question calmly after folding his hands across his chest. I gave him credit. He played it cool.

"Your grandson is dead."

He said nothing, but his jaw flexed. His hand grip tightened. In his lined face, I saw the menace that seeped from an old photo. It ran as strong as ever in veins beneath old skin.

"You better be goddamned lying to me."

"Nope."

Neither of us spoke for a minute.

The old man huffed an angry breath. "That fuckin' kid. Always had rocks in his head."

"Yeah. He studied geology. Rocks in his head. Cute."

"That kid was useless. So, what's he to you? You some kinda gay lover of his?"

"Was he gay?"

"Not as far as I know."

"Neither am I."

I gave him more silence. I think it irritated him.

"I'm gonna move my right hand and take off this goddamned sleep mask. You don't like it, shoot me."

I pulled the suppressor away from his forehead and poked it into his shoulder.

"This weapon is loaded with home defense rounds. You know what they are?"

"Fuck, yes."

"Mess with me, and the first shot goes into your shoulder. They'll probably save your life, but they'll take your whole arm. And I won't leave without putting a second round in the ball joint of your other shoulder. Got it?"

"Screw you."

I smiled. The man had nerve. "Aren't you going to tell me I'm already a dead man?"

"That's a given." He lifted his right arm and found the mask on his face. He pushed it up.

Anthony Caniglierie, the darling of six decades of Philadelphia mob bosses, looked up at me with cold, dead eyes that gave me a chill. I could understand the terror his victims likely felt in their last moments.

"What do you want, asshole?"

"Do you really think you should be insulting me?"

He sighed. This time he let me fill the silence.

"Your grandson went by the name of Ray Minelli. Pretended to be a—well, I guess he was a geologist. He pretended to be writing a book, but he was actually looking for the loot from that Lufthansa robbery—you know—up at that lodge you visited in 1963 on your way back into the country from Canada."

As I said these words Caniglierie rolled his eyes. "That fuckin' idiot. That useless miserable idiot. Goddammit." Caniglierie abruptly pushed himself upright and leaned against the padded head of the bed. He didn't seem to care about the gun pressed to his shoulder. He all but brushed it off. He sat for a moment staring dead ahead, working saliva around in his mouth.

"He was hunting for the rest of the loot. The two thirds I'm guessing you didn't find after you murdered your partners."

Caniglierie shot me a cold look. "And what? You come here looking for it? You're fucking dumber than he was."

I said nothing.

Caniglierie shook his head. "Wanna know something? Lemme tell you something, asshat. There is no loot. There never was. The whole fucking thing was a story. A goddamned made-up story. I'd'a given my left nut to be on that crew that did that Lufthansa job, but I'll give you odds they all wound up dead or worse. That loot was never found. None of it. Goddamned insurance company probably has it in a vault somewhere. I was never within a thousand miles of that job."

"Am I supposed to believe that?"

"I don't give a shit what you believe. You think I'm gonna bullshit someone pointing a gun at me in my bedroom? How the fuck did you get in here? Never mind. I don't give a shit. Somebody's gonna pay. That's for sure. Starting with you, asshole."

"Let's dial it down a little, Tony. I'm the one with the gun, remember?" He scowled at me. I think he didn't like me using his first name. "You're saying the whole thing was a lie?"

"Best lie I ever told. Shit, I didn't even have to tell the lie. People spread it around me. All I had to do was not deny it. Yeah, sure, I offed those two amateurs up there in Buttfuck, Minnesota. I don't even remember how or what I did with 'em. But that was after a job we did in Montreal. Sixty or seventy grand or some such. Not bad for the day. I saw no future for those guys, but I saw plenty of future for that money. I bought my way in, see? I made a career outta that money. I fuckin' grew it like Madoff. Look around you. That money was the seed that planted all this. But hell—that Lufthansa shit? Pure legend."

"A legend you told your grandson."

"What grampa doesn't tell his grandson stories? How was I supposed to know he'd take that bullshit seriously?"

I almost laughed. I almost lowered the gun and laughed and wished the old man a good night. Almost. Then I thought about Lieutenant Turinski taking his kid fishing on Candice's generosity. I thought about the horror at the ravine. Dr. and Mrs. Yuan on their way to celebrate an anniversary. Candice told me they had three kids.

Andy thinks I don't have it in me. Murder. But I do. It's in my heart. It lives there like a tiny, lethal seed. Maybe it's in all of us. Maybe it just takes the right moment, the right formula to nurture it, to let it grow and cut the bonds that restrain it.

I've had moments that came close.

This was one of those moments.

Caniglierie split open a nasty grin. "You wanna know something else about my grandson? He was a fucking mooch. I paid for that bullshit rock collecting education of his and I paid for this and for that and I got squat for a thank you. He was a mooch right up to the end. You know that? Right up to the end. He never stopped asking me for shit. Never."

"I can't say I'm shocked."

The nasty grin stayed. He aimed it at me for a minute. A minute too long. He had something up his sleeve. I started to wonder if he had a panic button in his pajamas, and if the door to the bedroom was about to burst open.

"Wanna know the last thing that mooch wanted from me?"

"Do I care?"

"You should. Hand me that phone. On the night stand behind you."

I didn't. This did not feel right.

"Fine. Don't. But on that phone, there's a photo. The kid sent me a photo because he knows I have resources. Resources you can't imagine. Fuckin' little mooch sent me a photo because he wanted to know who it was in the photo. Some guy and a little blondie. Are you getting me? Are you getting the picture here?"

Not even diving into Renell Lake in May had I ever felt such a shot of cold in my guts.

"Turns out the photo is some asshole named Stewart and his girlfriend named Page. Not too hard to track down. Guy was in the papers a while back. I guess my grandson took the picture when he met the two of you before—what? You killed him?"

"Wasn't me."

"Doesn't matter. You own it now."

The cold, nasty grin remained fixed on me. My arms felt watery. My finger felt weak on the Beretta trigger.

"Stewart. William Stanley Stewart. Married. Wife's a cop. Andrea. And the little blondie. Page. Cassandra or some shit, I think. It's all in my phone."

I felt sick. Disoriented. He did not let up.

"Go ahead. Put a bullet in me. That's a nice piece of hardware in your hand.

Expensive. You've got a beauty there. You brought your own gun, you stupid shit, and the cops are gonna know exactly who shot me. I killed more mother-fuckers than that gun has bullets, but I never owned a gun in my life. Go ahead. Plant some evidence."

Except the evidence wouldn't point at me. It would point at Andy.

He leaned into it.

"I don't think you got it in you. Fucking pussy with your home defense bull-shit. If you're gonna shoot somebody, you shoot 'em dead."

To make his point, he reached for the gun. Not trying to be fast or overpower-ing. Like it was a toy to be taken from a child. I jerked it back out of reach. He sneered.

"Here's what's going to happen, Stewart. You're gonna take that shitty mask off and you're going to kneel at the foot of my bed. And you're going to put that gun to your head and blow your fucking brains out, because if you don't, what I will do to that wife Andrea and that girlfriend Cass is going to *TAKE FUCKING DAYS!* Do you hear me, asshole? *FUCKING DAYS!* They will run out of ways to beg. You got only one out, here. Only thing gets me to not peel their skin off is your corpse at the foot of my bed."

The grin widened. A glistening line of spittle dripped down his chin.

My heart pounded. Deep in that pounding, the black seed germinated. Cold. Ruthless. It was there all along. It stirred when I watched Dickie Farwell claw the water over his head. It flourished now. It would not be denied.

I slid backward holding the gun on him. Retreating. He mistook it for victory. The grin grew into a sneer.

I reached the edge of the mattress and stopped.

I shifted the weapon to my left hand and reached for his phone. He watched me lift the device from the nightstand and slip it into my jacket, and for a sliced fraction of second I saw what I needed to see. A flicker of weakness. A moment of doubt. Realization.

What he knew about me and Pidge existed only in his phone. He had no backup because his mooch grandson's request was just one more pointless and annoying proof that the idiot turned out useless. Not shared. Not taken seriously. In that flicker of hesitation, I saw that the old man didn't delegate his research to an associate. Why add to his embarrassment for his worthless grandson?

The kid with the rocks in his head.

I swapped gun hands again, and then pulled the balaclava off my head. The gesture might have been interpreted as surrender, but the narrowing of my eyes and the slit of an awakening smile was anything but.

When he did not speak, I did.

"That's not going to happen."

2

He struggled at first. Not when I ordered him out of the bed. Not when I ordered him to exit the bedroom onto the marble deck outside. Not when I made him walk across the deck with the gun pressed to the back of his head.

He struggled when I tucked the gun in the holster and grabbed him by his thin corded neck and made him vanish.

Fwooomp!

He cried out when I kicked the stone underfoot and we shot into the air. His arms flailed. He struck me, but I held him at arm's length. The blows were weak. He tried to claw me until I made it clear that if I let go he was on his own—that this magic only lasted as long as Tinkerbell kept a hand on his throat. He stopped swinging.

He demanded to know what was happening. I said nothing.

He cursed and threatened. I ignored him.

We rose several hundred feet in the air on the kick launch before I shifted him to one side, rotated us, and worked the BLASTER out of my pocket. I aimed the power unit away from him. He trailed like a human banner. His flimsy silk pajamas flapped. He reached up and found my grip on the back of his neck, not to peel himself free, but to hold on. His bony fingers dug into mine.

Demands drew no response from me. Curses sparked no reaction. Offers of a big payoff went unanswered. He fell silent, then began to shake involuntarily as fear swallowed him. His reliable menace deserted him in the face of something he never dreamed possible, never imagined. He heaved his breath in and out until I thought he might hyperventilate.

Three hundred feet up we touched the low-hanging mist of a dense overcast. The dark golf course fell behind us. City lights streamed by below.

He asked if I was real. If I was sent from God. I told him he'd better hope not.

He begged to be let down. He swore he didn't mean it. He swore he'd forget this ever happened. He said he didn't mean what he said about my wife, my girl-friend. He said their lives were sacred to him now. That he had power. That no one would ever dare touch them.

I said nothing.

He gasped and made sounds that might have been crying or near-silent screaming. He made an animal sound that merged with a sworn apology.

This went on for most of the journey.

I NOTED the map feature on the flight in. Habit, I guess. Tall towers are marked on aeronautical charts. The Roxborough Tower Farm in Philadelphia grows a cluster of them, the highest over 1,200 feet tall. I knew where to look. The tower farm rises off the northeast banks of the Schuylkill River, not terribly far from Grays Ferry where the old man had roots. It didn't take complex navigation to locate the cluster of thirteen broadcast towers. Beneath the low cloud ceiling, the hazard lights blinked out warnings that guided me.

I picked the tallest, the candelabra tower erected in 2003. I flew to the base where the transmission buildings were dwarfed by the galvanized steel structure and taut support wires overhead. Caniglierie settled into a breathless whimper.

"Please please please please…"

"Is that what they said to you? The people you killed? Is that what they sounded like?"

"I didn't mean it please please I didn't mean it…"

I wondered if he'd wet himself. Soil himself.

Where's your menace now, Tony?

I carefully avoided the steel cables anchoring the tower to the earth. At over a thousand feet tall, the structure and its support wires posed a significant hazard to aviation.

I shifted from horizontal to vertical flight. We shot upward. The geometric steel frame flew by us at a dizzying speed. We almost immediately slipped into the instrument conditions that dogged my flight into Philadelphia. Lights below us faded into mist that spread an ethereal glow around us. Heavenly, when seen from above. Against this white/gray world, the triangular steel streamed by, sections painted white and red. The color alternated, intended to alert aviators who fly too near tall towers.

At intervals, aerial hazard lights lit up the cloud, blinding in their intensity. White. Then red. Then white. Onward and upward.

I almost collided with the candelabra top when we reached it. I fired off a solid shot of reverse thrust to bring us to a halt and stabilize us yards below the three white transmission tower arms. I leveled off below the supports that angled outward. Lines and cables ran down the central triangle structure, which was a lot larger than I thought it would be at this height. I expected something narrow, something a man would have to squeeze into. This tower spanned fifteen or twenty feet on all three dimensions. Missing from a tower was anything resembling a ladder. Cables suggested that maintenance workers used a lightweight elevator. The idea of climbing 20 feet down to the next crossmember made my head spin.

My hand clutching the old man's thin neck started to cramp.

I rotated Caniglierie and put him between me and the tower. Holding him out with one hand and pulsing the BLASTER in the other, I steered him toward a vertical support. The steel had a powdered finish, painted white.

"Grab on."

I bumped him against the vertical beam. Beneath trembling terror, I felt him wiggle. He let go of my hands.

"Got it?"

He made a noise. I felt the shift. I felt him tug away from me. Good enough.

Fwooomp!

An electric snap bit into my hand. I let him go and hoped for the best.

Caniglierie appeared against the misty night, a man clinging to a vertical steel beam in empty space. Gravity sucked him down. His shin banged off the horizontal beam. His crotch slammed into the angled support beam. He cried out, but he didn't have much air to give it.

His face had changed dramatically. Menace and confidence drained. Unhinged fear sucked the blood from his skin.

The topmost light above us flashed red at intervals. When it illuminated, the mist all around us burst into a hellish glow. When it went out, Caniglierie was a ghost, lit only by thin city light filtered through clouds. Both ways, his face was a mask of terror. His chin dripped drool. His nostrils flowed with snot. His eyes bulged. He shivered.

I used BLASTER power against a steady wind to hold position a few feet away. He didn't look for me. He stared blindly.

"*Take me down! Please! Take me down! I'll do anything!*"

"Tell me again, Tony, what you were going to do to my wife. To my friend."

"*I never meant it!*"

"Tell me, Tony. How long were you going to make it last?"

"*Please! I'll confess. I'll confess to all of them!*"

"How many, Tony? How many have you done that way? How many wives? Sons? Daughters?"

"*Please! I'll confess. I'll confess to all of them!*" He clawed at the steel to hold on. The pain from the angled steel support in his crotch had to be excruciating. He tried to lift himself to relieve it, but his old arms were weak. His legs dangled. He'd lost one of the slippers he insisted on donning when I drove him from his bedroom. His silk pajamas fluttered in the wind. Released from the comfortable cool sensation induced by *the other thing,* his skin broke out in goose flesh against the bite of cold air at altitude. He shivered. Snot strung out from his nose and whipped in the wind.

Murder.

It crawled up out of the deepest, dimmest recesses of my heart. I knew what this was. I also knew what my choices were. He made the rules. Not me. He only needed to tell me his intentions once. I knew he meant it.

I looked down. Even without seeing the ground a thousand feet away, this was utterly terrifying.

I could bargain with him. Ask him if he learned his lesson. Accept his confession and call it a day. The old man clutching steel in this sky-high nightmare would fervently agree to anything. He would beg and plead and make promises and swear to forget he ever saw me or Pidge.

But the man leaning on his chrome-edged Caddy in the old photo would have his payback.

I took one last look at the Philadelphia mobster, the untouchable, the Teflon killer whose least crime was one crime too many.

"You shouldn't have lied to your grandson."

He shivered in the flashing red light, bony and weak. I drifted. Distance grew between us.

I called out to him.

"You're free to climb down, Tony. Or you can wait for someone to spot you. This weather should clear in a few days. Somebody might see you. A passing airliner, maybe. Just remember…when the sand runs out, panic."

DIVISIBLE MAN – THE ELEVENTH HOURGLASS

Saturday, March 25, 2023 to Saturday, June 17, 2023

ABOUT THE AUTHOR

HOWARD SEABORNE is the author of the DIVISIBLE MAN^{TM} series as well
as a collection of short stories featuring the same cast of characters. He began
writing novels in spiral notebooks at age ten. He began flying airplanes at age
sixteen. He is a former flight instructor and commercial charter pilot licensed in
single- and multi-engine airplanes as well as helicopters. Today he flies a twin-
engine Beechcraft Baron, a single-engine Beechcraft Bonanza, and a Rotorway
A-600 Talon experimental helicopter he built from a kit in his garage. He lives
with his wife and writes and flies during all four seasons in Wisconsin, never far
from Essex County Airport.

Visit www.HowardSeaborne.com to join the Email List
and get a FREE DOWNLOAD.

DIVISIBLE MAN

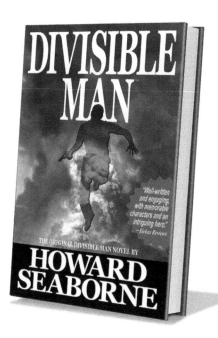

The media calls it a "miracle" when air charter pilot Will Stewart survives an aircraft in-flight breakup, but Will's miracle pales beside the stunning aftereffect of the crash. Barely on his feet again, Will and his police sergeant wife Andy race to rescue an innocent child from a heinous abduction. *Will's new ability might make the difference between life and death…if it doesn't kill him first.*

Available in print, digital, and audio.

Search: "DIVISIBLE MAN Howard Seaborne"

Join our Reader Email list at **HowardSeaborne.com**

DIVISIBLE MAN: THE SIXTH PAWN

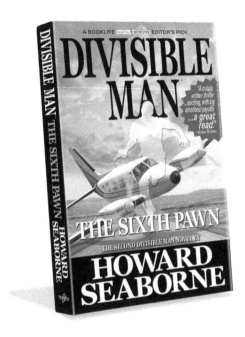

DIVISIBLE MAN: THE SECOND GHOST

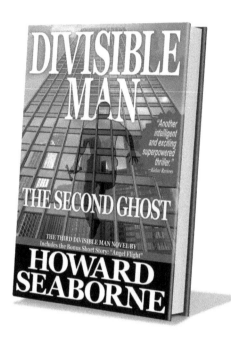

Tormented by a cyber stalker, Lane Franklin's best friend turns to suicide. Lane's frantic call launches Will and Andy Stewart on a desperate rescue mission. When it all goes bad, Will must adapt his extraordinary ability to survive the dangerous high steel and glass of Chicago as Andy and Pidge confront the edge of disaster. **Includes the short story, "Angel Flight," a bridge to the fourth DIVISIBLE MAN novel that follows.**

Available in print, digital, and audio.

Search: "DIVISIBLE MAN Howard Seaborne"

Join our Reader Email list at **HowardSeaborne.com**

DIVISIBLE MAN: THE SEVENTH STAR

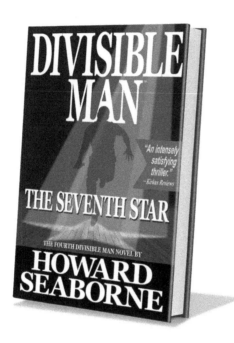

A horrifying message turns a holiday gathering tragic. An unsolved murder hangs a death threat over Detective Andy Stewart's head. And internet-fueled hatred targets Will and Andy's friend Lane. Will and Andy struggle to keep the ones they love safe, while hunting a murderer who is supposed to be dead. As the tension tightens, Will confronts a troubling revelation about the extraordinary after-effect of his midair collision.

DIVISIBLE MAN: TEN MAN CREW

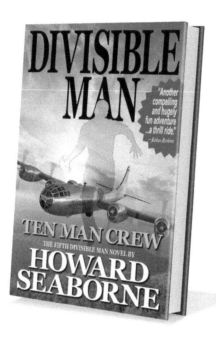

An unexpected visit from the FBI threatens Will Stewart's secret and sends Detective Andy Stewart on a collision course with her darkest impulses. A twisted road reveals how a long-buried Cold War secret has been weaponized. And Pidge shows a daring side of herself that could cost her dearly.

Available in print and digital.

DIVISIBLE MAN: THE THIRD LIE

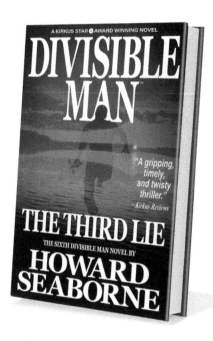

Caught up in a series of hideous crimes that generate national headlines, Will faces the critical question of whether to reveal himself or allow innocent lives to be lost. The stakes go higher than ever when Andy uncovers the real reason behind a celebrity athlete's assault on an underaged girl. And Will discovers that the limits of his ability can lead to disaster.

A Kirkus Starred Review.

A Kirkus Star is awarded to "books of exceptional merit."

Available in print and digital.

Search: "DIVISIBLE MAN Howard Seaborne"

Join our Reader Email list at **HowardSeaborne.com**

DIVISIBLE MAN: THREE NINES FINE

A mysterious mission request from Earl Jackson sends Will into the sphere of a troubled celebrity. A meeting with the Deputy Director of the FBI that goes terribly wrong. Will and Andy find themselves on the run from Federal authorities, infiltrating a notorious cartel, and racing to prevent what might prove to be the crime of the century.

Available in print and digital.

Search: "DIVISIBLE MAN Howard Seaborne"

Join our Reader Email list at **HowardSeaborne.com**

DIVISIBLE MAN: EIGHT BALL

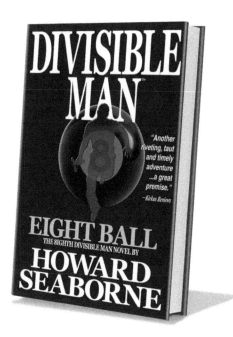

Will's encounter with a deadly sniper on a serial killing rampage sends him deeper into the FBI's hands with costly consequences for Andy. And when billionaire Spiro Lewko makes an appearance, Will and Andy's future takes a dark turn. The stakes could not be higher when the sniper's ultimate target is revealed.

Available in print and digital.

Search: "DIVISIBLE MAN Howard Seaborne"

Join our Reader Email list at HowardSeaborne.com

ENGINE OUT AND OTHER SHORT FLIGHTS

Things just have a way of happening around Will and Andy Stewart. In this collection of twelve tales from Essex County, boy meets girl, a mercy flight goes badly wrong, and Will crashes and burns when he tries dating again. Engines fail. Shots are fired. A rash of the unexpected breaks loose—from bank jobs to zombies.

Available in print and digital.

Search: "DIVISIBLE MAN Howard Seaborne"

Join our Reader Email list at **HowardSeaborne.com**

DIVISIBLE MAN: NINE LIVES LOST

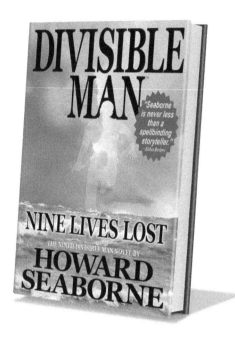

A simple request from Earl Jackson sends Will on a cross-country chase. A threat to Andy's career takes a deadly turn. And a mystery literally lands at Will and Andy's mailbox. Before it all ends, Will confronts a deep, dark place he never imagined.

Available in print and digital.

Search: "DIVISIBLE MAN Howard Seaborne"

Join our Reader Email list at **HowardSeaborne.com**

DIVISIBLE MAN: TEN KEYS WEST

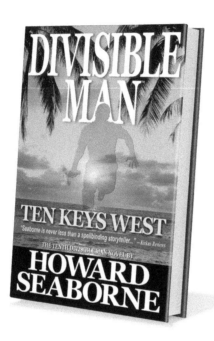

A terrifying incident lands Detective Andy Stewart in the grip of an indelible nightmare.
A scheme to raise a fortune reveals that no life has value when billions are at stake. In this
nail-biting adventure Will and Andy must enlist unlikely help to keep Will's secret from
being exposed to the world.

Available in print and digital.

Search: "DIVISIBLE MAN Howard Seaborne"

Join our Reader Email list at **HowardSeaborne.com**

DIVISIBLE MAN: THE ELEVENTH HOURGLASS

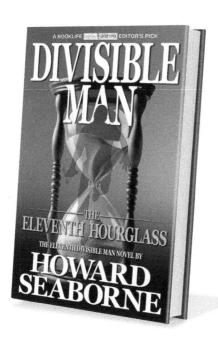

Printed in the USA
CPSIA information can be obtained
at www.ICGtesting.com
LVHW071232081123
763182LV00015B/144/J